To KEENA! Best

The Trouble with Gold...

a Promising Treasure from Cripple Creek

Jim Davis

Maps & illustrations by the author

Deep Creek Press
Golden, Colorado

Copyright © 2003 by James F. Davis

All rights reserved. No part of this book may be reproduced or transmitted in any form or by any means, electronic or mechanical, including photocopying, recording, or by any information storage and retrieval system, without permission in writing from the publisher or author.

Library of Congress Cataloging–in–Publication Data

Jim Davis, 1933–

The Trouble with Gold...
A Promising Treasure from Cripple Creek

ISBN 0–9663347–1–x (soft cover)

PCN 2003103627

Published in the United States of America
by Deep Creek Press

www.deepcreekpress.com

Preface

Cripple Creek District, Colorado: On November 24, 1914 a large natural void was blasted open by underground mining at a depth of 1200 feet in the Cresson Mine. The walls of the cave were encrusted with glowing crystals of gold and gold-tellurides. Heaps of gold littered the floor.

Superintendent Roelofs, a scrupulously honest man, of the Cresson Mine secured the find with an iron door so that none of the yellow treasure could be stolen (highgraded) before it could be mined. The Cresson Company then quickly mined it using trusted miners under strict guard.

But could something so rich and tempting really escape the avarice of man?

The Trouble with Gold... is a tale of what could have happened. The promise of the golden treasure was great to those who sought to steal it. But would the gold keep its promise? There is no one alive today who might know the real truth.

The land and places in the novel are as I have seen them, adjusted to the novel's time frame of 1914 to 1919, less than a generation before my advent into this world. Much of the countryside of the novel is little changed today from what it was ninety years ago. There was an active mine and a hotel at DePass, Wyoming before 1920, but there is little left today.

The early years of the 20th Century in the American West saw the final transition from the frontier west to a more civilized region. Towns flourished and travel became easier, yet hardy citizens were still required for the hard work and unforgiving climate. The land demanded tough ranchers, rugged cowboys and miners, resolute women and empire builders.

Several characters in the novel are loosely based on people of the time. Charles Siringo, the famous range detective, was the model for the novel's Charlie Surcingle.

Angus Lowe, the resolute Scot sheep rancher, epitomizes the strength and determination of many early settlers such as John Love on Muskrat Creek.

Paddymack was modeled after a notorious thief (highgrader) who worked many of the Colorado gold districts in the late 19th century.

The rancher-entrepreneur, JT Stokes, embodies the tough ranchers and empire builders throughout the West who were resolute and unforgiving of weakness or those who got in their way.

Dutch, the story's protagonist, exemplifies the robust men such as Butch Cassidy who tried the outlaw life for its adventure as well as its illicit awards. Some of these men were basically good and a few later lived an honest life. It has been written that Butch Cassidy was not killed in Bolivia but returned to the U.S. and lived out his life in Spokane, Washington!

Cat Teason, on the other hand, embodies the feckless, sometimes likeable, but forgettable outlaw who chose the easiest way through life in the waning days of the wild frontier.

Ella Price, the heroine of the novel, is beautiful, intelligent and a wonderful person, but she has a past she wishes to forget. Is Ella the well-known but vanished outlaw queen who had those same attributes?

Any other similarity of the book's characters with real persons, dead or alive, is coincidental or the result of a combination of personalities to embody characters of the time.

The old Cresson Mine has been swallowed up by a modern Cresson Mine, a giant open-pit mine. 300 ton trucks, instead of mules, haul very low-grade ore out of the new Cresson Mine.

There is a glossary of mining terms in the back of the book.

Jim Davis, April, 2003

CENTRAL WYOMING

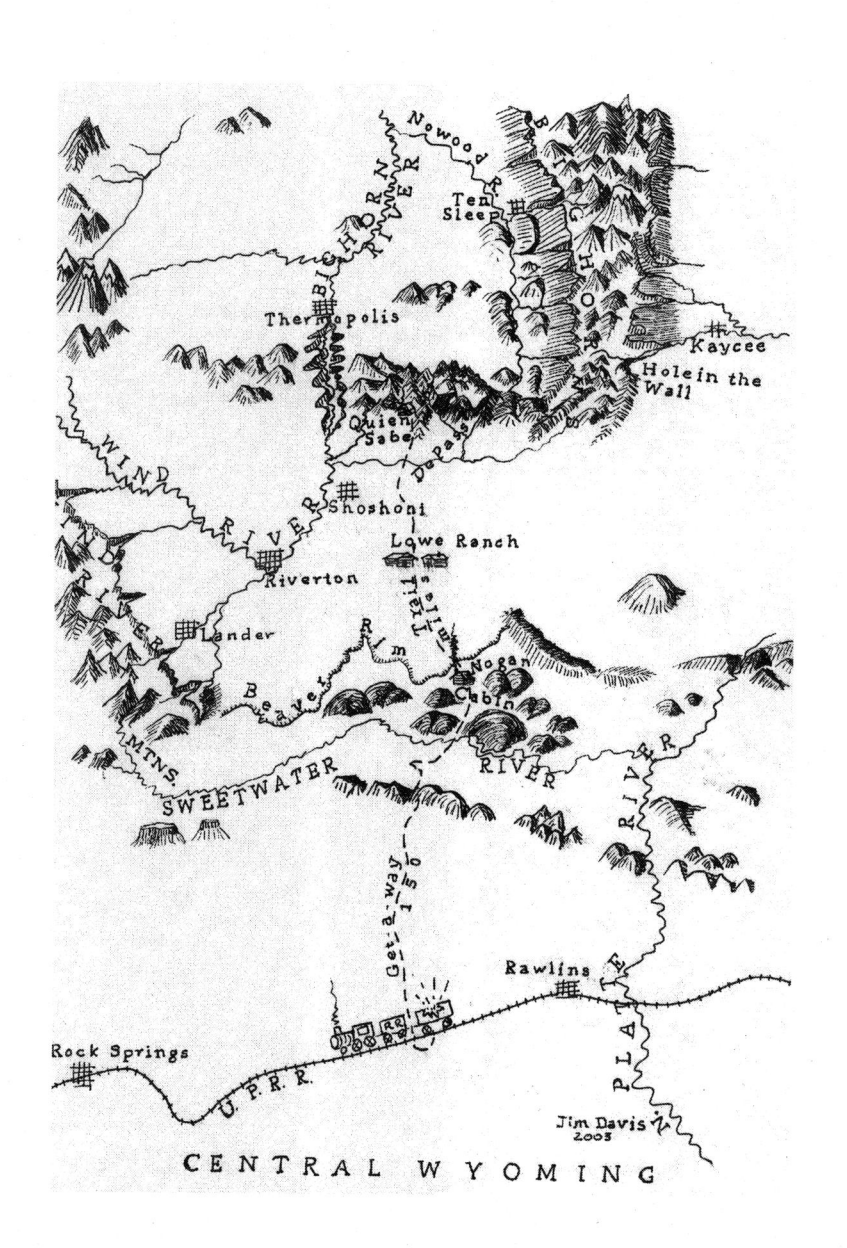

*To Mom
in memory of Dad*

Thanks for inspirations from both.

Chapter 1

The Volcano

Flashes of red lit the night sky as the volcano shook the earth in thunderous eruptions. Clouds of volcanic ash filled the valleys and swept out onto the plains. During the day the sun was blotted out as the young, building mountain flaunted its pubescent power.

As the volcano grew, tropical waters seeped deep, meeting white-hot magma below. Steam produced by the marriage roared and hissed up the throat of the volcano, blasting the rocks apart into a jumble that collapsed back into the innards of the volcano. The chimney of broken rock, a diatreme in geologic terms, reached from grass to Hell.

Hot water, a hydrothermal, metal rich brew, boiled up from the depths and flowed through the voids and cracks of the broken rock. Slowly, over a million years or so, minerals of gold and tellurium grew and crystallized with geometric beauty.

It was then, almost thirty million years ago, that the robust volcano's hot juices boiled into a cave-a vug-far beneath the giant sequoias that cloaked the mountain's flanks. Crystals of pure gold and calaverite, chemically wedded gold and tellurium, slowly formed and lined the giant geode with a treasure trove so wonderful that God must have had a hand in its creation. It might have been a cathedral, but when miners found it they called it the Cresson Vug and mined it in a matter of days.

After the waters cooled there was little activity but the inexorable wearing down of the lifeless volcano. Bit by bit rains washed the mountain's silt into streams, then to rivers which dropped the now ignoble mud onto ocean deltas.

The process of evolution and climate tried out various forms of life and weather on the mountain and its valleys. Tropical plants took root. The giant rhino-like *Trigonis* browsed on plants and in turn vicious saber-tooth tigers ripped down the browsers. But for the most of 28 million years the place was quiet. The area of the volcano had no name–not until man came and gave it an unlikely label– Cripple Creek.

Well after the other major gold discoveries of the west, the volcano at Cripple Creek in Colorado hunkered down like an ancient wise man, worn but hiding a rich legacy of gold. The mountain's once youthful exuberance was hidden in the chronicle of its rocks and the genes of its minerals. Erosion's etchings had reduced once towering heights to rolling hills, apparently useful only for summer pasturage.

* * *

The mountain serenity of the grassy meadows along Cripple Creek was broken in 1891 when a cowboy named Bob Womack found a strange form of gold in the cold waters of Cripple Creek. For a while no one believed the cowboy had anything of value–that his "gold" was a whiskey induced illusion. The gold he found was mixed with the element tellurium and had a silvery luster rather than the heart quickening yellow brilliance prospectors normally looked for.

Promoters – friends of Bob Womack, –had faith in his find and put money there. Cripple Creek soon became one

THE TROUBLE WITH GOLD...

of the greatest gold camps in the world. At one time as many as four hundred mines were operating within the six-mile diameter of the old collapsed volcano. For twenty-some years gold ore poured from the depths before production declined.

The district seemed to have passed its apogee when, on a cold November morning in 1914, a cage loaded with men descended to the 1200 level of the Cresson Mine. The foreman went ahead in the drift to check out the working face before giving the order for his men to start mining.

The shift-boss was puzzled, for where there should have been a solid face of rock there was, instead, a large hole. He shined his light into the void and was astounded by a wondrous sight.

His mouth dropped open in slack jawed amazement. He rubbed his hand across his eyes, thinking his vision must be playing tricks on him. *Maybe it was that bad whiskey from last night.* Standing on the broken rock from the last round of blasting he peered through the hole into a cavern that glowed with a blinding, golden brilliance in the rays of his mine lamp. The rock itself seemed to be on fire. Scintillating reflections danced like flames as the miner moved the light back and forth.

"It must be quartz or iron pyrite," he muttered, knowing it wasn't, but unable to comprehend the obvious. He leaned into the cavern, the size of which challenged the limits of his light. A vaulted ceiling rose far above him and the walls shimmered with an eerie glow. His heart raced with excitement and he fell to his knees as his legs quivered with a sudden weakness. "Gold! My God! The place is bloody filled with gold!"

Scattered about in rich profusion were pure, softly glowing gold crystals the size of a miner's thumbnail. Silvery crystals of calaverite, feather-like, seemed so delicate that a man's breath might dislodge them. Veinlets of pure gold filled cracks in the of the breccia walls, confirming the richness of the lode.

Some of the miners, wondering at the delay, walked up the drift and saw the sight. They were quick to recognize the opportunity. A few stuffed their pockets with gold before the foreman chased them out and sent a messenger to notify the mine superintendent.

In short time, contents of the golden trove made the mine owners rich, transformed working men into thieves, and prompted others to steal from the thieves. Lives were changed and lost. Sometimes subtle and patient with its power, the gold hastened the demise of the undeserving and tested the resolve of good men.

* * *

The Cresson Mine

THE TROUBLE WITH GOLD...

Within hours of the discovery of the Cresson Mine's golden cave, the entire Cripple Creek community vibrated with excitement. Housewives gathered on their porches to dream of jewels and dare to hope for good times, patrons in the saloons debated the gold's value, and owners of almost depleted mines felt renewed hope. The normal drudgery of miners was forgotten for a time as they eyed the muck piles for gold that they might surreptitiously stash in their lunchboxes or in the nether regions of their bodies.

Chapter 2

Dutch

Deep in the Portland Mine, a mile from the Cresson excitement, the hoist cable creaked and snapped as it stretched between the man cage and the spinning hoist drum two thousand feet up the shaft. As the cage gained upward momentum in its trip from the depths of the mine, its guides bumped sporadically on the shaft rails. Heavy grease on the rails smacked like a crude miner eating with his mouth open.

Dutch Wyatt felt the cage shudder as it passed rough spots on the worn rails. Momentary flashes of light marked the mine stations at hundred feet intervals as the rising cage whispered past. Dutch yawned to release the pressure building in his ears.

Dutch and a fellow miner, Tom Hoskins, their faces grimy with drilling dust, stood in the cage as it took them from the warm dampness of the mine toward the inevitable chill wind of November on the surface.

Hoskins broke the silence that usually rode with them at the end of a day. "Dutch, did ya hear about the cave full of gold they found on the 1200 level at the Cresson? Every miner in the district is trying to figure out a way to high-grade some of it."

Dutch, stooping slightly to fit his tall frame into the cage, pursed his lips and tugged at his sweeping mustache. "Yeah, I heard. They're fooling themselves to think they can get any of that gold. Old Dick Roelofs is nobody's fool. I hear tell he's put in a solid iron door there. Nobody will get into that cave except the mine bosses. They'll just shovel the gold into sacks, then keep a shotgun with every bag until it's locked in a railroad car."

Dutch thought of times, long past, when he had helped Butch Cassidy rob a train or two. "If I were in Roelofs' boots I'd load the train half with gold and half with guards. Nope, I'd as soon work down here in the muck of the old Portland as try to steal some of his gold."

Dutch preferred to lose himself in thought but today his partner was excited about the news from the Cresson.

"I bet old Paddymack will find a way to get his grubby mitts on some of it."

"I doubt it. Paddy's a clever thief alright, but he won't get any of this stuff."

Dutch put the Cresson gold out of his mind. He'd been at the Portland Mine for more than three years now, and the dollars were slowly adding up. But it was honest money, and in a couple more years he could buy a ranch somewhere up in Wyoming. There the breezes keep the views sparkling clear for a hundred miles and you can ride for three days and not see a soul.

I'll buy a few cattle. Just enough to make a living so's I'll have time to fish and read some good books. It'll be a quiet life. A hell of a lot less adventure than robbing trains, but at least I won't have to worry about getting caught and sitting in prison while the songs of spring are calling.

Dutch had been in jail once, falsely convicted of stealing a horse, and those few months had been pure hell.

Damn, I'm near to forty. I'd best get this dream to happening. I wasted too many years chasing money. Bad money for the most part. Spending it for the moment instead of making my dreams come true. A Wordsworth phrase floated across his mind and the words were unsettling.

*"The world is too much with us; late and soon,
Getting and spending, we lay waste our powers."*

"Dutch"

Dutch worked his mind hard to imagine the feel of his horse under him. To hear the soothing creak of saddle leather. To breathe deeply of the rich incense of sagebrush. The image faded as the cold air sweeping down from Pikes Peak found its way into the upper reaches of the mine. He closed his eyes tightly, wanting badly to feel warm spring sun on his back. *Damn. Two years is a long time to wait for a dream to happen.*

I wonder how many guards Roelofs will have on the gold train? The train would wind through rugged hills on its way down the mountain to Colorado Springs. An easy place to stop a train. A posse would need hours to mount a pursuit. He gritted his teeth, angry at his thoughts. The dismal walls of the mine fomented forbidden ideas, ideas that ran through his mind like the devil's messenger. *One good heist and I could take away more than this job as shift boss will pay in five years. Enough to buy that ranch.*

No, Dammit!

Shaking his head to dispel Temptation's voice, he impatiently waited as the hoist neared the surface. "Up to grass." Instead of taking the electric trolley that ran from the mines to Victor, he walked off Battle Mountain to his little cabin at the lower edge of town. He always walked when he needed to cleanse his mind of Temptation's badgering. His rented cabin cost a little more than the boarding houses, but he liked the quiet. Within the boarding houses snores of a hundred men crowded out sleep, dreams and even wakeful thoughts. Only nightmares seemed to survive.

As Dutch walked in the twilight of the cold November evening, he reminisced again about his train-robbing days.

Those were the times when train robbers enjoyed a certain degree of respect that other bandits didn't command. It was different then, not so many people out west and a lot easier to disappear–or at least be where nobody asked questions. I wonder what it would be like today?

As he walked, the snow crunched and squeaked under his boots. It would be a cold night. Normally he felt good about getting to his cabin and cooking a meal, but tonight the whispers of past devils seemed to haunt him.

"Damn, I belong in the sun, not in the bowels of the Earth."

He felt a shiver, not from the cold, but from an inexplicable sense of dread mingled with excitement. It was a familiar feeling. He always felt it just before a hold-up.

CRIPPLE CREEK GOLD DISTRICT, COLORADO

Chapter 3

Cresson Gold

At first word of the bonanza, Superintendent Roelofs hurried down to the 1200 level of the Cresson. He stared in silent awe, then exclaimed, "We have burrowed into Eldorado!" Turning to the foreman he snapped an order. "Get a crew down from the machine shop. I want an iron door in this drift before the day is out. I'll wait here while you get two good men and rifles. Put a twenty-four hour guard on this. Except for you and the guards the 1200 level is off-limits until we get this stuff hauled out. Ever damn highgrader in the district will be trying to worm their way into this." That afternoon Roelofs called one of the mine owners and told him to make all haste to Cripple Creek.

That evening, one of the lucky miners who had pocketed a spectacular piece of the Cresson gold quickly slurped down his meal of grits and sowbelly at his cheap boarding house and headed for the Gold Coin Saloon in Victor. Crowding his way through the smoky, noisy throng of miners and ignoring the clutching whores, he approached Paddy Mackabee at the bar. "Hullo, Paddymack. I got somepthin' that might int'rest ya." In a false show of nonchalance, he spat a stream of thick tobacco juice towards the dirty brass spittoon near the whore pressed against Paddymack.

Paddymack occupied his spot at the bar as if it were a princely throne. "Can't ya see I'm busy?" Paddymack squeezed the floozy's ample hip with his rough hand. The whore giggled, heavy paint on her aging face preventing any visible sign of a smile.

The miner slapped down fifty cents with an elaborate show. "It's good enuf I'll buy ya a shot if you'll listen a minute." He leaned close to Paddymack and spoke in a conspiratorial voice. "I got some stuff from the Vug."

Paddymack rolled his buggy eyes and shrugged his shoulders, but then pushed away the hapless whore and pulled the miner into the space vacated by the woman.

A rough, hulking man, Paddymack sported several days' growth of whiskers over his grimy face. A low hairline barely allowed a forehead above his thick eyebrows. Thick cauliflower ears and wild unkempt hair completed a countenance that made him look like a stupid lout. His cocksure demeanor, however, suggested he was no ordinary miner. Those who had a bit of filched gold to sell knew that he always had quick cash.

Paddy Mackabee was, in fact, as shrewd as he was unsavory. He was a notorious ore thief, a highgrader. He eyed the miner up and down and snorted, his mouth cruel in an odd, twisted way. A solitary yellowed snag showed in his mouth and one eye bulged abnormally from its socket–the result of an improperly healed cheekbone broken in a fight. He tossed down the shot of whiskey, blinked his eyes once and burped with a drawn-out crescendo.

"Well, let me take a look at whut ya got. I'm a busy man. Ain't got all night." He leaned to one side, lifted a leg slightly and farted.

The miner carefully looked around, then slipped the gold from his pocket and held it close to his belly. Paddymack deftly grabbed it and tossed the rich ore slightly to test its heft. To the miner's disappointment, Paddymack registered only a mild interest in the sample. "I might give ya five dollars fer it." He turned back to the bar, more interested in another whiskey than in the gold-rich rock.

"I ain't here to sell ya this piece. But I can tell ya how ya might get a lot more of this stuff. I might remember more when I ain't so thirsty."

Paddymack snorted. "Begorra, man, they's got that cave covered wid guards like Pike's Peak's covered wid snow in January! He grunted with a wave of casual dismissal and downed another shot of whiskey with a noisy sucking slurp. "Me offer stands, five bucks for thet piece."

"I know a lot more. Like about meybe what they's gonna do wid it." The miner leaned close to Paddymack and in a conspiratorial voice muttered, "I heared things. Secrets I 'spect. I seen the Vug, Paddy, and even you never seed nuthin' rich as this."

"Awright, 'ere's what I'll do. Ten now an' a ten more when I sell the gold, if I can get enuf and ya tell me everthing ya know." Paddymack again belched loudly, and smacked his thick lips, savoring the recycled whiskey fumes.

"It's wuth a lot mor'nat. I'd need mor'nat jus to keep me mouth shut about tellin' ya how they're gonna guard it."

At this Paddy's left eyebrow raised until it was almost lost in his unruly hair. He glared at the miner with a bulging, baleful eye, squinting the other almost closed. "I don't scare into deals. Now tell me whut ya know or get lost."

"Ah hell, Paddy, I'z jus' makin' a point. I'd not say nuthin to nobody." Emboldened by Paddy's mild show of interest, the miner bravely upped the price. "Let's say ten now and a hunert if'n ya get more gold, an' maybe ten percent of the gold ya get." He added the last lamely.

Paddymack glared at him with his bulging eye and blew explosively through his thick lips. "If'n I gave that kind of deal to ever' damn miner what come in here wid a story like yers, I'd done been broke 'fore I started." With that said, Paddy tossed down the rest of his whiskey and turned to leave.

The miner was bewildered. He looked at the bottle. He needed another drink, but all of his money had gone for the first round. "Oh, hell, Paddy, I guess yur deal is okay if you'll throw in the rest of thet bottle."

Mackabee smiled smugly. "B'gorra, ya must be a mick. Ya drive a hard bargain. Now let's sit and 'ave another shot or two whilst ya tell me what ya know. I'm buyin'."

Ten dollars richer, the miner turned on his stool and winked salaciously at one of the dance hall girls. The money was as good as spent.

Paddymack roughly grabbed the dallying miner by the arm. "Ya can play with her later. First, I want ya to tell me everythin' you know about that cave of gold." He doubted if the miner's information would be of much help in stealing more gold from the Vug, but the golden rock, with its beautiful crystals of gold, would bring fifty dollars. But first, the gaudy specimen would be useful in other ways. The rich ore sample could be a persuasive tool in his quest for help in a felonious plan.

THE TROUBLE WITH GOLD...

The miner tossed down his whiskey and looked expectantly at the bottle that Paddymack held firmly in his fist. He told Paddymack what he knew, embellished with his Irish skill.

"I was the first to see it. The light blazed out of the hole like as how we'd broke into Hades. I could grab only one piece before the shift boss ran us off. I stuck around whilst the boss talked to the super. They was purty excited." He looked hopefully at the bottle.

"Hell, man, you ain't told me nuthin' yet." Paddymack poured more whiskey into his own glass but kept a tight grip on the bottle.

The miner coughed to emphasize his dry throat. "Well, later I heard some more stuff, a lot more. After Roelofs looked at the cave he ordered an iron door built in the tunnel and a guard put there all the time until the cave was mined out. But I heard somethin' else, somethin' purty important." He looked around, coughed again, then waited expectantly.

Paddymack filled the miner's glass. "Well, what was it?"

The miner gulped from his glass then set it down closer to the bottle. Paddymack poured a little more whiskey into the glass, not filling it this time. The miner shrugged and leaned closer to the highgrader. "They is shippin' ever'thin' to the sample plant to be graded and sorted and sealed in bags. Ain't nobody knows that. Most ever'body thinks that the gold is going right onto guarded railroad cars. Ten guards for each car!"

Paddymack blinked his good eye in surprise. He too had assumed that the highgrade gold would be loaded directly into a guarded railroad car and shipped to the mill in Colorado City to lessen chances for a holdup. Apparently Roelofs, the superintendent, wanted to know the value of what he had before it left the mine. Paddymack shoved the bottle towards the miner and chuckled to himself. *I'll have some of thet Cresson stuff or me name ain't Paddymack.*

*   *   *

Over the next few days Paddymack heard more details of the bonanza. Crystals of gold were literally being scraped off the cavern walls. Superintendent Roelofs had guards watching every aspect of the operation. The Cresson Mine resembled an impenetrable fortress. Paddymack knew that it would just take a little more patience and planning.

Paddymack gleaned bits of information from every possible source. He learned that the cavern was a dozen feet wide by forty feet high and extended back thirty or so feet. He got detailed information on the richness of the gold and how it was being handled from the vug to the surface. None of this knowledge was of any help in using his usual methods to filch some of the gold. Normally he would have purchased lunch pails spiked with gold, but regular miners weren't allowed in the cavern. A select few of the mine bosses dug out the gold by hand. Canvas sacks stuffed with gold and gold tellurides were hoisted to the surface. Armed guards accompanied the treasure as might the Queen's guard protect her majesty's jewels.

The gold was brought to the surface at night so that the darkness and the clever use of dummy bags filled with waste obscured the final destination of the gold. If it were going to the sample plant Paddy was certain that he could highgrade some of the Cresson gold with the assistance of the sample plant operator. The man was a previous associate in crime at another mine. Paddy found his man at the Silver Dollar saloon, but the sampler only shook his head and shrugged his shoulders when Paddymack asked him about gold from the vug.

THE TROUBLE WITH GOLD...

The bulging eye glared white with frustration and the black eyebrow arched up into his unkempt hair. Now that he knew just how rich the Cresson Vug was, he desperately wanted part of its contents. This was the first time that this particular sampler was unwilling to assist Paddy. *Or is it that he is unwilling to help? I bet the bugger is lying.*

That night Paddymack made a stealthy visit to the sample plant. He wiggled under the fence that surrounded the sample building, unmindful of the snowdrift against the fence. Staying in the shadows he wormed his way to the building and around it until he found a small, grimy window he could peer through.

Inside, the sampler weighed small piles of ore on a large brass balance scale. He was dumping the contents of canvas bags that had been secured with a tightly twisted wire and clamped with a pressed lead seal. Paddymack watched as the sampler sorted through the samples and selected certain pieces. His heart quickened when he saw the glitter. It was almost pure gold and the gold telluride, calaverite. This was no ordinary ore. It was from the Vug!

Paddymack was puzzled that the sampler was separating out only a small fraction of the total gold. He knew that this was not the usual method that would assure a representative cut. The sampler weighed the smaller portion and poured it into an unmarked canvas bag, which he tied and slid under the bench. He then weighed the remainder of the gold, put it into a larger bag stenciled with the company name.

Paddy noticed another unusual thing. The sampler was not recording the weight of the smaller samples in the official sample ledger. He was, though, penciling a notation in a small notebook he kept in his shirt pocket. "Begorra!" Paddymack whispered to himself. "The bloke is skimmin' off the best stuff fer someone."

Paddymack was abruptly startled from his observations by the sound of footsteps approaching. A dark, looming figure rattled the chain and unlocked the gate, letting himself in. He turned and replaced the lock, then walked directly towards Paddymack. It was too late to escape.

Paddymack squeezed into the shadows at the bottom of the building, stiffening his body in an attempt to resemble a mine timber. The door to the sample plant was a bare six feet away and he knew that the light from the open door would shine full on him when it opened. His muscles tensed. Mentally he swore, knowing if he were seen that security would be beefed up even more. The man crunched across the icy plant yard, approaching the door.

He rapped on the door. "Open up."

"Just a minute," a muffled response from inside. "Who is it?"

"Sam, open the gol-durned door. It's me. The boss."

A moment later there was the sound of the bar being lifted from inside the door. Paddymack tensed, ready to sprint for the hole under the fence. The door groaned open. Light flooded out, shining full on Paddymack for a brief moment. The visitor quickly entered the building and closed the door. Paddymack slowly let out his breath. The bar dropped into place with a loud thump.

Paddymack slowly pulled his numb body up along the building until he could see through the grimy window. He recognized one the mine bosses under the dim, shade-covered electric bulb. The two men walked towards the bench where the scales sat, talking rapidly. Holding his breath Paddymack could make out a few words. The boss man did most of the talking, and from the tone of his voice, Paddymack could tell that this was not a usual conversation about the sampling operation.

As he watched and listened, the sampler slid the gold laden bags from under the bench. The boss laughed, his lips curling in a greedy leer as he gave orders to Sam. Paddymack strained to catch the words.

THE TROUBLE WITH GOLD... 19

"Divvy up... Get the best stuff... small bags which... three ways... your share... gold for silence... lead between the eyes for squeal... ship to bank at San Fran..." A nearby mine skip dumped its load with a clattering roar and masked part of the conversation.

Paddymack hardly breathed. He heard only a few words, but they were enough. Enough to lay the next part of his scheme. From the voices he could tell that the boss was giving orders and the answering voice of Sam was whiney with a touch of fear. Paddymack's pulse raced with excitement. *Begorra! This may be my key to riches.*

The next night he again wiggled under the fence. This time he rapped boldly on the barred door. "Sam, it's Paddy. I need to talk to you."

"What the hell are ya doin' here. Ya know I can't let nobody in. I'd get fired for sure. I ain't lettin' ya in. Yer not even s'posed to be inside the fence." Sam's voice cracked with alarm.

"Sam, this is official bizness." Paddy drew himself to his full height and pounded on the door again, this time more forcefully.

"I ain't no fool. Yus'd be the last one on the hill to have bizness with this mine. Leastwise honest bizness. Now get out of here before we both get shot."

"Sam, I know about the plan to divvy up part of that haul from the Vug. An' I knows yer sendin' it to a bank in San Francisco. Yer partners want me to make sure nuthin' happens to it before it gits to the bank."

Sam paused as he contemplated Paddymack's surprising knowledge of the operation. "Whut's their names then?"

Paddymack guessed that Sam likely didn't know who, other than the shift boss, was involved. "You know the shift-boss is the only one what knows who all's involved."

Paddymack obviously had knowledge of the large-scale gold skimming scheme that was going on with the

Cresson Vug gold. "Why would they hire you?" he asked cautiously.

"Sam, think about it. They wouldn't 'ardly hire the Sheriff fer the job, now would they?" He chuckled.

"Wal, I guess ya must know whut's going on, but I still dasn't let you in. They's got special security rules fer this. I'd get fired fer sure or maybe shot. Whut da ya want?"

"Ardly nuthin, Sam. Ardly nuthin' a'tall. Just enuf infermation that I can make sure nuthin' happens to thet gold between here and San Franciso. Stop by the Gold Coin tomarra' and I'll buy a whiskey."

Chapter 4

An Offer

Dutch sat in an old rocker smoking his pipe and reading *The Sea Wolf* for the second time. The fire crackled warmly in the kitchen stove and the smell of hot iron was comforting on a cold night. For a moment Dutch fixed his gaze on the polished bas-relief of the ocean-going steamer on the oven front. The picture and the words around it, *The Great Majestic*, always gave him a sense of adventure and at the moment fit the book in his hand.

A sharp rapping on the door shook him from his thoughts. With one smooth, intuitive action born from his outlaw days, he put the book aside, drew his pistol and stood off to one side of the door. "Who's there?"

"It's Paddy Mackabee. I want to talk some business."

"You have the wrong place. I don't need any business with you."

"Jus' give me yer ear fer a minute."

Reluctantly Dutch opened the door, holding his .45 at his side. "Like I said, Mackabee, I don't have any business with you and don't want any. So get it off your chest and get out of here."

Paddymack sauntered in with a smirk on his grimy face. From his pocket he pulled out a fist-sized piece of ore shot through with gold. "How would ya like a few hundert ounces of that?"

"Paddy, I'm a miner, not a gold buyer. I see gold ore every day. Not much that good, but I get paid for the rock I mine whether I can see the gold or not." Dutch took the heavy rock and examined it closely. "This came from the Cresson Vug didn't it? There's no way you'll get any of that stuff. Roelof's got it sealed off with an iron door."

Paddymack snickered. "Who says I'd have to get it through the door? I got me ways. The company won't know its gone neither."

"I suppose you got your own tunnel into it!" said Dutch sarcastically.

"If I did, I wouldn't need no train-robbin' expert. Wyatt, I know whut ya did in the old days. I know thet you was one a da best. I heard that whole trains shook when ya got near. Onc't anyways." Paddymack laughed at his joke, an eyebrow lifting to show the bulging eye. His solitary tooth glinted yellow through his grimy whiskers.

He plopped himself down on a kitchen chair and with no encouragement from Dutch continued. "Ya know as well as I do that twic't as much gold came outa that Cresson hole as they claim. There's pieces all over town and I figure we oughta have some ourselves." Paddymack emphasized his belief by vigorously scratching his beard. He belched, his breath smelling of the corned beef and cabbage and raw onion he'd eaten for supper.

He held the gold up to the lamp so the flickering flame could work magic on the gold. "I cain't tell ya anymore 'til I knows if you'll help. I'm talking about a big take. Thousands of ounces, an' it ain't even perzactly stealin'. Leastways ifn ya don't count stealin from company thieves a criminal activity." Paddy snorted a laugh and wiped his nose on his sleeve.

THE TROUBLE WITH GOLD...

"Macabee, that train will be loaded with guards. You're crazy if you plan to pull a heist on it." Dutch remembered that he'd already considered the possibilities.

"I ain't worried about *that* train. Just one leetle hint for ya to think about, Dutch." Paddymack giggled, leaned forward and cocked his head. "A lot of the Cresson gold is gonna be shipped to a bank in San Francisco, an' the company ain't doin' it. What's more, it'll be shipped on the Union Pacific Railroad!"

"Paddy, I'm not sayin' you're lying, but why in the hell would anybody involved tell you? I know Roelofs, and he's as honest as they come."

Paddymack looked over his shoulder and continued in a conspiratorial voice. "It's some mine bosses. Maybe it ain't Roelofs, but it's some a them what work for Roelofs! They's stealin' their company's gold. Dutch, I ain't lyin'. Ya pick the place to knock off the train. Make us rich, it will, and takin' from thieves ain't wrong anyhows!" He snickered hoarsely.

"I'm not in the robbing business. You'll have to find another train robber." Dutch walked to the door and opened it.

Paddymack rose and stepped out into the cold, his breath billowing clouds of white. "Nuthin' ain't gonna happen soon, Wyatt. Think about it. I got time. They ain't shippin' the gold 'til things settle down, meybe not 'til spring."

"I wouldn't bet on much gold getting past Roelofs. I wouldn't even try."

Paddy cackled, his yellow tooth gleaming through his whiskers, "I got me ways. I'll be talkin' with ya later, Dutch."

Dutch lay awake for a long time that night. It bothered him that he couldn't immediately dismiss Paddymack and his foolish scheme. *Why do I let myself be tempted?*

He still remembered the last words his mother spoke to him thirty years ago. Knowing she was dying of consumption she put her eight year old son on the orphan train from New York City to the West. "It's the best thing, Henry. You'll have a chance to be somebody out there, I know I will be proud of you."

The car was jammed with other children. Many were crying, others looked stunned, and several had the look of having seen it all. Gripping his little black pasteboard suitcase he pushed his way through the mass of kids until he could look out the window. His eyes blurred with tears so that he could barely see his mother, head bowed in dejection and pain, as she slowly walked away and was soon lost in the milling crowd at Grand Central Station. She stopped once, as though to turn, but then moved on and was lost from his sight forever. At that moment Dutch vowed to live up to his mother's hopes.

At Omaha two days later the children were herded off the train to a platform crowded with farmers and their wives. One burly farmer in dirty coveralls walked up to Dutch and grabbed his arm. "I'll take ya. Ya look like a strong boy what'll do good on the farm."

Dutch remembered kicking him hard on the shin. The farmer swore and called him a stubborn little Dutchman. Little Henry Wyatt decided right then that the name Dutch might warn off troublemakers.

*   *   *

Thinking about it now, Dutch was glad his anger hadn't stopped a kindly, older couple from luring him with promises of pets and home-cooked food. Treating him as their own, the couple had taught him to appreciate music and most important to read, especially the classics. When he came home from school he and his foster father would talk about what he had learned. Tapping the cover of Washington Irving, O. Henry, Mark Twain and even

THE TROUBLE WITH GOLD... 25

Shakespeare, he told Dutch, "When you go out into the world there are lots of things to experience–some good and some bad. These books can be your compass in life. Just like a ship needs an anchorage, or the prairie, a mountain on the horizon, you must have something to hitch yourself to. Learn to read good, no, great books and you will know where to sail your ship. Now and then you'll get lost, but your port will be there if you know to follow the right signs."

Life had been good until his foster parents died during an influenza epidemic. Dutch, fourteen years old, found himself once more an orphan. He wandered west, wanting to be a cowboy. His intentions were good, but life's circumstances conspired to put him off on the wrong fork of the road. Sometimes he felt akin to Don Quixote, Cervantes' hapless hero.

It seemed easier and more lucrative to rob trains than wrangle cows. Most of all, it was the adventure. Always being on the move, outwitting the law. With Butch Cassidy he'd learned that smart thinking could pay off. Sometimes he remembered the wisdom of his foster father, but he was having too much fun to heed the words. *Besides, robbing trains isn't so bad as long as nobody got hurt. That was Butch's motto, too.* After a time, though, he could see that banditry employed mostly losers. There were exceptions – Butch, Sundance, and Cat Teason. Sundance was likeable but he had a wild streak. Cat Teason wasn't too smart but a decent enough chap considering that he was an incorrigible thief and gambler. Dutch considered himself a decent person but he wondered if he was any better than his outlaw cronies.

He'd tried homesteading up on the Powder River in Wyoming but some of the big ranchers took umbrage at his branding maverick calves on the range. He'd gone back to robbing trains.

From the depths of his mind Temptation again mocked him, bringing him back to the present. "Of course, you might make enough in robbing that gold on the train to get that ranch now." Temptation was indeed back-urging, ridiculing, sometimes subtle and arrogant. Dutch shoved the dissonant taunt from his mind, like an alcoholic fighting to stay on the wagon, or the lonesome, needful men trying to resist the painted women posing seductively in the windows of their cribs on Myers Avenue in Cripple Creek.

As much as he disliked working in the earth's innards and the mine owners treating the miners like indentured servants, he would keep with mining until he could afford his dream honestly. He was more tired of running from the law than working in the mine. With Temptation silenced, Dutch slept.

During the winter months Dutch's life took on a routine that didn't vary much. The shifts were long and he read during the rest of his waking hours. Sometimes he calculated how much longer he would have to work before he bought a horse and looked for a homestead. He worried that there would be no places left to buy. *Maybe I should have paid more attention to Paddy's offer. Of course, nothing has come of that anyway.* He paused, disgusted with his thoughts. *Damn, here I am back to thinking of the easy way.* He clenched his teeth in anger at his thoughts. *I will do things right. No more stealing.*

By the calender it was spring, but the evenings were cold and piles of dirty, weary snow clung stubbornly in shaded areas. Still, Dutch could sense the changes that signaled spring in the high country. Spring always made him restless to move on, to find new challenges. He strode quickly down the trail to his cabin, anxious to start a fire and eat an early supper.

When he approached his cabin he saw smoke rising from the chimney. Someone was inside. He turned the knob and booted the door open.

"Hullo, Dutch. I got cold waitn' fer ya outside so's I came on in an' started a fire. I figured ya wouldn't mind."

THE TROUBLE WITH GOLD... 27

Paddymack stood with his back to the stove, his yellowed tooth protruding through a tangled beard.

"Paddy, I told you I want no business with you and I meant it. Now get on out of here before I shoot you for trespassing."

Paddymack cackled, and made no move to leave. "Jus' listen fer a minute, Dutch, and think about it fer a bit.

"Thet gold will be on the train to San Francisco in two weeks. I'll stop by tomorra night wid whut I knows if'n yer interested. It's bigger'n I thought, mor'n a thousand pounds a' gold! Rich, by golly. It's damn rich, Dutch. Them thieves picked out mostly pure gold from them tellerides. Jus' think about it." Abruptly Paddymack walked to the door. At the door he turned. "Don't fergit, the law wouldn't know to chase us, cause it's already thieves' gold when we gets it." Paddymack sniggered and disappeared into the darkness before Dutch could tell him to go to hell.

That night Dutch tossed and turned, wondering about Paddymack's scheme.

"It's a dark, dank hell of a place to work, down in the mine." Temptation was back.

Conscience spoke up, but with a weaker voice. "Your work is honest. Won't be much longer and you'll have that nest egg."

Temptation snorted. "You'll be an old man by the time you have enough money for a ranch."

Adventure chimed in. "You can outwit them. You need some excitement in your life."

I could get caught and go to prison.

"Don't be silly. It's stolen gold to start with. It'll be an easy job. Think of that log cabin on the banks of a crystal clear creek. Elk down in the pasture. The sun shining all day."

Towards morning Dutch sat up and in a prayerful tone, said aloud. "I can do it for a couple more years, by

God, I'll stick with the mine." He felt bone-tired now, but it was time to go to work.

Down in the mine, groggy from his sleepless night, Dutch walked to the drift where one of his jobs was to check the muck blasted at the end of the last shift. His friend, Tom Hoskins, accompanied him to pry loose rock from the back. Dutch looked over the muck pile and stepped back while Hoskins used a steel bar to pry loose rock down from the back. He was having trouble getting the last of the loose rocks pried down. Dutch moved up to help. "Give me that bar Tom, and I'll finish. You go back and bring up the rest of the boys."

A small trickle of rock dirt dribbled from the back. In the split second before Dutch could warn his friend, a large rock slab swung loose. For an awful moment the rock seemed suspended, then with a sickening thud it landed on Hoskins in a cloud of dust.

It was over in a moment–from a breathing, joking, hard-working miner to a lifeless form crushed by the rock. A look of terror was frozen on Hoskins' face as sightless eyes peered from under the edge of the deadly tombstone, the spreading blood glistening red on the mine floor. The sudden accident sickened Dutch and he bent over, retching violently, then turned and stumbled back to the shaft station.

He felt an overwhelming urge to get out of the mine. To feel the reassuring solace of the hills. To breathe fresh air. As he helped bring the dead man to the surface Dutch knew he was riding the cage for the last time. He walked from the shaft into the cold spring day and looked heavenward. "Forgive me, God, for what I am about to do–for breaking my promise." Once again he felt a chill, but also excitement.

Later that evening at Dutch's cabin, Paddymack gave him the details on the shipment. "May tenth. Early Monday morning, Dutch. The train will leave Rawlins after midnight. Two wooden crates in da' express car. We'll split down the middle."

"Whoa! Just a minute Paddymack. If that's the deal, you can stop talking right now. I have to share my take with someone to help me with the holdup and the getaway and we'll be taking all the risks."

Paddymack twisted his mouth into a grimace. "Okay, Dutch, don't get yerself uppity. Shouldn't be much risk for you though. The law and the railroad won't know what the shipment is so they shouldn't be chasin' ya very hard. Let's make it sixty for ya."

"You're telling me there won't be any guards on that train? No U.S. marshal? No railroad bulls?"

"Well...Hell, Dutch, you know the railroad always has somebody wid the mail car. Probably some cash along with the mail. That'll be sorta extra gravy for ya."

"What about the gold shippers, Paddy. I'd think they might want a little extra protection."

"Well, I heared they hired a guard to look after their interests, but he shouldn't be a problem. Some worn-out, old cowboy. Fellow by the name of Charley Surcingle. Just shoot him if he gets in the way." Paddymack cackled at the thought, vigorously scratching his beard.

Dutch stared at Paddymack. "Charlie Surcingle! Good Lord, Paddy, he may be old but he's still the best damn range detective in the country. Surcingle changes everything. First of all, I don't cotton to shooting. Secondly, I've got to get a good-sized poke to make it worth matching wits with Charlie Surcingle, not to mention the Union Pacific for knocking off one of their trains." Dutch shook his head, wondering if the job was worth the risk.

"Meybe ya'd better if I told you there was almost ten thousand ounces what's gonna be shipped to San Francisco."

"Okay, Paddy, here's the deal. Take it or get out of here. I'll do the job for ninety percent."

Paddymack's mouth dropped open and he belched. His eyebrow lifted, and he glowered. "Ye'r a god-damned worse thief than... than me!"

"I'll still make you a rich man, Paddy. If there's as much gold as you claim there is."

"Hell, Dutch," Paddymack whined, "I need more to get into the Homestead House. A fancy whorehouse like that ain't gonna be cheap."

Dutch thought that it would take more than money before Paddymack could get into the elegant Homestead at Cripple Creek. "With that much gold you can probably find some fancy whore to marry – then you won't need to join the Homestead House." Dutch had laughed, thinking to himself that a woman would have to be down on her luck in the worst way to marry the likes of Paddymack, gold or not.

"Come on Paddymack, ten percent will make you a rich man. I'll be lucky to ever spend mine. I might likely end up in prison or in a coffin."

Paddymack slowly rose and walked to the door. His hand on the latch, he turned with a black scowl, "Yer makin' a mistake Dutch."

"You heard my deal, Paddy. Make up your mind. Right now or never.

As quickly as it came, the scowl passed from Paddymack's face. "Hell, I guess ya got me, Dutch. Tell me how I'll get me share."

"I'll have your share of the gold waiting for you at Rock Springs. Here's what you have to do." Dutch spelled out the details. "And Paddy, no double-cross, thinking you might pick up a reward as well. Believe me, I'll have that angle covered."

The next day Dutch found Cat Teason, one of the former Wild Bunch, at Crapper Jack's on Myers Avenue in Cripple Creek. Cat was an incorrigible thief from the old train robbing days and fancied himself quite a clever gambler.

"Dutch! Hell, you're just in time to stake me in a big pot. I need a little financing. I'll split 50-50 with you."

"Forget it, Cat. I'm here to offer you a job." He grasped Cat firmly by the arm and pulled him away from the table. "We'll split something that's worth a lot more than any poker pot you ever played for."

Cat looked pained, his straggly mustache bristling as he screwed up his face. "A job? You mean work? No thanks, Dutch, work makes me tired."

"Too tired to lift your share of a few thousand ounces of gold off a train?" Cat's pained expression was rapidly replaced by a grin. "Hell, I'm ready, Dutch. I was just kiddin' about work, especially if it pays that well."

Dutch didn't tell Cat about Detective Surcingle.

Chapter 5

Just Like Old Times

Two weeks later Dutch and Cat rode out of Rawlins towards a rendezvous on Wyoming's Red Desert with the gold-bearing train. They rode fresh horses, leading four pack-mules. The mules were outfitted with pack frames to carry the gold.

"Dutch, I'm a mite bothered." Cat tipped his hat back and tugged at his ear. "If we get a posse after us, we won't have a chance draggin' these damn mules behind us. Why don't we just bury most of the gold and get it later?"

"What are you going to do, Cat? Tell the train crew not to peek whilst we dig a hole? Anyway, if anybody tracks us they'd see digging signs for sure. We don't know for sure how much gold there will be, but if there is a lot the mules will do better than horses. Don't worry Cat, I have a few tricks up my sleeve that will buy us some time."

The days were longer now, but the sun was setting when Dutch and Cat arrived at a tiny water-filled depression in the Red Desert a mile north of the railroad. A rim of greening grass surrounded the pond. "We'll camp here for the night and leave two of the mules here in the morning."

THE TROUBLE WITH GOLD...

"Dutch, maybe I'm dumb, but why would ya leave two of the mules way out here? Seems like as how it'd be easier to load everything right at the train."

"You'll see soon enough, Cat. Right now let's look things over. It always pays to get a feel for the area. I don't like surprises."

Over a hill to the south of the railroad they came upon a band of sheep grazing the fresh spring grass. "Right where I hoped they'd be. You can tell what day of the month it is by where old Juan has his sheep. Let's ride over and say howdy to the herder."

"Dutch, I don't get it. We're going to all kinds of trouble to be secret and you want to say howdy to a sheep herder?"

"Buenas dias, Juan." Dutch raised his hand in salutation then rode over and spoke a few words in Spanish, gesturing as he talked.

Later, as they rode away, Dutch explained. "I helped Juan out here a few years ago when I was on the run. He'll be sure to give some bad directions to anyone following us. I left a few bucks with him. That'll buy us a few hours head start."

It was dark when Dutch and Cat finished their supper. A crisp chill of the high desert settled over their camp. They hunkered close to the glowing embers and sipped tea while Dutch explained his strategy to Cat. "First of all we don't know just how much gold there is. I'm hoping there will be enough to overload two mules. Anybody set to give chase will figure to catch up with us pretty quick, seeing how heavy the mules are loaded. They'll be in a hurry to catch us. They'll be careless and make some mistakes."

"Heck, it'll take plenty of time to get a posse on our trail anyway." Cat pulled at his scraggly mustache, feeling better now that it seemed to be an easy heist and a rich one at that.

"Cat"

"Well, there is one little thing I hadn't mentioned, Cat." Dutch grinned to himself in the darkness, already savoring Cat's certain reaction. "The thieves will have their own guard on the train. I suspect he will be in the car with the gold, but he might be anywhere. With any luck he'll be in the caboose. Now let's try to get a few hours rest before we have to go to work."

Cat yawned and spread out his blankets. "I don't guess one guard will be much of a problem. A lot easier than that hold-up at Wilcox with Butch. The thieves probably hired some over-the-hill railroad bull."

"He isn't any retired railroad bull, but you might remember him from a few years ago, Cat. He gave the Wild Bunch a bad time. Paddymack told me they'd hired Charlie Surcingle."

Cat sat up straight in his bedroll, his face faintly reflecting a red glow from the dying fire. "Dad blast it, Dutch!" Cat exploded in anger. "Are you joshin' me? I would'na come if I'd knowed that."

"That's why I didn't tell you." Dutch grinned.

Cat pulled at his ear, then his mustache. "We should'a least brought more help."

"Just don't shoot him, Cat. We'll tie him up if he's in the express car. If he's in the caboose, we'll cut it loose and let it roll back. It'll go a mile or two. Now get a good night's sleep."

Cat mumbled something unintelligible as he rolled up in his blankets.

Dutch slept lightly and rose when the night was at its darkest, long before the first light of dawn. The grass was white with heavy frost. He shivered abruptly from something more than the chill air. *Maybe the train went by early. Maybe Cat was right. There should be more of us. I didn't have to make a deal with Paddymack. I don't know why I agreed to do this.*

But he did know why, and it made him angry. Once again Temptation had knocked him off the wagon that Conscience had been so carefully guiding. Of course, the gruesome death of Tom Hoskins had tipped the balance.

Dutch hated to admit it, but other factors, too, had mustered him out of his vow of an honest life. There was the heady excitement of robbing a train one more time. After all, the gold was already stolen. "I wonder if two wrongs make a right in this case? Stealing stolen gold!" He laughed.

"What did you say, Dutch?" Cat asked groggily, poking his head out from the warmth of his bedroll.

"Nothing, Cat. Except I suppose we should get ready. The train should be showing up in an hour or so."

Dutch felt exhilaration, a heady combination of planning, danger, and the rush of excitement that surged through his body. His previous premonition faded.

Cat echoed his excitement. "Hell Dutch, it's kinda like puttin' all yore money on one roll of loaded dice. We can't hardly lose but we don't know just how much we might win."

"Yeh, I guess it'll be like the train stickups we used to do a long time ago. What the heck, Cat, it'll be fun to shake up the railroad one more time."

"What about them mine thieves, Dutch? They're gonna really be pissed! Especially if they have Surcingle on the job."

"I reckon they're going to be more than pissed, but I wonder how a thief gets the law to help look for something he stole? They can't even tell the railroad what they're shipping. By the way, the shipment is marked Lead Ingots for Press Type."

"Maybe the railroad won't put anybody on our tail if they don't know we stole anything valuable." Cat sounded hopeful.

"I wouldn't count on it. For sure it's the worst sort of insult to challenge them. That will stir them up more than losing somebody else's goods. I'm most worried about Charlie Surcingle. He'll hound us to the end of creation if we don't lose him at the beginning."

In his mind Dutch again rationalized the harmlessness of stealing from thieves. Again Conscience found its voice, *"Baloney! It is not an honest way to start a ranch."*

"Dammit. Dammit to Hell." Dutch muttered angrily.

A distant and familiar sound wiped out the anger. The lonesome wail of a train whistle flowed over the hills.

THE TROUBLE WITH GOLD...

Like flooding water, it sought out every space and filled it. A faint chugging followed as the train clickity-clacked across the desert.

"Come on Cat, let's go." Dutch pulled his bandanna up over his lower face and silently swore that this would be his last job. He tightened the cinch and swung into the saddle.

Cat adjusted his own bandanna that made his jug ears stand out. He made several rapid draws with his pistol to make sure it slid smoothly from its oiled holster. After the last draw he twirled the weapon on his finger and expertly shoved it back in its holster.

"Remember, this is different from the old days. There aren't as many places to hide, and there's more people to look for us, especially if we shoot somebody. That's only a couple of the reasons there aren't any train robbers anymore. We don't need any shooting today."

"Aw hell Dutch, let me just ricochet a round or two off the engine. We could scare 'em a little and they'd be more accomadatin'."

Dutch remembered that Cat was a good hand–not overly smart, but tough and willing to follow orders. With most things he could be trusted, but he could be a little impulsive when it came to using his gun. What Dutch liked most about Cat, what made him a good partner in crime, was his unflinching loyalty.

"Cat, if Surcingle is on the caboose we might get by without alerting him if we don't make a lot of noise. We'll unhitch the train behind the express car. If Charlie's with the gold we'll have to get the jump on him and tie him up. If he's in the caboose he'll roll back a mile or two before he knows what's going on."

Cat nodded with a show of disappointment and slid the gun back into its holster as they approached the tracks. He liked the reassuring sound; cold steel against the oiled leather. He knew a whizzing bullet could hurry things along in a holdup, but he respected Dutch's caution. *Hell, I guess I was born to follow a man like Dutch. I reckon he's sorta' the father I never knew.* The huffing and puffing became more labored as the train climbed the slight grade approaching the barely discernible Continental Divide. Showers of sparks outlined the black smoke against the star-studded sky. Drawing closer, the engine loomed demon-like out of the darkness, a snorting cacophony of steam and clanking metal. The engineer signaled with the whistle and the train slowed as Dutch waved a red lantern from side to side as a signal of distress. Dutch had picked the stopping point to be on the grade where the train would be slowing, but most importantly, it would take longer to get up to speed after the holdup. When he'd worked as a sheepherder here he'd noticed how the freight trains labored and slowed on the long grade east of Tipton station.

The train came to a stop, its wheels screeching with a shower of sparks from the rails, as Dutch rode up along side the engine with his gun drawn. He waved his pistol menacingly and yelled at the engineer. "Keep that thing stopped until I tell you to move it on."

The engineer nodded his head vigorously but the fireman made a move as to jump from the far side of the train. Cat aimed his pistol at the fireman. "Put yer hands up and keep 'em there." The light from the firebox reflected the menace in his eyes. He quickly rode back and uncoupled the rest of the train from behind the express car. Dutch deftly swung aboard the engine and with motions of his .45 commanded the engineer to move up the tracks.

Leading Dutch's horse, Cat rode alongside the engine. Dutch hoped Cat would keep his finger light on the trigger. If he kept his cool they would be well on their way with the loot by the time Charlie Surcingle figured out what was going on.

Behind them the uncoupled cars slowly began to roll back down the slight grade. In the glimmer of dawn Dutch could see them increasing their distance from the moving engine and the express car. When Dutch judged that there was a mile separating them, he ordered the engineer to stop and motioned Cat toward the express car. Cat carried four sticks of dynamite bound in two bundles. According the Paddymack's information there would be two strongboxes in the express car. "Open the dad-blamed door!"

There was a muffled curse in the express car. "Go to hell!"

"I'm in a hurry, mister. You got five seconds an' I'm count'n now before I light a short fuse on this dynamite."

The express door slid open and a guard jumped down, raising his hands as he hit the ground. He wore a Union Pacific guard's uniform. Cat shoved his pistol into the guard's ribs. "Who else is in the express car?"

"Nobody." Cat pushed the gun a little harder. "Honest, mister, there ain't anybody else here. Don't shoot, I won't try nuthin'."

"Where's Surcingle?"

The guard hesitated briefly before another nudge from Cat encouraged him to talk. "He's back in the caboose."

Cat disarmed the guard and shoved him over to where Dutch was binding the hands of the other crewmen. When he had finished tying them up, Dutch pushed them to the ground behind some rocks, "Keep your heads down boys, there'll be one hell of a bang pretty quick."

Cat found the two strongboxes, just as Dutch had described. He centered a dynamite bundle on each of them, then molded a few handfuls of mud over the dynamite. The mud would direct the blasts into the boxes, assuring that they would be laid open neatly. He attached the fuses and then looked around until he found another heavy wooden box marked for shipment to Mr. P. Mackee, Rock Springs, Wyoming. He pulled the box off to one side where it would not be damaged by the explosion. He called down. "I found 'em all."

Cat cut the fuse lengths for fifteen seconds and lit the ends together. As they started spewing out sparks from the burning powder he leaped out of the car and ran for cover behind the engine.

"...four, five, six." Cat counted out the seconds as he ran, knowing that even fifteen seconds would seem impossibly long. It was always that way when you were waiting for the fuses to burn and wondering if the damn things had misfired. He'd learned to count off the seconds after getting knocked off his feet once.

Nearby, Dutch waited. *Good Lord, the fuse must have been bad. It's been way too long.* The guard slowly raised his head as if thinking the same thing. Then a shattering explosion blew out the roof of the mail car. Pieces of the car rained down around them. Mail and cash fluttered from the sky, picked up by a morning breeze born on the heels of night.

Dutch and Cat hoisted themselves up into the express car. Surrounded by litter of the destroyed strongboxes were two piles of canvas bags. One of the bags had spilled its contents across the floor. Despite the darkness they could see a dim glitter of the ore from Cripple Creek. Carefully they scooped the spilled treasure into an extra sack they had brought along.

Cat held some pieces of the gold in his hand. "Dutch, it's heavier than sin. Come daylight I want to get a good look at what our future looks like. I reckon its gotta be more beautiful than 'most anything!"

"Come on Cat, get a move on. Surcingle will have his boots on about now. Keep an eye on the crew."

Cat jumped down and led the two mules to the side of the express car where he and Dutch loaded the heavy bags into sturdy panniers, the leather containers they would bind to the pack frames on the mules. Dutch marveled at the amount of gold. Paddy had exaggerated, but not by a lot. "Be sure and clean up all of it, Cat. I bet the Union Pacific doesn't know what's in these crates. It will be just as well if they can't figure it out. Those mine thieves sure didn't want to advertise by identifying the contents."

They loaded the two mules up with as much gold as they could carry, leaving a generous amount for Paddymack's share.

Dutch found the small trunk destined for Mr. P. Mackee. From his pocket he retrieved a key and opened the hefty padlock. Inside were several pieces of granite, tightly packed with wadded newspaper. It was just as he and Paddymack, alias Mr. P. Mackee, had planned. Dutch hurled the pieces of granite out onto the prairie on the side away from the train crew. He placed the remaining bags of gold into the crate, packed them tightly with the newspaper and secured the lid. The gold weighed about the same as the seventy or eighty pounds of rock that it replaced. *This is more than ten percent,* Dutch thought. *Oh well, he'll need it to get into the Homestead House.* He laughed as he remembered one of Paddymack's arguments for a bigger cut.

"This'll fix ol' Paddymack up for the rest of his worthless life." Dutch commented to Cat as he locked the little trunk. Together they shoved it back into a corner of the car.

"Dutch, I don't understand you sometimes. Why should we leave anything for Paddy? He ain't here to know and wouldn't know where to find us."

"Well, Cat, there's two reasons and either one will do. One, he earned it. And two, there's more gold than we can pack anyways. Now let's take care of that telegraph line."

Dutch tossed his lariat over the telegraph wire that ran alongside the track and pulled it down as Cat reached up and cut it.

"That'll take care of the telegraph back to Rawlins. We'd better get a move on, Cat." Mounting their horses and leading the mules they crossed the tracks in front of the engine and headed southwest. The heavily laden mules left deep tracks in the sand.

"Have you lost your mind, Dutch?" Cat said in a husky whisper. "You're going the wrong way." Cat pointed back to the other side of the railroad track where they had left the other mules.

"Yesterday I told the sheepherder that we would be headed for a hideout in Brown's Park. Old Juan knows that's not true, but he'll pass the word to anyone on our trail. It would be a logical place for us to hide."

"But Dutch, what about the other..."

Dutch held up his hand to silence Cat. They rode on, Cat shaking his head and muttering to himself.

As they rode over a hill they saw Juan's band of sheep slowly moving out from their bed-ground. Dutch and Cat rode ahead of them, then turned sharply west. Looking back Dutch watched as Juan sent out his dogs to turn the leaders, heading them over the tracks of the horses and gold bearing mules. It would take some time before a tracker could find where their tracks emerged from the overprint of several hundred sheep. Juan raised his arm in farewell.

Ten minutes later Dutch turned back north. They crossed the railroad tracks out of sight of the stopped engine. Cat threw back his head and laughed as he figured out Dutch's plan.

They soon reached the other mules and quickly redistributed the gold. The little caravan started out across the Great Divide Basin towards the Quien Sabe Ranch hideaway nestled next to Hoodoo Creek on Copper Mountain, 150 miles and three day's ride away.

Looking back, they watched the engine's plume of smoke as it moved back to recouple, the engineer pulling angry blasts from the whistle. Dutch knew that news of the heist would be on the wires from the next station beyond the cut wire. From Rock Springs, more than sixty miles to the west, it would take hours to get a posse organized and start pursuit across the desolate land.

The Great Divide Basin is a daunting place. More than a hundred miles across, it is a mile and a half above sea level. The wind blows incessantly, unfettered by any vegetation higher than scrubby sagebrush. The main inhabitants are herds of pronghorn antelope that graze the shortgrass with the safety of vast vistas ideal for their telescopic vision.

Snow can fall during any month of the year and the spring storms are often the most dangerous. Only occasionally can the rare traveler, anxious for landmarks, spot the distant peaks of the Wind River Mountains far to the northwest, and rarely the Sierra Madres to the southeast. Robbed of majestic mountains to define its location, the continent's divide seems lost and takes two courses, forming the Great Divide Basin where the rare waters of inconsequential draws wander until lost in the sands of the desert.

Dutch hoped that this great reach of almost trackless countryside would prove a good route for their escape. Shifting sands could wipe out tracks in a matter of minutes. During the heat of the day the sun's intensity often made shimmering images that danced and distorted ones ability to distinguish distant objects. With luck he and Cat, with their gold-laden mule train, would be safe at their Quien Sabe Ranch hideout while any pursuers were still searching the hidden canyons of Brown's Hole.

Dutch looked up at the stars, rapidly fading as the day began. The North Star was barely visible. He confirmed their direction of travel, due north. His inate compass rarely failed him, but he liked to have confirmation. He scanned the horizon. There would be no storm today. Intuitively Dutch knew the signs of nature that told him the time and the day's upcoming weather. Even his own mood was a signal of weather changes. He knew that in this country there would be wind later in the day. "Cat, I reckon it'll be a nice spring day. Of course that might be good or bad, depending how soon Mr. Surcingle finds our trail."

Cat stood in his stirrups and looked back. "I don't see anything back there yet. Maybe we've lost him." Cat's words were hopeful but the tone of his voice was not.

As the sun showed its first glimmer Cat looked across the seemingly endless desert. Not a tree was in sight and even the sagebrush had a low, windblown profile. "My God, we'll never find our way across this hell." His voice was tight.

"Don't worry Cat. See that yonder hill with the little bump on top? That's the direction we want. When we get there we'll check the sun and set our bearing again. We'll make Crooks Creek for camp tonight. There's a nice hidden meadow at Sand Springs in the dunes next to Green Mountain. We'll find a water hole or two between here and there. It'll be a long day's ride but there's nobody out here to see us."

"Shi-oot, I cain't even tell which direction we're going. I cain't even see that little hill with the bump anymore. And I don't 'spect we'll just stumble onto any water."

"Don't worry about that, Cat. There's low spots in dry lake beds. They'll have enough water there from the spring rains for the horses." Dutch whistled Swanee River, carrying the words in his mind. He would have liked to travel a little faster but they had to stop frequently to tighten up the pack frames.

"Dutch, when I was down on the border, I met some pack trains coming out of the mines down in Mexico. Them mules was loaded down with twice as much as ours and cinched up so tight that the loads didn't move at all. Seems like we could be using fewer mules and cinch up the bigger loads tighter. We'd make better time."

"I've seen those Mexican pack saddles. *Aparejos*. They're cruel things. The poor mules are cinched up so tight that they moan in pain and sometimes the rig rubs

THE TROUBLE WITH GOLD... 45

holes right through their hides. I felt like shooting the muleskinners for their stupid cruelty, then the poor mules to put them out of their misery. We'll make better time the way we're doing it."

Towards noon they rode over some small sand hills and down to a small depression puddled with recent rainwater. They stopped to let the animals graze and water. They pulled the heavy packs off the mules and tethered them in the little meadow that bordered the pond. The sun, at its zenith, soaked them with the delicious warmth of a Wyoming spring day.

"Dutch, how much gold do you reckon we've got?" Cat relaxed back against a large sagebrush and chewed on a piece of jerky.

"Well, judging from the mules' tracks and the weight of each sack as we loaded it I'd guess there's probably a hundred and fifty pounds on each mule. Let's see." Dutch pushed his hat back and he furrowed his forehead in thought. "That would be six hundred pounds, maybe a little more. Of course gold is measured in troy ounces instead of regular ounces. Regular ounces is butter or something ordinary and gold is sold in troy ounces. There's only 14 ounces of gold to a pound so we'd have to take that into account." Dutch rubbed his face to mask his grin as he waited for Cat take the bait.

Cat twitched his mouth, pulling his scraggly mustache to one side. He wrinkled his brow and rolled his slightly bulging eyes up in perplexed thought. "Sumethin' ain't right about your figger'n. Are you tellin' me that if that was butter on them mules, there'd be more of that than gold? Hell, Dutch, I betcha an ounce of gold weighs as much as a *pound* of butter!" Cat was quiet as he thought about the numbers. "What's an ounce of gold worth?"

"About twenty dollars, but..."

"Take twenty bucks times fourteen or sixteen or whatever ounces are in a pound. That times a hundred and fifty pounds times four mules is a lot a money, Dutch! Shi-oot! That must be a million bucks!"

"If it were all gold it might be, but this isn't all gold. It's pretty rich stuff but it isn't pure gold. We might have four or five thousand ounces at most."

"Dagonnit, Dutch, that cain't be right. If gold is so damn heavy it only makes sense that there's more than a few ounces in a pound. Are you pullin' my leg? I don't think we'd oughta be usin' them funny ounces."

I just know about troy ounces from when I worked in the mine." Dutch paused for a moment, mischief in his eyes. "I asked a banker once about troy ounces. The story he told me was that a long time ago over in Greece, Helen of Troy cornered the gold market by buying in troy ounces and selling in regular ounces. Or maybe it was the other way around, I'm not sure. So I guess it matters if you're buying or selling. And it'd be better if you were good looking like Helen instead of being ugly."

"Dammit, Dutch, you piss me off sometimes."

Dutch chuckled gleefully and climbed to the top of a nearby sand dune where he could see back on their trail and ahead towards Green Mountain. The only movement was a scattering of grazing antelope. Bluebirds flitted around the nearby sagebrush. It was a peaceful scene. Down below, Cat propped on his elbow, took out a deck of cards and deftly dealt a hand of solitaire.

Dutch scanned the open desert one more time. He saw nothing unusual. Back down in the hollow he scrunched down on top of a dense sagebrush, working himself around until he had a comfortable perch. Overhead a single white wisp signaled the early beginning of the spring afternoon's clouds. In a voice directed to no one he quoted a line of Wordsworth. *"I wandered lonely as a cloud that floats on high o'er vales and hills."* He leaned back and squirmed down into the sagebrush, pulling the brim of his hat down over his eyes.

"Dutch, you beat all. Where in heck do ya git them fancy words yer always spoutin' off." There was no answer. Dutch had drifted into a nap.

An hour later the two outlaws were on their way again. Dutch repeatedly scanned the hills behind, knowing their tracks would be plainly visible. The light colored hills shimmered, breathless, under the glaring sun. He hoped the wind would soon come up and cover their tracks with drifting sand. Low places in the desert would appear to be filled with water that would just as suddenly disappear. A distant bush would stretch to mock the image of a tree, then float mirage-like and disappear.

By late afternoon they reached the crest of a broad featureless hill, which was high enough to survey the countryside for miles. As Dutch scanned the desert he spotted a dark speck of movement on a sand dune they had crossed two hours earlier. It shimmered, then disappeared and abruptly was there again. He stared at it and was uncertain whether the shimmering object had moved. He wiped the sweat away from his eyes and looked again. The object, if there had been one, had vanished once again. "Cat, I thought I could see something moving back on that far sand dune. Can you see anything?"

Cat, immediately alarmed, reined in his horse, stood in his stirrups and twisted around to look. After staring for several seconds he shook his head. "It must have been a mirage, they sure are dancin' right now."

Still searching the distant hill Dutch shook his head. "I remember riding with Butch. It seemed like Surcingle was a mirage. We'd be certain we had made a clever get-a-way, then before we'd had time to catch our breath, there would be old Charlie high onto our tail. He'd just appear, like coming out of thin air. Just like that speck in the distance."

Chapter 6

The Range Detective

Charlie Surcingle was asleep in the caboose when the train stopped. Shortly after the train had left Rawlins, he had drifted into sleep, lulled by the steady clacking of the wheels over the rails. He struck a match and looked at his pocket watch. *About the right time to be taking on water at Tipton.* A minute later he could feel the train move backwards. *The dadblamed engineer must of overshot.* He yawned and turned over to resume his sleep.

Charlie had been hired by the crooked Cresson Mine boss to accompany the gold shipment to San Francisco. Not even the Union Pacific knew what was in the two heavy lock boxes or even which shipment Charlie was riding shotgun for. Charlie wondered if his job here was really necessary considering the boxes were labeled as lead ingots and only he and the shipper knew the contents of the shipment. Charlie didn't know the gold came from. Nor did he ask. The shipper was a long time friend from the days that Charlie had worked in the mines. Charlie's job was to see the shipment safely to its destination, San Francisco, where he intended to have a good time.

THE TROUBLE WITH GOLD...

He turned over and was dreaming of a long lost love when a distant "BOOM" brought him out of his bed. Charlie and the brakeman rushed to the window of the car and looked ahead but it was too dark to see anything.

"What do you reckon that was?" the brakeman yelled.

"I reckon either the boiler blew or we's being robbed." Charlie slipped on his boots, followed by his hat.

"My God, I hope there won't be a shootout!" The brakeman fretted.

"Won't be. If it's a holdup we'll play by my rules. Ain't no use gittin' in a dither until there's some light to see by. We're still movin' backwards. We might be disconnected from the engine. That blast was some distance away. Maybe you'd best get this thing stopped before we're too damn far away to do anything. Then help me get my horse out of the next car."

It took the brakeman several minutes to put down a ramp and walk Charlie's big horse onto the ground. Charlie quickly saddled his horse and loaded the saddlebag with rations. After a few minutes ride he arrived at the site of the holdup to find the train crew still struggling with their bonds. With his bowie knife he quickly released them.

"The bastard pistol whipped me," moaned the guard. He rubbed his head where a piece of the express car had hit him when he had peeked over the rock.

Charlie quizzed each of the crew separately, asking what they had seen or heard. The engineer was in a state of agitation. "Robbers! There was several of them and a bunch of horses. They had masks over their faces but I got a look at one of 'em. His ears stuck out like a jackrabbit's."

The fireman was the coolest of the crew. "I overheard the one in charge mention Brown's Park and they rode in that direction. Maybe there were more, but I only saw two of them."

Charlie climbed up into the express car and and saw the blasted strongboxes. There wasn't a trace of anything left to give a clue as to what was in the boxes except for the stenciled letters, *Lead Ingots.* "Nobody would go to this trouble for some lead ingots," Charlie muttered. "Whoever did this had inside information." Back on the ground Charlie searched the area around the express car for tracks and any other clues the bandits might have left behind. Gradually he expanded his search out from the train and found what he was looking for. Two horses and two mules had traveled across the drifted sand a few hundred yards south of the railroad. The mule tracks were deep. The tracks headed southwest towards Utah.

Charlie grinned to himself. "Hell, these fellows ain't gonna get very far or very fast with those loads. Those mules must be carryin' two or three hundred pounds apiece."

The loose sand made it easy to follow the tracks. *They're headed straight for Browns Park in Utah, all right.* Charlie knew that country well. It was a rugged place with the myriads of canyons that had been an outlaw hangout in the old days. He urged his horse into an easy lope. His eyes squinted with grimness as he realized there could be gunplay before the full light of day. It wouldn't take long to catch up with the bandits and their overloaded mules. "Heck, I'll get to San Francisco yet." A disturbing thought niggled his mind. *Maybe it's too doggoned easy.*

Then the outlaw's tracks were gone, wiped out by a large band of sheep. Spurring his horse a little Charlie continued in the same direction through the obliterating tracks of hundreds of sheep. Occasionally he had to slow and detour around the straggling back of the herd. It was some time before he managed to ride around the band of woolies. The tracks of his quarry were missing. Wheeling his horse he rode east for a quarter of a mile but still no tracks. Turning back he rode to the west. The outlaws and their loot seemed to have vanished into thin air.

Charlie reined in his horse and took off his dusty Stetson. He chuckled and pulled at his white mustache.

"By durn, maybe ol' Butch Cassidy did make it back from South America." As he topped a small ridge he saw the sheepherder a short distance away and rode over to him. "Howdy, I'm looking for two friends who rode through here an hour or so ago."

The herder looked at him and spread his hands. He shook his head. "No ingles."

"Dos amigos con dos mules."

The herder waved to the southwest, nodding vigorously with a broad smile.

"Gracias."

Patiently Charlie began a traverse southwest, beyond his earlier search. Nothing. "Clever buggers. They bribed that herder, sure as heck!" Charlie didn't know whether to laugh or curse. He rode back to the railroad tracks two miles west of the holdup spot. Riding along the bare ground near the rails he found what he was looking for. The outlaw's tracks were headed north. "Brown's Park, my raw butt!" He looked at his watch. They have a good three hours jump on me. "Well, hell's fire. We can catch them overloaded mules." He patted the neck of his horse.

Charlie looked up at the sky. "Butch Cassidy, you ol' SOB, I know for a fact that you're buried down there in the Andes. Why in hell did you have to come back and haunt me?" Charlie chuckled and snorted. "Well, you're not so gol-durn smart as you think."

Twenty minutes later he found the spot where the outlaws had redistributed their load onto four mules. "I'll be go to the devil and halfway back." He took off his hat and beat it against his thigh in momentary exasperation, then laughed. "Heck, this is going to be fun."

Charlie Surcingle

* * *

Night was approaching as Dutch and Cat neared Crooks Gap where two mountains squeezed the desert into a narrow neck before it opened again into the Sweetwater country. The long day was taking its toll on men and animals, but they were more than fifty miles from the pre-dawn holdup.

THE TROUBLE WITH GOLD...

"I reckon Surcingle will figure on us camping at the old stage station in Crooks Gap. It's too dark for him to track us now. We'll detour a bit where he's not likely to see us." Dutch led the way into a hidden oasis a few miles east of the old stage stop. There they made camp next to a bubbling spring. Sand dunes formed a perfect shelter along the lush, grassy banks of a small stream fed by the spring. Water poured sweet and cold from the spring.

"I don't like it, Dutch. We're wastin' time strayin' off the road like this."

"If Surcingle is on our tail it'll take cleverness instead of speed to lose him."

With the animals picketed by the stream, they ate a cold, sparse meal of jerky and hardtack. A fire would be too risky. Instead of hot coffee they substituted cold spring water, filtered through the sand. Dutch lay over the bank and drank long from the spring. The water was sweet and pure. "Hell, Cat, this stuff is better than any darn whiskey!"

"Dutch, you're g'tting' downright weird!" Cat scooped up some water with the dusty brim of his hat and drank from it, screwing up his face in distaste as he beat his hat dry against his leg.

Cat stared in disbelief as Dutch ate watercress that he pulled by the roots from the spring. Dutch laughed and handed a sprig to Cat who nibbled at it tentatively. "Well hell, it does sorta taste like radishes," Cat said, as he pulled another plant from the water.

The night was unusually warm and the sky cloudless. Dutch knew that the warm air probably meant a change in weather, but for now the heavens were clear. The Milky Way glowed, magnificent with its awesome silence. Down in Texas the cowboys on a cattle drive called it the Milkmaid's Path and claimed that if you looked carefully, you could see a beautiful woman's face in the shining galaxy. Dutch reckoned she was only visible to a cowboy who had been on the trail for a long time.

But Dutch did find her once, a long time ago. He was in love at the time. In unspoken love with that lovely, warm girl, Etta, who traveled for a while with Cassidy's bunch. Now, years later, he kept the memory of Etta alive in his mind but he could no longer find her in the stars. He wondered whatever had happened to her. He felt a sadness that he would never see her again.

"Cat, did you ever see the girl in the stars?"

"The girl where? Dutch, are you gettin' addled?"

"No, I'm serious. A pretty woman's face shows up plain as can be if you look at the Milky Way just right." He knew that Cat wouldn't see her. He didn't have much imagination.

"I'd rather see the real thing at the Ritzy Parlor after we cash in some of this gold."

Cat was, Dutch thought, practical, if not romantic. He stretched out under his blankets and looked up at the glowing trail of stars. The galaxy seemed so grandly immense it went beyond one's comprehension. Somehow it seemed to roar with its silence. *I wonder why the Greeks didn't have a god of the Milky Way, sometimes it seems to have more power than the moon.*

Dutch closed his eyes and listened to the gentle murmuring of the creek. His thoughts returned again to Etta. She had first ridden into Cassidy's Hole-in-the-wall camp with Harry Longabaugh. The Sundance Kid, they'd tagged the happy-go-lucky Longabaugh. Etta was wearing riding britches and sat astride her horse instead of riding sidesaddle, the way proper women did. It didn't seem wrong. Just something she did because it made more sense. She was that way. Choosing practicality over convention. She was slender, yet shapely, and her face–he'd never before seen a girl with such beauty. Beauty that emanated from a kind and happy soul. Hers was the sort of loveliness that seemed to grow because of her kindness and happy personality.

She was Sundance's girl, but Dutch had fallen in love with her. It was a secret love. Because of his friendship with Sundance, he had buried his feelings deep in the inner recesses of his mind. Sometimes he would watch Etta, drinking in the magic of her, when she would catch him and smile. He would grin, embarrassed, and hope she couldn't read his mind.

Unable to sleep, Dutch opened his eyes and looked again at the glowing trail in the night sky, wishing he could see Etta, at least in the stars. Then, just for a fleeting moment, he did. She was smiling, just as he remembered. Then she was gone. He rubbed his eyes but the haunting image would not return.

The next morning Dutch and Cat rose with the sun and ate their breakfast–a repeat of supper. This time, though, the meal was livened with coffee, made over a discreet, smokeless fire of dry willow twigs. After breakfast, Dutch climbed to the top of a large dune next to the creek and lay there for a long while, combing the distant desert and the area around the old stage stop for movement.

"If he's out there, Charlie will be watching for us to move early. Right now I'd reckon he doesn't know just where we are. Let's get out of here, anyway. I don't feel right about this place – just something in my bones, Cat." Quickly they saddled the horses, repacked the mules and moved out, riding up the steep flank of Green Mountain, through a pine forest on top, and down the other side.

"Dutch, why ain't we takin' the main road? We'd be making better time if we weren't flailin' through the sagebrush and trees."

"Maybe, but the main road goes through Crooks Gap. That would be a likely place for Charlie to ambush us. If he doesn't see our tracks he may wait for us and we'll have more of a head start. We'll take the long way and keep a little bit of fear in our hearts. Sometimes haste and bravery make dead fools."

A stiff breeze signaled changing weather as they descended into the broad, windy valley of the Sweetwater River. Sagebrush covered hills and dunes stretched for miles to the granite knobs along the Sweetwater River. Dutch scanned the country but it seemed that he and Cat were the only inhabitants of the valley. They rode down and crossed the dry bed of Crooks Creek then up to the stage road. Dutch dismounted and looked closely at the road. He saw no sign that Charlie Surcingle had passed this way. Dutch wondered if he was only imagining that the detective was on their trail. Perhaps it was only a mirage that he had seen the day before. He glanced at the darkening sky and smelled rain on the wind. Crossing the road he ripped up a sagebrush and clumsily brushed it over their tracks on the road.

Cat looked at him in puzzlement. "Dutch, I don't mean to be insulting but a blind man can see where you tried to brush out our tracks."

"That's exactly what I want, Cat. I figure if old Charlie is close behind us he'll be thinking rain. If he sees our tracks striking out for Lander he'll figure on picking up our trail tomorrow. Its not far down the road to the Rongis saloon and I'm thinking Charlie will opt for that instead of following us in the rain. Let's find a high spot and watch for a while. I'd like to at least know if it is Surcingle who's on our tail. It helps to know who you're up against." Dutch remounted and they rode in the direction of Lander.

As the wind picked up, Cat grumbled. "Hell, it looks to me that old Surcingle will be stayin' dry and we'll be out in the rain bein' miserable."

Towering thunderheads quickly moved over them, flashes of lightning glowing in the dark interior of the clouds. The following thunder increased its tempo like drummers with a marching army. On a dry flat of hardpan Dutch abruptly wheeled his horse to the south into some sandy hills. "Hold the animals here, I'm going to take a look back at where we crossed the road." He crawled to the top of a small hill where he could see the stage road leading out of Crooks Gap. It was not more than a few minutes before he spotted a movement on the road where it first appeared out of the gap. It was a solitary rider riding at a steady, determined pace. The man was bent forward in the saddle, looking down at the road and occasionally looking at the surrounding hills. Searching for signs of his quarry. Puffs of dust rose up from the horse's hooves and were quickly blown away by the stiff wind. The man rode easily, as one who has spent much of his life in the saddle. *At the rate he's riding he'll soon see where we crossed the road.*

Dutch turned and motioned to Cat. "Tie up the animals and come up here. Keep down." Cat tied the horses to sagebrush and hurried up the hill. As he'd crawled the last few feet to the top Dutch pointed ahead at the solitary rider. "Look at him, Cat. He's looking for tracks.

"Shi-oot!" Cat swore in a whisper, even though the rider was a mile away. "Do ya reckon that could be Surcingle? What if he decides to follow us? Hell, with these mules he could catch us in no time."

A strong gust of wind whipped a stinging flurry of sand over them. Dutch looked at Cat and grinned, shaking his head. He pointed at the darkening sky. Another squall brought a sharp smattering of rain. Dutch pointed to the black sky in the southwest. "That rain will soon be on us, Cat. There won't be any tracking once that gets here. Charlie knows that. I bet that right now he's thinking that it's time to stop the physical tracking and to start thinking like an outlaw. He'll figure we're headed for the pleasures of Lander and can catch us in due time. I'm betting he'll go to Rongis and wait out the storm."

They watched as the rider reined to a sudden stop where Dutch had partially brushed out their tracks. He turned in his saddle and looked intently in the direction they led. Finally he dismounted and followed their tracks on foot for a few feet off the road.

"What the hell is he doing?"

The man had dropped to his haunches.

"He's checking the grass where our horses stepped. He can tell just how long ago we made those tracks. He knows we're not far ahead. See him looking this way. Don't move. In a minute he'll get his field glasses." Dutch took out his own glasses and watched the man intently. "That's old Charlie Surcingle all right."

Dutch had called it right. For several long minutes Surcingle scanned in their direction with a field glass. Then he swung back onto his horse, looked at the approaching storm, and rode towards Rongis, disappearing over a rise in an easy lope. Cat laughed with relief. He looked at Dutch with admiration. He wished he could think clever like that. *Hell, I been thinkin' about women and poker.*

"Come on Cat, let's get out of here. He may double back yet. We're heading for Johnny Nogan's."

Spurring the horses into a trot with the mules trailing behind, they soon crossed the road and Surcingle's tracks. Cat glanced nervously in the direction Surcingle had gone, half expecting an ambush. A few large raindrops splattered. The horses picked up their pace, nipping at each other as they raced along with the freshening breeze. The mules, reluctant at first, raced along with the horses, showing their teeth in a jackass grin.

Dutch yelled at Cat. "I'm glad we tightened those pack cinches back there. If we hadn't, we'd be stringing gold all across the prairie." He laughed, accompanied by a burst of rain. Cat could only think of being wet and miserable. He hoped Dutch knew where they were going. There was no road, only stunted sage and sand. Ahead, towering granite monoliths loomed through the fog.

Holding the reins loosely in his teeth, Dutch reached back, untied his slicker, and pulled it on. Cat followed suit

THE TROUBLE WITH GOLD... 59

as lightning slashed the sky and stabbed into the nearby granite hills. A stubby pinon tree exploded in a whitehot brilliance. A quickly following thunderclap caused the horses to shy and lie their ears back with fright. Low clouds moved in rapidly with a cold wind and surges of wildly driving rain.

The heavens turned a slate gray and the rain settled into a steady downpour. The wet sand made the going easier except where the sand had blown free of the clay hardpan. The clay was as slippery as grease and they were forced to slow the horses to a walk, spurring them again when they reached another stretch of sand.

The two men rode in chilled, wet misery, slouched in their slickers. Small waterfalls poured off their hat brims, the wind swirling the water into their faces. Soon wet snow was mixed with the rain. As the temperature dropped, the snow intensified and plastered white against their rain gear. Their beards became ghostly lumps on their faces. Their efforts to hurry were further diminished when one of the pack mules lost a shoe.

Dutch could barely make out their location by the ghostly forms of the granite knobs as they approached the Sweetwater River. "We'll make Johnny Nogan's place soon. He'll fix that shoe for us. That is, if he isn't in Rongis on a binge. We'll stay at his cabin in any case."

"I wish the hell we were the ones going to Rongis instead of that damn detective. I could do with a drink and play a little poker." Cat grimaced and, one at a time, put a hand over his aching, cold ears. "Goldurnit, when I get to a decent town and cash in my gold, I ain't never gettin' on another horse cause I'm walkin' from the hotel to the saloon and back agin and they'd better be next door to each other. And the whore house will be upstairs at the saloon!"

The storm let up some by the time they reached the Sweetwater River. In spite of the rain, the Sweetwater, more of a creek than a river, flowed crystal clear over a bed of pebbles. Several large trout scurried under the banks. "If it weren't so damn cold I'd stop and catch a few of those trout. I bet ol' Johnny would fry them up for breakfast in the morning."

Cat didn't comment, but spurred his horse through the shallow waters to higher ground, hoping the breeze would dry out his clothes and melt the icy clumps from his mustache. He and Dutch rode on in silence, hunkered down in their slickers to keep warm.

With the detour and bad weather, they would barely make it to Johnny Nogan's before dark. The weather was so miserable Cat couldn't even keep a good daydream going. When he thought of being with a woman he could only imagine her telling him he was too cold to get in bed with.

The thick clouds brought early darkness as the bandits crossed expanses of low sandy hills and alkali flats. Like islands in the desert, dome-shaped granite monoliths jutted up into the low, raw clouds, their tops hidden from view. Wisps of fog swirled around the few juniper bushes that had gained a meager toehold in the granite cracks. Lightning flashes and rolling rumbles of thunder added to the otherworld scene. Dutch was fascinated by the display and barely noticed his discomfort. Cat was beginning to wonder if they would ever arrive at Johnny Nogan's place. Then Dutch pointed to a small cabin in the center of a desert plain that stretched between the granite hills. A lazy plume of smoke rose from the chimney.

* * *

Charlie Surcingle examined the outlaw's tracks where they crossed the road and knew he was close to his prey. He looked at the approaching storm and wondered if he could follow the tracks in the storm. A gust of wind swirled sand up into his face. Quickly he mounted his horse and turned towards Rongis. He swore as a sudden blast of wind drove the first stinging drops of rain into his back. *Wherever they go they will get a spending urge. Once they start cashing in the gold it'll be easy to track'em down.* Simultaneously the lightning stabbed at a nearby hill and the rain hit with a sudden soaking burst. He pulled his hat down hard over his ears. *Goldurnit! I should 'ave stayed on the rocking chair at my ranch.*

Chapter 7

Johnny Nogan

Johnny Nogan hurried out of his cabin, almost skipping with glee and a broad smile, "Begorra Dutch, I'm glad to see ya. I just butchered a lame steer and I got spuds in the cellar. Can ya stay the night?"

"Hell's fire, Johnny, we rode right on by Rongis, knowing the kind of fine cuisine we'd get here."

Johnny slapped his thigh and laughed. "Dutch, we gotta lot of catching up to do. It's been a few years since we cowboyed together." He shook Dutch's hand vigorously.

"Johnny, this is Cat. He and I are doing a little freighting job. Which reminds me. We'd sure appreciate it if you could reshoe one of our mules."

"Shor enough, Dutch, we'll get that first thing in the mornin'." He reached out and grabbed Cat's hand. "Good to meetcha Cat. If you can put up with this old sourpuss, you gotta be a pretty good sport. Come on in boys."

Johnny fixed supper while he and Dutch reminisced about old times. Dutch noticed that the usually profane Nogan hadn't used more that a couple of swear words since they'd arrived. "Johnny, I'm mighty puzzled by something. I haven't heard you cuss hardly at all."

"Dutch, I've changed me ways. I had something happen that made me realize the power of the Lord. From now on I'm His servant. But for the Lord's quick answer to me prayer I wouldn't be here with ya! Let's eat and I'll tell ya me tale."

That the Lord had called Johnny was, to Dutch, amazing. He and Johnny had spent some hell-raising nights at Lander. Dutch figured God would have higher priorities.

After supper they rolled Bull-Durham cigarettes and settled back as Nogan told them about his encounter with an enraged longhorn that had made him a religious man.

"Wal, I'd knowed 'bout this ol' mossy horn fer two or three years. He hung out in them breaks over by Lankin Dome, and a more clever critter I ain't never seed. He was onta' me tricks and always got away at the last minute. This time I outguessed him an' he ran right into a pen I'd built fer 'im.

"Now Dutch, ya know how smart them ol' steers kin be. They gits mighty ornery when they git outsmarted. Wal, he got mad all right. Then I did a real dumb thing. After I chased him inta the pen I jumped off me horse to wire up the gate. Would ya believe, I was so excited, stupid more likely, I found meself on the wrong side of the gate. I turned round, and by damn, er, dang, there was that critter lookin' at me real mean.

"Begorra, I swear that steer ad fire in his eyes and smoke was asnortn' from his nostrils. Course it was only his breath in the cold air, but ta me right then he shore looked bad enough to be the devil hisself! That critter stood for a bit of a second, na' ten feet away, pawin' the dirt into a big dust cloud thet was like smoke from hell. All the while he was bellowin' and swingin' his horns to and fro. Like me ol' friend Johnny Young use ta say, "Them horns ain't for ornamentin'!"

Johnny drew in a deep drag of smoke. Exhaling forcefully through his lips, he paused for a moment to let the suspense build. "Wal, that old bugger charged! He'd backed up a few yards to get up a good heada' steam and he came like a bolt a' lightnin'. That old boy had set his sights on me and was lookin' to dip them horns in blood."

Dutch and Cat were leaning forward in rapt attention. "Praise the Lord!" exclaimed Dutch, "I can't believe you're here to tell us this!"

Johnny paused, wanting to prolong his moment of glory as long as he could.

"Well, how in thunderation didya' get away?" asked Cat impatiently.

"Wal'," Johnny drawled, "course I didn't have time to jump on me horse. The truth be told I couldn't seem to move atall. Any direction I'da gone wouldn'a been enuf. I don't mine tellin' ya, I was scared as h...heck! I knowed it was payoff time fer all the hell I'd raised over the years. Me dear Ma, bless 'er heart, warned me I'd git me due some day." He stared at the flickering kerosene lamp, for a moment forgetting his audience.

"Wal, I seed that he wuz gonna hook out me liver with the first thrust of that horn. Then I figgered e'd finish me off by rippin' out the rest a' me innards and stringin' 'em round the prairie!" Nogan grabbed his belly and with a ripping motion spread his arms and swung them around to depict his gory fate. His face distorted with the imagined pain.

Dutch grinned at Johnny's theatrics. Cat's eyes bugged out in amazement as he leaned forward and waited for the outcome. He wondered if Johnny might rip open his shirt and reveal a ghastly wound.

"BeGorra, I didna' wanna die like that. I knowed it'd be mighty painful, less'n I was lucky and he caught me in the heart with that first charge." Nogan stopped, clutched his chest, then theatrically crossed himself. "I prayed to the Virgin Mother ta save me from pain with a quick death. Boys, that's what I prayed for and I meant it, ever' damn... er darn word.

"By Damn! Ahh - - -, dang! That son of the Devil swerved at that exact moment, and with a toss of his head gored me horse. Me poor steed dropped with nary a sound – didn't have time ta think about it. He'd been got right through his heart."

"Wal, I finely got some wits about me, pulled me pistol and shot that SOB right in 'is bloody horn. It knocked him out fer a while, but when he come to he'd got some manners, an' I was on the other side of the gate."

Nogan dabbed at his eyes with the back of his hand. "Old Star was me faverit' horse, worth a quid or two. Begorra, we worked good together, too."

Johnny's mouth quivered and he wiped another tear from his eye. Suddenly he smacked a fist into his open hand. "God DAMN that sons-a-bitchin' Devil!"

Johnnie jumped up. "Boys, that calls fer a drink!"

Dutch laughed, glad that Johnny wasn't taking religion too seriously. "Johnny, you're a dang lucky man!"

"Yep, I knows that Dutch, but ya know somethin'?" He winked at his friend. "I have a heck of a time expressin' meself since I got religion."

As the three sat around telling stories, they could hear the rain pick up its intensity, beginning with distant rolling thunder, then settling down to a steady downpour which only quieted when the rain turned to snow. Trickles of muddy water dripped down the inside walls from the sod covered roof. Contrasted with the miserable weather outside the dim glow of the lantern and the crackling wood stove produced an aura of warmth and security.

Later, Dutch lay in his blankets on the floor wondering if his various attempts to lose Charlie Surcingle had worked or only slightly delayed the chase. He had hoped to have some breathing room at the old hideout at Copper Mountain but now he doubted that. With Surcingle hot on their backsides this big country suddenly seemed smaller. Dutch tossed and turned for an hour about how they might best the old range detective. Then his saddle-weary body succumbed to sleep, lulled by water dripping from the ceiling.

Chapter 8

Quien Sabe

The morning sun dawned bright, reflecting a sparkling brilliance off the new snow. A totally clear sky promised a quick end to the snow and a warm day. Johnny was up early and shoed the mule before fixing breakfast. Dutch and Cat, after the hearty breakfast of steak and flapjacks, bid their good-byes to Johnny and rode north to Beaver Rim. From there they could see Copper Mountain, their destination, 60 miles away.

To most travelers who crossed this country, the land was a desolate expanse of few people, strong winds and cold winters. To Dutch the land had a freshness that brought him to life. A plan was unfolding in his mind that he hoped would take the steam out of Surcingle's chase. It would mean putting the gold into hiding for a while. His ranch and Cat's revelry would have to wait.

Dutch breathed in deeply, his nostrils filling with the scent of rain washed sagebrush. A few early paintbrush dotted the expanse of silvery sage with red. Where the skiff of snow had melted, low-lying mayflower clumps and single pink bitter-roots showed themselves, glistening with beads of water. Bluebirds flitted with azure flashes against the silver gray of the fresh sage. The sun shone warmly and the sky was a deep blue, washed clean by the storm. It all brought back a warm nostalgia of the carefree days when he was a cowboy.

"Cat. Don't ya reckon that a day like this makes up for a lot of the worse ones?"

Cat mumbled something unintelligible. His night on a hard floor hadn't helped his saddle beat body. He was ready for the comforts of a town.

Dutch, ignoring his partner's lack of enthusiasm, continued. "You know, its fortunate that most people only see the less desirable things about this dry country and keep away. Sometimes you have to have a lonesomeness to enjoy this wide-open space. That's part of its beauty people don't understand."

"You can count me as one of them." Cat muttered, "What can I buy out here with all this gold? Nuthin'. Not a dad-blasted thing!"

As they gazed across the great expanse of open country, Cat spoke up again. "Dutch I been worryin' all night about them ounces stuff–wonderin' if we should be sellin' as regalar or them Helen of Troy kind of ounces. It seems to me that we should know which one we're sellin' before the time comes. We'd seem sorta' stupid if we didn't know one ounce from the other."

Dutch sat quietly for a moment, rubbing a hand over several days' growth of beard, suppressing an urge to chuckle. "Yeah, you're right. I've been thinking about that too. Now I remember that there's a troy pound to fit with them troy ounces and it's different than a reg'lar pound. I reckon that's good, Cat, instead of six hundred regular pounds we've got more of the troy pounds."

Cat grinned with relief. "By dang, I been tellin' ya, Dutch, gold weighs more than butter."

"Well, in a way you're right, but there's a catch. Instead of 16 there's only 12 of them Troy ounces in a Troy pound."

THE TROUBLE WITH GOLD...

Cat turned and looked at Dutch in utter bewilderment.

Mischievously Dutch continued to confuse the issue. "Course there's another thing too. A lot of this stuff is tellurides that aren't pure gold. Tellurium by itself isn't worth a penny. We don't really know how much actual gold we have."

Cat slapped his thigh in exasperation, causing his horse to start. "Wal for the...!" For a moment he couldn't think of a word that was strong enough to match his feelings. "SHI-OOT!" He finally spat out. "We might as well jus' pour that stuff out on the ground and let the wind blow it away. Hell, it's worth less ever' time we talk about it. You mean we're usin' four of these stubborn mules when one might do? Why don't we open them bags and throw out the telleride stuff if it ain't worth nuthin'? I think you're trying to do a fast one on me!" He spurred his horse and headed off Beaver Rim in a clatter of loose rocks.

Dutch, his belly shaking, snorted a laugh through his nose and followed at a more leisurely pace. Finally Cat stopped and waited for Dutch to catch up with the pack mules. "Cat, settle down a minute and let me finish. It isn't as bad as you're thinking. Like I said, there's more of them troy pounds in the saddlebags than regular pounds– reckon probably more than seven hundred troy pounds.

"Wal, why didn't ya say it that simple in the first place. Judas Priest! So even better yet, I say we weigh in Helen's pounds and sell it as reg'lar ounces."

"That isn't exactly the way it works, Cat." Dutch knew it was time to stop kidding Cat. "Right now we don't know just how much gold there is. Some of it is pure and some of it is combined with the tellurides. The two aren't separated so you can't just get rid of the worthless stuff. But you can bet what we got is the cream of the stuff out of that cave in the Cresson Mine. My guess is that if we'd smelt down the tellurides to get the gold pure we'd have a couple or three thousand ounces. Multiply half of that by twenty bucks and you'll have enough to keep yourself surrounded by painted whores for a long spell!"

"Well hell, Dutch. That'd be a fair amount, wouldn't it? I reckon I can live in style on that and you can buy yer ranch."

Nearby a meadowlark trilled its spring song from atop a yucca stalk. Dutch wondered if he would be as happy as the meadowlark when he had a ranch bought with the stolen gold. *Well, it isn't exactly stolen, so maybe that's all right.*

It was late morning when they rode into Angus Lowe's ranch. They found Lowe and his two young sons fixing a broken corral post. "Well by the great horn spoon! Dutch, it's been years. It's darn good to see you. You fellows are just in time for dinner."

"Howdy Angus. You don't have to make that offer twice. Cat here isn't real fond of my cooking. Angus, this is Cat Teason. We're working together on a little freighting job."

Lowe looked at the mules and smiled slightly. "Thought maybe you were on a fishing trip. I was hoping you might be looking for work. I could use a couple more sheep herders." Lowe grinned down at his two young boys nearby. "These men do what they can but I hate to saddle them with all of the work." His Scottish burr and pleasant laugh laid out an aura of friendliness that made even Cat relax.

"How long has it been Dutch? More than ten years I reckon since you and Cassidy stopped by. It was more like you slowed down a bit as you rode by. As I recollect, you were in a hurry."

Dutch laughed. "I remember that. We were on an errand of mercy then–we would have been at the mercy of a posse if we'd stayed."

Lowe laughed, a twinkle in his eyes, white teeth shining behind his large, drooping mustache. "That wasn't the last time though. I well remember when you helped me round up some sheep just before a big blizzard. I was always thankful for that Dutch, but in the end, it's not God's elements that are the toughest." A bitter shadow passed over Lowe's face. "Later, when times got a little tough the banks blew in worse than any blizzard and just about stripped me out. We might as well of sat by the stove."

Dutch remembered the blizzard. The day before had been cold and windy, a preamble to a bad storm that was collecting its forces over the Wind River Mountains. Working into the night he had helped Lowe get his sheep to safety. The blizzard blew in that night and lasted for two days. Since then Angus had been a trustworthy friend.

*   *   *

That afternoon Dutch and Cat stopped at Lacey's horse ranch further down Muskrat Creek. They changed horses and mules for the last miles to *Quien Sabe*. For three days they had pushed their animals hard. At the time it had seemed important to put distance between themselves and Surcingle. Now Dutch wasn't so sure that speed had made much difference. *Sometimes thinking is better than running.*

It was twilight when Dutch and Cat rode the final mile into Quien Sabe. Dutch felt uneasy. The old ranch had been a haven in the old days but now it didn't seem as isolated.

"Cat, those mine company thieves are bound to be persistent. If it was my gold I'd want Charlie Surcingle keeping after it until I got it back."

"Dutch, I think you're worryin' too much. Heck, we lost him back there at the Sweetwater. I say let's stay the night here and take some of that gold over to Thermop'."

Dutch didn't answer, thinking about the potential dangers and the best course of action to shake Surcingle.

During his time with Butch Cassidy he had learned that good planning and executing the jobs with precision and attention to detail paid off. It would be dangerous to assume anything about Surcingle other than he would be persistent. Dutch knew what they had to do.

The *Quien Sabe* cabins and outbuildings nestled amongst the sagebrush-cloaked hills along Hoodoo Creek. Butch Cassidy had liked it here. He'd owned the little ranch for a while. That was when the Wild Bunch liked to hang out around Thermopolis, just over the mountain. The little town had saloons such as Tom Skinner's Hole in the Wall saloon and other places where the young and restless outlaws could find ladies for a price.

Dutch liked *Quien Sabe* too. It was a secluded and restful place, unlike the Red Wall country over near Kaycee where there was always the smell of trouble. *At least in the earlier days.*

Dutch had hoped they could hole up here until the chase had cooled off. The steep rugged canyons of Copper Mountain would be carpeted with lush green grass, a good place to hide out for a while. It would be easy for them to bury the gold and disappear for days if the law came snooping around. Back in the outlaw days, neighboring ranchers, what few there were, would even help with a change of horses. He'd thought about all of these factors when he decided to head here with the gold. Now everything changed, with Charlie Surcingle so close.

Just beyond the squat log cabin and the weathered outbuildings of Quien Sabe, Copper Mountain rose with abrupt ruggedness, belying the peaceful scene below. A melange of dark and light colored rocks formed a lithic zebra of platey black schists and swirls of crystal-laden granite. Erosion had sought out fractures and the softer of the dark rock units, forming a labyrinth of crevasses and canyons separated by vertiginous ridges of granite dikes. To the senses it is a cataclysmic place. To Dutch it provided not only beauty, but also a place for quick and concealed escape. He allowed himself a small sigh of relief.

They unloaded the mules, stashing the gold under a pile of hay in the barn. Cat broke the silence that comes with a long day. "Dutch, I been wonderin' why this here place has a Mexican name when it's a million miles north of the border. What does *Quien Sabe* mean?"

"Who knows."

"Wal, I sure as hell don't, else I wouldn't ask. You stayed here with Butch. You must know what the name stands for."

Dutch chuckled. "Who knows. That's what it means, Cat. In Spanish. Butch and I were high-tailing it from a posse back around '99 and I asked Butch where we were headed. He said *'Quien Sabe, mi amigo?* Who knows, my friend?' Well, we ended up here and Butch said that was a pretty good name for the place."

The rusty handmade hinges squeaked a noisy welcome as Dutch pushed open the rough plank door of the cabin. Inside he breathed deeply of the mixed redolence of old wood smoke, bacon, leather and the myriad of other smells that had steeped into the old logs. *This old cabin's been here almost thirty years, there'd be a story or two told if one could separate out all them odors and put them in a book.*

As he started a fire in the cook stove Dutch remembered when Etta Place had been here. She had made the place seem like a home that he would like to have someday. It was the last time he had seen her. Before she left she had given him a little book of poems and signed it, "Love, Etta." He knew her heart belonged to another, but when she was gone he had traced his fingers over her writing and dreamed that she was his. He shook his head to bring himself back to the present as he walked out to tell Cat of his plans.

Cat was wiping the sweat from his horse's back when Dutch came back out of the cabin. "Dutch, I been thinkin'.

Maybe tomorra' we could hide most of the gold a little better and take some over to Thermopolis. I'm ready to start spendin' some of this haul."

"Cat, you've got part of the plan right, but I have a strong hunch that Charlie Surcingle will be searching all the old outlaw hangouts and this place will be one of them. I've been doing some serious reconsidering of our plans. We'll stay the night here then bury it up in the breaks on Tough Creek first thing in the morning. Surcingle doesn't know who he's after so he will be looking for signs of the gold showing up at bars and whorehouses. If we hide the gold and disappear for a while, old Charlie won't have anything to look for."

"Well, I reckon I can hold out for a couple a' weeks." Cat looked at Dutch hopefully.

Dutch shook his head. "It'll have to be a lot longer than that. Charlie won't give in easily. We'll have to outwait him before we unload the gold and that might be a year or so."

Cat looked shocked. "Shi-oot, Dutch, yer imaginin' too much. I think we lost Surcingle for good. Hell, I say we spend some of that gold over at ol' Tom Skinners and stay at the Ritzy. We've earned it."

Dutch shook his head decisively. "Nope, we can't take a chance. Surcingle will be waiting for the gold to start showing up."

"Do you reckon Surcingle really is still on our tail? Hell, it was a hunderd miles back when we last saw him."

"Cat, I know Surcingle. Considering the size of our heist his employers will keep him looking for that gold. The best thing we can do for now is get it buried, forget it for a while, and act like as how we're a couple of cowboys. Just for a while you'll have to drink rot-gut instead of the finer stuff, dream of women instead of having the real item and sleep in your dirty old bedroll instead of staying at some fancy digs."

Cat winced, but he could see the wisdom in Dutch's thinking. *Dutch is different than most of us outlaws.* Cat knew that Dutch had actually given money away. It seemed like a dumb thing to do – to risk one's life then give the proceeds away to someone down on their luck. *Oh well, everyone is entitled to a weakness or two.*

Before sunrise the next morning Dutch and Cat loaded the gold and shovels from the barn onto the mules. Dutch led the way over a ridge and into the rugged, narrow canyon of Tough Creek. The sun was tinting the tops of the mountain ridges with pink as they rode into the canyon. "Wait here Cat, and come ahead when I go behind that big juniper." Cat could not see that there was a likely place to hide the gold, but he waited as Dutch rode up the canyon. Dutch rode around behind the large juniper next to the wall of the canyon and seemed to disappear. One second he was there and then seemed to evaporate into thin air.

"What the hell!" Cat spurred his horse, tugging at the balky mules as he hurried to catch up with Dutch. Behind the tree he found a narrow crevasse. He rode into the crevasse that gradually widened until it suddenly spilled out into a small grass-floored canyon surrounded by cliffs of granite and black schists cut with numerous vertical fissures. Dutch was waiting in the meadow.

"Butch showed me this place once when we had to ride out of the ranch in a hurry. The posse must have thought we had worked magic when we seemed to disappear into solid rock." Dutch laughed as he remembered. "Butch called the place his personal bank vault. I imagine there's still one of Butch Cassidy's stashes up here somewhere. Maybe there's still room for our stuff."

Riding up the gorge, Dutch found a fissure in the vertical wall that was just large enough to crawl back into. Working on their hands and knees he and Cat dragged the gold, one bag at a time, back into the crevice. Dutch had brought a shovel from the ranch and dug into the loose sand and gravel. As they prepared to push the bags into the hole Dutch had dug, Cat stopped him, "Hey, Dutch, lets take a look at some of that gold before we hide it. It was too dark to see much on the train and most of the bags didn't get blown open anyway. I want to have a vision of that yellow stuff in my mind."

Dutch laughed. "Geez, wouldn't it be awful if it were mostly pieces of lead like the box was labeled?"

With fence pliers from Dutch's saddlebag they cut the wire tie on the first bag. Cat reached in and pulled out a large piece of ore. They both gazed in amazement. Never had they seen anything so stunning, so captivating, as the crystal aggregate of pure gold that lay before them. In the darkness of the crevice the gold seemed to generate a glowing light of its own. Peering into the bag they could see more of the glistening metal.

They opened another bag. This time Dutch took out a piece. It was breccia, a broken rock cemented together with flecks of gold but a larger amount of silvery mineral that filled the spaces. "Hell's fire!" Cat exclaimed in dismay, lifting the piece and looking at it. "This looks like lead. I know there's a' lot of gold bein' mined at Cripple Creek, but I've seen more in one poker pot than we likely got in this bags." His face drooped like a wet rag.

Dutch took the piece and examined it closely. He scraped the pliers over the rock. There was a fine yellow dust on the scratch. "Cat, look at this. Cripple Creek is the greatest gold deposit in Colorado, but it wasn't found until twenty years after the other gold districts because there wasn't any of the usual placer gold at Cripple Creek. This is high-grade telluride ore. Most of the gold in Cripple Creek is in rock like this.

"There's plenty of gold here. It just isn't all gold like normal nuggets. A lot of the Cripple Creek ore is silver colored and nobody, except an old cowboy, recognized it. Bob Womack was his name, and he kept after it. Finally a friend of his tested it and by golly it was gold. Just like that ol' cowboy figured. Some of our gold is in the tellurides. It's like the stuff that Bob Womack found. We got a lot of it here but it should be worth a fair piece. They sure as hell wouldn't ship lead to a San Francisco bank in a strongbox! I saw a lot of this stuff when I was mining there. It ain't worth as much as the yellow gold but it's still pretty good stuff."

Cat seemed somewhat appeased with this explanation, if not totally convinced. In his mind notions of the magnitude of his new wealth continued to diminish. First there was the question of weight, then the delay before they could safely trade the gold for money and now this. Still the vision of that first piece of pure glowing gold stuck in his memory and soothed him.

They opened the rest of the bags and found somewhat the same mix that they had seen in the first two, together with a lot of orange fines that hefted like gold dust.

"Cat, I reckon you can rest easy when you cash in."

"Shi-oot, I'll be too old to do anything but buy my coffin."

After digging two holes they lined them with old tarpaulins then laid an equal number of the heavy bags in each hole. They finished by covering over the area with a natural appearing arrangement of gravel and rocks. The sweat was rolling off their faces as they smoothed out their tracks in the crevice with a juniper branch. At the entrance Dutch chipped a small "x" in the granite at eye level to guide them back later.

"Dutch, it seems that this place could be a trap. I don't see any other way out."

"Let's ride to the upper end of the meadow. I'll show you another secret." As they approached the end of the gorge it appeared to be a box canyon, but the color of the rock played a deceiving trick. The wall of granite was offset and a rib of rock jutted into the canyon obscuring a narrow gorge. "If you ride through this, you'll find a trail that leads over the top of the mountain."

The next day they rode over the mountain to Buffalo Creek where Dutch sold the mules to "Sixteen Mule" Johnson, an old-time freighter who was homesteading there. This gave them a little extra cash that Cat was eager to spend in town.

An hour later, as they rode into town Dutch handed Cat some of the money. "Here's half of yours, Cat. I'll hold on to the rest for our travels. We'll stay here a couple of days then we head south and let things cool down for a while."

Cat looked dismayed, then shrugged his shoulders and headed for the saloon. On his way he reached in his pocket and fingered the gold nuggets that he had spirited out of the bags before they buried them in the crevice at Quien Sabe. He smiled. *Hell, this will set me up with a good poker stake with enough left over for the girls at the Ritzy.* He whistled happily through his teeth and primped his mustache.

Dutch eyed Cat contemplatively, wondering what he had up his sleeve. "Cat, like as not we'll get separated before we get back to the gold. It'll be a year or more before either one of us should even try. I'm telling you now that what's yours is yours and I'll not touch your poke and I expect the same."

"Oh, hell yes." Cat exclaimed, "I wouldn't try to take yer's no matter what. You can trust me Dutch."

"I know you too well, Cat. I know you wouldn't take it for your own, but I don't want you taking it to a "safer" place on account of you figuring I'm dead. I'm gonna be mightily pissed if I get back and find my gold has walked away. When the time comes I got plans for it. Don't you think otherwise. You don't want me on your trail. I know how you think better than you do."

Cat nodded his head, twisting his mouth and mustache to one side and thinking that Dutch was always ahead of him in the mind-reading department.

THE TROUBLE WITH GOLD...

In Thermopolis, Dutch was up early every morning to check on the horses at the stable and to have breakfast. On the third day when Dutch came back to the hotel after breakfast he saw a familiar figure at the desk. The man wore a large white hat and sported a large drooping mustache. Dutch looked closer, then quietly slipped, unseen, into the hall.

Upstairs he shook Cat, groggy from a late night of poker and other pursuits. "Cat, get yourself up. I just saw Charlie Surcingle checking in at the desk." Cat groaned as he got out of bed and struggled into his clothes. Leaving money for the room on the dresser, the two men went down the back stairs, got their horses from the stable, and rode over the red hills east of town.

"Where do you reckon on headin' to, Dutch?" Cat fingered his remaining gold nugget, wishing he'd had a chance to spend it. He'd gotten sort of sweet on one of the girls at the Ritzy.

"We'll stay on the Big Horn Mountains for a while. I don't think it's a place that Charlie would expect to find us. We can look for the Lost Cabin Mine. It's supposed to be up in that country. I figure that what I learned mining at Cripple Creek could give us an edge in knowing what signs to look for. In a couple of weeks things will cool off a bit and we can ride down the other side of the mountains to Kaycee and find out what's going on. After that? Well, we'll see."

Chapter 9

On the Run

Dutch steadied himself against a rock on the first high ridge of the Bighorns and scanned the vast emptiness of the basin to the west. He spent an hour with his field glass watching every trail and road. There was no sign of pursuit. He hadn't expected any. Not even Charlie Surcingle would imagine that the two outlaws, who had gotten away with thousands of ounces of gold, would be prospecting on the Big Horn Mountains. Dutch and Cat camped at a pleasant spot with tall aspen and grassy meadows. A chattering stream flowed near by. It was a lazy time for the most part, as they found no gold in the stream, which meant no gravel to shovel and sluice. They found a couple of old cabins but no sign of placering nearby. Without telltale placer gold there was no reason to dig prospect pits looking for a vein.

One evening after supper Dutch leaned back against a tree, smoking his pipe and drinking his tea. "You know, I been thinking that this is the kind of country I'd like to settle in. Maybe down off the mountain where the snow wouldn't be so deep in the winter. What do you think, Cat?"

THE TROUBLE WITH GOLD... 81

"Shi-oot, Dutch, I'll tell ya what I think. I'm gittin' fed up eatin' nuthin' but fish, bored from not seein' even one nugget, and thinkin' the closest town must be New York City. Hell, this gold prospectin' seems silly when we got sacks full of the stuff back at Quien Sabe. I still cain't see that milkmaid in the stars! And I'm tired a lookin' at you instead of some woman."

Dutch laughed. "You're right Cat. I reckon it's about time to head on down to Kaycee. Maybe we can get the latest on the train robbery."

The next morning they packed up and rode down through the juniper-covered east slope of the mountains. They passed the red cliffs of the Hole-in-the-Wall, where Dutch and Cat had hung out for a while with Butch Cassidy's bunch. The place was now deserted except for cows and cowboys. Riding a few miles down the Powder River they stopped at the little town of Kaycee where they picked up a week old Buffalo Bulletin. On the front page a headline screamed out "Train bandits still in Wyoming."

"I'll be darned!" Dutch exclaimed as he read the article. "Cat, they say that the heist had the earmarks of the old Wild Bunch." Then he laughed. "They're wondering if Butch Cassidy might still be around. Listen to this. 'It is not known what the robbers were after. According to the Union Pacific, only a small amount of mail and cash was missing; hardly enough to warrant blowing up a train at the risk of innocent lives.' Hell, that's pretty funny, those mine thieves aren't about to fess up that they had gold on that train."

Dutch read on, "Railroad officials are suggesting that some of the former Wild Bunch may have been involved. 'Although it is generally believed that Butch Cassidy perished in South America, there are some who believe that Cassidy returned to the states and has been living under an alias. The railroad would not give out any more details but say they have some suspects in mind. A reward of $5000 is offered for information leading to the capture of the bandits.' Who do you suppose they're thinking of Cat? Heck, there's not many of the old bunch left. Except for you and me, and maybe Butch."

Cat swore, his face turning pale. "Hell, with that reward, everybody in the whole country is gonna be lookin' for us. Dutch, what the devil are we gonna do now?"

"They don't know for sure who the bandits are, Cat, or they'd put out our names. They're hoping somebody will squeal. I reckon we'll head south and stay out of the way. The interest will cool down pretty quick when there's no sign of us."

Cat tugged nervously at his mustache. "But with a big reward, I doubt if there is a safe place for long."

Dutch put a finger against his cheek. "I think we should go down to old Mexico. Surcingle will figure we'll stay close to the gold and won't expect us to go far with that heavy cargo. He'll be doing some pretty smart guessing, but we'll make sure he guesses wrong.

"You'll like them senoritas there."

"Dutch, maybe we oughta sell the horses in Casper and catch the train. It'd be a lot faster." Cat was thinking of the long ride on horseback.

"We're not in any hurry, Cat. By riding our horses, we'll have some control over who sees us. Someone spots us on a train and we'd have to jump off fast. There we'd be. Broken legs and all, and no horses to ride!" Dutch laughed.

Cat wasn't in a mood to be humored. "Shi-oot, Dutch, if we had to detour through Hell you'd make it seem like the only way to go."

"This won't be so bad, sort of a strung-out picnic. Lots'a places that'll put us up for the night. We even got enough cash to stay at a hotel once in a while. If worse comes to worse we've got our bedrolls. You'd best drag that one of yours behind for a while and give them Ritzy crab lice a chance to jump ship." Dutch, laughing, spurred ahead to escape Cat's curses.

THE TROUBLE WITH GOLD...

By the time they reached Silver City, New Mexico, Cat was tired of living on the trail and ready to stop and try his hand at poker.

"My butt is tired of horses, Dutch. I'm stoppin' here and I ain't gonna do nuthin' but sit at the card table fer a while. Let's you and me teach these miners a thing or two about cards."

"You know I'm no gambler. You'd better be careful yourself. You don't have that much of a poke to last 'til we get back to Wyoming."

"Gol darnit, Dutch, just cause I ain't got much now doesn't mean I'm about broke. Hell, after a week of poker I'll be a lot richer. You know I'm pretty good."

Dutch shook his head in resignation. "Cat, I'm telling you that eventually you'll want a bigger stake. You'll be looking to knock off a bank and sure as hell you'll end up in the hoosegow. Anyway, let's stop in this place and I'll buy you a drink."

They approached a table where a card game was in progress. "You go ahead and stay, Cat. I'll stick around for a couple of days, then I'm riding south to Mexico."

Chapter 10

Pancho Villa

One of the card players, a short fat man, laid his cards face down on the table and looked up. "Did I hear you say Mexico, my friend? Me and my partner is fixin' to head down and look for work in one of the silver mines in Chihauhau." He thrust out a pudgy hand, limp and damp with sweat. "Name's Carl."

Carl shifted his eyes from Dutch to another man at the table, a sallow, skinny man, who nodded his head just slightly. "We might be lookin' for a guide to help us find the way. Safety in numbers you know. Old Pancho Villa might think twice before he tackles three of us!" Carl snickered and slapped the table. His friend's thin lips parted, showing yellowed teeth in a mirthless smile.

Dutch smiled politely. "Well, I appreciate the offer and I'll sure think about it." He grasped Cat by the arm and led him to the bar. "Come on, Cat. I'll buy you a drink."

"Hell, Dutch," Cat grumbled in protest, "I was thinking about joinin' 'em for a friendly little game.""Forget it!" Dutch spoke in a low voice. "I recognize that partner of Carl's. He's bad news. Don't get yourself involved with

THE TROUBLE WITH GOLD...

him. He'd kill for a couple of dollars. One thing for sure, those two aren't miners."

Later, Dutch stopped by a store and filled his saddlebags with dried jerky, hardtack and coffee. He filled two large canteens of water, just enough to get him and his horse to a watering hole. That evening he inquired around and found an old prospector who gave him some valuable pointers on travel in Chihuahua.

"If I was a little younger, I'd go along." The old man sat on the front steps of his little log cabin, speaking wistfully of times long past. "You'll do alright as long as you don't try to push it in the middle of the day. There ain't no water in the cricks, just a little seep that you have to dig for. Meybe a spring here and there."

The prospector slowly rose to his feet and led the way into the cabin. "Somewheres I got a map. I don't need it no more. It might help you." He pulled a rolled-up, soiled paper from a kitchen drawer. It was a crude, hand-drawn map, crumpled to softness from years of use. The faded map showed trails and river courses, along with the names of an occasional village. He pointed at several small "X's" on the map. "Them's the water holes.

"I can tell from the looks of you that you know how to work with Ma Nature. You'll be alright out there. The biggest worry I'd have is ol' Pancho Villa. He got whipped bad down at Celaya a few months ago, and he's trying to recoup by plundering anything or anybody he can find along the border. I hear tell that he blames the Americans for that defeat and would as soon as not kill gringos. After he strips you clean."

Dutch thought to himself that the two card players who wanted go with him to Mexico wouldn't be any more trustworthy than the well-known Mexican rebel. He decided to leave before sunup the next morning to make sure he didn't end up in their company.

Dawn was barely a cool gray glimmer the next morning as Dutch saddled up. Cat came down to the stable to see him off.

"Cat, I sure wish you'd come along, it'd be nice to have some company on the trail. Excepting them yokels at the saloon. I wouldn't dare sleep a wink with them in my camp."

Cat tugged at his ear, then his mustache. He looked uncomfortable with Dutch's gentle urging. He cleared his throat as though to say something, but Dutch interrupted him before he could start.

"Oh hell, Cat. I know you got your mind set on staying, so don't fret yourself about it. Just remember, I'll be back for my share of that gold. It may be a couple of years. As a matter of fact I think it might be wise to wait that long. Charlie Surcingle is a patient man."

He swung up into his saddle, the leather creaking in the morning stillness. "You take care, Cat."

"Heck, I'll be a rich man when you ride back through here, Dutch." Cat turned and walked back towards the hotel. At the door, he turned. "Dutch, I..." His words trailed off as he saw that Dutch had urged his horse into a lope and was already at the edge of town.

Dutch had been two hours on the road when he looked back and saw two riders approaching at a full gallop. As they drew near he recognized the two card players, Carl and Thin-Lips, from the day before.

"Well, if it ain't our travelin' friend." Thin-Lip's words were raw with sarcasm.

"We thought you was gonna ride with us, or ain't we good enough for the likes of you?" Carl added with a whining voice.

Dutch smiled, ignoring the comment. "Sorry fellas, I didn't reckon you'd want to be traveling this early. I figured you could probably take care of yourselves anyhow."

Thin-Lips spoke again. "Or maybe it's because you might have some valuable cargo in them saddlebags thet yur proud of."

Dutch's eyes narrowed. "Mister, what I'm carrying is my business. Speaking of cargo, those loads of yours look pretty heavy. Seems mighty strange to be riding full tilt out of town this early in the morning. Now let's ride on down the trail before it gets too hot to travel or that posse catches up."

Betraying their guilt, the two men turned in their saddles and looked back at the road from town.

By noon the sun fixed itself straight above and blazed down without mercy as the three riders crossed the desert towards Mexico. Dutch kept the other riders slightly ahead. *Doggonit, why didn't I tell them I had nothing but hardtack and coffee. They'll be trying to get the drop on me first chance.*

An hour later the desert stones burned with a fire of their own, and heat mirages shimmered in the distance. Dutch reined in his horse. "You boys ride on if you want, but my horse and I are stopping for a siesta."

Carl, his pudgy red face dripping with sweat, turned in his saddle and looked at Dutch in disbelief. "Are you crazy? We've gotta move on." He looked back on their trail and wiped his brow. "We need water."

Thin-Lips squinted his snake-like eyes to slits, the yellow teeth ugly with a sneer. Like a blur of a striking rattlesnake, his revolver was suddenly aimed at Dutch. "You heard my friend, mister. We're ridin' on. You can take your siesta later." He motioned up the trail with his gun.

Dutch seemed unperturbed and swung out of his saddle. "Oh, I'm not sleepy, but our horses are getting pretty dry. If we push them on in this heat we'll never make it to the next water hole by nightfall."

The pistol wavered and dropped a little. "You're lyin', mister. I know there's a big river just over the next ridge."

"I reckon you're right, but did you ever see how much water flows at this time of the summer? Hell, it's nothing but a river of wind-blown sand!"

Dutch laughed brusquely as he loosened the cinch on his saddle. "You go on ahead, but tomorrow I'll find you staggering off from your dead horses. Another thing, boys," Dutch stopped and scanned the surrounding hills. "Pancho Villa is skulking around these parts and he's killing for a lot less than you have in your saddlebags."

"Dammit, you told me this would be an easy ride!" Carl muttered, glaring at Thin-Lips. His voice quavered as fear tightened his throat.

A hint of alarm showed in Thin-Lip's eyes. He slowly holstered his gun. His tongue darted swiftly from his mouth and wetted his lips. His eyes narrowed to hide the insincerity of his words. "No offense meant, mister, you just can't be too careful about people out here on the desert. You seem to know somethin' about this country. Guess we'd best stick together."

After a two-hour rest the three men rode until dark and camped at a tiny seep of water next to a ledge of platy limestone. Gray mesquite shrubs, clumps of short, dry grass and patches of large prickly pear cactus made up the landscape. Only a slight tinge of green moss and a rim of mud revealed the spring's location.

As Dutch crouched down to quench his parched throat the water picked up the reflection of the night heavens and stirred it into a sparkling image. *Are you there, Etta, my lost love, dancing with the stars?*

He shook his head to force a return to the reality of his situation. "Boys, we don't want Senor Villa riding in on us during the night. We'd better take turns keeping watch."

Dutch knew that as long as he could keep his two companions fearful of the wild country and Mexican bandits he could sleep without fear of being killed. He could handle the elements and the two gamblers well

THE TROUBLE WITH GOLD...

enough, but a surprise visit by the feared Mexican could indeed be lethal. They were now on a well-traveled trail, and it was prime country for ambush. It didn't help that brush and frequent arroyos made it difficult to see very far in any direction.

Neither man complained about guard duty, although Dutch could see resentment in Thin-Lips eyes. Carl sat down and started to remove his boots.

"You'd best keep those boots on. If the rebels show up we'll need to get away fast," warned Dutch.

The morning dawned with a cold stillness, broken only by the grumbling of Dutch's sleepy companions when he shook them awake. "Come on, boys, up and at 'em. No coffee this morning. We've got to hit the trail."

Carl rose up on one elbow. "We need more rest, and I ain't goin' nowhere without some coffee."

Thin-Lips sat up abruptly. "Carl's right, mister. I'm gonna make some coffee. Hell, them Mexican banditos is probably in Chihuahua sleeping with some senoritas."

Dutch ignored Thin-Lip's declaration and saddled his horse. The two men crawled out of their blankets. They moved slowly, their bodies stiff from the unaccustomed hours in the saddle the day before and the night on the ground.

Dutch swung up into his saddle. "I'm starting out. You two can catch up when you've had your coffee."

At that moment he heard a slight clinking noise on the broken pieces of limestone that littered the ground. Dutch reached for his pistol, but he was too late. A large sombrero appeared suddenly from nowhere out of the mesquite. Beneath the sweeping brim of the hat an expanse of white teeth was framed by an enormous, bushy mustache and a swarthy face. Two bandoleers of rifle cartridges crossed his chest. He held a pistol, dangling along his side.

"Buenas dias, gringos." The teeth glowed even brighter. A ray of the morning sun glinted off a gold tooth. Pancho Villa bowed in mock politeness. Casually he turned, and placing two fingers to his mouth, whistled shrilly. Several men with rifles materialized from the brush.

The swarthy Pancho spat out rapid orders in Spanish, assigning three of the bandits to watch the captives. One of them grabbed the bridle of Dutch's horse. Pancho strutted over to Carl's horse. With a flashing stroke of his machete he slashed one of the swollen saddlebags. A flood of bright silver dollars cascaded onto the hard-packed earth.

The Mexicans stared, transfixed at the sight. Their leader threw back his head and laughed uproariously. With two more deft swipes of his machete, he sliced open Thin-Lip's flimsy saddlebags. Another stream of silver flashed in the sun as it poured onto the ground. The bandits yelled in unison. *"Mucho plata!"* They fell to their knees to scoop up the scattered money. The bandit holding Dutch's horse let go and rushed to the windfall.

Dutch bent low on his horse and spurred him hard. The horse made a good start and was behind a shielding mesquite before the Mexicans started shooting. Dutch could hear Pancho screaming out orders and knew that his lead was short. He remembered the prospector in Silver City had told him that Pancho Villa was fond of fast horses.

The bandits dashed to their horses. Pancho Villa swore and ordered two of them to stay behind. While Pancho and the others rode in pursuit of Dutch, the two remaining bandits began loading the money into their saddlebags. They then removed Carl's and Thin-Lip's boots and pocket watches. Carl shook with fear. The Mexicans laughed, then forced him to strip. They argued over the possession of each piece of clothing. The bandits guffawed and made obscene gestures at his nakedness as they spoke rapidly in Spanish. Carl understood only one word: *muerto.*

While the bandits harassed Carl, Thin-Lips quietly pulled himself onto his horse and wheeled him towards the shelter of the mesquite. He lay low along his horse's side as he had seen Dutch do only minutes before and kicked the horse hard in the flanks. His bare heels didn't have the effect of spurs.

One of the banditos swore and shot just before Thin-Lips reached the shelter of the brush. The horse swerved and Thin-Lips plummeted into the thorny mesquite branches. There he lay, grotesquely suspended.

Carl stared in shock as Thin-Lips' body twitched. A wet spot appeared on his clothes and dripped steadily onto the barren soil where it rapidly soaked in.

Carl babbled for his life, his portly body pink with the cold. One of the bandits aimed his pistol and shot into the ground near Carl's feet, howling with glee when Carl jumped. Then the other bandit shot, yelling. *"Escaparse rapido."*

Carl turned and ran, bullets spraying fragments of rock and dirt against his exposed legs. He ran for his life, certain that the next bullet would rip into his back. There were more shots and he sprawled into a small arroyo. Instead of running again he lie still. Forlorn of hope, he heard the bandits laughing as they approached. One of them spoke to the other in Spanish. Carl understood the words. "Kill the gringo!"

In the distance there was a volley of shots. The two bandits stopped, listening. The shooting stopped, followed by a shrill whistle. Carl's tormentors hurried back and vaulted into their saddles. The sound of their galloping horses soon diminished in the distance.

Paralyzed with fright, Carl lay in the dirt, feeling a wet warmth spreading beneath him. He wondered how badly he had been wounded. Gradually, as his senses returned, his scraped body began to sting. It was then he realized that the warmth was not blood. He had urinated.

With a small sigh of relief that he wasn't dying, Carl pulled himself up, gingerly brushed the mud from his body and trudged back to his horse. He avoided looking at the body of his partner. As he began to dig through the remnants of his saddlebags he was startled by a voice. He jumped in fear, almost spooking his horse.

"Damn you, Carl, are you just gonna to let me hang here and die in this bush?" Thin-Lips struggled feebly, moaning and wincing with every movement. The long thorns painfully tortured every attempt to free himself.

Carl, recovering from his fright, giggled. "Damned if you don't look like some kinda magpie perched in that bush. I ought'a just leave you there for getting us into this predicament." Carl looked at the wet patch on the ground under Thin-Lips. "Are you shot bad?"

"Hell, I ain't shot. It's these damn thorns. I can't move."

Carl looked again at where he thought he had seen blood dripping. Thin-Lip's trousers were soaked, but not with blood. Carl giggled again and slowly pulled shredded clothes over his shivering body. He wrapped other clothes around his feet and ambled over to his partner. Gingerly avoiding the mesquite thorns, he helped Thin-Lips free himself.

They looked in vain for Thin-Lips' horse but he was nowhere to be found. In the dirt they found three silver dollars overlooked by the bandits.

Four days later Carl and Thin-Lips rode into Lordsburg, riding double on Carl's horse. They were thirsty, hungry and more dead than alive. They reported that Dutch had been murdered by Pancho Villa's bandits. They added that Dutch was fleeing with money robbed from a Silver City saloon.

*   *   *

Cat later heard the story with a mixture of dismay and doubt, knowing that Dutch didn't rob the saloon. He also thought about the gold and remembered Dutch's final words. "I'll be back."

Dammit, I wish he'd stayed in town and maybe he could help me rob a bank. Shi-oot I should'a knowed not to bet everything on that hand, but I thought I could bluff my way into that big pot.

Chapter 11

The King of Phrygia

A year later Cat Teason looked down on a great stone mansion that stood like a misplaced eastern sophisticate. All around, drab badlands stretched out from the Wyoming mountains. Newly greening cottonwoods around the castle-like place offered little graduation between the cultured and the wilderness. The ranch was a jarring anomaly in the midst of the barren hills, brown from the long winter. Near the three-story mansion, a commissary, bunkhouse and corrals showed this to be a working ranch.

Cat paid little heed to the setting. He had come to collect a small favor owed from the ranch owner. He rode towards the commissary store where a simple log cabin served as an office to JT Stokes, the mercurial owner of the Midas Ranch.

Several horses, their heads drooping languidly, stood in the corral. A flock of grackles filled the spreading cottonwoods with their raucous chatter. A white-haired cowboy, too crippled to work the range, puttered around the corrals.

Suddenly a shot shattered the peaceful scene. As Cat watched the old cowboy hobbled into the log cabin. Cat cautiously urged his horse closer. As he neared the ranch buildings, the old cowboy, his wrinkled face drooping in perpetual melancholy, came out the door. He gingerly carried a mangled packrat by the tail. Subconsciously Cat smoothed his long wispy mustache that stuck out along each cheek. Nervously he tugged at one of his jughandle ears. The old cowboy watched as Cat approached. He noticed the black vest and fitted leather riding gloves that Cat wore that showed the rider hadn't fixed much barbed wire fence, or done any kind of cowboying, for that matter.

"Howdy, where can I find your boss?"

The cowboy jerked his head in the direction of Stokes' office. Looking at the dead rat, he said, "The boss hates rats."

Cat nodded and swung smoothly off his horse. He stretched his lanky form and brushed the dust from his clothes. He flipped the reins neatly around the hitching rail and strode up to the open doorway, his boots galumphing noisily on the board porch.

Stokes glared up from behind his desk when he heard the visitor approach. He straightened his tie and adjusted his vest, finally twisting the ends of his waxed mustache to precise points. Irritated at the interruption from his work, his jaw clenched and his mouth tightened, drawing the mustache into a tight line. Reacting from an old habit he reached into the drawer and put his hand on the still smoking six-shooter.

"Howdy, Mr. Stokes, ain't you glad to see me?"

Stokes squinted at the figure silhouetted against the sunlight. "Come on in where I can see you. I know the voice, but I sure don't remember who it belongs to."

Cat strode into the room, his spurs clinking as he walked. "You owe me a favor, Stokes, and I've come to collect." He laughed as if enjoying a good joke.

"I'm sorry, but I can't place you." Stokes said brusquely as his hand tightened on the pistol grip, his finger resting lightly on the trigger. Stokes squinted his eyes as he tried to identify the visitor.

"Shi-oot, JT, remember when I pulled you out of the Platte River? You were fording it when your wagon overturned. You were in the process of drowning when I showed up."

"Ah, it must be Cat Teason." Stokes relaxed a little. "I didn't recognize you with the light to your back." Stokes took his hand off of the pistol and gently pushed the drawer shut.

"Well, I guess you did help keep my wagon from going down the river, but I was doing fine getting out by myself. I appreciate what you did, but I don't think it's any big debt as you make out. Hell, I'd heard you were in the pen down in New Mexico."

"Wal, I was fer a while. I took advantage of an open gate. Damn, that was a miserable place." Cat laughed harshly. "I was headed up to Thermopolis to try my hand at a little poker, but I have a feeling the federal marshal might be looking for me to show up there. I need a place to sit for a spell until things cool down." Cat brushed imagined dust from a sleeve.

"I don't know as I owe you anything, Teason. This is a ranch, not one of your outlaw hangouts, but I'll put you up until the heat is off."

"I think a week will do it and I'll be out of here." With a hint of sarcasm he added, "I do appreciate your generosity."

"Oh, don't misunderstand me," Stokes said, with a cold smile, "I'm glad to have you." He looked at the ceiling, pursing his thin lips in contemplation. He pulled a crisp white handkerchief from his vest pocket and wiped it over his shiny pate. "As a matter of fact I have a job you can take care of while you're here. Come on by the house for supper this evening and we'll talk about it. There's a spare cot in the bunkhouse. You can use it while you're here."

At supper that evening Stokes explained to Cat the realities of ranching in the arid West. "A band of sheep has to keep on the move to get enough grass during the summer, and there's barely enough good valley bottom land to raise hay for the winter. These homesteaders think they can make a go of it on 160 acres. They're fools. Hell, it takes at least fifty acres to run a cow on some of this God forsaken country. Most of the nesters have seen the light and sold out at a reasonable price but there are still too many who plop down in the middle of my range and try to homestead the creek bottoms."

Stokes sliced off a piece of steak and gestured with the fork. "This is tough country, Teason. No, by God, it's unforgiving country if one makes many mistakes or plays anything but his strongest hand. Do you know the legend of Midas?"

Cat looked blank and shook his head.

"Midas was the king of Phrygia and everything he touched turned to gold. Midas knew what to touch and when to touch it. Just like Rockefeller and Jay Gould took advantage of the industrial revolution to get rich."

Cat interjected, "Hell, they was just big-time crooks. They stole ever'thing from the workin' people."

"You think they were ruthless men but they did what they had to. If they hadn't, this wouldn't be a great country. They were builders, leaders." Stokes' steely blue eyes glowed with zeal as he stabbed another piece of steak. "They didn't steal from the people, Teason. They gave them jobs!

"That's the way it is here on the range. I'm doing what I have to to squeeze the riches from this land. The West needs help from powerful people. It has to be big ranches, not hardscrabble goat pastures. And it's more than

THE TROUBLE WITH GOLD...

ranching. We need mines, better roads, and industry. That's why I bought the DePass Mine up on Copper Mountain. Once I get it in production again it'll be the cornerstone for my empire. I'm not here on this stretch of badlands for the fun of it. This land can produce wealth, but not if a bunch of nesters plow it into dust and move on when they go broke." Stokes savagely cut another piece of steak.

Cat had been putting away the food while Stokes talked. He finished chewing a bite of t-bone and sipped the good whiskey, sucking the wet off his mustache. "So what's that got to do with me?"

Stokes took off his small wire-rim glasses and leaned forward across the table, stabbing them in the air to emphasize his next point. Without the glasses his face seemed strangely naked and less imposing. "These hold-out homesteaders are a real thorn in my side. Cat, it takes tens of thousands of acres, not hundreds, to make money. It might appear cruel when I force homesteaders out, but I am doing them a favor, and I am creating progress where there was nothing before.

"What it comes down to is this. The problem has to be...let's say, regulated. That's were I can use your help to get these nesters to move on."

Cat sipped at his whiskey. "Well Stokes, I guess it sounds interestin' but I got other business as soon I figure the law will have given up looking for me in the old hangouts."

"Then you had better park here for a week. I'll pay you a hundred for every property deed you get signed over to me. Now let me tell you where to find these fellows." Stokes went on to describe the location of the bothersome homesteads.

Cat laughed, "Hell, you want me to pick up some '.30-30 homesteads.' I'll have to practice my aim."

Stokes ignored Cat's attempt at humor. "I'll pay them what their land is worth. I'm not running them off at gunpoint."

"Okay, Stokes, I'll give you a few days, but this is chicken feed compared to what I'm about to get. I got my own Midas just waitin' in the hills." He downed the last of his whiskey and rose from the table.

Cat opened the door to leave, then turned back. "Some of these guys aren't going to leave easily. I'll need a bonus if I have to shoot any of them."

Stokes' eyes bulged. "Good Lord, man, we're talking about men, not coyotes. I want you to help me stay in business, not get me run out of the country. Those kinds of tactics won't play anymore. You will do no killing or even wounding. I don't care if you make them think you might kill them, but, by damn, you shoot anybody and I'll be in the posse hunting you down!"

The next morning Cat saddled up and rode south out of the Midas Ranch. Just before noon he arrived at a crude shack roosting forlornly on a greasewood flat above Poison Creek. The homesteader was building a barbed wire fence around a small plot of ground that could be irrigated by the creek. A few head of cattle grazed the dry treeless hillside just beyond. The man had a black, full beard. His battered hat had little to flaunt but a sweat-stained leather band. The nestor raised his hand in greeting. Cat did not return the greeting nor did he dismount or offer his hand.

Noting the lack of frontier etiquette, the homesteader eyed Cat with suspicion. His rifle leaned against the cabin a hundred feet away. "Howdy, mister, reckon yur just in time for grub."

Cat didn't acknowledge the invitation. "Yur name Welks?"

"Reckon so, mister. What's your business?"

"Stokes sent me over to collect the loan he made to you."

THE TROUBLE WITH GOLD... 101

"Collect the loan? Hell, that's not due for another three months. After I take some cattle to market. He must be thinkin' of someone else." The homesteader turned back to staple a strand of stretched barbed wire to a crooked post.

"Mister Welks, I'm not here to argue. I saw the loan papers and there's a due date all right but the papers give Midas Ranch the option to call in the loan early if it appears there may be a default due to business circumstances. Seems to me that there are some bad times on the horizon and you'd be lucky to get out now."

The man laughed harshly. "So maybe I ain't ready to move on. I got a legal homestead goin' here and I reckon I'm stayin'." Tacking in another staple the man continued. "Now why don't you get down offn' yer horse and join me for some victuals." He looked up to find himself looking down the barrel of a single action .45. Behind the pistol, Cat's gray, unflinching eyes made the nester involuntarily shudder.

Cat's words flowed out like icy silk. "Here's a check and bill of sale for yer cows. Mr. Stokes is pretty generous. If it were me, I'd pay a lot less. Now sign the quitclaim and I'll git on out of here. I'll be back by tomorrow. You'd best be gone by then."

Looking at the papers, the homesteader flushed red in anger. "That's not what this place and the cows are worth an' Stokes knows it. He's got to give me a chance. I'll pay what's due in cash come fall. Dammit, I have some..."

Cat's single action barked and splinters flew from the post. The well-placed shot severed the wire, shutting off the man's protest. "Sign the paper before I lose my temper."

The nestor could see the gleam in Cat's gray eyes. Again he felt a cold chill run up his back. Angrily, but without further protest he took a stubby pencil from his overalls pocket, signed the quit claim and threw the paper to the ground. Cat dismounted and retrieved the document, tempted to nick the hapless homesteader as he walked to his shack.

"I must be git'n soft in my old age." Cat muttered as he mounted and rode away.

For the next several mornings Cat rode out from the ranch. He returned most evenings with signed quitclaim deeds, which he turned over to Stokes. Stokes would later record the quitclaim deeds at the county seat. The acreage wasn't large but the land would fit nicely into his ranch operations. On one particular day Cat reported the "purchase" of three homesteads.

Stokes rubbed his hands together in satisfaction. "Teason, it's too bad I have to be seen as ruthless with these poor souls. Eventually they will thank me for saving them from an effort destined to end in failure. Times are hard right now. These fellows will do better if I get them off their hardscrabble squattings."

Cat fidgeted while he waited for Stokes to finish his speech. He didn't care about Stokes' vision or what happened to the nesters. Visions of the golden cache hidden up in the granite crevice loomed larger in his mind. "Stokes, I'm leaving in the morning."

Stokes looked slightly relieved. "Cat I appreciate your help. I'm headed up to the mine in an hour, so I'll pay you off now." He opened the safe behind his desk and took out several bills. "Here, this should take care of you."

Cat leafed through the greenbacks. He smiled, looking at the safe and wondering how much money Stokes kept there. *Guess that wouldn't be right, with what he just paid me.* He put the thought out of his mind. After he picked up the gold there would be no need for petty theft.

The next morning Cat "borrowed" one of Stokes' packhorses and rode toward Quien Sabe and the gold. Even by putting part of the gold on his own mount, the packhorse would be overloaded. Not for long, though. He intended to cash in some of the gold in Thermopolis. He wondered if Victoria–or was her name Veronica?–would still be at the Ritzy.

Chapter 12

Cat is the Mouse

Cat rode lazily, his eyes half-closed, happily calculating the value of his buried wealth. On the prairie along the road, antelope grazed on the new green grass–grass that would be brown by the start of summer. The sun was warm on his back, making him comfortably drowsy.

As he approached the yucca and sage-covered foothills that rose gently between the flat plains and the mountain two miles beyond, movement on the road ahead startled him from his reverie. A solitary rider on a large white horse rode into view where the road emerged from a dry wash.

The rider slumped in his saddle. As he came closer, Cat could see that he was an elderly cowboy. The crown of his large hat was punched out round and a large graying mustache drooped as if reflecting low spirits. A red bandanna was tied loosely around his neck.

The old man touched the brim of his hat in greeting. "Howdy. Guess you're planning to catch a big mess of fish to load up that pack-horse?" The cowboy grinned, a twinkle in his pale blue eyes.

"I might, lessn' I find somethin' better. Like maybe a beautiful gal!" Cat laughed, flipping an ear with his hand.

"Wal, keep lookin' stranger, but I didn't see her up this way. Just a bunch a' gol-durned bawlin' cows." The cowboy brought his hand up in a farewell salute as he gently urged his horse down the road.

Cat found no one at the *Quien Sabe*. After putting the horses in the corral, he warily entered the cabin. Someone had recently been here. The stove was slightly warm and a half-full pot of coffee sat on the back of the stove. Cat felt a little uneasy, until he realized that the old cowboy must have stayed here while moving his cows onto the mountain. He fetched a blue enameled cup from a board shelf and filled it with lukewarm coffee, sipping while he looked around the place and thought about his next move. He remembered playing some mean poker here with the Wild Bunch boys several years back. *It's too bad that old codger ain't still here. Maybe I could get him to play a little poker.*

The main cabin had three rooms and for a bachelor cabin it was a pretty decent place. Still, it wasn't the Ritzy in Thermopolis. Cat grinned at the thought of arriving there loaded down with gold. He would stash most of it but he'd keep enough handy to impress the girls at the Ritzy. *Hell! Four or five ounces will buy me everything I want and stake me to a start in some poker. Matter of fact, meybe I ought just take a little over to Thermop. That way I can have a good time and not have to worry about where to stash it. Later I'll get the rest and move on.*

Cat hadn't thought through how to dispose of all the gold but figured he could sell a few ounces at a time without raising suspicions. *Hell, I bet we could'a cashed in a year ago, instead'a burying the gold and runnin'. We could'a waited and sold it after Surcingle left. People are always crazy to get their hands on gold. Dutch was just too naïve and careful. Dammit, he wouldn't have got killed if we'd stayed here.*

Cat decided to wait until morning to ride up to the buried gold. He would leave at dawn, dig out the gold and be in Thermopolis before evening. He felt strangely agitated as he paced around the cabin, drinking coffee. He lifted up a stove lid to see if the embers were enough to start a fire but there were only a few sparks glimmering in the ashes. He began to worry if it were wise to stay at the cabin. If someone did come along they might wonder what Cat's business there was. *Especially with a packhorse in tow.* He wished he'd loaded the pack-saddle with a shovel and supplies so that he could pass as a prospector. He cursed inwardly at his lack of planning. *Damn! Dutch would've had that figured out.*

In times of uncertainty Cat had always let somebody else make the decisions, but now he was on his own. He walked outside where the sun shone warm and comfortable, its rays tempered with a cool breeze that wafted out of Hoodoo Canyon. Cat hardly noticed. Something was wrong, but he couldn't put his finger on what it might be. He should be happy. Unconcerned. Like that old cowboy. *That old cowboy?*

"My God! That was Surcingle!" The sudden realization brought a sharp pang of fear that made him feel short of breath. *I remember now. He was riding a big white horse when we saw him on our trail at Crooks Gap!*

No, I'm just imagining things. Why would he be here a year later?

"Shi-oot! I'd better get out of here just in case." Cat peered intently back down the valley but there was no movement on the road. He went back into the cabin where he picked up his bedroll. He grabbed a can of beans from the cupboard and hurried outside. *Surcingle could be watching with his rifle from a dozen places.* Cat moved quickly, thinking he might spoil Surcingle's aim. He noticed that birds had left the cottonwood tree and there were no chickadees flitting about the willows on the creek. To Cat it seemed that it was a silence holding its breath.

Waiting for something to happen. *Damn, I wish I knew how to read outdoor signs. Dutch always said, "You've got to trust the voices."* He saddled his horse and with the packhorse on a halter rope rode out of the gate towards the mountain.

He kept as much as possible to juniper patches where he could ride somewhat obscured. High on ridges of rock above him, a few gnarly pine trees, their half-dead trunks bleached by the winds, grasped any available crack. There were a thousand spots for ambush. *Surcingle could pick me off easy if he were up there.*

Dutch had told him about the secret little glades tucked between the ridges. He had scratched out a map in the dirt and pointed out trails and canyons. The creeks had intriguing names. Birdseye, Tough, Hoodoo–and other ones that Cat couldn't recall.

Though he couldn't remember the details of the map Cat thought he could probably find one of the hidden crannies in the rocky crags above Hoodoo Creek. It would be a good place to disappear for the night. As he rode, he was careful to keep on the bare rocks as much as possible so as not to leave easily traceable signs. The horses sensed his nervousness, shying and snorting as though every tree might harbor a mountain lion or bear.

Cat found a spot where he could lie in the sun and keep watch while the horses contentedly grazed in a secluded meadow no larger than a saloon. To spell the tedium he took out a deck of cards and practiced dealing with various sleight-of-hand tricks. Tiring of that, he took out a well-thumbed copy of Erdnase's "The Expert at the Card Table." Dutch had always tried to get him interested in books and he'd found this one at the library in Denver where Dutch took him once. He didn't tell Dutch that he'd stolen the book.

When evening came Cat chewed on a few pieces of pemmican and hard tack that he had brought from the Midas Ranch. Later he ate part of the cold canned pork and beans. As the bright constellations began to decorate the sky, Cat rolled up in a couple of blankets. For a few minutes he looked up at the stars. Idly he remembered Dutch's girl on the Milkmaid's Path but his mind wasn't up to finding her. Dutch had tried to show him the various constellations but all he could see were the individual stars. Dutch had shown him how to find the North Star by lining up the two stars on the Big Dipper. That had seemed like a useful thing to know until Cat looked again the next morning before dawn. The Dipper wasn't there. When he mentioned the missing Big Dipper Dutch had laughed and showed him where it was, but upside-down from the night before.

"Now what good is that if the doggoned thing is always in a diff'rent place?" He'd complained to Dutch. "Anyway, what's the use of seein' pictures in the sky?"

The only sounds in the night were his horses munching grass nearby and the swoop of the nighthawk overhead. The sudden noise startled him every time. From somewhere over the ridge a coyote howled its mournful cry and Cat wished he were lying in a bed at the Ritzy Hotel. He wondered how much gold he might have. *I'll leave Dutch's share buried. At least for the present. I couldn't carry it all anyway. If Dutch doesn't show up in another year there would be nothin' wrong with taking the rest of the gold.* With a pang of loneliness that surprised him, he wished that Dutch were here – he would have a plan that considered all the angles. He was soon asleep and stirred little until the dawn was showing over the mountain ridge to the northeast.

* * *

Cat's sense of foreboding had been right.

Charlie Surcingle did not have proof of who had robbed the train, but had put lots of twos and twos together. With meager clues and intuition he figured he

THE TROUBLE WITH GOLD... 109

had a pretty good notion of who might have done the job. Cat Teason was one of his guesses.

For the past year Charlie Surcingle had waited and kept his ear to the ground. When he heard of Cat's escape from the New Mexico prison, he played a hunch that Cat might show up at Quien Sabe. When he'd trailed the two outlaws from the robbery a year ago, he'd come close to catching them in Thermopolis. One of the thieves had used a few nuggets for barter at a gambling hall and the Ritzy Hotel. It was Cripple Creek gold, but not another ounce of the gold showed up. The outlaws had come to Thermopolis with only their two horses and no pack mules. Obviously they had already stashed the gold. They abruptly dropped from sight only hours before Charlie was ready to pounce.

The rugged country around *Quien Sabe* would be a likely place to hide the loot. *This wouldn't be the first time booty had been buried in those hills,* Charlie thought, remembering Butch Cassidy. *I wonder if Butch Cassidy really could be alive.* There had been rumors and this job certainly had the Cassidy earmarks of careful planning.

Charlie had camped for over a week in the old cabin at *Quien Sabe.* Sadly he'd concluded his hunch had been wrong. This morning he rode out, anxious to get back to his own ranch.

Now here was Cat Teason, literally walking into his grasp. Surcingle couldn't believe his good fortune. With a little patience he'd get the gold as well as one of the outlaws.

Charlie knew that Cat wasn't clever enough to plan the train robbery, but it was easier to put together the clues that pointed to Cat. Years ago Charlie had seen a wanted poster with Cat's picture on it. He remembered those prominent jug ears and the straggly mustache that couldn't seem to make it to maturity. The best break had come, though, when he found that tiny amount of the Cresson gold that had been spent at the Silver Dollar saloon and at the Ritzy Hotel whorehouse in Thermopolis. The description of the man who had spent the gold initially at these places matched those of Cat. Unfortunately the bandit and his companion disappeared–until now, a year later.

Charlie had watched Cat ride towards the Quien Sabe. *By golly, I reckon my hunch was right after all.* He'd had the first laugh he'd had in a week.

Once Cat was well out of sight Charlie took off his hat, beat off the dust, sharpened a crease into the crown and placed it at a jaunty angle on his head. Wheeling his horse around he headed for the high country above the ranch where he could keep track of Cat's activities. He whistled a cheerful little ditty, thinking of the packhorse being led by Cat. It was not loaded down. That could only mean that his quarry planned to pick up something. *If my hunch is right it will be gold!*

Charlie rode to the top of the mountain where he had a good view of the *Quien Sabe* ranch and the surrounding country. From his perch Charlie watched Cat as he hurried away from the ranch. Something was up. He could see Cat looking back down the road. *Hell, I bet he finally figured out who that was he met on the road. He figures I might come back to the ranch. Well, I'll just have to keep a close eye on him.* Though it appeared that Charlie's patience would pay off with Cat, he wished that both of the gold thieves were in sight.

* * *

The next morning Cat rose early from his hard bed on the ground. He ate the beans and hard-tack left from the night before and wished for a hot cup of coffee, but was afraid to build a fire. *Tomorrow morning I'll have a cup at Thermopolis with lots of sugar and cream. I'll need it for the hangover I plan to have after partying tonight.* With those thoughts, Cat felt better. *Hell, I gotta stop imagin' things. Like thinkin' that Surcingle was down the road.*

The canyon where he and Dutch had buried the gold looked different than Cat remembered and he searched for more than two hours before he found the concealed passage that led to the ravine where the gold was hidden. *Damn. If Dutch were here, he'd know right where to go. He knows how to get around in the wilds. That son-of-a-gun must carry maps in his mind of anyplace he's ever been.* It took Cat another hour to find the crevice with the chiseled "X" on the canyon wall.

He crawled back into the gap and anxiously scooped away the loose sand with his bare hands until the top of the bags were uncovered. "Damn! I'm a rich man. What the hell am I waiting for," Cat muttered to himself, "I'll take all of my share right now."

In his excitement he forgot about leaving part of his gold until later and anxiously began to pull the heavy bags from the sand. One of them ripped open. To Cat's dismay he found other bags that were rotted or chewed by rockchucks. He remembered seeing some empty gunnysacks at *Quien Sabe*. Cursing, he crawled out of the crevice and rode his horse back to Quien Sabe. He grabbed several sacks and rode back to the gold. By the time he had the gold loaded on the packhorse and in the saddlebags of his own mount, it was afternoon. He pushed the sand and rocks back over Dutch's gold then brushed over his tracks with a juniper branch.

Hurriedly he mounted his horse and rode out of the narrow gorge with the heavily laden packhorse in tow. He found the trail and headed for the top the mountain. Thermopolis was just a few miles down the other side.

* * *

Charlie Surcingle watched Cat from his lookout high on the ragged granite pinnacles. Although he couldn't see the gold's hiding place, Charlie smiled with satisfaction when Cat came into view leading the loaded packhorse. Now the gold was out of hiding. He would wait for the right moment to nab Cat Teason and his loot. Charlie stepped down behind the rocks and stretched his limbs, stiff from his long wait. He saddled his horse and rode over the mountain to wait for Cat's arrival.

* * *

As he rode up the canyon Cat's anxiety once again increased. He nervously scanned the surrounding terrain, half expecting to hear a rifle shot. Once the packhorse dislodged a rock that rolled off a ledge and crashed below with a reverberating echo. Cat flinched so abruptly that his horse stumbled and they almost fell on the steep, rocky trail. Cat's eyes darted from side to side as he studied the trail for tracks and watched the countless shadowed crannies for movement. His worries mounted as the steady plodding of his horse's hooves echoed off the canyon walls as though counting off the seconds to some eminent date with doom.

"Shi-oot!" he muttered, "Meybe I shouldn't go to Thermop. I shoulda' brought just a little of the gold like I'd planned. Damn! Maybe I should take part of the gold back and hide it again." But he didn't. Instead, Cat focused his thoughts on the sweet pleasures that awaited him in town.

Near the top of the mountain he stopped. Uncertainty continued to hound him. "Shi-oot, I shoulda' waited in case Dutch might be back." After checking the cinch on the packsaddle, he continued over the ridge towards Birdseye Pass. From there it would be a quick ride down the mountain to the Ritzy Hotel. Cat yelped with elation and spurred his startled horse.

As he crested a small rise he saw a tall man standing beside a white horse on the trail a hundred yards distant. Even at that distance Cat knew. The horse, the hat. Cat

THE TROUBLE WITH GOLD... 113

couldn't yet see the face, but there was no doubt about it. It was the old cowboy he had met the day before. The man he and Dutch had spied on their tail as they fled the train robbery. Surcingle!

Damn! Cat's entire body jangled in alarm. A numbing mantle of dread spread over his face and down his back.

Slowly Cat pulled his carbine from its scabbard and then, in a quick movement, brought the gun to waist level as he cocked the rifle and fired. Surcingle had spotted the move and dropped to the ground behind a rock a split second before Cat pulled the trigger.

Cat shot twice more before wheeling his horse and dashing for the protection of the ridge. His back felt terribly exposed and he expected bullets to rip his flesh and shatter his bones. He spurred his horse, but the packhorse was like an anchor.

Surcingle steadied his rifle over the rock, elevating the sight for the distance as he smoothly swung the rifle to match the movement of his target. He slowly squeezed the trigger. Even before the report echoed off the hills he smoothly levered in another round and aimed again. He had to hurry before Cat disappeared over the hill.

Cat heard the buzz of the first bullet as it passed close to him. He knew and dreaded that sound. It was followed closely by the boom of the rifle, the report echoing sharply off the bare granite hills. Another few yards and he would be safely out of sight. Then he could take cover and wait for Surcingle. Turning in his saddle he pulled off two quick shots. He could hear the bullets' wobbly whine as they ricocheted off the rock that protected Surcingle.

At least meybe I spoiled his aim. At the top of the ridge Cat leaned down to make a smaller target for Surcingle to shoot at. He was a second too late and felt the excruciating pain as a bullet ripped through his upper arm. He yelped in pain. Two more shots missed him as he rode over the ridge, lying as low as he possibly could along the side of his horse.

When he was well out of sight, he spurred his horse until they were out of sight behind a large granite outcrop. A wave of nausea swept over him as he slid off his horse, pain racking his body. Gritting his teeth he clumsily bound up his badly bleeding arm with a bandanna. He could tell that the bone had not been broken.

He knew that Surcingle would likely approach cautiously from one side. That would give him a little time to turn the tables. Quickly he decided to hide the gold here and try to outrun Surcingle. He found a narrow crevice in the rocks and dragged off the gold-laden saddlebags using his one good arm. Sweating with the painful effort, he tossed the bags into the shallow cleft. Hurriedly he threw dead sagebrush in on top of the bags, hoping it would appear to be a packrat's nest.

Wincing and gritting his teeth, Cat tied two of the empty burlap sacks onto the pack frame. He laboriously loaded the sacks with loose rocks. He picked up a piece of sagebrush and slapped the packhorse on the rump. The horse, startled, leaped forward. The sacks of rocks slammed against the pack frame. The horse, panicked at the unexpected movement, bolted across the sagebrush-covered flat.

"That's the way! Go like hell!" Cat silently cheered as the horse galloped off, bucking and kicking. When he stepped in a hole and stumbled, Cat caught his breath but the horse recovered and disappeared over the edge of the mountain into the Hoodoo Creek gorge.

Cat led his saddlehorse behind a knob of granite. Pulling his rifle from the scabbard, he laid it on the rock. Holding a quieting hand on his horse's nose, he waited for Surcingle.

The bleeding from his arm had slowed. Cat felt that he would survive one more life. He believed that the nine lives superstition applied to him as well as felines. It gave him a certain comfort. He hoped that he could accurately fire the rifle with his good arm.

THE TROUBLE WITH GOLD...

He didn't have long to wait before he saw movement behind a small outcrop and pines. Cat shook his head to focus his eyes. The trees seemed to sway, dim and almost disappear. He stared at the spot where he'd seen something move. He felt lightheaded. The rocks seemed to move.

Meybe he's not there. My eyes are playin' tricks on me. I wonder if he is creepin' up on the rocks behind me. Cat felt a surge of hopelessness and panic as he realized that he could be shot anytime. He was about to mount his horse and make a desperate run for it when he spotted another movement in the trees. Straining to clear his head he saw Surcingle framed by a gap in the tree branches, barely two hundred yards distant. The detective was being cautious, moving only slightly, then stopping to listen and watch.

Cat leveled his rifle over the boulder. Taking a deep breath he lined up the sights onto the range detective's chest and moved his finger to the trigger. Before he could squeeze off the shot, the image of his target doubled and swam in and out of his vision. The rifle's sights blurred. Then everything went black. Cat silently crumpled behind the rock, gripping the unfired rifle. In vain he attempted to see, but there was nothing. The world swirled away in strange images and unearthly voices beckoned him. He wanted to resist but was powerless. *I wonder if this is how death begins.*

Cat felt the pain in his arm as consciousness slowly returned. He had no idea how long he had been out. He sensed movement nearby, but his eyes were still unseeing. He wanted to claw himself away from the unknown danger.

Then Cat felt cold steel against his forehead. He had often thought of death, but always thought it would come in a fight where he would have at least an even chance. Now here he was, powerless, his life soon to be snuffed out by a bullet through his brain.

In his nightmare of blackness Cat could feel the presence of someone standing over him. He imagined Surcingle's face twisted in a dog-like snarl as he slowly levered a round into the rifle's chamber. Once again he felt the cold steel against his head. Cat squeezed his eyes tight, waiting for the shot he would never hear, but feared it as he had never feared anything before.

He felt the cold steel move and press harder against his face. "For God's sake, get it over with!" he pleaded.

Cat's plea was answered by the familiar sound of a horse mouthing his bit. Equine smelling drool dripped onto Cat's cheek. He slowly opened his eyes to find his horse standing over him, the steel bit touching his face as the curious horse investigated his prostrate rider. Slowly Cat looked from one side to the other.

There was no one else, just the horse. Cat pulled himself to his feet and looked up to the heavens. He sobbed with relief. Carefully he peered out over the boulder to where he had last seen Surcingle.

There was no sign of the detective. He was gone. *He must have followed the packhorse.* Cat looked at the sun, low over the limestone cliffs above the Birdseye stage station and knew he hadn't been unconscious for more than a few minutes. *Okay, so I won that round, but he'll be back. It might be minutes or maybe it'll be a day. Whatever, I'd better get out of here fast.*

* * *

After the last shot, Charlie watched Cat disappear over the hill. Assuming he hadn't mortally wounded him, it would now be a contest of wits. He had to be careful. A badly wounded man would be desperate. Rather than pursuing Cat directly he circled around to a hidden point in the trees and rocks. Here he could see much of the area around where he had last seen Cat. He cursed inwardly at his lapse of patience in trying a long shot at a moving target. *There was a time when I wouldn't have missed. I should quit this business and stay on the ranch.*

Surcingle surveyed the mountain with his field glasses looking for a clue to Cat's whereabouts. He didn't hear or see anything. Slowly he inched ahead, intently scrutinizing the countryside. It seemed that Cat Teason had disappeared into thin air. The quiet seemed ominous and Charlie dismounted to watch from better concealment. *That little two-bit devil will get me in his sights if I'm not careful.*

At that moment Charlie's horse turned his ears toward the gorge that dropped off the mountain. Charlie heard a faint clattering of rocks as something moved down the steep mountainside. He hurriedly remounted and spurred his horse forward to the edge of the mountain. Far below a pall of dust hung in the air at the edge of an aspen grove. Carefully he urged his horse down the steep mountain into the gorge. He stopped often to listen, sometimes hearing the faint clatter of hooves echoing off the rugged granite cliffs. Charlie followed at a measured pace, certain that he could soon catch his gold-laden prey.

An hour later Charlie rode out of Hoodoo canyon above Quien Sabe. Darkness was settling in when he spotted the packhorse grazing quietly in a meadow. The packsaddle was on the horse and obviously loaded. Cat was nowhere in sight. Charlie swore silently and dismounted. Keeping low in the dry wash he examined the tracks where the trail came out of the narrow canyon. There was only the one set of tracks, that of the packhorse. "Damn. Damn. Damn! I let that jug-eared thief get the best of me. He traded the gold for his freedom. Well I've got this much any..." He opened one of the bags tied on the packframe and stared at the chunks of barren rock.

For a moment Charlie was stunned. Then he laughed, taking off his hat and slapping it on his thigh. "By dang, Cat, you're not so dumb after all. Hell, you must've been takin' lessons from Butch Cassidy. Or just maybe, Dutch Wyatt."

Charlie's quarry didn't often get the best of him, but when they did it just added spice to the chase. He knew that he would likely win in the end. He reshaped the hat with a jaunty crease, and headed for Shoshoni. *Tonight I just might get drunk.* "Beer today, gold tomorrow!" He laughed at his little joke.

* * *

Cat knew that, without a packhorse, the gold would have to stay where it was for now. Surcingle would be back tomorrow or even tonight. Cat's mind, numbed by the pain in his arm, struggled for a solution. With his wound the options were few. He desperately needed help. *Dutch, why in the hell ain't you here?*

The only other person he could think of was Stokes. Of course, Stokes might not be of a mind to help. Cat had "borrowed" his horse. At best, he would extract a steep price for helping. "The bastard might even turn me in," Cat muttered.

He remembered that Stokes had said that he would be at the DePass Mine for a few days. *Maybe I can find him there. It should be only a few miles to the east. I can keep to the backcountry to get there.*

Standing alongside the crevice, Cat slowly turned to identify reference points that would get him back to the gold. This was a trick that Dutch had showed him. At the time he thought it was a silly thing to do. *If I'd paid more attention when we hid the gold at Tough Creek then I would've saved hours and got away instead of gettin' shot.*

Cat could see a knob of granite looming just above him with a profile that resembled an Indian brave. In the other direction two lone pine snags lined up. Finally he paced the distance to the snags. He could find the place even a year from now.

THE TROUBLE WITH GOLD...

He felt woozy as he struggled to mount his horse. He cursed when he realized that he'd be in no shape to get another horse and ride back for the gold anytime soon. He wouldn't be able to return before Surcingle, who would certainly be here tomorrow.

Cat turned his horse along the mountain crest in the direction of the DePass Mine. As his mind began to clear he realized he would have to deal Stokes in on the gold in return for his help. "Shi-oot! That old shyster will want a big cut!" Cat could see his gold poke diminishing.

Picking his route to keep out of sight, Cat nervously scanned every rock outcrop where a man might hide. It was easy to imagine another ambush. After an hour of riding Cat worried less about being shot and fretted over how much Stokes' help would cost him. "Hell, if I can hang onto even half of the gold I can still live a life of luxury." He would have to be careful. Stokes didn't like to share wealth at all; even if it belonged to someone else.

Night was filling the mountain valleys when Cat crested the high ridge west of the DePass Mine. On the valley floor below lights glimmered invitingly from the windows of a white building. Cat guessed it to be the hotel. Stokes had told him it was built for housing miners in the boom times ten years earlier. He had reopened the hotel and hired a hotel manager, a Miss Ella Price.

Cat had heard cowboy talk around the Midas Ranch bunkhouse that Miss Price was a beautiful woman. The cowboys chortled among themselves that Stokes was more interested in having her around than needing a hotel.

Cat rode down the hill cautiously, his feverish mind wondering if Surcingle might be waiting at the hotel. He could see the mine on the far side of the valley where it pierced into the granite high on a barren hillside. The mine portal itself was almost obscured by a large dump of broken waste rock. Streaks of orange iron oxides and broken rock, not yet camouflaged with lichen, set the dump off from the natural outcrops and silver-gray sagebrush of the adjacent mountainside. A light glimmered in a building next to the mine. With any luck that would be the mine office.

A shiver ran through his body and he felt slightly faint from the loss of blood. "Damn! I need to get some whiskey on this before infection sets in," He mumbled, gritting his teeth as the pain worsened. "Stokes, you old bastard, I hope you're there, I can't hold out on my own much longer." Cat gripped the saddle horn tightly as he rode slowly across the valley and up to what appeared to be the mine office.

"Who there?" Stokes' gruff voice was more of a challenge than an invitation to enter.

"It's Cat." Cat pushed the door open, letting out a stream of yellow light from the Coleman lantern. He stepped in and quickly closed the door.

"Well, I'll be damned. I figured you'd turned horse thief and I wouldn't see you again. One of my boys rode over from the ranch and said you'd taken a horse." Stokes leaned forward across his desk, his face grim. As he peered at Cat in the dim light his expression changed. "My God, old boy, you look terrible. What's happened?"

Cat wobbled slightly on his feet and slumped into a chair as dizziness overcame him. "Sorry about the horse. I only needed it for a couple of days. He should be back at the ranch by now." Drawing in a deep breath he continued, "I've been shot. I need some whiskey to treat this damned arm and if you can spare it I could use a little inside as well."

Stokes looked startled. "Dammit man, let's have a look at that." He quickly stripped off the bandanna and Cat's shirt, grimacing at the ugly wound in Cat's arm. He turned, and reaching in a glass-fronted cabinet, took out a bottle of whiskey. From a desk drawer he brought out a clean bandanna, soaked the cloth with whiskey and wrapped it tightly around the bleeding wound. Cat grunted with the stab of pain as the alcohol penetrated into his flesh.

"Cat, that's a bad looking thing, you need more help than I can give you. You need a doctor."

"No!" Cat exclaimed vehemently. "I can't risk it. That range detective, Charlie Surcingle, shot me. He's workin' for some people who think I stole their gold."

Stokes took two glasses out of the cabinet and poured whiskey into them. "Surcingle? Who's he working for? It must be pretty important if he's involved. How much gold is there? Do you have it with you?" Stokes fired questions at Cat.

"That's my business." Cat exclaimed, as his mind swirled in the confusion of his mounting delirium. "Thanks for the doctoring, but I can take care of myself now. I'd better get out of here before Surcingle shows up." He downed the whiskey with a quick motion and stood up abruptly. The room seemed to tilt and Cat collapsed to the floor.

When Cat came to, he was lying on the floor of the mine office. Stokes lifted his head and put the glass of whiskey to his lips. Cat sucked up a little of the fiery liquid. He felt better and his mind cleared a little.

"Look here, Cat, you don't have a bunch of options. I can help you but you've got to level with me before I can know what to do. Right now you're not in any condition to get the best of Charlie Surcingle. I know him. He won't stop until he tracks you down."

Cat moaned with a sudden throb of pain. "I've got to head out for Canada. I can't stay here. I'll be caught for sure."

"You're in no shape to travel, let alone take care of your gold, however much you have. I reckon if you needed my horse it must be heavy." He laughed, then with a sympathetic tone implored, "Cat, I can make sure Surcingle doesn't find you, but there has got to be something in it for me to make it worth the risk. I don't know how much gold you have hidden out there, but lets see what we can do to keep it. The mine is the perfect place for you to hide out with the gold. I've got a hoist operator on duty during the day. I can put the gold down in the mine until the coast is clear."

Cat responded with a grimace of pain.

"You won't be in shape to keep ahead of that detective for a week or two. You don't have a choice, you're staying here. Now you've got to tell me where the gold is. We don't have much time."

Cat's mind reeled, both from his wound and from what seemed like the good sense of Stokes' entreaty. He thought about the gold that he had stashed in the rock outcrop. Surcingle would know by now that he had been duped by the rock-laden packhorse. He would be back looking for the gold. *Yes, he will find it in time, probably tomorrow, if I don't beat him to it.*

Stokes shook his head in amazement as he listened to Cat's story. He made Cat repeat the location of the gold and memorized the landmarks that Cat described. "I'll have to get over there tonight. You can bet Surcingle will be back early tomorrow. There's a cot in a little storage room back of the office."

Cat stood on his feet. "Hell, that whiskey helped, but I do feel a little tired." Stokes showed Cat into the small room. "You'll be safe enough here, Cat. I'll send Ella up in the morning with some breakfast."

"Who's this Ella woman. I don't want anyone else to know I'm here." Without answering Stokes slipped out of the door and was gone.

* * *

Stokes had his doubts about finding the gold stash at night. At least if he got there tonight he could find the gold first thing in the morning and be gone before Surcingle returned. If Surcingle were there already he would use the excuse of riding for cows and attempt to mislead the detective with a bogus story.

A mile east of the Birdseye stage station he found what he assumed to be the area that Cat had described. The moon cast an eerie bluish light that made it difficult to identify the landmarks, let alone crevices where the gold might be hidden. After midnight he gave up the search and wrapped in a blanket to wait for dawn.

At the first glimmer of morning Stokes resumed the search and quickly spotted the Indian profile on the rocks. That was what he needed to find the critical marker trees. After only a few minutes of searching crevices in the rock outcrop he heard a distinctive change of sound as his probing stick tapped a leather saddlebag. Pulling out loose sagebrush, Stokes peered back into the crack with a lighted match. He could dimly see the sacks. Cat had hidden the gold well.

Stokes' face beaded with nervous sweat as he climbed a large boulder and scanned the surrounding countryside. Seeing nothing alarming, he removed his fedora, squeezed into the narrow space, and tied his lariat onto the saddlebags. As he started to drag them out they wedged tightly in the narrow cleft. Cursing, he crawled back into the crack where it took several precious minutes to release the tightly stuck bags. Unused to the exercise, Stokes was soon soaked with sweat and his heart was racing. Finally he managed to drag the bags out. Gasping from his exertions, Stokes loaded them on the packhorse.

"Holy smokes!" Stokes gasped in surprise at the gold's weight, then cursed as he realized that the packhorse would be overloaded. "Dammit anyway!" *Too bad Cat didn't tell me there was this much gold. I would have brought another horse. There must be a lot more than two hundred pounds. It'll take me hours to get back to the mine.* He looked at the heavily laden horse and laughed softly. *Here I am worrying about too much weight. Hell, I've got a bloody fortune here.*

He felt a great resolve issue from his very soul. *This will be seed for a great mine at DePass.*

His jubilation was tempered by the thought that Charlie Surcingle might not be far away. Surcingle's exploits were legend, from his pursuit of Billy the Kid to hounding other outlaws throughout the West. It seemed that detective could be in two or three places at once.

Stokes guided his horses through a rocky area where tracks would be difficult to see. Anxious to get back to the mine and hide the gold, he pushed the horses hard. This kind of physical adventure made Stokes nervous. His forte' was the money chase. He much preferred cleverness to confrontation. He was not a coward, but the possibility of injury or death made him uneasy. With a clever adversary like Charlie Surcingle there was real danger involved. Surcingle was certain to eventually show up at the mine. Both the gold and Cat would have to be well out of sight.

An hour's ride from where he picked up the gold, Stokes rode down off the high mountain ridge into a large open valley. As he turned south toward the mine he rode past a herd of cattle that would soon obliterate his tracks.

He felt exposed, riding across the open expanse of the valley. A chill crawled up his back like a snake, as he contemplated the rocky points above the valley where Surcingle could get the drop on him. With the loaded packhorse slowing him, it seemed like an eternity before he entered the draw that took the road up through De Pass. From De Pass, a notch cutting the mountain crest, it was only a mile or so down into the mine camp.

On the pass, Stokes stopped and carefully searched the open country behind him. There was no sign of anyone following. Cows grazed peacefully on the hills where he had just passed. He breathed easier. *Once I get back to the mine I can make my own rules.*

The morning sun was already warming the mountain valley of the DePass Mine as Stokes clattered down the wagon road with the valuable cargo. The road was a rocky

THE TROUBLE WITH GOLD...

one and he felt good that there would be no sign of his travel since he had turned south. He began to make plans. Plans for Cat's gold.

As he neared the mine, Stokes conjured up a little ditty that he sang in time with the rhythmic beat of the horses' hooves.

"Listen up, Mr. Rockefeller.
JP Morgan, keep your dirty steel.
JT Stokes is coming up fast.
Those Colorado mines will pale.
DePass will go past!
This goose will lay its golden egg."

He sang the last line with all the gusto he could muster. As his last note echoed in the ravine he felt suddenly embarrassed that someone may have heard him. He never let anyone see any other than the stern business side of him.

Stokes laughed aloud as his mind whirled with elation. *This gold will be the catalyst for grand accomplishments. First I'll have to convince Cat. That should be easy.*

* * *

Cat awakened early from a fitful sleep. From the first light of dawn he nervously watched the road. When Stokes rode into sight, Cat drew a deep breath and exhaled with relief. The dark curtain of foreboding that had been with him since the shooting lifted from his mind. He knew he owed Stokes a big debt, but it was worth it. He hurried out as Stokes rode up the hill to the mine.

Stokes dismounted and took off his hat to fan his ruddy face. Beads of sweat glistened on his shiny head. "Well, here's our gold. I'd better get it down in the mine. If my hunch is right, we'll soon have a visitor looking for it. You'd best stay here, Cat. I'll take it down to the fourth level where it'll be safe. That will be a good hideout for you too. They'd never look for you there. I'll fix it up with plenty of grub and a bed if things get too risky up here."

"Stokes, I ain't stayin' long enough to need no hideout. I'm leavin' as soon as I find a place to trade the gold for cash. Even payin' you for your help and sellin' the rest at two-bits on the dollar, I'll do all right."

"It would be suicide to unload this stuff now. I can take care of the gold safely and you'll make even *more* that its market value. Now that's a hell of a lot better than a quarter of its worth! I'll stop around later this morning and we'll talk about it. And I won't take a big cut like I would if you left now."

Cat, too weak and sore to help, watched as Stokes loaded the sacks of gold into a mine car and prepared to push the car into the adit. "Wait a minute, Stokes, I don't think I heard you right. You're tellin' me that my gold is worth *more* than its weight in gold? You're funnier than a damn cocklebur under a saddle blanket. That sounds like some sort of magic trick. I don't need none of that, thank you."

Stokes didn't smile. "Don't jump to conclusions. I think you'll like what I have to say. We'll talk about it later. I'm beat right now. I'll put this stuff where it's safe, then I'm going down to the hotel and rest for a couple of hours. You'd better stay here in case Surcingle comes around. He'll likely be here by tomorrow, maybe even today. I'll have Ella bring you up some coffee and breakfast."

"Stokes, I asked you before. Who is this Ella? I don't like the idea of anyone else knowin' I'm here."

"You needn't worry about Ella. You probably can trust her more than you trust me." Stokes laughed and pushed the ore car into the adit and to the shaft station. He maneuvered the car onto the cage and signaled for descent to the fourth level.

Four hundred feet down the shaft the mine was eerily quiet except for the echoing drip of water in the dark tunnel. The track sloped up slightly so that water would drain toward the shaft. Stokes strained to get the car back into the unused powder magazine. Putting his shoulder to the heavy door, he pushed it shut. The waterlogged door wedged tightly in its jam. It would be difficult to open even with a pry bar.

Chapter 13

Ella

Ella looked in satisfaction at the flowers she had planted to replace the dusty yard in front of the hotel at the DePass Mine. Her chestnut hair, piled in large loose curls over her head, glowed with the early sun. Ella's fine-boned beauty contrasted with the stark mining scene as much as the flowers she admired, yet her poise and steady green eyes spoke of an inner strength greater than that of a tough miner. Her face retained a demure beauty of youth even as she matured into her mid-thirties. Only a few tiny lines on her forehead marked the passage of hard times in her past, but otherwise Ella's face had an exquisite loveliness that embodied her good nature and intelligence.

This morning she felt on top of the world. She loved this wild, rugged country and the opportunity to make something out of the old hotel, and her life. Her happiness ebbed a little as she wondered if Stokes would ever get the mine going as he had promised. She had been here for a few months, and there were few signs that the mine would

Ella

be producing anytime soon. The only miner working was the hoist operator. Stokes had hired him so he could go down into the mine periodically to check on the pumping progress. Stokes had mentioned that nothing could be done until the mine was dewatered. Ella suspected that a lack of money was the real reason for the delay.Ella had met Stokes on the train from Denver to Omaha when she was returning from a trip west to find friends from fifteen years past. It had been a fruitless search. Most of her former acquaintances were dead. That wasn't surprising, since they were all outlaws. She had ridden with them in search of youthful adventure and romance. The West was much different now and those memories of train robberies and exciting pursuits by posses seemed more of a dream than foolish reality. The one man she most hoped to find had disappeared without a trace.

JT Stokes, obviously a lonely man, had introduced himself and took the train seat next to hers. Stokes talked about his large ranch and the mine he had recently purchased. "Miss Price," he enthused, as he talked about the DePass Mine and its potential, "once I get the mine running I'll need a place to entertain bankers and investors visiting the greatest gold mine in the west. I'm going to fix up the old hotel at the mine." Stokes's plans were interesting as well as grand, and Ella had responded to his enthusiasm with genuine interest and suggestions about refurbishing the hotel.

As the train neared Omaha, Stokes abruptly turned to her. "Miss Price, come to work for me. I need someone to run my hotel. Together, we can make the DePass Hotel famous. I want it to be known for its fine wines and elegant cuisine. A shining star in the wilderness. It will help convince investors that the mine is worthy of their money."

THE TROUBLE WITH GOLD...

Ella had thought for only a moment before accepting Stokes' offer. She was tired of teaching school in the east, and she loved the west. When Stokes finished his business in Omaha she returned to Wyoming with him.

Ella convinced Stokes to loan her the services of a man to help fix up the hotel. With surprising expertise, an old cowboy from Stokes' ranch had painted the hotel and constructed a curving flagstone walk in place of the loose planks that had been there. He built a low rock wall around the garden and was now framing a veranda over the exposed entrance.

Next to the walk, delicate lavender crocii were fading. Along the rock wall, a patch of alyssum plants showed the beginnings of what would soon be a mass of color. Yellow, blue and purple pansies filled in the garden next to a row of blue and white iris.

Ella could imagine the hotel when she had finished. A lattice of climbing roses would flank the veranda. In front of the windows, framed by lace curtains, tall hollyhocks would be visible from the lobby. And when the spring flowers faded, black-eyed susans would take over.

She listened to the mellow burble of the small brook as it exited from the cooling cellar. The hotel had been cleverly constructed over the stream. There was a trap door from the kitchen down into the little stone-lined cellar and it was a perfect place to keep foods fresh. Ella smiled, thinking it would also keep bottles of French wine at the right temperature. She had taken a room next to the brook so that she could hear the tinkling of the water at night. *I only hope that the mine will be as much of a success as Stokes claims it will be. I hid out once, a long time ago, not far from here. Those days are past. Now I'm hoping to find my future in almost the same place. Life's turns can be strange.*

* * *

Photo courtesy of Joyce Fuller
The DePass Hotel, 1916

With the gold hidden and Cat safely out of sight, Stokes walked down to the hotel for breakfast. Ella could tell that he was in an agitated state of mind. He seemed both exhausted and exuberant at the same time. His eyes were red and bleary and he obviously needed sleep, but he lingered over his coffee, stirring it constantly with a spoon, as though wanting to tell her something.

"Ella, a fellow rode in here last night. He's been shot in the arm and needs some help. I know him a little, he's done a couple of jobs for me. Anyway, I felt sorry for him and agreed to let him hide out up at the mine office until things blow over. Apparently he stole something from a band of thieves. Scoundrels, by the sound of it. Anyway they put a man-hunter on his trail. An old-timer by the name of Surcingle. Surcingle ambushed him over near Birdseye."

At the mention of Surcingle's name Ella stifled a gasp and, unnoticed by Stokes, turned pale. On the pretense of getting more coffee, she went to the kitchen where she took a deep breath to compose herself. *It's been almost fifteen years and he didn't actually ever see me. It was just that portrait that Butch and Harry insisted on having done in New York before we left for South America. Pinkerton's got a print and used it on a wanted poster. I just hope I'm forgotten history to Surcingle.* Taking a minute to compose herself, she returned to Stokes' table with the steaming pot of coffee.

"Ella, I've got to get some rest. Take some breakfast up to our wounded friend. I think he needs a little more doctoring than I could give him, but he doesn't want to risk having a doctor see him. The wound ought to be cauterized. I don't think there's any broken bones, but the bullet carried a lot of his shirt into the flesh."

He rose from the table and started up the stairs to his room, then stopped and turned. "By the way, this fellow's name is Cat Teason. I guess he spent some time with the Wild Bunch back in their heyday."

For the second time this morning Ella felt a sense of shock. She put her hands on the back of a chair to steady herself. It seemed that her past was overtaking her like a freight train. *Cat wasn't a big man in the Bunch but he'll remember me. I guess it was bound to happen. After fifteen years I can just hope my indiscretions will be forgiven as the truth leaks out.* As she thought more about it she realized that Cat Teason probably didn't want to open up ancient history any more than she did. *Oh God, I'm so tired of hiding.*

Ella wasn't anxious to have her past revisited, but knew she'd have to face Cat. *The sooner the better.* She put a plate of eggs and bacon, hot biscuits and a pot of fresh coffee into a basket and, with a bucket of hot water for nursing in the other hand, climbed the steep road up to the mine office. She knocked and quietly called out his name as she opened the door. Cat's eyes opened wide in surprise.

"Hello Cat. It's been a long while."

"My God, I never expected to see you again." Cat said when he recovered from his surprise. "When Stokes said he'd have someone look in on me, he said Ella. I never guessed it might be someone I knew from the past."

"I thought I'd left that past behind, but I guess it's inevitable that it catches up with one sometime. And I *am* Ella now." Looking at his arm with its bloody wrapping, Ella's eyes softened with a sudden concern. "Let me look at that. JT told me you were wounded but I didn't know how bad." She took his arm and gently undid the makeshift bandage. She could smell the whiskey.

Ella gently washed the wound with the warm water. "If we keep the wound clean you might not get infection." She carefully picked out pieces of shirt from the torn flesh. "This will sting for a minute or two." she dabbed on some medicinal alcohol. "We might not have to cauterize the wound if infection doesn't get started."

Cat winced and gritted his teeth, holding back a groan, as the antiseptic seemed to burn to the bone.

"I'm sorry, I know that hurts, but getting the wound clean will help avoid infection better than the whiskey I can smell." She held her hand gently on his forehead, checking his temperature. "You men seem to think booze is a cure-all for everything," she teased.

"Thanks, Et...Ella." He closed his eyes as she placed her soft hand on his feverish brow, then frowned in disappointment when she took it away. "Look, Ella, I won't say anything about knowing you before, but someone is likely to be around looking for me and..."

Ella laughed. "Are you forgetting that I've handled this kind of situation before? I'll be back tomorrow to check on you," Ella opened the door to leave, then turned back. "Cat, I don't want to know why you're here or why you got shot. I do have one question though." She hesitated for a moment, biting her lip as if afraid to ask. "What ever happened to Dutch, Dutch Wyatt?"

"I saw him a year ago, down in New Mexico He went across the border into Mexico and I stayed in Silver City. I heard that he had a run-in with Pancho Villa. Uh... Ella, I don't know. I heard that he was...Well..." Cat stopped, not wanting to finish. He went on with a pretense of certainty. "Well hell, knowin' Dutch I'd give you odds that he's still around."

Ella paled and her voice broke a little as she spoke. "Oh God, I hope so." She said softly, almost as a prayer. "Surely he's okay. I...He's a good man." She turned and hurried from the room. On the way back down the rough road to the hotel she stumbled and almost fell as her eyes brimmed with tears.

* * *

Cat, intent on his own problems, did not see Ella's distress, but felt exuberant after her visit. *She always brings out the good side of people. She'll find the bright side of things and make others feel the same way in no time.* Cat thought back to the days many years ago when Etta interjected a gentling influence on a gang who were largely ruffians. He was always amazed at her sincere air of sophistication, yet she had an equal ability to ride a horse and shoot. She rode with a regular saddle too, and still managed to look feminine. Even though she was good with a pistol he was sure she'd never shot anyone, let alone even point the gun at a person.

Cat remembered how her smile would seem to light up a room. Just now, when she smiled at him, he thought she must be the most beautiful woman in the world. He recalled how she could even get Harvey Logan to smile. Logan, who went by the name Kid Curry, was so cold and full of meanness that it could be dangerous to risk setting off his short temper. Ella wasn't fazed by the Kid's reputation and he seemed buffaloed by her. Cat remembered that the usually dismal outlaw camps were a much better place while Ella was there.

I wonder if there's anything between her and Stokes? She deserves someone better than that stingy old bastard.

He dug into the breakfast with the appetite of a bear after a long winter.

Chapter 14

The Golden Goose & the Egg

At the hotel, Stokes lay awake in his bed, his need for sleep denied as he wondered how to use Cat's gold to start up the DePass Mine. Restless, he rose and looked out his window. To his tired mind the mine buildings and equipment emanated an ominous aura. High above the hotel, next to the portal, the hoisthouse loomed over the valley with its hulk of rusty corrugated metal. Some of the sheathing hung loose and flapped idly in a late morning breeze, clanking and screeching mournfully. The portal itself stared across the valley like an empty eye socket in the mountainside. Near the hotel, the ore processing building sprawled like a prehistoric monster, loose boards hanging like shedding scales. Here and there, a clutter of abandoned equipment showed the progressive rust of disuse.

To further emphasize the depressing scene was the disaster that had shut down the mine only a few years before. The mine foreman and two miners died when deadly gases seeped in from a fault deep in the mine. The mining company died with them.

In the midst of the tragic story there were persistent rumors that the last rounds of blasting had intersected a rich gold vein in the deepest level of the mine. The truth was now under a few hundred feet of water in the mine shaft. After the accident Stokes bought the mine. He knew of the rumored bonanza. More importantly, he found the last shipping records. The gold grades had progressively been getting better with each shipment. Stokes was convinced that a gold bonanza lay just beyond the present mine workings. Unfortunately the financial pressures of his ranch prevented him from doing anything with the mine.

The dismal scene before him seemed to mock his dreams, as a dilemma nagged at Stokes. There was plenty of gold to finance the mine startup, but he had the same problem he had warned Cat about. *How will I convert the gold to cash? Then, what if I don't find the bonanza before the money runs out?*

Stokes finally gave up getting any sleep. As he climbed the hill past the dilapidated buildings and rusty equipment to the mine office, a plan suddenly materialized. He would use the gold, but he wouldn't have to convert it to cash. With the money raised he could buy new pumps and miners would be driving toward rich ore. *What I'm going to do isn't dishonest, it's just priming the pump. Nobody will know except Cat and me, and Cat won't need to know the details. In the end, everyone will make money.* First, he needed to make a deal with Teason.

Stokes entered Cat's little room brimming with enthusiasm about his plan. "Teason, there isn't a safe place where you can cash in this gold right now. Surcingle will have the word out. Even if you could sell it out on the open market you'll be lucky to get ten cents on the dollar. And you'll get caught for sure. I'll make you a deal to get *more*, not less, than the real value. And with no risk."

"Come on, Stokes, I'm not a buffoon who just rode in outa' the hills." Cat blustered. "Why and how could you give me more than it's worth? And don't give me any crap about regaler and troy ounces."

"Teason, do you know what leverage is?"

"All I know is, I've got a lotta gold and I intend to keep most of it until I can trade it for cash."

"Ah, but why settle for a little bit of cash." Stokes smiled with confidence. "I'm talking about you getting a lot more cash than you ever dreamed of. We won't just sell that gold to some fence for pennies on the dollar, I'll make that gold work for you. Your gold will be feed for the goose that will lay many golden eggs. That goose will be the DePass Mine. With your gold as a primer our goose is worth a lot more than the one egg you have now. You will be a major shareholder in the DePass Mine. Unlike your gold, the shares will be legal."

Cat rubbed a hand over his eyes as Stokes' spoke. He started to object but Stokes held up his hand.

"Let me finish, Teason, then you'll see the wisdom of my plan. I'm going to start up the DePass and it will make us both rich. Here, I'll show you why." Stokes opened a desk drawer and pulled out a brown pasteboard portfolio wrapped with a shoelace. "Here are the official shipping records from the mine before it shut down a couple of years back. Look at the gold values."

Cat took the sheaf of shipping receipts and looked at them blankly for a moment, then tossed them back on the desk. "Those are just numbers to me. They don't mean beans. If ya' already got gold down there then why do ya' need mine?"

"Here." Stokes impatiently stabbed his finger at the numbers, his face growing red. "The dates of the shipments are down the left side. This is the ore weight and these three columns show the assays for copper, gold and silver. Now follow down the copper column. See? The copper values are decreasing. The mine was running out of copper ore.

"Now look at the gold values. The gold values are getting better. It's not a big change but it's important because each shipment is several blast rounds further into the vein on the lowest level.

"That might not seem too important, and by itself it wouldn't be. The last miners found rich stuff but they didn't live to tell about it. There's a bonanza waiting six hundred feet below where we are now. I'm certain there's a lot more gold than you got from that train. A hell of a lot more!"

Stokes enthusiastically spread his arms wide as though to grasp the lode. "We'll get the mine back up and follow that gold vein as it gets even richer. First we need to get some excitement generated. We can prime things with a few ounces of your gold. A little in the mine and a little with the bankers. With some money I can get the company organized. With your gold and some publicity, the share value will go up like crazy."

Cat, his head spinning, sat down to think more clearly. Stokes was going too fast for him to comprehend. "Why in the hell would I want to trade good yellow gold for a share of a fly-by-night mine venture that might not find anything but worthless rock, let alone a bonanza?" exploded Cat. "No thanks. I'll take my lumps and get what I can out of the gold. I bet I can get fifty cents on the dollar."

"Before you decide, let me explain what I have in mind. For only half of your gold I'll give you shares in DePass Mines Unlimited with a par value equal to all of your gold. What's more, we don't have to find a lot of gold to cash in on this mine venture. You've seen the trend showing more gold. The trend is there, the gold values will keep increasing."

Cat pulled at his ear as he thought over Stokes' proposal. It was sort of like playing poker – *Should I cash in or put it in the pot for another game?*

"Believe me Teason, the DePass Mines stock will skyrocket. Besides, the bankers will have only a little bit of your gold. I dare say that after we get started, they will be glad to trade that gold back for some of your shares in the mine. Look at it this way," Stokes continued persuasively.

"If you leave with your gold today, minus some for my trouble, you'll be lucky to get ten thousand dollars. *If* you can find a place to trade it. I'm betting that your share of the mine stock will easily be a quarter of a million dollars once I get this thing going. One more thing. I looked in some of those bags. There's a hell of a lot of lead ore in there. It's not all gold!"

"It's not lead, them's gold teller-ides, which is worth damn near as much as the yellow gold. I know that for a fact." Cat blurted out. Still, the words "quarter of a million dollars," softened Cat's resistance. "Stokes, you're a slick talker, but what if your work down there runs out of the gold vein?"

Stokes laughed, knowing that Cat was headed into the chute. "It won't! The values will get better and better. Your gold will take us to the mother lode!" He exclaimed in a convincingly firm voice.

"Hell, I've talked with a miner friend about veins. He says that they's mighty unpredictable. You can't know anything ahead of what ya' see." Cat winced as a stab of pain reminded him of his wound.

"We'll make sure that doesn't happen with a little salting of the vein. A few ounces of that gold dust in your poke will make sure the new development looks good until we get into the real stuff. It's not really cheating because there will be better ore out there. All the signs point to it."

Cat perked up at Stokes' reference to cheating. "Wal, I shore like it better when the odds are stacked in our favor like that."

"I tell you what, Teason. I'll take a few of the nicer pieces of gold around to some bankers. That will get their attention and getting loans will be easy. I won't tell them the samples are from the DePass, but I won't tell them they aren't either. They will think what they want to think. I can't help that." Stokes rubbed his hands together at the thought. "I could tell them it wasn't from the DePass, but they'd think I was just being cagey and get even more stirred up." Stokes chuckled at the thought.

"These bankers and stock promoters know that old carpenter Will Stratten made millions with his mines at Cripple Creek. They are anxious for the next big opportunity to come along and won't take a chance on missing out." He continued in a tone as if the deal was done. "Later, we'll take a few ounces of the fine gold and I'll show you how to salt the vein so that it assays like the real stuff."

Cat liked Stokes' scheme but he was reluctant to part with his sacks of golden treasure. He tugged at his ear again. "Well, let me think about it a while."

"We don't have much time. Each hour brings Surcingle closer. You're going to need my help to stay out of his clutches until you get healed. If Surcingle finds you here you can bet the gold is a goner. I don't like to think what his clients might do to you!

"If you're not happy with the way things go after I get this thing underway I'll buy back your stock. You do what you want with the rest your gold. Better yet, I'll take that off your hands too, for a better price than you would get from a buyer who might squeal on you. Hells fire, Cat we're sitting right on top of another Cripple Creek."

Cat thought for a long minute. He knew his options were limited, considering his bullet-torn arm. Right now he just wanted to lie back and rest. Stokes was right. It would be no small trick to sell the gold. The thought of getting caught and having to face up to the mine thieves made him shiver. Then, too, was his love of a game, especially if the odds were stacked in his favor by a trick card or so. He would rather bet on the chance of a big win rather than run with a smaller pat hand.

Meybe this will be the biggest game I've ever played. A vision flashed in his mind, the cards so clear that he could feel them in his hand – *Four aces!*

"Stokes, I oughta' have my head examined, but you got a deal."

"Good man!" Stokes grabbed Cat's hand to seal the partnership. "Your gold will be safe down in the mine. It's well hidden in an old powder magazine on Level 4. As soon as you're up to it I'll take you down there so you know where it is. I'll go to town today and stir things up a little with the newspaper. Keep a lookout for anyone coming in. If you stay out of sight here, Ella will make sure no one comes up to the mine. She'll bring up some extra grub and you can lie low."

Later, Cat wondered if he'd been taken, but it seemed like a pretty foolproof deal. Just the same he'd keep a close eye on Stokes. He wished he knew how much the gold weighed. He should have mentioned the weight business again so Stokes would know that he knew something about gold.

Stokes hurried back to the hotel, anxious to put his plan in motion. Over lunch with Ella he excitedly told her of his plans for the mine, although he didn't mention Cat's involvement or the gold. "Ella, I've come up with a plan to get the mine started up. I'm going to town to finalize some things. I have a feeling that this plan will move along pretty fast. We're going put this place on the map, and it's going to coin money, lots of money. It will be our Midas touch," he paused and added, "if I don't fall into the River Pactolus first," referring to the mythical river that had been King Midas' downfall. He laughed at his joke, which was lost on Ella.

"You'll need to hire more help here at the hotel. Get a good chef. Make this a show place. We'll have plenty of investors who will want to see the mine that's making them rich. Make sure we have some of the finest whiskey too."

Ella was a little surprised. This was the first mention about financing of the mine. He'd idly talked about the mine's great potential but she thought it wishful thinking until his creditors were in a happier mood.

* * *

Charlie Surcingle knew he wouldn't likely find the stash of loot when he returned back to the place where he had shot the outlaw. He'd already concluded that he would have to follow the thief and the gold. He looked for a while and found where someone had clumsily tried to wipe out his tracks near the rocky cleft. Cat, or an accomplice, must have returned with another packhorse and retrieved the gold. Charlie's practiced eye told him that one horse carried a load of more than two hundred pounds, much more than the other horse and its rider.

Charlie followed the tracks onto a patch of rocky terrain where the tracking became slow. Rather than wasting time, Charlie played a hunch and wheeled his horse along the mountain ridge. A half-mile away he picked up the trail again.

The tracks soon disappeared again on the rocky terrain along the backbone of the mountain but Surcingle continued to let his intuition work for him and continued east, dropping off the high ridge into a cow camp. No one was there and a herd of steers had been grazing over the valley, wiping out any tracks that might have been made.

Charlie reined his horse to a stop. Removing his hat, he put himself in the outlaw's place and weighed the alternatives. Then Surcingle gently nudged his horse in the direction of the DePass Mine. The bartender in Shoshoni told him that the hotel at DePass had the best steaks in the country. "And," the bartender had added with a knowing lift of his eyebrows, "they're served up by the most beautiful woman in these parts."

Charlie Surcingle had retired twice but found he missed the excitement and adventure that had been his life for over thirty years. Still a handsome man, he longed for the romances he often found on the road. He knew that he presented a fine figure that women seemed to like. "What the hell, I might even get some useful information at the hotel." He spoke out loud to convince himself that there was a legitimate need for the detour.

The horse agreed with a snort and a toss of his head. Without further urging the horse picked up his pace.

It was late afternoon as Charlie rode down the narrow, rock and sagebrush rimmed ravine that led into the DePass Mine camp and hotel.

* * *

Through a window, Ella watched Charlie approach. He rode with an erect military posture. As he approached the hotel he smoothed his drooping white mustache and brushed the dust from his clothes. A neatly tied scarf covered his neck above a gray vest. His dark trousers were neatly pressed. He fit to his big roan horse as though he was part of it and together they presented a commanding force. Ella had never seen him before, but his appearance left no doubt about his identity.

Surcingle tied his horse to the hitching rail and tilted his hat at a rakish angle with a deft lift of a finger under the brim. Ella could see that Charlie was an attractive man and she wondered how many broken hearts he had left behind in his travels. She wondered for a brief moment if he would be attracted to her. She mentally chided herself and felt her cheeks flush slightly.

He strode into the hotel, *My God, the Shoshoni bartender was right, she is beautiful.* He doffed his hat and as he looked at her he had the feeling that he'd seen this woman somewhere before, but he couldn't recall just where or when. "Ma'am, I need a room and dinner for a night or two and I'm looking for work as a miner. I worked in the mines down in Colorado." Then he looked at her with a smile. "By the way, haven't we met somewhere before?"

Ella smiled at Charlie, looked him straight in the eye for a moment. She shook her head slightly with only the hint of a smile that indicated that she'd heard that line many times before. She gripped the register book firmly to conceal the trembling in her hands as she slid it across the counter to him.

"Supper will be served at 6 o'clock. The bar is open anytime. If you want hot water for a bath that will be 15 cents extra." Looking at the name he signed, Charlie Anderson, she continued. "I don't know about work Mr. Anderson, but I could use someone to wash dishes." Ella laughed and flashed a warm smile.

As Ella got the room key off the hook he appraised her with the practiced eye of a man who made it his business to learn what he could of everyone. The West left its deep mark, good and bad, on those who stayed here long. As attractive as Ella was, with her smooth complexion and youthful face, Charlie could see a record of some hard times. A ready smile and a musical laugh covered that hint of toughness. Or was it, Charlie wondered, sadness he saw. She seemed to be unaware of her attractiveness but carried herself with a statuesque poise that emphasized her shapely figure.

Charlie was certain he had seen or met her somewhere before. He said nothing else to her about that and she showed no signs of recognition. Charlie concluded that he must be mistaken. *If I had met her before I would have wooed her and we would both remember.*

* * *

Cat, keeping a nervous lookout from the mine office perched high above the road, saw the rider come down the road and dismount at the hotel. It was Surcingle. Cat's face broke out in a cold sweat, fear overriding the throbbing pain of his wound. He cursed under his breath. "Damn, I should have ridden out when I had the chance." He forced himself to calm down, realizing that he was in no shape to evade capture. He took his revolver from its holster and spun the cylinder, checking that it was loaded. He laid the gun on the bed beside him. *Hell, there's no reason I can't lie low here and be okay. That detective won't stay long if he doesn't see me. Ella will get him on his way.* He paced to and fro, his pain compounded by worry about his stalker just below at the hotel. *Could he have seen some sign or track and knows I'm here? Why doesn't he leave?*

Cat worried about the gold and wondered if Stokes had told him the truth. Was it really in the mine car, safe in the depths of the mine? Cat's mind was in a whirl. What worried him most was that Stokes had seen the gold. That amount of wealth could warp men's minds. He'd seen men kill for a lot less than his gold.

When Stokes returned he would demand to see it and maybe move down into the mine where he could hole-up and keep an eye on the gold at the same time. No one was likely to come down in the mine looking for him. This mine office was too exposed and the hill behind too steep for a rapid escape. Cat finally lay down on the cot, feverish and dismayed by his predicament.

* * *

After enjoying a warm bath, Charlie Surcingle dressed in his best clothes and found that this little hotel did indeed serve fine whiskey and tender steak. As Charlie openly admired Ella's beauty there was something about her face, especially when she looked contemplative, that rang a bell in the depths of his mind. Once Ella had caught him looking at her and she met his gaze with an unwavering one of her own then smiled slightly as she turned and went through the kitchen door. Finally, giving in to the rigors of the past several days and the hard night in Shoshoni, Charlie turned in for the night.

* * *

Stokes rode the twenty miles to Shoshoni and sent a telegram to a friend at the stock exchange. His message announced that he would be reopening the DePass mine. Examination of samples taken before the mine had closed showed the presence of high-grade gold-telluride ore. That was all–he didn't elaborate or make any glowing predictions. He would feed the information out gradually although he did show a piece of gold-rich rock to the newspaper editor. Suspense would be cultivated. News of the western world's greatest new gold mine would come gradually as the exploration work advanced and identified formations with limitless potential. Not only would the new exploration sampling be beyond expectations, but start up mining in the exploration drift would support the samples beyond any doubt, *thanks to Teason's gold.*

Stokes arrived back at DePass the next day, jubilant with the conviction that the mine would make him a rich man. He went directly to the mine office where he found Cat pacing with mild delirium and his mind running wild with imagined conspiracies. Stokes calmed him by giving him the details of the powder magazine on the fourth level where the gold was safe behind the heavy door. "Teason, I'll put some food and a bedroll down there. It will be a safe hiding place if you need it, and," He added soothingly, "you'd be right there with your gold."

Cat's low spirits rose and he felt a rising sense of relief–Stokes had taken care of his concerns even before he had a chance to voice them himself.

"Anytime you want to check it out I'll take you down."

"I feel better about the gold being down there but I'm worried about that detective hanging around. I think he must have some idea that I may be nearby. Maybe I should try and get the drop on him before he surprises me."

"Don't do something foolish. Whoever hired him probably knows his whereabouts. If he disappears we'll have a whole flock of lawmen prowling around the countryside. He claims he's looking for work as a miner. I reckon he wants a reason to stay around on account of Ella. He isn't the first man to stay over because of her. Don't worry, she can handle him."

Cat laughed, nodding his head in agreement. "Ella's a nice reason to stay around and she's a pretty good nurse too."

Stokes scowled. "I haven't told Ella about the gold. I trust her but there's no need for her to know." He looked at Cat's arm. "It's looking better but I think you ought to see a doctor. I have a friend in Shoshoni, a doctor, who you could trust.",

"Like I said, Stokes, I'm not going to take the chance with a doctor. Especially as long as I'm gettin' better."

* * *

Charlie Surcingle's intuitive sense told him that his prey hadn't gone far. Still, his stay at the DePass hadn't produced anything more than some good whiskey and tender beef, adding up to an expensive bill at the hotel. Ella continued to be immune to his charms and it made him feel old. In the past women could seldom resist him for long. Even worse, Charlie felt he could fall in love with the beautiful Ella.

Charlie would have liked to have the chance to snoop around the mine but there was no logical reason to do so. He'd talked to Stokes about a miner's job but Stokes told him it would be a few weeks yet before he would need to expand his crew. After two days Charlie decided that it would look suspicious to stay longer.

It was fascinating to Charlie how much value man seemed to place on the lure of a hole in the ground. Even more interesting were the clever men who did well by capitalizing on others' attractions to these man-made perforations in the earth. Often there was only the allure of the expectation rather than the gold itself. He wondered if this mine was real or a seducer. One of Charlie Surcingle's greatest tools was his knowledge of how greed directed the actions of dishonest men. He knew that a mine could be a magnet to this greed so it was with some reluctance that he gave up and left DePass. He would be back soon, knowing that surprise might reap rewards.

Chapter 15

The Salt of the Earth

Cat shivered as he grasped the side of the mine cage. He felt he was dropping like a rock into the blackness. "How in the hell deep is this?" Stokes ignored him. Cat wanted to tell Stokes to take him back to the surface. But he had to see his gold. His cap-lamp showed only a blur of the shaft walls and his ears popped as the mine cage descended four hundred feet down the shaft.

Stokes was carrying a shotgun and a rolled up tarp. "What the hell are you going to hunt down here?" Cat laughed nervously, wishing he'd strapped on his pistol.

"Sometimes the rats nest back in these old mines.

"Let's go back up. I don't like this hole to hell."

"Teason, you're a gambler. I'm going to deal you in on a new type of game. This won't be two-bit poker. The stakes will be larger than you'd ever dreamed of. And the odds will be much better. Best of all, you won't have all of your poke in the pot. Right now, I want you to see for yourself that your gold is here."

"I'm listening Stokes, but right now I'm planning to hit the trail as soon as the arm is a little better. Maybe I'll sit in on your game for a while but the payoff had better be good." He felt uneasy, still wondering why Stokes had brought the shotgun along. The rat excuse seemed unlikely. He wondered if Stokes intended to kill him, or worse leave him down here to die. *Why the tarp? It's about the right size to roll a body up in.* Cat kept thinking about what gold could do to a man and what he might do to have it.

"Shi-oot, Stokes, I think we oughta go back up and talk about this a little more. Maybe I'll just give you what gold I owe you and head out with the rest." Before he could say more, the cage halted on the fourth level, springing up and down as four hundred feet of cable stretched and rebounded with the stop.

"Good God! What's happening?" Cat's voice cracked with panic. Stokes opened the steel gate and Cat stumbled out of the cage. He felt queasy and needed to feel solid earth under his feet. He hadn't realized the passage was so small; he could reach both sides easily at the same time, and often had to bow his head to avoid banging it on the back. The rocks seemed as though they might suddenly squeeze in on them as they walked along the narrow drift.

The hissing carbide lamps on their helmets illuminated only a small area in front of them, and the gloom beyond was heavy with dampness, as though cloaking sinister spirits. The air smelled of musty, wet timbers. Water dripped into puddles, echoing an eerie plink, plink, plink. The dark walls, slimy with mud, pressed in closer as they walked along the drift.

Cat's breath came in short gasps and he felt the panic of not enough air. Putting his hand on the wall to steady himself he touched the cold sliminess of the muddy rock. He drew his hand back quickly, wiping it on his trousers. Shaking his head to ward off claustrophobia, he tried to suck in a deep breath, but tension constricted his lungs. He hurried to keep up with Stokes, who walked along briskly in his rubber boots. Only the need to see his gold kept Cat from fleeing back to the shaft.

At the powder magazine it took both of them to pry and pull open the sodden door. As they entered the powder magazine, Stokes spoke again. "When you're in a high-stakes game you don't just get out when you feel like it. I need to know. Are you in or out?" He gestured with the shotgun. "If not, then I can't risk you staying here at DePass. If you don't have the guts to stay, we'll haul this stuff back to the surface. I'll sell you a couple of packhorses and there'll be nothing keeping you. But if you stay, don't think you can cash out whenever you take the notion. We have to play the hand out."

The powder magazine was a small room formed by a short crosscut drift that inclined steeply upward. The door separated the room from the narrow drift they had walked through. The bags of gold were neatly stacked in the ore car. One bag had been opened and the gold dumped into an empty dynamite box. The gold in the box reflected the mine lamps like a blaze of fire. Cat could almost feel the warmth. He sucked in the damp air. His chest no longer felt as if it were in a vice.

"I reckon you're right, Stokes. I ain't been thinkin' right since I was shot. I'll keep my word to stay until you get things goin', but you got to tell me what you have in mind. I want to be sure I'll still have some of it when I leave." He nervously eyed the shotgun, which Stokes cradled next to his side.

"Just watch." Stokes leaned the gun against the mine wall near his side. "You'll see what it's all about." He spread the canvas tarp out on the floor. Taking a sack from the ore car, he poured the gold onto the canvas and rolled it back and forth to separate the gold and telluride fines from the larger pieces of rich specimen ore. He scooped up all of the finer portions into the bag, then put the larger pieces in the dynamite box where the light from the flames of the carbide lights glistened spectacularly off of the gold. Cat felt immensely better. For the moment he forgot the shotgun.

"My God Teason, you made a real haul!"

"It looks pretty nice, don't it? But I don't understand why we need to separate the fine gold from the other. Looks to me like it all ought to be worth about the same."

"These fines will be just the ticket for a little salting of the mine samples until I hit the real thing. I told you that I have a plan where we're going to get more out of this gold than you would by selling it. Have a little patience and you'll ride out of here in a few months with most of your gold and a lot of cash to boot."

Cat wrinkled his brow in puzzlement and pulled at his ear. "Stokes, you might as well be talking Chinese, I still don't get what your game is."

Stokes chuckled. "Hell, it's sort of like cooking. If the soup doesn't taste quite right you salt it a little. We'll go down to a lower level and I'll show you how we can do the same with a mine."

Stokes picked up one of the chunks of gold-laden ore and turned it in the light. "When I show a few chunks of this good stuff around it will bring in investors and their money to DePass like bears to honey.

"There's a mother lode down here, somewhere deeper or further out. These upper veins are only tentacles leading to the main prize. I just have to get there, and with the financing generated by the excitement of this gold, I'll get the job done. DePass stock will be sought after around the world."

"Hell! I can't see how there'd be any damn gold in this muddy rock!"

Stokes ignored him. "What we need to do is give this mine some momentum. We're going to salt it with a little bit of these gold fines. You can stop fretting about the shotgun. That's what I'm going to use it for – salting the mine." He looked at Cat with a shadow of a smile.

"I've already calculated how much gold to put in a shotgun load. It will only take a few ounces to salt a hundred samples." Stokes sifted out a teaspoon of the Cripple Creek highgrade gold fines and mixed it with some dirt from the mine floor. He poured the mixture into a shotgun shell from which he had removed the shot. "Now, we'll wad up this piece of paper and tamp it into the end of the shell. I'll shoot this into the sample location. The rusty colored gold telluride isn't obvious and will blend with the rock better than the brighter gold but it will still show up good in an assay. When the investors send in an engineer, I'll have these sample locations ready to sample."

Carrying the shotgun and a heavy bag of the fine ore they walked back to the shaft. Stokes signaled for the hoistman to lower them to the next level. They walked back several hundred feet into the gloom as Stokes systematically marked the walls of the workings for sampling locations.

Stokes then aimed the shotgun at the vein above the sample point and shot the gold into the rock. The shotgun blast echoed so loudly that Cat thought it would surely be heard all the way to the hotel. He clasped his hands over his ears.

At the end of the drift Stokes poured some of the fines directly from the bag onto the pile of broken ore at the mining face. Cat winced as Stokes sifted his precious gold onto the muddy rock. "It looks to me like it's takin' a helluva lot of my gold to do that."

"This will upgrade the ore so that a sample of it will assay as good as bonanza ore."

As they walked back down the drift, Stokes explained the salting process. "Let's say that two pounds of rock sample represents a hundred tons of ore. It doesn't take much of your gold to make a two-pound sample look good. With a two pound sample the sample to ore weight is a ratio of one to a thousand. If a ton of good ore contains two ounces of gold, then that sample only needs one thousandth of that. By hell, Teason, that's only a pinch of gold in that shotgun blast to make the vein look good! The values will be spectacular but the vein isn't wide enough here to mine at a profit. Investors will be clamoring for us to make all speed to find the giant bonanza. Now let's get the job done."

Cat's brain felt numb with the overload of information. "Are you sayin' you only need three or four ounces total?" Cat liked this deal better all the time.

"We'll probably need a little more from time to time for a muck pile, maybe a hundred ounces total before the exploration hits the high grade. But hell Cat, you've got thousands of ounces here."

"What about the upper parts of the mine? Won't you want to salt that too?" Cat was feeling an interest in the plan.

"It's a little like your card playing strategy, Cat. The previous mining didn't show much gold in the upper levels. But," Stokes rubbed his hands vigorously in satisfaction, "that makes things even more dramatic as we show higher grade as the mining progresses deeper. It'll be obvious that we're getting close to the bonanza!"

As he watched the salting procedure, Cat was impressed. He felt a devious pride at being crucial to the scheme. "Hell," he chortled, "this could be better than an ace up my sleeve! Looks like you're dealing out a good hand!"

"Darn close to a sure bet! By the way, I'm going to take several of the nicer pieces of your gold up to the office. I need something to show stockbrokers and investors. There's nothing like gold to loosen pocket books! Don't worry, I'll keep it locked away. It'll just be a few pounds anyway."

An alarm rang in Cat's head. A few minutes ago Stokes was talking of using a few ounces, now it was pounds. His euphoria was diminished a little. His gold was in Stokes' control but he liked the plan.

During the next few days Cat continued to help Stokes with the salting. He hated going down in the mine but felt the need to keep track of how much gold Stokes was using. He never felt comfortable underground though. Each day he found it harder to get in the cage and drop into the depths of the mine.

Sometimes they rode the ore skip, which was nothing more than a large iron bucket. As the bucket tipped and rocked, Cat was fearful they would be spilled into the shaft. Back in the narrow drifts the black gooey rocks and dank air were a gloomy nightmare.

As Stokes became more involved in other aspects of the mine start-up Cat went down in the mine less and less. Finally he went down only to the fourth level every several days to inventory his remaining gold. Stokes had stopped salting the older drifts with the shotgun. Miners were now mining along the vein and Stokes was salting only new samples from the vein. This salting was taking a little more gold than Stokes had said, but not enough to alarm Cat.

The initial results brought about by the salting and the old mine records proved an attractive bait for investors. Stokes soon had the financing to make his dream a reality.

Chapter 16

A Full House

Cat spent his time playing solitaire in the little room back of the mine office. Sometimes, to ease the tedium, he practiced dealing cards from the bottom of the deck. The excitement he'd felt about the mine salting had worn off and again he worried about his deal with Stokes. *Damn, I wish I'd never let Stokes in on this. I shouldn't have agreed to let him use my gold. I could have given him a little for helping me and I'd have been done with it.*

He saw Stokes at the mine office several times a day and would ask about the mine progress, but Stokes was preoccupied with the start up and keeping investors' interest up. He barely spoke when Cat questioned him.

After several days, Cat's concerns and worries, heightened by boredom, became unbearable. Casting caution aside, he wandered down to the hotel. Ella looked surprised and a little concerned to see him at the hotel, but greeted him with her usual cheerfulness as he sat down at a table. He nodded to an equipment salesman who had just arrived and was sitting at the bar. "Ella, I need a drink. Pour me a shot of that Red Dog and set up one for our friend at the bar. I feel like splurging."

"Thanks, mister," the salesman turned around on his stool. "I guess drinking is about the only entertainment around here. This place ain't much of a match for Cripple Creek down in Colorado. If it weren't so far, I'd ride down to Shoshoni for a little poker." He looked around to see if Ella was out of earshot. "I might even stop by the Blue Goose. Have ya' seen the girls there?"

He looked at Cat intently and thrust his head forward, his brow knitted. "Say, I've seen you somewhere. Yeah!" he exclaimed with smug satisfaction, "I used to see you at the tables in places on Myers Avenue in Cripple Creek."

Cat was startled. He hadn't thought about being recognized here at DePass. Any sign of recognition meant possible trouble. Then he realized that the man didn't know his name. "Yeah, I reckon I played a few hands there from time to time."

"Well, hell, I bet you'd be up for a little poker if you're as bored as I am."

Cat, relieved, nodded his head in agreement. "Sounds good to me." He glanced at Ella, who had returned to the bar.

"I don't mind you playing a few friendly hands, just leave your guns at the door and no cheating." She looked meaningfully at Cat as she handed him a new deck of cards and chips from under the bar.

The salesman looked at Ella, then laughed, snorting coarsely as he drew his breath in through his nose. "Ma'am, I ain't no gunslinger." He sat down in a chair and pulled it up to the table with a scraping of wood on wood. "How about a little blackjack to start?"

Later, Cat walked back up to his room behind the mine office as darkness was falling. He felt a little drunk from more whiskey than he had been used to in the past several weeks. He smiled though; he had played without cheating and still won a little money. Not much, but it felt good to deal out the cards in a real game. He would have played longer but Ella had gently shut the game down as suppertime approached. In spite of Stokes' warning to lie low, he stayed for supper with the salesman.

The next morning Stokes sat down for breakfast with Ella. The sun streamed over the hill above the mine and a shaft of sunshine beamed onto their table. "Ella, it looks like we are headed into good ore. We're getting some good results in the lower drifts. There's a bonanza out there. I can feel it! The pumps are keeping ahead of the water, and we haven't had to timber in the drifts. Things are moving better than I expected. I'm going to take the train down to Denver and get some big investors fired up. I think you'd better hire a full time cook. This place is going to get busy."

"I'm glad it's going well JT, I'll make sure the hotel is ready for a crowd." Ella stirred sugar into her coffee and put down her spoon. "By the way, I wanted to talk to you about Cat. He came down to the hotel late yesterday. I could tell he's getting bored sitting around up there. He said he wants to get back on the road but his arm isn't up to it just yet. He asked me about setting up a table for poker in the bar. JT, I want to keep this place on the level and I'm not exactly anxious to have him gambling at my hotel. I know..." Ella caught herself, "I think that he fancies himself a smooth gambler, but..." She hesitated, biting her lip, and clearly showing her doubts. "I told him I would ask you about it."

Stokes removed his glasses and vigorously polished them with his handkerchief and put them back on. He smoothed his mustache carefully with his fingers, one side at a time, then twisted the waxed ends to a precise point. "I understand your concern, Ella. But to tell you the truth, he's been driving me to distraction at the mine office. Maybe it wouldn't be a bad idea for a while. He could entertain the guests a little."

THE TROUBLE WITH GOLD...

Ella nodded her head. A slight frown clouded her face. "I just hope he doesn't try to be too clever with some grifting. That could mean trouble."

Ella talked with Cat after her discussion with Stokes. "I don't want any cheating at cards in this hotel. If I see any of that, I'll shut your table down. And no all night or Sunday games either. I want you out of here at ten o'clock."

"Sure, Ella. It's your place. Heck, I ain't no idiot." Cat said defensively. "I can win without cheating anyway. Mainly it beats sitting around up at the mine office all day." *It's funny, Ella's a lot younger than me but she treats me like I'm a kid.*

* * *

Cat found a willing partner for poker almost every day. As the mine activities picked up, equipment salesmen and miners looking for work gathered every evening except Sunday for a table of stud poker. Cat, though rich with gold, was short of real money so he sold Stokes a few ounces of his remaining gold at a deep discount to get some cash.

When Stokes paid the cash for some of Cat's gold he cautioned Cat not use the gold for gambling. "It's too risky Cat, with these mining types around someone will recognize that Cripple Creek gold ore."

Cat knew poker. He'd memorized the odds of winning hands, and usually did well without cheating. One night though, after a run of bad luck at five-card stud, he lost not only his winnings of several nights but the cash Stokes had advanced him. His pile of remaining chips was pitifully low. Cat sensed that his luck was about to change. He had the chips for one more hand. *What the hell, it's piss in the ocean compared to my gold.* "Boys, I'm good for one more game then I'm done for the night."

The dealer dealt out the first round face down to the five men at the table. The next card was up. Cat's was a nine of hearts. His was the highest card showing. Slowly he lifted the corner of the buried card. *An ace of clubs.* He let it snap back to the table with an air of boldness. *I'll bluff on the nine.* "Twenty bucks on the nine!"

The dealer called out the possible hands as he dealt, first to Cat then on around the table. "A nine of spades to make a pair and possible three of a kind! A pair of eights for this gentleman and a possible straight flush here." The dealer finished dealing out the third round. Cat's pair of nines was high. "What do the nines say?"

"Fifty bucks."

"Too rich for my blood, I'm out." The pump salesman tossed in his cards.

"Me too." The rancher from Bridger Creek pushed back his chair and headed for the door.

The pair of eights stayed, along with the dealer's deuce and three of hearts.

"See it and weep," the dealer said and dealt out the fourth card, face up. "Hell's fire! An ace to go with them nines! Another eight, three of 'em. That's lookin' mighty good. And I get a dad-burned queen of spades. Whata' ya say, you with them three eights?"

"Three eights" looked at Cat's pair of nines and the ace, scratched his head. "I'll bid ten bucks." He said with a poorly concealed reluctance.

Cat spoke with a confident voice. "I'll see your ten and raise you fifty."

"Three eights" blanched and hesitated a split second, but put in the fifty.

The dealer tossed in his hand with an explosive snort. "Might as well be cow dung!"

"Down and dirty!" He dealt out the last cards face down to Cat and "Three Eights."

Cat wondered if there was an angel of poker. He inwardly prayed for the right card. Slowly, his face devoid of expression, he lifted the last card. *An ace of hearts!* He felt his heart rising up into his throat. *An ace and nine in the hole and two nines and an ace up. A full house!*

The tiniest hint of a smile played on his tight lips.

He watched his opponent's face intently as the salesman lifted his card. The man's jaw clenched slightly and a grim expression, like the passing shadow of a scudding cloud, passed over his face. Straightening up in his chair, he bid, his voice unnaturally loud. "Two hundred bucks."

Cat felt good. *The man's trying to buy the pot with a bluff! I can't stop now, I've got the greenhorn S. O. B.!* His opponent had only a hundred dollars worth of chips left. "I'm out of cash but I'll put up my horse if that's okay with you. He's worth more than five hundred."

The man nodded his head in agreement.

Cat quickly scribbled out a bill of sale and tossed it in the pot. "Okay then, I'll meet your two hundred and raise you two hundred." Tension hung like an invisible backdrop over the drama playing in the still room. The salesman cursed and pushed out his remaining chips. He dug into his pocket and brought out two fifties that he tossed into the pile of chips and the bill-of-sale. "Damn, I'm near to flat busted. I'm calling. I 'spect with them nines and what you got in the hole you can beat this." He turned over his hole cards.

Four eights!

The blood drained from Cat's face. The ticking of the Regulator clock on the wall measured out the seconds as the others waited for Cat. His mind swirled in frustration and anger. *The bastard bluffed me good. Fooled me into thinking he had a smaller full house than mine!* For a moment he wished he had his pistol. With a shrug he pushed his cards, down cards unseen, into the pile of cards on the table and rose from his chair. "Shi-oot, mister, you got me. Maybe tomorrow I'll be up on my luck. I'll see you then." He strode briskly into the night air and stumbled up the rocky road to his room next to the hoist house.

Chapter 17

All the Way to Hell

Stokes hired Alvin Bates, a young mining engineer, and put him and a crew of miners to work extending the fifth-level workings. Stokes was anxious to start work on the sixth level where he expected to find the bonanza ore, but the water level had barely dropped below the fifth level.

"Bates, we've got to get that water pumped down faster. I can't see much progress since yesterday."

"I'm sorry, Mr. Stokes. I think the water is coming in almost as fast as we pump it out."

"Then do something, Bates. Get a bigger pump if you have to. I'll expect you to be on that sixth level in a week." Stokes had heard of bonanza veins in famous districts and knew that often they had been discovered only as a result of persistence and guts. He could imagine the quartz glimmering with streaks and crystals of gold. Meanwhile he would have to use a little more of Cat's gold to build up excitement for what might lie below. *Not too much. Just enough to keep the money coming in until we can get to the real thing. Just enough to make it appear that the vein is improving as the mining progresses.*

On one of Stokes' trips underground, Bates took him to the end of the fifth level drift where he excitedly pointed out that the country rock next to the vein was shot through with smaller quartz veins that filled the cracks in the shattered rock.

"Mr. Stokes, the geology is getting more favorable for ore formation. I recommend we drive a cross cut out into the country rock. There could be more veins out there. I have something else to show you. Take a look at this." He handed a fist-sized piece of vein rock to Stokes, pointing to the freshly broken surface.

With his magnifying glass Stokes peered at the rock illuminated by the engineer's mine light. Imbedded in the smoky quartz a particle of free gold was clearly visible. "I'll be damned! From this muck pile?" Stokes queried.

"Yup." Bates was pleased with his boss's response. "After each round I look through the muck pile to see what's going on with the vein. I just a while ago whacked this rock with my pick."

Stokes was elated. He could hardly contain his glee. "Mark my word, Alvin, my boy. We're getting there. When we do, this ore will go all the way to Hell!" He slapped Bates on the back.

Bates beamed.

Later Stokes showed Ella the pinhead-sized piece of gold. She looked at the gold with the glass. "I don't understand, JT, I can't see as much gold as in the other samples you showed me."

Stokes was momentarily taken aback. "Those were samples from the old deep mining. We probably won't see that kind of rich ore until we get down on the sixth level. This is a good indication though, that the gold values are picking up as we drive out on the vein. In any case, I need to get a company incorporated and get some serious investors on board. I'm going to take the train to the

THE TROUBLE WITH GOLD... 167

mining exchange in Colorado Springs. It's time to launch my flagship, DePass Bonanza Mines, Incorporated. By the way, Ella, I want you to profit in this too. The hotel is an important part of the operation. I'll put some stock in your name."

"Thank you, JT, that's exciting. I'll do everything I can to make the hotel the best in these parts." Ella laughed, "Of course, it's the only hotel!"

Stokes barely smiled. "You've already been working hard, Ella. Why don't you come to Denver with me? We can catch a play and see the sights."

Ella put her hand over her mouth to hide a slight gasp. She quickly regained her composure. "That's nice of you to ask, JT, but I'd better keep things going with the hotel. There are a lot of things to look after. After all, I'll soon be part owner."

Stokes didn't persist and Ella was relieved when he went back up to the mine.

* * *

A few days later Stokes drove his buggy to Shoshoni and boarded the train. He carried several pieces of Cat's best gold and a DePass mine map showing the new assay results. Bates' map was a masterpiece of drafting. The veins, portrayed in red, contrasted strikingly against the light blue that represented the country rock. It was easy to see that the branching veins could add up to a substantial reserve. A vertical section showed the gold values increasing with depth. The map illustrated beautifully that this was a bonanza mine in the making.

Stokes stopped over in Cheyenne, where he could always find a few ranchers from the big spreads. He unrolled the assay maps for the men at the exclusive Cheyenne Club. "It's really too early to celebrate, but you can see why I'm enthused." Stokes traced the course of the new workings with his finger, pointing out the gold assays.

Tom Hysun, a rancher from the Sweetwater country looked at the maps with interest. "Maybe Wyoming will overtake Colorado? I hear that production at Cripple Creek is dropping off."

"Well, I wouldn't go so far as to claim that Tom, although if we can find a lot of this sort of stuff..." Stokes took out a piece of Cat's gold from his pocket, "then we just might."

"Holy Moses! This is from the DePass? Where can I buy your stock?"

"I'm on my way to get the company incorporated. The company, DePass Bonanza Mines, should be listed within a fortnight."

At the mining exchange in Colorado Springs, Stokes presented his story and showed the gold specimens to a small group of brokers. "We're not down to the main ore body yet, so we don't know just how much we might have."

The brokers nodded their heads knowingly. Stokes knew that every one of them was eager to hit the street with the story. One broker looked closely at one of the specimens. "Hell, I believe this might be calaverite, like the ore at Cripple Creek. You may have another gold rich volcano up there in Wyoming. If you do, then this stock will go crazy." This comment gained credence and the word spread.

On his return, Stokes stopped in Shoshoni where he ordered a Model T touring car. "I need some faster transportation." Stokes told the Ford dealer. As an afterthought he showed him a piece of the high-grade.

"Mr. Stokes, if I showed that piece around I could interest a lot of my customers in buying your stock."

"I tell you what, Jake, I'll just leave the sample with you for a week or two until I get back to pick up the automobile."

THE TROUBLE WITH GOLD... 169

Back at the mine, Stokes found engineer Bates anxious to show his progress.

"We got the water drained down to the sixth level and the mining crew has been working there for three days. The main vein is splitting into several smaller veins but the gold values are holding pretty good."

"That's fine, Bates, but how much visible gold is there?"

"Well, just an occasional speck here and there, and that's what puzzles me. I've seen nothing like those good samples you showed me earlier."

"I wouldn't worry about that, Alvin. Those rich samples probably came from rich pockets that got mined out. We'll just have to drift until we find where everything comes together. We'll get some assays on the ore you've been taking out. Remember, if you can see gold at all, it can still run a pretty good assay."

"I should have thought of that, Mr. Stokes. The way this vein is splitting might be a good sign. I'll take some samples and bring them up to you later today."

Stokes went back to the surface feeling good. He stopped by the office before he went down to the hotel for supper. Cat sauntered in as Stokes was preparing some fine gold to salt the samples with that Bates would drop off later.

"Glad you're here, Teason. I want to bring you up to date on the mine. Things are looking pretty good. As a matter of fact I have this for you." He handed Cat a stock certificate.

"DePass Bonanza Mines, Inc., 2000 shares, par value $1.00." Cat read aloud. "This is a pretty fancy lookin' piece of paper. Two thousand dollars worth? Shi-oot, that ain't nuthin' for what my gold's done to get you started!"

Stokes laughed "Ah, but that's the *par* value, Teason. It doesn't have anything to do with what the stock is selling for today or tomorrow."

"Two thousand or five thousand." Cat pulled at his ear. "Not a helluva lotta difference for all the gold you've used. Looks to me like I'm g'tting' hornswoggled."

Stokes' face reddened with impatience. "Before you get too worked up, listen to this. I checked the market price yesterday. That stock is worth twenty-one dollars per share and going up fast."

Cat's eyes opened wide in surprise. He tugged at his ear, his lips moving as he calculated. Then he tapped the certificate. "You mean this is worth more than forty thousand bucks?"

"That was yesterday. It will be higher today, and I expect it'll go a lot higher."

Cat sat down abruptly, staring at the stock certificate. "What about the gold? How much will I have left?"

"Things are going well down in the mine. We're starting to pick up some gold in the vein extension on Six. I'm just using a little of your gold for salting some of the samples and a few of the larger pieces for show. You'll leave here with half of your gold. Minus maybe a few hundred ounces."

Stokes pursed his lips and looked at the ceiling, his brow knitted. "Hell, you're making more than a hundred bucks an ounce! I'd say that's better than twenty." He laughed, "Or maybe only five for stolen gold!"

Cat rubbed the stubble on his chin and suddenly grinned. "Well, I 'spect maybe as how I can live with that!"

That week Stokes added another crew so that two headings could be worked at the same time. One drift would follow the original vein and the other would branch off to explore for additional veins. Within a week work on the "Old Vein," as Stokes called it, encountered good gold values across a vein width of five feet. At the same time the rock began to show signs of weakness. Several rock falls and minor cave-ins forced the crews to put in square sets–massive timber supports, to shore up the drift.

With the added task of timbering the drifts, progress along the veins slowed considerably. Stokes was in and out of the mine continually, berating the engineer and miners below and working above to keep brokers and investors happy. After a week the mining progress had improved and Stokes took time to pick up his new Ford touring car.

The dealer gave Stokes a brief driving lesson but was anxious to talk about the mine. "Mr. Stokes, I don't mind telling you that the piece of gold you left with me has sure stirred up interest. It's pretty good advertising for both of us." He went to his safe and handed the gold to Stokes.

Stokes laughed, "If it's working for us maybe you'd better hang on to it for a while." He handed the piece of ore back to the dealer. "I'll bring the car back for a check-up and get it then."

Ella heard the automobile approaching and stepped out on the veranda to see who might be coming in a motor car. Stokes drove up to the hotel and shut off the engine. Laughing, he jumped down, took off a pair of driving goggles and beat the dust from his clothes. "How do you like the newest piece of mine equipment?" he asked, grinning proudly at his new acquisition.

"This is yours?" She asked in amazement.

"I thought I'd surprise you with it. I'll show you how to drive it. The old horse and buggy just take too long to get to town. I..."

Stokes was cut short by a commotion up at the mine portal. Looking up he could see the dayshift hurrying out of the portal. He looked at his watch. "It's not time for shift change. What the devil is going on?" He hurried up the road to the mine. Ella could hear him yelling at the hapless engineer long before he got to the portal.

"Alvin, what the hell is going on? Get those men back in the mine!"

"It's water! Water's coming in bad down on Six, Mr. Stokes. The pumps won't keep up with it. We went through a big zone of fault clay. It was like we broke through a dam!"

"Then get the new pump going!"

"It's pumping and we're still losing ground. If we had another one like it we'd be okay."

"Then you'd better go to town and get one ordered. Better yet, I'll take you down in the car." Impatiently he added. "We've got to get more ore mined. I told some of the investors we'd have some gold poured by next week." Stokes started back to the hotel.

Alvin hurried to catch up with him. "Mr. Stokes, there's no vein on the other side of the fault! There's nothing but barren country rock."

Stokes stopped dead in his tracks. For a moment he stood still then slowly turned. "Did you say you've lost the vein?" Stokes's face turned red then ashen. "How in hell can a five foot wide vein just disappear?" He asked in disbelief.

"It's a fault. The veins were cut off and displaced when the mountain broke and slid on the fault. I'm guessing that the veins we have been mining were pushed up in a wedge of rocks."

Stokes broke in abruptly. "You guess? I'm not paying you to guess!"

The young engineer wiped beads of sweat from his forehead with his sleeve. "Mr. Stokes, it's sort of like this." Alvin held the palms of his hands together and tipped them up to the angle of the vein. Holding his thumbs together to represent the vein he slipped his hands. His thumbs showed the displacement of the vein.

"The vein continues all right, but the main part is deeper, beneath the mountain. It's hard to say how much movement there was along the fault. These fault movements can be several thousand feet, which would be the amount of offset we'd have from the root of the veins.

"I think we might back up and sink on the higher grade ore shoot we went through. If the fault is pretty

THE TROUBLE WITH GOLD...

steep we could go a long ways before we hit the fault again. I'm guessing we'd have ore along the way."

"You 'guess' this and we 'might' that! Good Lord, man, we've got to do better than that." Stokes blustered, then quickly recovered his composure as his mind raced, seeking a way out of this unexpected predicament. "We'd better get something going. Keep this quiet. Play it down if anybody finds out. Bad news would raise hell with the stock. Anyway I'm sure it's only a temporary problem. By the way Bates, I'm putting a hundred shares of DePass stock in your name. There will be more when you get these problems resolved."

Later the next day, after sending several telegrams to equipment companies, Bates reported more bad news. "I wired several places but another pump can't be delivered for a week."

Stokes' jaws clenched and his face turned red with frustration. He mopped his bald head with a handkerchief. "We'll just have to get by. See if you can put together something from the old equipment down by the mill." He managed a wan smile. "We'll think of something."

The engineer hurried off, relieved that he wasn't again the focus of Stokes' wrath. *I'll rig up something. It should be worth a few hundred shares.*

Stokes stomped into the hotel and sat down in one of the large leather chairs in the lobby. "Ella, bring me a glass of that Irish whiskey."

"JT, what is the matter?" Ella had never seen him drink before dinnertime.

"Everything is going wrong just when I'm planning to have some big investors in to look at the mine." Stokes fumed. "I'll have to do something to divert attention away from the mine problems for a while. I'll take my dinner early tonight. I need to get a good rest so I can resolve these problems with a fresh mind."

Later, sleepless in his bed, he systematically went through the possibilities. *At this point more salting won't work as long as the mining was shut down. It will take something dramatic. Something unique and positive, to bridge the time while the mine problems were being solved.*

Before first light the next morning, Stokes woke from a vivid dream. In the dream he was down in the new drift right after a round had been blasted. Smoke and dust swirled, making it difficult to see as the light from his lamp refracted in the dust. He turned off his light but something bright glowed in the mine ahead of him. Dropping to his hands and knees he crawled in the darkness until the bright object was directly in front of him. It seemed strangely out of place. When he reached out to feel the object, it faded and disappeared.

Downstairs there was a clanking as Ella started a fire in the cookstove. Stokes wakened from his dream with a start. He tried to hold on to what it was that he had seen in his dream. Whatever the bright object was, he was convinced it would be the answer to his dilemma.

Damn, damn, damn! What was it? He closed his eyes tightly and pressed his hands to his eyes until spots of light flashed. "What was it?" He muttered again. He cursed the sounds from the kitchen.

Frustrated, Stokes found a match and lit the gas lantern on the table beside his bed. He stared at the bright hissing flame, struggling to bring up the vision of his dream. More and more the dream faded and finally he turned off the light and lay back on his pillow. *Maybe if I can get back to sleep I can go back to the dream. Damn, I must remember!* He closed his eyes, but the bright mantel of the lantern had burned its image into his retina. At first it was a glowing yellow block surrounded by a bluish halo. Slowly the yellow faded to a red, as though cooling.

Suddenly Stokes sat upright, unaware that he was shouting. "That's it! That's the revelation in my dream."

A bar of gold, just poured, hot then cooling! That's what I'll do. Pour a bar of gold to show just how rich those few tons of ore from the new drifts really are. That will give me the time I need to get the mine back on track He swung his feet out of bed and hurriedly dressed. *The news will push DePass shares to a new level of interest in the mining houses from Denver to London.*

Ella looked surprised when Stokes entered the kitchen. "Good morning JT, you are up early. I'm sorry, there isn't any breakfast yet. The cook starts a little later on Sunday. I'll fix something for you."

"Just some coffee, Ella. I have a lot to do this morning." He poured a cup of coffee, but sipped only a little before he got up and headed up the hill to the mine.

Stokes knew it would be a risky venture. It would take most of Cat's remaining gold to produce the results. *I'll have to deal with Cat's tantrum when he finds out. I can imagine his reaction when he finds his gold gone. He'll want to shoot me. Of course most of the gold will be recovered. It will just be in a different form.*

By mid-morning Stokes had hauled Cat's gold from the fourth level powder magazine to the concentrating jig in the mill. The jig would concentrate the heavy fraction minerals, including any free gold, by gravity separation from the barren, lighter part of the ore. The problem was how to melt the gold down. He'd seen it done in the assay laboratory, but that small furnace produced only a button of gold at the best.

He explained his needs to Bates. "Alvin, I need you to do something to the assay furnace so I can smelt down enough gold to make an ingot. I need something a lot bigger than an assay button."

"You mean five or six ounces?"

"No, no, Alvin I mean big. Maybe fifty pounds or so."

Bates' eyes grew large. "The only way I know to get an ingot that large would be to send it to a custom smelter if we had enough concentrate with that much gold. Right now we don't have nearly enough."

"Don't worry about that, Alvin. I found some high-grade stuff stockpiled from earlier mining. I don't have time to send it out to a smelter. You figure out something." Stokes turned and left, leaving the young engineer to wonder just how he was going to do the impossible.

After a moment he hurried after Stokes. "Mr. Stokes, we'd need a much larger furnace and the smelting would be complicated. We'd have to scorify or maybe cupellation. We'd need more..."

"Alvin, just do it. I don't care about the details. Build a bigger furnace if you have to. I'm sure you can figure something out."

*   *   *

Cat's attention had turned back to gambling which kept him busy. He had sold more gold to Stokes for gambling money and was keeping ahead with his winnings. He was relieved that he didn't have to go down in the mine.

One evening at dinner, Ella mentioned that the preacher would conduct services at DePass on the following Sunday. "Cat, you might enjoy what he has to say. Why don't you come to the services?"

Cat shuddered at the thought and on Sunday he stayed in his room. As he fidgeted impatiently he realized that it had been some time since he had checked on his gold. As much as he hated to be underground, he decided he needed to see it. He picked up a miner's hat and a carbide lamp and headed into the mine. Back at the shaft, he found the hoist engineer making adjustments on the equipment. Cat knew that Stokes was busy at the mill and the miners were not working today. It would be a good time to check on his treasure. "I need to go down to level four," he told the hoistman. "Stokes wants me to sample something for him. I shouldn't be more than fifteen or twenty minutes."

THE TROUBLE WITH GOLD...

"Sure, just ring the bell when you're ready to come back up. Hope everything is alright, Mr. Stokes was down several times yesterday."

On the fourth level Cat forced himself to keep calm. He wanted to turn back with each step. To be down here with someone was bad enough, but to be alone with the darkness and the eerie echoes gave Cat a terrible sense of claustrophobia. Stooping low in the small drift he hurried back to the powder magazine. Within minutes he was prying open the door.

Inside the dank little chamber he unlocked the box and lifted up the lid. For a moment he stood, paralyzed by sight of the virtually empty box. As though not believing his eyes, he felt in the box for the gold that should have been there. He uttered an involuntary cry of dismay. Only a handful of the large rich pieces and none of the fines remained. "My God, where is my gold?"

His gold had seemingly evaporated, leaving little more than the dregs of its former abundance!

Cat's angry bellow echoed shrilly around the powder magazine and down the drift. Then he remembered the hoist operator saying that Stokes had been down several times. *Why was Stokes coming down when the miners weren't working?*

The obvious truth burned at Cat's brain. *Stokes has stolen my gold!*

Blind, hot anger replaced Cat's fear. He slammed the big door shut and ran back down the drift onto the cage and rang the signal to be hoisted to the main level. He hurried out of the mine and to his room where he strapped on his six-gun. After checking the office to make sure Stokes wasn't there, Cat ran down the hill. He could hear the jig vibrating in the mill building and a loud rumble in the assay lab. He burst into the mill building where Stokes was standing beside a shaker table watching finely ground ore as it neatly separated into tails of different densities as the vibrations carried it down the sloping table.

"My gold! What have you done with my gold?" Cat screamed. Savagely ripping his gun from its holster, he aimed it at Stokes.

Stokes looked at him calmly, ignoring the gun. He pointed to the pulverized material on the shaker table. "It's all there. When I'm done with it you won't recognize it." Stokes picked up a handful of material from the moving concentrates. "This will be worth more than when I started with it this morning and no one can trace it to the Cripple Creek gold."

"Dammit anyway, Stokes! Don't bamboozle me. You're stealing my gold. You told me it would only take three or four hundred ounces. Now almost all of it is gone. By God, you'd better make good on payin' me somethin'! I want it settled now! And not with some damn worthless paper stock either." Cat's eyes glared and his voice cracked with fury as he waved the gun at Stokes.

Calmly Stokes held a hand up. "Patience my friend. Put that gun away. Trust me, your gold isn't gone. Let me show you something." He reached in his pocket and pulled out a shiny gold button that he had smelted down in the assay lab. "Your gold will look like this, only a lot bigger. A hell of a lot more valuable than that telluride ore you've been packing around. Now give me a hand."

Cat, disarmed by Stokes' calm demeanor, holstered his gun. "This had better be good. I ain't in no mood for givin' up any more of my gold."

Stokes, ignoring Cat's warning, shut down the shaker table and picked up one of the buckets containing the heaviest fractions. "Here, take this."

Stokes led the way outside to the open yard next to the assay office. Cat, staggering with the weight of the heavy concentrates, followed Stokes outside. A pulsating roar unlike any noise Cat had ever heard came from an enclosure next to the assay building.

THE TROUBLE WITH GOLD...

"This is like an assay furnace only a lot bigger," Stokes explained. "I told Bates what I wanted and he put it together. From the noise, I'd say it's working." Stokes opened a door and they were hit by a blast of intense heat and light that forced them to hold their arms in front of their faces. Flames were shooting with a thundering intensity into a furnace built of stacks of firebricks. An opening in the furnace contained a heavy steel cauldron that glowed orange with the heat generated by a blast of compressed air and gasoline.

Stokes nodded to Bates, who shoveled the heavy sand-like concentrate into the glowing vessel. After he had put in the concentrates, he ladled in several shovels full of a white material from a large drum.

Acrid smoke poured up from the cauldron as Stokes shouted to make himself heard above the roar of the furnace. "The concentrates still contain a lot of impurities with the gold. Other metals like tellurium and iron. The white stuff is flux. It will combine with the impurities and make a glassy slag that will separate out on top of the melt. Now watch. In a few minutes Bates will pour the melt into the crucible."

The engineer, protected by heavy gloves and standing behind a metal shield, pushed up on a long handle connected to a pivoted vessel containing the molten concentrates. The glowing melt cascaded out of the caldron into a quart-sized, cone shaped crucible that Bates had fashioned from fire bricks and clay and bound with iron straps.

"When it cools, we'll knock off the slag and you'll have an ingot worth several thousand dollars! We'll make a couple of those," Stokes shouted above the roar of the furnace.

Cat had calmed somewhat but still looked dubious. "It ain't all that big. It looks to me like some of the gold disappeared somewheres between my stash and here."

Stokes laughed. "I'll bring you back here after it's cooled a few hours. You'll be surprised." He glanced at Cat's holstered gun and added. "And pleased."

They returned later and watched while Bates hit the cold ingot with a hammer. The basal portion of the cone-shaped ingot shattered into green glass leaving a nondescript cone-shaped ingot of metal.

"Where's the gold?" Cat's doubts were returning with the sight of the dirty looking metal.

"Here, put on these leather gloves and pick it up." Cat could not move the slug of metal with his one good arm. The ingot was much smaller than the crown of a hat, but he couldn't as much as slide the ingot across the top of the smooth table.

Stokes nodded to Bates, who levered under the ingot with a sharp chisel, lifting it on one side. Grasping it with both hands he pushed it over on its one side until it crashed over, shaking the table it was on. Cat tried again to lift it. By pulling with all his weight, he could barely slide the gold ingot on the table.

"Shi-oot! I thought for a minute it was bolted down. How much does it weigh?" Cat was sweating in the warm room where the furnace, now silent, was slowly cooling.

Stokes pulled a small notebook from his pocket and jotted some numbers. "I'd guess it's at least forty pounds. And it's yours, Cat! It's not pure gold, but pretty damn close!"

Cat pulled at his ear, then broke out in the best laugh he'd had in weeks. "By golly, that poor packhorse will be lopsided as hell when I ride out of here. We'd better melt down the rest to balance him out!" Later that day Bates poured a second ingot. Stokes and Cat hauled it into the mine and down to the fourth level where they stored it in the dynamite magazine.

Stokes had other plans for one of the gold ingots. For now it would be a distraction to keep attention off the mine problems that were going to take a little time to

THE TROUBLE WITH GOLD... 181

resolve. He put one ingot on display at the Shoshoni bank under a twenty-four hour guard. The Shoshoni paper heralded the good news.

DEPASS GOLD – The first pour from only a few hundred feet of exploration work on the sixth level of the DePass Mine yielded several hundred ounces in two gold ingots. The owner and General Superintendent of the mine, JT Stokes, stated "This will be another Cripple Creek."

Stokes was elated. "Ella, the stock is going crazy and we aren't even in the main ore yet. Everybody is talking about DePass. Everywhere from here to Denver, and on the New York and San Francisco exchanges. Within a week the stock will be a lively item in London as well. The mining exchanges were ready for some exciting news and this new mine is it."

Stokes wondered if he should tell Ella about the mine's troubles. He decided there was nothing to be gained by mentioning temporary problems to Ella. *Especially in light of what I am going to ask her.*

"That's wonderful JT. I'm grateful to be part of this venture. I'll do everything I can to help."

Stokes cleared his throat. "There is something else, Ella" he hesitated, then blurted out, "Ella, I want you to marry me. Right away. I'll get the license next time I'm in Shoshoni."

Ella was glad she was already sitting down. Her head was spinning at the sudden and unexpected proposal. It seemed more of a demand than a proposal. She swallowed hard as she tried to think of a way to answer without upsetting Stokes. "My goodness, JT. When you decide to move you don't waste time!" She laughed, "You'll have to give me a little time to think. I didn't know...You hadn't..."

"Ella, I'm not one to go through some make-believe courtship ritual. That's for young people. I need a good woman beside me. There will be lots of powerful people and you will be my hostess. I can find someone else to run the hotel and I'll put you in the mansion over at the ranch. You take your time in thinking about it. I won't be going into town for a couple of days anyway." Stokes walked out of the hotel and over to the mill building.

After Stokes left, Ella went into the kitchen, poured herself a cup of coffee and looked down the valley where the willows were turning red and yellow with a lingering touch of green. Further on, the cottonwood trees in the narrow canyon glowed like yellow flames against the gray walls of granite. Suddenly her mental confusion gave way to disbelief and then to anger. *Why, he proposed as though he was bidding on livestock! He didn't even try to kiss me!*

* * *

Stokes felt good that investor excitement about DePass stock was still on track. *My plan is invincible. I just need a little more time to get back on the vein.* He examined his face in the mirror of his office, twisting the ends of his waxed mustache. *Yes, it is the face of success. With a beautiful woman by my side, my world will have no limits.* He smiled at his image in the mirror and polished his bald pate with a snowy white handkerchief.

Chapter 18

Deep Enough

Engineer Bates was quite proud of the pump he had built and installed. He showed Stokes where the water had been before the pump was installed. "I cobbled this pump out of some old parts in the bone pile. I made a few improvements and it seems to be working quite well."

"That's good, Alvin. Now we need to get back to finding ore and we don't have a lot of time. How long will it take you to get the water pumped back below the sixth level and start drifting?"

"I've been thinking about that Mr. Stokes. If you want to get into ore quickly I think we should sink on that old winze on the fifth level. I sampled the vein down in the winze and the gold values seem to picking up toward the bottom. We would be in the vein all the way from level five to six. The second crew can extend the drift on five at the same time. We can keep both crews busy and we won't have to wait for the water to get pumped down in the main shaft."

"That's a fine idea Alvin. Let's get on with it. You keep thinking like that and we'll make a real mine out of this." The young engineer beamed.

* * *

Down at the hotel, Cat's poker luck was back on track, thanks to more cash from Stokes, who bought most of Cat's remaining raw gold ore at twenty-five cents on the dollar. "Shi-oot," Cat said jubilantly, "keep that stock price going up and I may sell you my gold ingot.

"By the way, Stokes, I need a horse for when I ride out of here, but I want to keep the rest of the gold I have. If you'd sell me that roan gelding I'll give you an IOU until I get some cash. But don't tell Ella," Cat pleaded. "I didn't tell her I lost my horse at poker. She doesn't like high stakes games."

"She's right. I don't want this place to get the reputation as a gambling hall. You had better limit the bets to a hundred dollars. If you do that I'll keep quiet. I'm on my way to town, I'll check on the stock price. It just keeps going up. That gold ingot has really worked wonders." He clapped Cat on the back.

Cat gritted his teeth as Stokes walked away. A hundred dollar limit? *Damn, everybody wants to run my life. It's time to put my line in another stream. My feet are getting itchy anyway.*

* * *

Stokes stopped by the hotel before he left. "Ella, I'm going to town. Is there anything you need?"

"JT, we need to talk. I..."

Stokes brusquely interrupted. "Can it wait, Ella? I've got to call my broker now. I'll be back later today. We can talk before I go back to town again in a couple of days."

Stokes had been gone less than a couple of hours when Ella saw his Model T returning in a cloud of dust. She knew he hadn't had time to drive to Shoshoni, conduct his business and drive back. *Something must be wrong.* She went to tell Cat, who was sitting at a poker table playing solitaire. They both hurried outside as the car clattered up and Stokes turned off the engine.

"Teason, Surcingle is headed up here with a posse. We don't have much time. I'll lower you down to level four. You can hide out there until it's safe. There are plenty of supplies and some blankets. It won't be the most comfortable place, but for only a couple of days it's better than prison."

As Cat and Stokes hurried up the hill to the mine, Cat asked. "I wonder what made him decide to come back?"

"When you lost your horse in that poker game, you made a mistake. Surcingle spotted your horse in town and questioned the new owner. Good Lord, you might as well have sent Surcingle a letter!"

"Shi-oot!" Cat punched a fist into his hand. "What'll you tell him, you and Ella?"

"Don't worry about that. We'll coordinate our stories before the posse gets here. I told the sheriff on the road that I'd better come back to show them around. All we know is that you rode out of here yesterday. I'll tell him I didn't know who you were and sold you another horse. By the way, Ella doesn't know about your gold or the mine salting."

They stopped in Cat's little room to make sure nothing remained that would show that he had been there. Cat loaded a few personal items and his DePass stock certificate into a saddlebag. Stokes glanced down the valley. He could see the posse as they appeared over a rise about a mile from the hotel. "Let's get going. The posse will be here soon."

Cat seemed resigned to the situation. "Hell, it won't hurt to have another day or two. This arm is still a little weak. I'll practice up on dealing. I'm telling you though, Stokes, this is it. You've had plenty of time to get the mine goin' and you shouldn't need me or my gold. As soon as it's safe I'm gittin' outta' here."

Stokes nodded, "Maybe. Lets see how it looks when things cool down. I would lay you odds that Surcingle will keep an eye on DePass for a while, since he knows you were here. You had better stay down there for a couple of days anyway.

"I'll lower you down. The hoistman is off. I've got the mine crew working in the mill today. It's probably just as well that no one besides Ella and me knows where you are anyway. By the way, I strung an air hose back to a hole in the powder magazine. I'll make sure you have some air coming in from time to time."

This time Cat felt more comfortable walking up the drift to the powder magazine on level four. He was glad to have the place to hole up with his gold. He would soon be on his own, anyway. Mostly he was angry with himself for making a stupid mistake that put Surcingle back on his trail.

After lowering Cat down into the mine, Stokes hurried back down to the hotel where he and Ella had a few minutes to agree on a story before the posse came up the road. The sheriff, an old acquaintance of Stokes, rode up first. "Howdy JT. Thanks for comin' back up to show us around. Didn't have time to introduce you to Charlie Surcingle. Guess you've heard of him?"

"Well, damned if I haven't! Everybody's heard of you Charlie, but the last time I saw you I thought you went by the name of Anderson." Stokes laughed, joined by Surcingle.

"Nice to see you again, Mr. Stokes. Sorry about the alias, but I had to keep my cover when I was here before. I thought I was g'tting' close to my man." Surcingle shook

Stokes' hand, his eyes boring into Stokes'. "I hear you had a gambler workin' here. What can you tell me about him?"

"He didn't work for me. He stayed here for a while. It was right after you left that he showed up, hoping for some work. He didn't have the experience I needed, so he left. He was quite a gambler all right. Kept some of the hotel guests entertained with blackjack and stud poker for a while. Guess he pushed his luck too far when he lost his horse. I sold him another horse on an IOU. If I hadn't of, he'd still be here. Said his name was Carl Tyson."

"That was Cat Teason, a longtime outlaw. I'm pretty damn sure I winged him a few weeks ago. He was tryin' to get away with some considerable amount of loot he'd stolen in a train robbery a year or so ago."

Stokes looked mystified, "Well, he sure didn't show any signs of having a lot of money when he was here, other than what he won at poker. Fact is, he still owes on his hotel bill. Hell, he only left early this morning!"

Ella walked out on the front step of the hotel to listen. Charlie gallantly doffed his hat, flushing slightly.

Ella smiled. "Hello Mr. Anderson. You are a day too late to help. I'd been trying to get that man out of here. He showed up here right after you left. His gambling was wearing thin with me. He did have a bad arm, but no wound that I could tell of." Ella wondered if she was talking too much and stopped to collect herself.

Stokes chimed in. "He came up to the mine a couple of times, but quit doing that when what little work I had didn't suit him."

The sheriff asked. "Would you mind if we looked around, JT?"

"Absolutely not. Feel free to look anyplace. I can get you lowered down in the mine if you want. Right now we're pumping on the sixth level, but the other levels are open. First, let's have some lunch. Ella, set up something for the sheriff and his men."

During lunch Charlie glanced at Ella as often as he could without being obvious. He couldn't get over her beauty and the haunting feeling that he knew her from somewhere. *I should return later and look for more clues.* He wasn't sure if that thought was a legitimate hunch or just wishful thinking that he might eventually have some success in wooing Ella. *Maybe, with a woman like her, I would be ready to settle down on the ranch for good.*

After lunch Charlie stopped by the kitchen to thank Ella. "You run a mighty nice place here Miss Price."

"Why, thank you, *Mr. Anderson!*" She emphasized the name he had used during his earlier stay.

Charlie looked momentarily flustered. "Miss Price, I fear I have gotten off on the wrong foot with you. With your permission I would like to return and make amends." At the door he turned and smiled as he touched the brim of his hat. Ella returned his smile with her eyes twinkling. Charlie wasn't sure what Ella's smile implied, but felt more encouraged than he had before.

The sheriff talked briefly to Surcingle, then turned to Stokes. "JT, Charlie wants to look around the mine buildings if you don't mind. I hate to be a bother, and we certainly don't mean to imply that you might have known anything about Cat Teason's past, but one never knows what clues a criminal might leave behind."

"Hell, I'm glad to help, although I don't know what he could have left behind. If you find him I'd like to get my horse back. And the money he owes me," he added. "Come on up and I'll show you around the mine area. If you want we can go below."

"Did Teason ever go down in the mine?" Surcingle asked.

"I took him down to help me sample, but he was nervous underground and wasn't much use. That's when I told him that I didn't see any work for him."

Surcingle swung down off his horse and looked for tracks on the trail above the hotel. "How long has he been

THE TROUBLE WITH GOLD...

gone? I can't figure out why he didn't want two horses. I'm sure he had some loot stashed. Maybe he had an accomplice. Did he mention bein' with anyone?"

"No, but he seemed to be anxious about something. Always looking up the trail that goes over the pass to Thermopolis."

Charlie Surcingle rubbed a hand down over his face and mustache as he thought. "Did he see anybody who seemed to know him?"

"To my knowledge he was alone. Of course he played poker with several men who came by the hotel but they were all here for mine business."

As they walked up the hill, Stokes pointed out the mine portal. "The main shaft is several hundred feet in on this adit. I can get you lowered down to the fifth level. You can signal when you want to come up to the next level. I can tell you though, that the only way that your man could have gone down without us knowing would be the ladder. Hell, he was scared to hell just walking up a drift. He wouldn't try the ladder." Stokes turned and entered the mine portal.

The sheriff hesitated. He pulled out a large pocket watch on a silver chain and looked toward the clouds forming over the distant Wind River Mountains. "I'm wonderin' about the weather for the rest of the day. What do you think Charlie? If we leave now we still have time to ride over to Thermopolis. If you want to search the mine we'd better stay here for the night."

Charlie Surcingle pushed his hat back on his head and stroked his mustache. *By God, it is tempting to stay here and get to know Ella Price a little better, but...*

"Sheriff, I've got a notion we ought to ride on. If Teason has an accomplice and is packing that gold, we could still catch up with him. Better to use the time doing that than looking for clues here. We already know he's been here."

* * *

Later, as the sheriff and Surcingle rode over the mountain towards Thermopolis, Surcingle asked about Stokes and Ella. "Sheriff, what's the story on those two? Are they...Well you know what I mean. Together?"

"Wal, there's lots a rumors. Personally, I doubt they have anything goin'. Stokes, he's too busy with himself to have much of a relationship with anyone, leastwise the kind that Ella would want." The sheriff thought for a moment and nodding his head with a slight smile, said, "Ella's one of a kind. About as straight a shooter as I've ever known. She's smart, knows what she's doin'. Everybody likes her. More'n I can say for Stokes, I reckon."

Surcingle pressed further. "Do you think Stokes is givin' us the straight story?"

"I can't think of a reason why he would protect an outlaw. He wouldn't do anything foolish to jeopardize his business reputation. Nope, I don't think he'd throw in with an outlaw."

"Even for fifty thousand dollars worth of gold?"

The sheriff abruptly reined in his horse. "How much did you say?"

"*Fif-tee* grand!" Surcingle proclaimed the amount distinctly. "Maybe more. I told you earlier that I'm sure Teason was in on that UP train robbery a year or so ago. What I didn't tell you was that there was a secret shipment on that train. It was a sizable lot of damn rich gold ore! It was the only thing taken."

"Holy damn," exclaimed the sheriff. "That's news to me. I thought it was cash."

"Oh, there was a little cash and some mail. Likely most of that blew away across the Red Desert. For reasons I can't tell you, the gold isn't even known to UP. Officially, Cat Teason and his associate, whoever he is, are wanted only for mail theft and blowin' up the express car. I have some private clients though, that would like to get their property–the gold–back. I'd appreciate it if you forgot that part."

"Wal sure, Charlie, but goin' back to yore question. I still don't think Stokes would be involved. He's a tough businessman but no outlaw. This here mine's got him goin' and I'd bet he'll make somethin' of it. Tell you what though. If you want, we'll stop by here on our way back in a couple a' days."

"Good idea, sheriff. I have a hunch that Teason is still somewhere in these parts, and I'd bet he's got somebody workin' with him. Just in case he might be lurking around here-a-bouts let's post a lookout up here on the pass for a day or so. Now tell me what else you know about Ella Price."

* * *

Stokes waited almost two days to make sure Surcingle wasn't watching the mine before he felt it safe to check on Cat. Stopping by the mine office Stokes picked up a bag with several smaller gold specimens and a bottle of good whiskey.

Signaling for the hoist he took the cage down to the fourth level and walked back to the powder magazine.

"Cat, open up."

Cat kicked at the door, which stuck for a moment and then swung open. "Dammit, Stokes, I'm glad to see you. It's too damn quiet down here, except for that air hose. When it comes on it sounds like a damn snake. Are they gone? I've had it with this hole."

"We'll have to play it safe for another day or so, Cat. One of my cowboys from the ranch said he saw someone lurking around the pass. I reckon Surcingle probably posted a lookout.

"Here, maybe this will help." Stokes handed Cat the bottle of whiskey.

"Won't hurt none, but I'm ready to take my chances with Surcingle. Hell, I can ride out at night and he'll never know. I'll sell you my DePass stock and take my gold."

"Cat, you don't want to do that. The stock price is still going up. Wait for Surcingle to clear out of the country. I've got to go down below now and spice up some of the last ore from the end of the fifth level drift. I'll stop on my way back up in a couple of hours. We can figure out something that makes sense and keeps you out of Surcingle's clutches." Without giving Cat a chance to argue Stokes walked out of the powder magazine and pushed the big door shut.

Cat sat down, the carbide lamp lighting the cards on the dynamite box he had set up for a table. He poured himself a glass of whiskey and resumed his game of solitaire. The whiskey warmed him and he felt a boozy sense of optimism. *Hell, I've hid out in a lot worse places and I didn't have any gold to look at either.* The cone-shaped gold ingot reflected the light of the lamp and the golden glow made the place almost cozy. Cat poured himself another glass of whisky and leaned back with his bedroll as a pillow. As the whisky took effect, he closed his eyes and listened to the incessant hiss from the air hose. He soon drifted off to sleep.

Charlie Surcingle crept along the drift as stealthily as a rat. In place of his rifle he carried a long shovel. Cat watched as the detective neared the powder magazine. His eyes glowed from the flaming torch he carried. A skull and crossbones was emblazoned on the crown of his white hat.

As Surcingle came within range, Cat prepared to shoot. He tried to raise his pistol, but the gun seemed to be glued to the floor. Using both hands, Cat struggled again, to no avail, then saw that the gun was solid gold, too heavy to lift. Even the bullets were made of gold. Cat grabbed a handful of the bullets and threw them at Surcingle.

Surcingle laughed and covered the air hole with shovelfulls of mud and rock. Then, his white mustache gleaming, Surcingle closed the door and wedged the shovel against it. Suddenly he was gone and in his place an ominous silence smelled of death.

Cat woke up gasping, the dream vivid in his mind. The carbide lamp had gone out and the total darkness frightened him even more. He leaned back against the bedding and breathed deeply to rid himself of a growing panic. The air seemed heavy and he couldn't breathe deep enough. His labored breathing was the only sound in the powder magazine. Cat realized then that there was no air coming from the air hose. Frantically, he crawled to the bulkhead and felt along the planks until he found the hose. It was still there. There was no mud and rocks in its place, but no air hissed from the hose. Then he remembered. Stokes had told him that the air would be on intermittently.

Feeling his way along the bulkhead, Cat found the door and pushed at it. It didn't budge. Something was holding it shut. Cat braced his feet and pushed harder, then stepped back and repeatedly drove his shoulder into it. The door was as immovable as the surrounding bulkhead. *Was Surcingle really here? Hell, maybe he's trapped me here. He'll shoot me like a coyote in a den, or worse leave me to die. I couldn't do anything about it.* He shook his head to rid himself of the dream. "Dammit to hell Cat, get ahold of yourself!"

Exhausted, he groped his way back to his bedroll where he sat down. He felt around and found the lamp and the can of carbide. Unscrewing the lamp, Cat poured some carbide pieces into the lower chamber and replaced it. He opened the valve and spun the flint wheel with his hand. The flame popped on with a welcome light that flooded the mine walls and glimmered off the gold ingot. Cat looked at his pocket watch. It was going on four hours since Stokes had left with a promise to return in two. "Damn his deceitful hide. He planned to leave me here!"

As he rested, Cat saw several planks that had been laid out as lagging on the cap timbers above. Stretching up, he found one that was loose and pulled it down. He skidded the heavy, sodden timber until one end of it was under the door. Grasping the other end he lifted up. Water oozed out of the wet plank as it squeezed against the door. For a moment nothing happened, then the door creaked slightly. Cat put his shoulder under the pry and heaved with all his strength. With a reluctant groan, the door moved slightly, then popped open.

Hurriedly, Cat put the few remaining pieces of Cripple Creek gold into one of the saddlebags. He rolled the gold ingot into the other saddlebag and pulled them out of the door. Slowly he dragged his treasure toward the shaft, his going made somewhat easier by the slimy floor of the drift.

* * *

After he left Cat on level four, Stokes rang to be lowered to the fifth level. He stepped out of the cage into a torrent. The water cascaded with a roar into the shaft below. The water level in the shaft was rising at a much faster rate than the pumps could handle. Alarmed, he walked rapidly back into the drift, his boots sloshing through the swiftly running water that spread from wall to wall.

"Damn, more water must be coming through the fault." Stokes muttered, thinking that he would have to hurry back to the surface and have Bates get another pump going. *First I'd better find the muck pile and salt it. I want this investor to see something spectacular. Better that than him focusing on a few temporary problems. We'll have to get some extra pumps to get this water under control before he gets here.* His mind raced as he stumbled along the drift through the water.

Shining the beam of his carbide light ahead Stokes could see nothing but the slightly rippled surface of the water as it flowed toward the main shaft. The water was silent but for an occasional swishing against the rock wall. Stokes shivered. The dark water seemed alive with a menace that chilled his bones. The current surged strongly against his rubber boots as though it was a demon gripping at his ankles. *Maybe it's the Pactolus.* Stokes thought of the legendary river that cleansed King Midas of his golden touch. He angrily kicked at the water. "By damn, no water is going to wash my gold mine away." He resolutely strode ahead, intent on accomplishing his mission.

Suddenly he was sinking. The floor of the mine dropped away beneath him. With a numbing wave of shock and fear he realized he had walked into the winze that was submerged and hidden by the rising water. Flailing his arms in an attempt to regain his balance, Stokes pitched forward into the cold water. He realized the weight of the gold would be like an anchor and flung one bag away. He saw it break against the mine wall, spreading its glittering contents into the flowing water. He thrashed his arms and legs wildly as he fought to keep his head above the surface. Desperately he gasped one last breath of air before he went under. As he sank he ripped at his coat, trying to shed it and its ballast of the remaining gold samples. He felt his boots against the slanting wall of the inclined shaft and frantically clawed for a handhold, finally finding the access ladder.

As he struggled to pull himself up, his foot slipped through the ladder and his leg wedged between the ladder and the rock next to it. He fought to free himself, but his air-starved lungs involuntarily breathed in deeply. He screamed but there was no sound. Stokes felt the agony of drowning for only a moment before blackness mercifully overtook him.

* * *

It took Cat a half-hour to reach the shaft. He grabbed the bell cord and signaled for the hoist, hoping that the hoistman would still be on duty.

He heard the hoist start up and could see the cable moving as it brought the cage from below. *That's strange. If Stokes had gone back up the cage would been left at the top. Either Stokes is still down there or someone is working there.* He could hear the cage rattling against the guides, becoming louder as it neared. When he saw the cage Cat signaled for a stop. He dragged the saddlebags onto the cage, then signaled to be hoisted. I'm damn glad I learned those bell signals.

Just a few minutes and I'll be out of this place. Cat heaved a deep sigh of relief as the cage stopped. *Thank God.* Cat opened the gate. Something was wrong. He was only at the first level, a hundred feet below the main adit. Cat listened, but there was no chugging of the hoist engine. The cage hung silently, swinging slightly from its sudden stop. The faint roar of falling water came from somewhere below. Frustrated and with a sense of foreboding, Cat rang the bell again.

In a few moments, the hoistman shouted down. "Sorry Mr. Stokes. We've got a problem with the hoist. It may take a while to fix. Are you okay?"

Hell, Stokes must still be down in the mine. It won't hurt if they think it's him signaling for the hoist. Cat trusted that the echo up the shaft would disguise his voice adequately so that the hoistman would assume it was Stokes who answered. "I'm okay. I'll just climb on out, you'd better get to work on the hoist."

Grasping the heavy saddlebags Cat began the slow climb up the ladders. He looked down fearfully. *Thank God there are landings every twenty feet.*

Starting up the first flight of ladders, he tried to hold the saddlebags, lopsided and heavy with the gold, with one hand as he steadied himself with the other. He soon found this too uncertain. When he reached up to grab the next

THE TROUBLE WITH GOLD...

rung with his free arm he teetered momentarily out of control. After two rungs his sore arm was loosing its strength and he dropped back to the landing.

"Damned arm!" He muttered. Finally he was able to sling the saddlebags over one shoulder and laboriously climb to the next landing. The twenty feet seemed like a hundred. When he looked back down he felt fear tingle in his fingertips, knowing that one side of the ladderway was open to the deep shaft. He pulled himself onto the landing and collapsed, his breath coming in gasps.

"One done and four more to go," he said to himself as he looked up to the next landing. After a ten-minute rest, Cat felt better. "Shi-oot, I can do it. One step at a time. Twenty steps to a landing. Then rest, and up to the next landing." Cat felt some comfort in talking his way up the ladder. "That damned horse had better be ready. We are headin' out of here fast." He pulled himself to his feet, stooped to get the saddlebags over his shoulder and started up the next course of ladders.

Whispering, he counted each rung as he climbed. "One, two," he stopped and rested, "three..." He had counted to fifteen when his load started to slip from his shoulder. He stepped back down to elevate the shoulder, but the bag was already too far out on the point of his shoulder. He felt it slipping even more. The weight overbalanced him but he dare not let go of the ladder with his other hand. Awkwardly he grabbed for the saddlebag as it slipped off his shoulder, catching the bottom of one side just in time to keep it from falling. The side of the saddlebag that contained the heavy gold ingot hung with its open top at an angle.

Cat watched helplessly as the gold slid from the overbalanced bag and plummetted to the landing below. Flashing in the beam of his carbide lamp the ingot crashed to the platform. Like a bullet, the pointed mass of metal penetrated the wooden floor of the landing. He heard it hit the next landing and for a second it rolled. Cat held his breath, hoping the gold had rolled to a stop on the landing. Instead, he heard it bounce off the walls of the shaft. Cat held his breath, as if willing the gold to stop. After what seemed like a long time there was a faint splash.

It was as though the ingot had never been. Cat stared in unbelieving horror at the splintered black hole–the only proof that the gold had been there a moment before.

Dazed, Cat pulled himself onto the next landing. His mind was a whirl of disbelief that bordered on shock. For a long time he lay motionless on the wet wood of the landing, not caring if he could get on to the surface or not. Finally he reached into the other saddlebag where he could feel the few remaining pieces of rich ore and the little bit of cash that Stokes had paid for the last gold Cat had sold him. At least he still had the Midas stock and that was worth more than the gold. He gasped an involuntary sob as he rose to his knees then grasped the first ladder rung and pulled himself up. One rung at a time he willed his dispirited body up the shaft.

Even without the heavy gold ingot, it took him a half hour to reach the main adit. He staggered towards the sunlit portal. The light was blinding, and he had to peer between his fingers to shield the glare. He cautiously walked out of the mine, staying low as he passed around the building.

Until now the shock of losing the gold had completely muddled his mind. Outside, the fresh air revived him. He remembered Stokes' warning about Surcingle having a lookout, and moved into the shadows of the mine office where he could survey the surrounding hills.

Nearby, Stokes' horse stood in the shade of a small shed. The horse was saddled. *Stokes must be plannin' on doing some ridin' when he gets out of the mine.* Cat scanned the pasture but could not see his own horse. He found his own saddle in the shed where he had stored it. He grabbed the saddle and his other gear and tied it on

THE TROUBLE WITH GOLD...

behind Stokes' saddle. *Sorry Stokes, you SOB, I'll just borrow your horse and saddle. Soon as I find my horse I'll turn yours loose.*

A mile out of DePass he found the horse Stokes had sold him. He saddled up the horse and securely lashed on his saddlebags. Then Cat tied the reins over the neck of Stokes' horse and, with a slap, sent him back in the direction of the mine.

Cat swung up into his saddle, but sat for a moment. *Damn, I wonder if I oughta' go back and see if I can find that ingot. Maybe the hoist is fixed by now and I could go all the way down. Shi-oot, I'd probably run into Stokes and he'd find a way to make me stay. I'd better not take the chance.* "Well, what the hell," he muttered, "at least I've still got my shares in the mine. Cat spun the cylinder of his revolver to check its load, then rode up a narrow side draw and across the mountain without looking back.

Chapter 19

The Other Half

On wind-swept Beaver Rim, Dutch Wyatt looked fifty miles across the high desert basin to Copper Mountain. The shadows of autumn's low sun portrayed the canyons of the rugged mountain in stark relief. *Like wrinkles in an old cowboy's face. Hell, I reckon that mountain is lots older than any cowboy!*

A shadowed cleft cut the flank of the distant mountain, then the narrow canyon turned abruptly near the bottom, as if reluctant to drain its cool mountain waters into the parched badlands. "Tough Creek." Dutch said out loud. "It's been more than two years since Cat and I buried the gold there, Rosy." There was no one but his horse to hear him. After his brush with death at the hands of Panco Villa, Dutch had found work in a Mexican mine where no-one understood English. At least his horse, Rosinante, didn't look puzzled when Dutch spoke English to him. "That's our stake for the future, *mi viejo caballo*. Unless ol' Cat got away with all of it. Guess I wouldn't be surprised if he had figured me for dead. After all I'm on the wrong side of 40, a ripe old age for an outlaw." Dutch urged his horse down the steep, dusty trail.

"Ah, my faithful cayuse, we'll find that ranch where the pastures are green. When winter comes there'll be a barn, smelling of fresh hay and a full bin of grain. No more of these long rides. Just a frisky trot every morning then back to the barn for oats."

Dutch remembered when he and Cat had ridden down this same trail, arguing about how much gold they had taken from the train. "Troy ounces or them kind you weigh butter in?" Cat had wondered. Dutch chuckled at the memory. *I kind of miss the rascal.* Dutch had heard about the jailbreak and Cat's escape a year ago. *Cat may be the one that's gone. Sometimes he didn't play life too smart. He's always lucky though, or maybe it's because of his nine lives.*

Dutch shook his head to clear away thoughts of Cat and the gold. He felt ill at ease when he thought about the gold, even though it could make a lifetime dream come true. *The trouble is, just thinking about the booty lying buried in that crevice back in the mountain makes me feel like a felonious bandit again.* "Damned mettlesome conscience!"

Why feel that way? Temptation whispered. *The stealing was something in your past. Think about the future. You're no kid. The gold is the only way to go straight now.* It was as though the gold empowered that old voice that he worked so hard to put down.

"Hell!" He spat out, moving his thoughts to something different. *Right now the only gold I want to think about is the gold in those autumn leaves.* Off to the west, a patch of yellow under Beaver Rim showed the presence of aspen trees below the cliff of gray rock.

Probably a spring and the site of an old Indian campground where I could pick up arrowheads, Dutch mused. *I bet there's teepee rings on the rim. Below the cliff, in that aspen grove, there'll be a spring flowing sweet water.* Think we would have liked to chase buffalo with the Indians, Rosinante?"

Rosinante turned an ear in equine acknowledgment. Dutch knew his horse liked being talked to. Dutch sometimes quoted Cervantes from Don Quixote for their entertainment on a long ride.

The afternoon sun of Indian summer was low in the deep blue sky. The September warmth soaked into Dutch better than other times of the year. It was like he needed to store it up for the winter. In many ways he could feel the friendliness of this place. It was not at all like the oppressive aura of the Mexican desert.

The steady plop of the horse's hooves in the soft dust and the creaking of the saddle leather were comforting. *I'm finally in the country where I belong. It has been a long time coming.* Were it not for his habit of constant alertness it would have been easy to doze off in the saddle. An occasional cooling breeze helped to keep him vigilant, even though his body was tired from the long ride up from Rawlins.

He'd ridden the train from Denver to Rawlins, shipping his horse along in a cattle car. It was a Union Pacific train. The same U.P. Railroad Company that he and Cat had held up two years before. The conductor punched his ticket just the same as the other passengers. Dutch laughed at the irony of it. *There was a time when the UP dicks would have liked to punch Butch Cassidy and me full of lead. That was a long time ago and there's probably no one left who would care.*

There's Charlie Surcingle, though. He would remember. It's been more than two years since our great gold robbery. If anyone could figure out a connection between me and the gold it will be Charlie Surcingle. Dutch remembered the Buffalo Bulletin quoting Surcingle saying that the job had the earmarks of Butch Cassidy, Dutch's onetime mentor. Surcingle said it couldn't have been Butch Cassidy, claiming to have it on good authority that Cassidy had been killed in South America.

Of course there was also a rumor from a reliable source that he, Dutch Wyatt, had been killed down in Mexico. Ambushed and murdered by Pancho Villa. He laughed to himself, "Hell, I feel pretty good for being dead. From now on I'll be Henry Longfellow, or some other suitable moniker." Rosinante nickered.

Earlier in the day Dutch had detoured off the main road to stop by Johnny Nogan's cabin, hoping to spend the night and be regaled by Johnny's stories. There was no sign of Johnny. He was sorry Johnny wasn't home, feeling a loneliness that needed the companionship of old friends. He headed for Angus Lowe's ranch.

As he rode down Muskrat Creek below Beaver Rim a ferocious, gusty wind brought an abrupt change from summer to fall. In a matter of minutes it changed from a pleasant day to a disagreeable one as the wind increased. *Typical Wyoming. This country can have about three seasons in the same day!* He liked it, though. The weather was an element that added variety to the day to day tasks.

Before he left Mexico, Dutch had shaved off his handsome handlebar mustache, thinking he might not be recognized. The mustache had been a part of him for twenty years and he didn't like losing it, especially after he had heard that Pancho Villa had killed him. Without his mustache he felt like a different person. *Hell*, he'd thought to himself, *if I'm going to be someone new then I should feel and look different. Maybe I shaved off some bad habits along with the mustache.* He rubbed his smooth upper lip, missing the mustache and thinking he might grow it back. *Unless Charlie Surcingle gets wise, I'm not a hunted man any more. Maybe this time I can retire from the robbing business.* "No, by God, no maybes! I *am* retired. As of now." He leaned forward in the saddle. "Did you hear that you frayed old cayuse? I'm done being an outlaw. Period! I'll just pick up my gold and mind my own business."

The horse plodded on without any reaction to Dutch's declaration. Not bothered by Rosinante's lack of interest, he continued. "Hell, I'm tired of hiding and not having a place to call home or a wife to be with. I'm going to buy that little ranch to call home. I don't reckon I can even find some old widow to marry. Guess I'm just a broken down old bandit turned cowboy with nobody but a gol-durned broken down old horse!" Rosinante tossed his head, yanking at the reins and snorting.

From the crest of a hill east of Muskrat Creek, Dutch could see the buildings of the Lowe Ranch. Further down the creek was a massive reservoir used to collect the meager rainfall. Out on the flats various shades of green and gold marked the fields where Lowe grew barley, alfalfa and a large garden.

My God, what a feat! To build an oasis in the middle of this desert. Dutch felt a surge of envy, followed by anger at himself for wasting so many years. He knew the time was long passed to start a ranch from scratch. He'd have to buy one. *That's okay, the gold will be enough to buy a nice spread and the cattle to run on it.*

The gusting wind picked up velocity, threatening to take Dutch's hat and forcing a chill through the weave of his shirt. He pulled the bandanna from his neck and tied it over his hat, then reached back, untied his great coat, and slipped it on. He spurred his horse up the road towards Angus Lowe's ranch house.

Angus Lowe greeted Dutch. "Howdy, stranger. Stop and stay a spell, supper is just about ready."

Dutch smiled at the Scotsman. "Hello, Angus. It's Dutch. Dutch Wyatt." Lowe looked at Dutch closely. "Dutch? By the great horn spoon! I sure didn't recognize you without that dandy mustache. Get off your horse and tell me what you been up to." He smiled, "At least what you can. If I remember right, it's been about two years since you and that Cat fellow came through. You were sort of in a hurry as I recall." He chuckled as though he knew the secret of that furtive trip. Dutch dismounted and grasped Lowe's outstretched hand. Dutch felt totally as ease with Angus, a true friend. He'd first stopped by Lowe's ranch in the company of Butch Cassidy more than fifteen years ago. He knew that Lowe was aware that he and Cassidy were in the robbing business but never mentioned it, nor did Lowe judge his friends with that in mind.

"Angus I've been looking forward to talking to you ever since I left Mexico. Actually that was the second thing I thought of. The first was sitting down at your fine table with you and your family. I wish I was younger and knew a good woman. I envy you Angus."

"Laddy, you're no older than I was when I got married. You just need to be discovered by some filly who knows a good catch when she sees one!"

After supper that evening Lowe toured Dutch around the ranch buildings and up to the long dam of the large reservoir, now, in the early fall, retaining only a small amount of water. "Dutch, I'd hoped this dam would be the difference between making a success of this place or going broke. There's good soil here, but darn little water. I figured if I could string out the snowmelt and spring rains, I might have a chance in irrigating some good crops. The dam worked for a while, but a big storm washed it out. Of course I had to depend on the patience of the banker on top of everything else. Sometimes a whole lot of one's life turns on one decision that doesn't work out because of events you can't control."

Dutch furrowed his brow. "I've always prided myself in planning my jobs and not taking risks that didn't have a potential payoff, but I'd never really thought about one deed or action having the force to change my whole life." He looked out across the immense land, silent with his thoughts.

Then Dutch continued. "I've always wanted a ranch like this. Now I have the where-with-all to buy one and I'm not sure if it's the right thing to do."

"Well, Dutch not everybody is cut out to beat their heads against a wall on a ranch. I'm Scotch so it comes naturally." They both laughed.

"No, Angus, I want to have a ranch. And I can afford to buy one. It's just...Well, I'd feel beholden. Not to bankers, but to my conscience." Dutch groped for a way to speak his mind without mentioning the gold.

"I think I understand, Dutch. Maybe what you're talking about comes back to the importance of one decision. If it's a decision that affects everything after it...well, I'm reminded of a friend over in the Crooks Gap country. He worked hard on a little place and had done pretty well. He had a wife, a pretty little gal, but she couldn't get used to that barren country and the lonely life that goes with it. It pretty near drove her crazy. I guess it did sort of. Well, anyways a stranger came by, and after a little sweet talk and a shoulder to cry on, my friend's wife ran off with this fellow.

"My friend took that to be unforgivable. He could not understand her lack of appreciation for all the hard work he had done to make a better place for her.

"Well, my friend came through here, hot on their trail, his rifle loose in the scabbard and bent on revenge. He was primed to kill them both and devils take the hindmost.

"He wanted to change horses, borrow a fresh one of mine so he could run them down. 'Sure,' I told him, 'but before you leave, tell me what you want done with your ranch after your hanging. You and your wife will both be dead, so you ought to have some plans.' For a minute he stared at me like I was daft. I could see some of the craziness begin to go out of his eyes. He swung down off his horse and I suggested he stay for a bite to eat.

"After supper I walked out with him. He turned to me and shook my hand. 'Angus, I won't be needin' that horse. I've got to get back to the ranch and move some cattle to another pasture where they can get to water.'

"I reckon his decision was a whale of a lot bigger than my reservoir. I guess a person has got to look down the road and figure out where each fork is going to take him. And which one can he live with."

Dutch stayed the night at Lowe's bunkhouse and was up at dawn as Angus started his chores. Dutch saddled up his horse and fondly shook his old friend's hand, promising to return soon.

"Dutch, when ya' get tired of batching, stop by the old DePass Hotel sometime, I hear they serve a pretty good steak." His teeth showed in a broad smile behind his bushy mustache.

It was late afternoon as Dutch rode up the broad valley where Hoodoo creek sliced out of the rugged mountains. The large cottonwoods that shaded the buildings at Quien Sabe shimmered with the vibrant gold of fall. Along the creek the willows were still green but showing spatters of red and yellow. The stream was so clear he could see the trout scurry for deep holes beneath the banks.

Dutch breathed deeply of autumn. He loved the pungent fragrance of the fallen leaves and the ripe grasses. Even the lichen on the sun-soaked rocks had its own redolence. Occasionally a breeze brought in the smell of sagebrush from the parched hills and rattled the yucca pods. The low sun gave up only a grudging warmth. A noisy flock of blackbirds swept over, preparing for southern travel. Dried leaves rustled as brief cat's-paws swept out of the hills and whispered through the grass. Dutch's mood too, changed. He felt more relaxed, welcoming the semi-hibernation of winter.

Dutch approached the ranch buildings through the broad meadow, wondering if a cowboy might be there for the fall roundup. It didn't matter. Dutch figured he'd be welcome to spend the night. Then he would ride on back into the rugged breaks where he and Cat had hidden the gold.

Cat, old friend, if my share of the gold isn't there, you'll have some serious explaining to do when I catch up with you. Cat tended to be impulsive, but would probably think twice before he tried to get away with all of the gold.

Dutch was relieved to find the ranch deserted. It would be good to be alone with the mountain. Mountains spoke his language. He understood what it and its children said. The soft gurgling from the little stream and the rattling of the leaves in the big cottonwood. The willows along the creek sighed with the sound of autumn. Chickadees chirped as they flitted around in the willows.

Often, in the past, a subtle change in nature's voices had warned him of dangers, but now, for once in his life, he could relax. This time the sounds were reassuring. There was no bulletin out for his arrest and Charlie Surcingle, his most persistent nemesis, had likely returned to his ranch in New Mexico. Besides, he reminded himself again, he had never been tied for certain to the heist of the Cripple Creek gold from the train. His better known aliases were presumed dead. If he were careful, the gold, if it were still here, would be his nest egg. *Conscience be damned.*

Thinking of the gold he once more had some pause about taking it from its hiding place. He wasn't particularly superstitious but he couldn't help thinking of bad omens that followed gold. Shakespeare had said something about saint-seducing gold. *But then I'm certainly no saint, so maybe I'm safe. Besides I'm in no hurry to liberate the loot from its vault in the rocks. I'll feel better about it when the need comes to dig it up.*

He thought about the importance of a singular decision that Angus Lowe had talked about and wondered

THE TROUBLE WITH GOLD...

about the man whose wife had run away. *I can't compare the gold with a woman.*

As the long shadows of evening encroached into the valley, Dutch sorted through his saddlebags for some fishing line and a hook. *A few fish will be a nice change.* He was tired of tortillas, beans and hot peppers.

Dutch tied his line to a willow and crawled on his belly through the tall grass to the edge of the little stream. Almost immediately there was a sharp tug at his line and Dutch pulled out a dinner size trout. In twenty minutes he had caught three more, enough for dinner and breakfast in the morning. Back at the cabin he soon had a crackling fire and cooked two of the fish. The cabin's cupboards were well stocked with the basics such as flour and he baked a two-day supply of biscuits.

Later, after he washed the dishes, he took his cup of *lapsang souchong* tea and stepped out of the cabin into the pitch-black night. The stars pierced the cold with a shimmering brilliance. Above the rugged heights of Copper Mountain the Big Dipper pointed its bowl to the North Star. It had been his beacon on many a night ride.

His eyes followed the Milky Way. *I'd still rather call it the 'Milkmaid's Path' and remember my lost love.* Dutch's eyes misted with a pang of lonesomeness and the stars of the nebula coalesced into a blur.

As he gazed at the galaxy, the image appeared. Etta! The sensuous lips with a promise of soft kisses. Her eyes twinkling with good humor. He remembered the reddish tinge of her hair when the sun shown on it. The way it framed her face in an innocently seductive way.

Dutch closed his eyes with a powerful longing. He recalled Etta's joyous, musical laugh. He dared not look again, for he felt terribly lonesome.

In the morning Dutch rose at first light and walked through the frosty grass to wash in the ice-rimmed creek. He felt a thrill as of the bugle of a bull elk echoed down from Hoodoo Canyon. After breakfast, Dutch saddled his horse and rode through the rugged breaks behind the Quien Sabe and into the hidden canyon where he and Cat had buried the gold. He found the marked crevice and slithered into it. The rocks and sand looked undisturbed.

He and Cat had divided the gold and buried each half separately in the bottom of the crevice. He scraped around several places with a shovel until he felt the softness of a canvas bag. Quickly he moved a few rocks and scraped the sand away. He pulled out a canvas sack and then a leather pannier. They were both heavy with a weight that could only be gold.

Dutch opened the leather flap on the pannier. *Thank God, look at that!* Pieces of yellow gold mixed with the shimmering crystals of calaverite. The glittering cargo was intoxicating. Just as before, the gold was bright and clean and glowed warmly, even in the darkness of the granite abyss. He pulled more bags out until there were no more in the hole. Dutch dug around until he was convinced that Cat had retrieved his share.

Dutch closed his eyes and smiled in relief. Then Temptation laughed from the recesses of his mind and quoted Plutarch. *"Gold is the kindest of hosts when shining in the sky."* He laughed at the beckoning promise of the gold, then remembered the next part of the phrase. *"It becomes an evil guest unto those that receive it in their hand."*

"Dammit!" Dutch exclaimed, his voice echoing hollowly. "Why do things like that come wandering into my mind?"

Suddenly feeling uneasy, he covered up the bags, deeper this time, and rearranged the cover of sand and rocks. Crawling back out to the mouth of the crevice, he crouched in the shadows for a long time, his eyes examining every cranny in the surrounding rocky hills, his ears listening for danger. The blue jays and squirrels were quiet, and Rosinante grazed contentedly in the meadow.

THE TROUBLE WITH GOLD... 211

High above, a hawk silently rode the currents of warm air rising from the sun-warmed rocks.

Dutch's sharply honed senses told him that he was alone. There was no one else around. Yet he felt a sudden urge to hurry away from the gold. *Maybe I'd best wait until I figure out a plan trade the gold for cash. I could buy any ranch I want but maybe I just need a little cabin like Quien Sabe where I can sit back in the sun and contemplate nature.*

Of course the gold could help me find a wife. But would she be marrying me or the gold? "Damn, I guess I don't know what I want to do." He muttered the last under his breath.

"At least there's one thing for certain. I'm through with the outlaw business." He repeated his vow, as though he needed to reinforce his resolve. Times were changing. There was no romance pulling off a train or bank heist. Except for lucky ones with a reputation like Butch Cassidy the title of outlaw had become sullied. And Butch was gone. The Pinkerton agency said so.

Dutch rode back to the cabin where he built a fire in the stove. He brewed a pot of coffee and he spent the rest of the day reading old books and magazines he found stashed in a wooden dynamite box. He was tired after the adrenaline rush from seeing the gold again. As the sun dipped low, Dutch walked down to the creek and dropped a line into the water again. After cleaning the two trout he'd caught, he stripped down and jumped into a deeper part of the creek. The water was frigid and Dutch hurried out of the creek and ran to the cabin to dry off. Soon after the sun set below the western hills a wind came up. A line of clouds raced overhead and it turned cold. Dutch knew the signs were signaling an early autumn storm.

He rode his horse up into the patch of juniper scrub and with his lariat dragged in several dead branches. The juniper would burn hot. After supper, he banked up a fire in the stove and shut the damper to keep a bed of embers alive through most of the night. Gusts of wind buffeted the cabin and smoke puffed from around the stove lids but the cabin was well chinked to keep out the cold. The warmth inside and whistling of the wind outside made Dutch drowsy and he finally turned in for the night.

Before he dropped off, Dutch heard the sharp clicks of sleet against the windows. In the morning he was surprised that there was only an inch or two of snow on the ground. He fixed breakfast and read a National Geographic. The exotic places in the magazine made him restless. He felt an urgency to go somewhere. He didn't want to see or think about the gold today. Quickly he packed up his few belongings and saddled his horse. Without an immediate destination in mind he headed down to the main wagon road and turned east, away from the gold.

Instead of enjoying his retirement he was feeling aimless. "Rosy," he addressed his horse, "this life of leisure will take some time to get used to. Maybe we'll just visit around for a few days and then hole up for the winter at Thermopolis. Those hot springs will be good for us."

He knew he would have to do something with the gold but he realized that was going to be difficult without attracting unwanted attention. "Not today, nor tomorrow, maybe come spring I'll worry about it." Rosinante had no comment.

The snow was melting on the main road down from the ranch. The clayey surface of the road was slippery and the riding was miserable until the road skirted along a series of rusty-yellow sandstone cliffs. There, the sandy soil made for easy going and Dutch urged his horse into a gallop, trying to outrun an inexplicable sadness. *Maybe I'm not ready to retire from the excitement of train and bank robberies.*

"Damn!" he exclaimed, feeling anger for being so ambivalent about his destiny. The echoes that came back from the hills accentuated his frustration. He slowed his horse to a walk and let his mind wander back in time. In Mexico he'd almost married a lovely young senorita, but her intellect was wanting. She did her best though, to make up for it in other ways. She was a good woman, but married they wouldn't have been happy for long.

Dutch felt a deep sense of lonliness, an overwhelming desire to mix with people, to see someone he knew.

The road crossed a draw and climbed up a dug-way onto a sandy ridge where the main road turned. At the bend in the road a dim road turned off to the left–towards the mountain. A weathered sign stood at the junction. He reined in his horse.

DePass Hotel
E. Price, prop.
Lodging and Fine Food
3 miles

"E. Price? Mr. Price, what in the world are you doing with a hotel way back off the beaten path?" Then he remembered Angus Lowe's comment. "Stop by the DePass Hotel if you're in that part of the country. I hear tell they've got good steaks."

Dutch bent over and looked at the sign more closely. He could see that the words *DePass Mine, DePass Bonanza Mines, Inc.* had been painted over.

"The mine must be closed, but if Angus thought to mention the hotel, it must be worth a detour." *I remember he was grinning at the time. I wonder if he was pulling my leg?* "Rosie, let's go find out!"

Dutch turned his horse onto the hotel road, doubting that the place would be open for business. The road showed little sign of travel.

Twenty minutes later, from a low ridge that split the valley, he could see several mine buildings and a two story, white building at the upper end of a green, meadow. Dutch assumed the white building to be the hotel. A mine and hoisthouse perched high on the bare, rocky hillside above the valley. Rust-colored rocks of the mine dump contrasted with jagged outcrops of gray granite that jutted from the sage hills surrounding the valley.

As he rode up a grassy meadow below the hotel, Dutch saw a buggy parked by the hotel. Smoke drifted lazily from a chimney at the hotel. There was no sign of activity at the mine or mill. He doubted the hotel would be open for travelers and was surprised to see a sign hanging from the gingerbread scrolls above the main entrance: *OPEN*.

Dutch dismounted and tied his horse to a hitching rail just out from a flowerbed still colorful with sunflowers. He wondered how such a remote lodging could stay in business. *Probably, E. Price just didn't get around to taking down the sign.*

In spite of his doubts, the place had a homey feel to it. It beckoned Dutch with an allure to all his senses. The site was beautifully rugged with the large green meadow framed by granite pinnacles. The autumn touched willows gave off a sweet aroma and as he approached the hotel there was a fragrance of fresh bread. A small stream tinkled pleasantly as it flowed out of a springhouse under the hotel. An inexplicable sense of relief washed over Dutch as he entered the hotel.

Chapter 20

Down from the Milkmaid's Path

The hotel kitchen was pleasantly warm from the big iron cookstove as Ella loaded the oven with several pans of bread dough. Ella baked much more than the hotel business would justify. She would trade some of it for a few token vegetables to help a widow at her hardscrabble homestead on Bridger Creek. Ella stood at the window waiting for the loaves to brown and looked down the valley at the yellowing leaves. It was fall and she hated the thought of spending another winter at DePass. *But what else can I do?* There seemed to be no neat answers. *Good Lord, twenty years from now they'll call me that crazy old woman who lives at DePass.* She laughed at the specter. *Somehow I will come out of this better than when I started.* "I will, dear Lord, *I will!*"

A year had passed since the mine had closed when Stokes disappeared. The promises and hopes of DePass Bonanza Mines vanished into a morass of legal problems and ownership questions. Gone were the steady stream of salesmen, brokers, miners and job seekers. *Did Stokes leave because of me? Because I couldn't give him the answer he wanted. That's silly. JT Stokes wasn't that enamored with anyone but himself.*

The hotel was still open a year after the mine's closure because of Ella's enthusiasm and popularity. She could see, though, that the end was in sight. Aside from an occasional community dance, only a rare prospector or hunter stopped for a night or two. The hotel was just too far off the main roads. She had thought about selling, but who would want to buy a hotel without a town or a mine? Often, from the kitchen windows, she watched the road down the valley, hoping to see a savior arrive who might revive the mine. *Maybe, with the country at war, it could be started up again for the copper. That's wishful thinking. No one is going to come up that road and make this place well again*

A wave of loneliness swept over her. "Charlie Surcingle, you old rake, I'd even welcome you today. Maybe you could tell me something about Cat at least."

As if on cue, a rider rode out of the canyon far down the valley. Ella felt her heart quicken, then chided herself. *Whoever he is, he won't solve my problem. I've got to do it myself.*

Oh, my God! Maybe it is Surcingle. I should be careful what I wish for. Turning away from the window she opened the heavy oven door a crack to check the bread. A blast of hot air and baking aromas swirled around her face and she quickly closed the door.

Ella turned again to the window to watch the approaching rider. There was something in his bearing that was familiar–the way he sat tall in the saddle, his neat appearance, and the tilt of his hat. *No, it couldn't be. It's been too many years. I'm hallucinating.* After looking again, though, she hurried to her bedroom where she washed the flour from her hands and inspected herself in the mirror. She smoothed her hair with a brush, then pinched her cheeks to bring up a bit of color. Hurrying back to the kitchen she stole a quick glance out of the window. The rider was just below the hotel, his face barely visible in the shadow of his hat. He had no mustache, but she was certain anyway. *It's Dutch!* Ella suppressed a sob as a thrill of excitement surged through her body. She hurried to the lobby.

As he entered the hotel's lobby Dutch was startled when a woman's soft voice greeting him from the shadows of the room. "Dutch, where have you been? I've been waiting!"

He recognized the happy, lilting laugh that followed, but doubted his ears until he saw her. As Ella walked to him she swept through a ray of morning sun that danced in her chestnut hair. Dutch reached out and took her in his arms. He could feel a quiet emotion shake her shoulders. The years seemed to fade away as he held her in his strong arms. He hugged her tightly, then held her at arm's length and laughed with a joy he hadn't felt in a long time. He had found the girl in the stars, that elusive face in the Milkmaid's Path.

"She was a phantom of delight
When first she gleamed upon my sight;
A lovely apparition... still."

Ella laughed, and a tear glistened on her cheek. "You haven't changed, have you? You always were the romantic. Please don't stop, I love it." Putting her hands on the back of his neck she pulled him to her and kissed him, her lips briefly on his. "Dutch, I've been praying to find an old friend. It's a lonesome place out here."

"My God, Etta," Dutch exclaimed, feeling dizzy from the kiss. "I never expected to see you again, certainly not here. Are you..." he paused, his eyes betraying a shadow of concern, afraid of the answer, "alone?"

"Yes. Too much so. I'm the cook, the maid, everything, including the owner of this fine establishment. Here, sign my register and stay awhile." She pushed the register book towards him and laughed with happiness she hadn't felt for a long time. "By the way, my name is Ella, Ella Price."

He grinned. "You look just like a girl named Etta I once knew. I wanted to run away with her, but she didn't know that!"

"Maybe you should have asked her." Ella laughed.

Dutch looked at her in surprise. Then he signed the register, thinking a moment before he did. "Henry Wyatt, Quien Sabe Ranch." Ella turned the register around, examined the entry and looked at Dutch with a quizzical expression.

"Quien Sabe. Isn't that just along the mountain a few miles? Have you been there long?"

"Well no, Et...Ella, I was just there a day to check on something I left there a couple of years ago. I've been in Mexico for two years and I don't know where I'm headed. Quien Sabe means 'who knows.' It seems to fit for the moment. When I returned to the states, I heard that Pancho Villa had killed me. I decided it was a good time to make a new start. I shaved off my mustache and took on a new name."

"Henry doesn't fit you. But the mustache did. You will always be Dutch to me and you'll just have to grow that mustache back!" Ella made the statement with such finality that Dutch looked at her in surprise. "I've been Ella for a few years now and I can't go back, besides, it's pretty close to my old name anyway!"

Dutch could see that the matter was settled.

"Oh, my gosh! I almost forgot the bread." Ella hurried into the kitchen and took the pans from the oven. She placed the hot loaves, perfectly browned, on clean muslin laid over the porcelain work counter. She poured two cups of steaming coffee from the big pot simmering on the stove and carried them into the lobby.

"Dutch, I was so flabbergasted at seeing you that I haven't asked why you're here." She set the cups of coffee on a small table between two large leather chairs and sat in one, folding her legs beneath her.

THE TROUBLE WITH GOLD... 219

"It all started more than two years ago in Colorado." Dutch related his story: the highgraded gold, the train heist, the gold stashed at Quien Sabe and finally his escape to Mexico. He didn't mention Cat's name. "Ella, Wyoming is where I plan to stay. I'm looking for a ranch to buy. That's my dream. There are lots of details to tell you about, but first tell me how you got here."

As Dutch spoke, Ella studied his face. She saw a face marked with creases and wrinkles that told of hard work and kindness. *He is a handsome man. His arms felt good around me...* The thought trailed off and she felt her face flush. His voice, too, had the firmness and confidence of a truthful man. *How could such a good person become a bandit? Oh my gosh, how can I wonder? I believe I'm a good person and I rode with the outlaws!*

"Remember, Dutch, when I went to Argentina with Butch and Sundance? They thought we could make a new start. It was fun for a while, but I became ill and Sundance took me to Buenos Ayres. That's the last I saw of him. I finally came back to New York on my own. Pinkerton claims Sundance and Butch were killed in a standoff after a robbery at San Vincente in Bolivia." Ella stared into space as though into the past. "I'm not so sure." Almost imperceptibly she shook her head. "Anyway that's been a long time ago. I would rather live for today.

"I tried teaching for a few years but I was restless. I had a yearning to see my friends from those days, so I came back west. I remembered the adventure, the dangers and, most of all, the friendships. I knew a few of the old bunch were killed in gunfights. When I did find a couple of them still around, I found we had nothing in common anymore. Most of that old gang were a seamy lot, weren't they? Maybe we thought we were friends at the time only because we all shared the same dangers.

"I was on my way back to New York when I met JT Stokes, who owned the mine and a ranch over the mountain. He hired me to run his hotel. He had big plans for the DePass mine.

"Oh, by the way, Cat Teason was here for a while about a year ago."

Dutch's eyes widened in surprise and he leaned forward in his chair. "Cat was here? At DePass? Ella, Cat was my partner on that gold heist! I figured he'd been to Quien Sabe to get his share of the gold, but why did he come to DePass?"

"He was shot in the arm by that range detective, Charlie Surcingle. Cat hid out here and I nursed him back to health. He had done some work for Stokes earlier at Stokes' ranch and was riding north for Canada when Surcingle surprised him. I never did know what trouble there was between Surcingle and Cat, but I guess the stolen gold explains that."

"Charlie Surcingle was apparently hired by the thieves who first stole the gold. Obviously they couldn't go to the law. Surcingle is a persistent cuss. He was on our tail from the minute we took the gold off the train. It's been two years, I wonder if he's given up yet? And I wonder if he recovered any of Cat's gold?"

"Cat sure didn't act rich while he was here. He stayed here for several weeks and did quite a bit of gambling. When Surcingle and a posse came looking for him, Stokes hid Cat out down in the mine. He stayed there for a couple of days at least. I never saw him leave, but his horse and belongings were missing. I assumed he had ridden out at night. It was strange, Stokes disappeared at the same time. I haven't seen either one of them since that time over a year ago."

"Ella, I'm sure that Cat dug up his share of the gold at the Quien Sabe. Did he ever mention it?"

"Cat never mentioned any gold to me. I made it clear to him that I wouldn't put up with any crooked gambling, so I don't suppose he would have mentioned stolen gold."

"Did Stokes know about the gold?"

"I don't know, but I doubt if Cat would have said anything to Stokes."

"Tell me more about Stokes and the DePass Mine."

"Stokes had big plans for the mine. He was convinced that there is a lot of gold in veins beyond where the mine stopped when it operated for copper. He had been laying the groundwork for a couple of years and had been working on financing to get it running. He got the money lined up and started mining right after Cat arrived.

"When Stokes disappeared I thought something had happened to him down in the mine, but the hoistman said he had come out of the mine that afternoon. He didn't see him, but Stokes answered his call when the hoist broke down. The cage stopped on the first level. Stokes called up that he would climb up the ladders. After he climbed out he must have ridden into the hills to check on cattle and had an accident. His saddled horse showed up the next day. There was something odd though. The reins were tied over the horse's neck. Hardly something he could have done if he'd fallen or been thrown. Everybody in the area helped search for him, but there was no sign of him anywhere."

"Sounds like some kind of foul play. And it sure doesn't look good that Cat left at the same time."

"Cat may have cheated at cards but he wouldn't have killed Stokes. They weren't exactly friends, but I can't see where Cat stood to gain anything by killing Stokes. With all that gold it sounds like Cat was rich anyway."

"Did Stokes have many enemies? The sort who would have killed him?"

"I have thought about the possibilities. A lot of people didn't like Stokes, but not so much they would have killed him."

Dutch rubbed his face in thought. "Maybe Cat had some kind of deal with Stokes. I saw where Cat dug up his share of the gold at Quien Sabe, but you never saw it here.

I wonder what happened to it? What kind of person was Stokes?"

"He was a tough businessman and knew when to take advantage of a situation, although he was always fair with me. He imagined himself as the reincarnation of King Midas. It did seem that everything he got into made money. One time he said that the mine was going to make a lot of money if he didn't fall in the river first. In fact, he even mentioned the name of the river, which seemed strange. I had never heard of it."

"Was it the River Pactolus?"

Ella looked at Dutch in amazement. "Why yes, I believe it was! How in the world did you know? Where is it?"

Dutch laughed. "Midas was the king of Phyrgia. According to legend, Midas was kind to a captive named Silenus, the spirit of wine. For his good deed Midas was granted a wish. Midas wished that everything he touched would turn to gold. That was wonderful at first, but Midas soon found he was starving to death because all his food turned to gold. Even worse, his daughter became a statue of gold when he touched her.

"Midas begged to be released from his wish. He was told to bathe in the River Pactolus. That solved the gold problem, but Midas made such a fuss about losing his gold that the god Apollo gave him the ears of an ass."

Ella laughed. "I wonder if JT knew the whole story? There was something else, though. He wanted me to marry him. He asked me, or rather told me, only a few days before he disappeared."

Dutch, looking slightly perplexed, asked, "And what was your answer?"

"I put him off. I didn't want to hurt his feelings. I didn't love him and I doubt if he loved me. We'd never even kissed. He was thinking of his social life, and needed a wife to go with all the money he was going to make. Oh, I liked him as a business partner, but I was surprised when

THE TROUBLE WITH GOLD... 223

he said he wanted to marry me. I've wondered if my reticence had anything to do with his disappearance, but I'm sure he was far too self-centered to be affected by that."

Her forehead wrinkled, "I'm confused about Cat, Dutch. He never acted like he had much money and Stokes even loaned him money. Surcingle almost caught Cat because he lost his horse in poker. It doesn't sound like he had much of anything if he gambled away his horse. Surcingle must not have gotten the gold or he wouldn't have still be chasing Cat."

"Maybe Cat was financing the mine startup with his gold. The gold was worth plenty–fifty thousand or so. Stokes might have extracted a steep fee for hiding Cat."

"Oh, my gosh!" Ella's eyes widened. "That much? JT did make a rather sudden announcement about starting up the mine and he hadn't been to town to make any arrangements there. Do you really think there could have been a connection?"

"It's hard to say. Tomorrow let's look around the mine and see if we can find any clues."

"We can go up to the mine office and the room where Cat stayed, but the mine is filled with water to the main adit. It would mean a lot to me if we could get some answers.

"Dutch, you mentioned buying a ranch. Will you be happy with that?"

"I realized a long time ago that I didn't want to be an outlaw. I love this Wyoming country, and I want to settle on a piece of it before it becomes too crowded. There's already been lots of changes since I came west from Nebraska."

"I always knew you were a good man. That makes me happy. Life seems too precious to waste it by taking advantage of others. When I learned how our former cohorts had dissipated I was glad to leave those days behind forever. It was heaven sent luck when I met Stokes and he asked me to run the DePass Hotel. I like running this place." Ella rose and walked into the kitchen, returning with a fresh pot of coffee, a plate of hot, fresh bread and a jar of raspberry jam.

Spreading the fragrant jam on a slice of bread, she continued. "Stokes was good to me and he admired what I had done. The hotel even started to make money on its own. For once in my life I found some stability. I liked Stokes too, in spite of his strange ways. He needed a confidant, someone he could trust. I guess we both needed someone." Ella paused and looked at Dutch. "No, I never would have married him. I know what I want–though I may never get it–and it isn't to be a fur-draped wife of a rich cattle and mining baron."

Dutch suppressed a sigh of relief. He wasn't sure just why. After all, there had never been anything between Etta and himself. Why should he care if she'd had a few lovers? He remembered conjuring up her face in the milkmaid's path on many a night and wondered if she had ever thought of him in the past years. *No, probably not. She was Sundance's girl.*

Ella continued. "Things were going well here. Stokes believed in the mine and the mine was doing well. Then things turned around and everything seemed to crash down at once. First the ore vein was lost and the mine flooded when the drift went through a fault. Then Stokes disappeared. The mine closed after all that and the value of the stock dropped to a fraction of what it had been the month before."

Ella closed her eyes and rubbed her hand across her forehead as if trying to wipe away a bad memory. "I have a thousand shares of DePass Bonanza Mines stock. I was fabulously rich on paper for a while, but now it's worthless."

"What about the hotel? How did you manage to keep it out of the legal mess?"

THE TROUBLE WITH GOLD...

"Fortunately JT had put the hotel in a company separate from the mine. He sold me the hotel and I was to pay him a nominal amount out of my profit. I paid into an escrow account after he disappeared."

"It's strange that Cat didn't talk to you before he left. Unless he had some trouble with Stokes."

"I wasn't surprised that Cat left suddenly. He was scared to death of being caught. Cat was desperate to get out of here from the moment he came. I think he left as soon as he felt Surcingle wasn't watching the mine any longer. Maybe that just coincided with JT's disappearance. That's all I know about Cat.

"Now tell me about the train robbery, I bet you ruined another day for the Union Pacific."

"I'm sure the railroad brass were furious about us blowing up their express car, but the funny thing is, they didn't know what we'd gotten away with. The gold had been highgraded from a rich deposit of gold in the Cresson Mine by one of the mine bosses. He was secretly shipping it to a vault in San Francisco. I went along with a scheme to highjack it because it was already stolen goods and it didn't seem wrong to take gold from a thief. Of course the risk was greater with Charlie Surcingle on our trail."

"Doesn't that bother you, even now? When he stopped by here, Surcingle seemed to be pretty determined."

"It's been over two years since the robbery and I reckon the mine thieves would have tired of paying Surcingle to keep up the chase. I think it's time to put my share of the gold to an honest use. I'm tired of running from my conscience."

Ella frowned. "I'm afraid my conscience would still be nagging at me. I would always remember how I'd gotten the gold."

"I'd agree with you if we had stolen from its legitimate owners. We were careful not to hurt or kill anyone. That was the last train heist I'll ever do."

"Cat got hurt, and he was scared for his life all the time he was here at the mine. Dutch, I can't help it. I'll be scared too, once you take that gold from its hiding place."

"Once you see the gold, you'll feel better. When I sell it I'm going to make darn sure that I don't leave any clues that can be traced back to me."

Ella smiled, but there was a note of sadness in her voice. "Please be careful Dutch, I...I don't want to lose you again."

"After what I've been through so far, the rest will be easy. After all, I escaped Pancho Villa's troops!"

"It must have been terrifying! What happened?"

"I made up my mind to work in the Mexican silver mines for a couple of years. I met up with a couple of unsavory gringos as I rode out of Silver City. They weren't my choice of ideal companions but they hooked up with me anyway. One of them was a pudgy little scam artist. The other one was a man with a cruel slit of a mouth. I recognized him as a vicious killer and thief from Utah. They told me they were looking for work in the Mexican silver mines. It was obvious they weren't miners. I figured they had probably just busted a bank and were looking for me to guide them into Mexico.

"On the first night we camped at a little spring. Pancho Villa and his band got the jump on us the next morning. Pancho slashed open one of their saddlebags and a river of silver dollars cascaded out. While the Mexicans were occupied with the money I slipped onto my horse and lit out like a heathen out of church!

"I was out of sight in the brush before they could get a bead on me, but I'd heard that Pancho collected fast horses, so I knew I didn't have much time. I leaned over and told that to Rosinante, my horse, and he left those Mexican ponies in the dust. That's about all of the story."

"But what about the rumor that you got killed in that chase? Were you wounded?"

"No, they didn't even get any close misses, thanks to Rosinante. When I got back to New Mexico a couple years later I heard that the two gringos managed to get back. They'd been stripped of everything but a few clothes and one horse. I guess they told around that I had been shot. They also laid the blame for their robbing of the silver dollars on me."

The next morning Dutch and Ella walked up to the mine office. Inside everything was in the same place as it had been when Stokes disappeared. The only changes were piles of mouse droppings. A dusty desk was littered with chewed up papers. A file cabinet was covered with rock samples. In a corner behind the file cabinet was a wooden box bound with riveted iron straps. It was secured with a large padlock and labeled "ore samples."

In a desk drawer Dutch found several shotgun shells and a cigar box half full of lead shot. There was also a cloth sample bag full of a heavy material. Dutch opened the bag. It was filled with rusty-colored dirt. He hefted the bag to feel the weight. "Ella, I think this is high-grade gold ore, maybe a concentrate from the mill. Maybe Stokes *was* onto something!" Dutch closed the drawer.

"I'll show you where Cat stayed." They walked outside and behind the office. Ella opened the door of a little shed-like room. It contained only a cot, dilapidated wardrobe and a small cast-iron stove. The flyspecked windows were hung with cheap cheesecloth curtains. The windowsills were layered with dust and dead flies. There was a dingy, musty darkness about the room.

Ella shuddered and pushed open the flimsy curtains. "Cat didn't bring much with him and there is nothing left that belonged to him."

From Cat's former quarters they went into the change room in the hoisthouse where they put on miner's hats. Dutch charged two carbide lights with water and carbide. Ella unlocked the big door at the timbered portal and they walked back into the main adit. Ella had been back in the mine with Stokes, but she still found the tunnel dank and uninviting. Dutch clicked open the valve on the carbide lamps to let water drip into the carbide chamber. With a deft swipe of his hand he spun the sparking wheel on each lamp. The acetylene gas ignited with a pop and the hissing flames lit up the dark tunnel. He and Ella cautiously walked into the dark mine, their footsteps echoing down the drift.

Ella shivered, not with the cold, but with a foreboding that she was entering a place where she didn't belong. "It's a few hundred feet back to the shaft that goes down six hundred feet. Do you think it's safe?"

"No mine is completely safe, but the air is moving, apparently up through old workings to the surface. We won't have to worry about bad air. I'll keep an eye open for loose rocks in the back."

When they reached the underground hoist station, Dutch carefully crawled up to the edge of the shaft. Putting a silencing finger to his lips, he dropped a rock down the shaft. He silently counted until the rock splashed below. "My guess is that the water level is down between a hundred and two hundred feet. The water is probably rising fairly slowly now, but even if we could get the pumps going it might take months to lower the water down to the bottom of the shaft. When was the last time anyone was down in the shaft?"

"After JT disappeared the sheriff looked through the mine down to level four. He didn't find anything, but the water level was already above the fifth level."

They walked back out to the portal. Ella was relieved to be back out in the sunshine. Below them the green meadow stood in sharp contrast to the gray sagebrush higher on the slopes. Smoke wafted from the hotel chimney, layering a thin cloud down the valley in the cool morning air trapped by the surrounding hills.

THE TROUBLE WITH GOLD...

At the hotel Ella fixed breakfast for the two of them. As they ate she could tell that Dutch was deep in thought. "What is it Dutch? Is there something wrong?"

"I'm going back up to the mine office. I saw something that puzzles me. Maybe it's a clue, maybe not."

At the office Dutch rummaged through several papers in the filing cabinet. Most of the papers were sample assays and shipping records from mining done in earlier days. He scanned through the assays, noting a few moderate gold numbers, but no highgrade. He looked at the locked wooden chest. He attempted to move it out of the dark corner. The box would not budge. *This is either bolted down or damned heavy.* He sat on the floor and braced his feet against the wall. He grasped one of the iron handles on the box and inch by inch, slowly slid it out into the room. He looked through the desk drawers and on the wall for keys but couldn't find any that would fit.

"Well, heck. Being a former bandit I should be able to get this open without a key." Dutch worked at the lock with the leather punch of his pocketknife. The lock soon fell open. At that moment he heard footsteps on the wooden landing outside. He felt a surge of alarm and drew his pistol. He whirled around as the door swung open.

"Dutch, are you in there?"

It was Ella. Dutch exhaled in relief and slid his gun back in the holster. He didn't know why, but he had half-expected trouble.

"I couldn't stand it. I had to know what you saw that made you come back up." Ella saw Dutch's hand on his pistol. "I didn't mean to surprise you. Are you finding any clues?"

Dutch laughed, "Sorry Ella, I'm always nervous when I'm picking a lock.

"I have a feeling that several things may add up to an idea about what happened between Stokes and Cat. First of all, let's see what's in this heavy chest. I just picked the lock on it. Go ahead and open it up."

Tentatively, Ella lifted up the heavy, iron-reinforced lid of the chest. The hinges creaked with the rust of disuse. The contents were covered with a piece of burlap. Dutch picked up a corner of the burlap and took it out.

They both caught their breath. Ella clasped her hand to her mouth. Dutch, on the other hand, was not totally surprised. The contents glittered just like when he and Cat had buried the gold in the crevice at Quien Sabe. In the box were several pieces of almost pure gold and highgrade calaverite. It was some of the Cripple Creek ore. Dutch picked up card a heavy manila paper that was on top of the gold. It was a sample description form. On the location line was neatly lettered: *"500 level decline, DePass Mine.'*

"I've never seen such beautiful gold." Ella said as she picked up a piece of gold. "I didn't know they had found anything this rich before the flooding."

"Ella, I don't think they did. You're looking at some of the Cripple Creek gold that Cat and I took from the train two years ago." Reaching into the box, Dutch took out some of the larger, richer specimens. "This is gold from the 1200 foot level of the Cresson Mine. Not the 500 level of the DePass Mine! My guess is that Stokes was using this to salt samples from the DePass."

"I don't understand. What do you mean by *salt*?"

"He was using this high-grade ore from Cripple Creek to make the samples from the DePass mine look good."

Ella took another piece out and was admiring it when Dutch exclaimed. "What's this?" He quickly removed the remaining pieces of gold and calaverite, revealing a piece of canvas well above the bottom of the box. Holding the corners to keep from spilling the remaining fine gold, he lifted out the canvas. The bottom of the box was filled with barren broken rock. "Why would have Stokes put this waste rock in here?" Dutch removed the rocks one by one, examining them for possible vein material. None of the rocks showed anything of interest. He removed all of the rocks until only a canvas sample bag remained in the bottom of the box. It apparently contained another sample. Dutch grasped it by the ties that kept the bag closed and pulled. "It seems to be nailed to the box." He took out his pocketknife and sliced through the bag, spreading it open. Dutch and Ella gasped at the lone item. A glittering yellow cone-shaped ingot of gold the size of a coffee cup stared at them with the brilliance of the midday sun.

Dutch tried to lift the smooth sided cone of precious metal from its place. He could not get hold of the sloping surface to lift it out. "Give me a hand Ella. We'll lift one end of the box and dump it out." They lifted the box and the gold ingot tumbled out on the floor in a crashing cloud of dust. With the ingot on its side Dutch was able to lift it.

"Good Lord, this weighs 30 or 40 pounds."

"Dutch, I think I know what this is. I heard a loud roar in the mill one day and Stokes told me they were smelting down some of the ore concentrates from the mine. He mentioned something about stirring up a new level of interest in DePass Mine stock. It did, too. But there were two of these. He had one on display in Shoshoni for a while."

"I wonder...?" Dutch lifted the ingot again, then hefted each larger piece of ore, mentally adding the weights. He walked to the desk where he rummaged around until he found a pencil and some paper. He wrote down several numbers and did some calculations. "Ella, if there were two gold ingots, plus the pieces of ore here in the box, I figure that accounts a good part of the gold Cat would have had. I think I know where the rest of it went!"

"Maybe Cat took the rest of it with him."

"He might have taken a little, but I have a hunch something else was going on. I have a notion of what it might have been. Some of the best specimens are still here. The most valuable ones. Why didn't Cat take these?

"There was quite a bit of fine gold, too. I think I know what might have happened to it." Dutch retrieved the cloth bag from the desk and poured the contents out onto a piece of paper. "Take a close look at that and tell me what you see. Your eyes are better than mine."

"Well, it looks sort of like rusty dirt to me." Ella bent closer to the paper and spread the powder out over the paper. "Oh, I see! There are little specs of gold all through the powder, but there isn't much here."

"That's because the rest was used for salting the mine." Dutch opened the desk and took out the cigar box with the loose lead shot and the shotgun shells. "Here's the salting equipment."

"Shotgun shells?"

"These pellets have been removed from shotgun shells and were replaced with gold-rich fines. Some paper wadding would hold in the material until it was shot. I think Stokes was salting the DePass Mine by shooting gold, Cat's gold, into the vein with a shotgun.

"Stokes, or whoever it was, marked where samples would be taken in the mine drifts. The person doing the salting would shoot a couple of blasts into the vein at those locations, enriching the rock with the high-grade gold. Stokes probably had an independent engineer doing the sampling to make it look convincing. It wouldn't take much of this stuff to make low-grade rock assay pretty good. A couple of ounces mixed with regular rock dust would go a long way. I've seen salting tried in some of the Colorado mines when they were for sale. It's an old promoter's trick for selling played-out mines."

"But why? JT told me that there was gold in the DePass. That was before Cat ever came around. He said he wasn't interested in selling the mine."

"Stokes probably needed to generate excitement about the mine to get better financing for more mine development. When I first came up here after breakfast I saw some old shipping records from several years back that showed there were better gold values down in the deepest part of the mine. These were shipments made before the mine closed down in 1912. Stokes must have been a real optimist. He probably was convinced that the mother-lode existed down there somewhere but needed to raise money to find it."

"JT believed he could make anything happen if he wanted it. He didn't consider himself dishonest but he did believe that his goals justified whatever was necessary to get there.

"Dutch, we still don't have any idea about what happened to Stokes or where Cat took off to, do we?"

"No, we don't, but it does appear that Stokes was using Cat's gold. They must have had some kind of agreement. Cat must have figured on getting something out of it or he wouldn't have stuck around as long as he did."

"The whole thing gives me a headache. Let's go have a cup of coffee." Ella took Dutch's hand and pulled him in the direction of the hotel.

For several days Dutch combed the area around the mine but came up with no other clues. Late one afternoon, Dutch stopped at a small marshy area that had formed in a pond built for mill water. He cut a bouquet of cattails and reeds with his pocketknife. *I reckon I've never given a woman anything like a bouquet of flowers.*

Ella was as thrilled as if the cattails were beautiful roses. She arranged the dried plants in a vase and placed it on the lobby table while Dutch started a fire in the big pot-bellied stove. The days were pleasantly warm but with the nights came a chill that encouraged a crackling fire in the stove and the comfort of the big leather chairs.

After dinner Dutch read a few chapters from Mark Twain's *Roughing It* to Ella while she sat contentedly wrapped in a blanket in front of the stove. When Dutch finished reading, Ella smiled at him. "I'm so glad you're here, Dutch."

Dutch felt a warm glow. "Ella, I feel more civilized and glad to be alive than I have in years, having tea and reading to you. Being with you, I..." He stopped, afraid to say what was in his heart. He had been at DePass for more than a week and he and Ella had built a warm friendship. Every day he felt more in love with her, even though there was no overt romance. It was as though in telling her of his love he might find it was solely his fantasy. *I should just tell her, she might be waiting for me to say something. If she loves me as well.*

Ella reached out and put her hand on his arm. "You were going to say something else?"

"Ella, I'm ready to buy a ranch. When Cat and I were on the run a couple of years ago we rode across the badlands country to the Big Horn Mountains. At the foot of the Big Horns I saw some mighty nice country where trout-filled streams flow out of magnificent canyons and meander through rich valleys at the foot of the mountains. That's where I want to look for a ranch."

"So how soon are you leaving?"

He looked at Ella in surprise. "How did you know?"

"Dutch, you've been fidgeting all day. I guessed what you had in mind, and at least some of what you thinking." Ella felt a stab of dread as she continued with a question. "Will you be back...soon?"

"Well, I'd like to if you don't mind."

Ella smiled, her relief evident. "Was there something else you wanted to tell me?"

Dutch looked into her eyes. There was a gentle, open softness, as though she wanted him to gaze into her very soul. "Yes, there is, Ella. I reckon I love you! I always have, but since I've been here my love for you is greater than I can ever tell you."

With a small cry and tears on her cheeks, Ella went to Dutch. Sitting on his lap she put her arms around his neck. Her lips found his as he responded with a gentle passion. When they broke apart she looked into his eyes. "I love you, Dutch. I don't want to ever be without you."

"I think I must be dreaming. I promise not to be gone very long. I should be able to find out soon enough if there are any ranches for sale over in the Nowood country."

"Dutch, remember when we rode together with the Wild Bunch? I'd like to do it again. Take me with you."

"Well, I'd love to... But what about the hotel?"

"There's hardly any business to worry about, especially this time of the year. I have two horses and a nice buggy. We could travel in style." She puckered her lips and wrinkled her brow in mock petulance. "I won't let you take my horses unless I can go along to take care of them. Besides that, I've saved up some money. I want to help buy the ranch."

"All right. You've convinced me, but I have enough gold to buy a ranch." He kissed her and laughed. "When can you be ready?"

"Well, this afternoon while you were deciding how to tell me that you were leaving, I got together some food from the kitchen. I'll make up my bedroll, pack my travel bag and be ready first thing in the morning." Dutch looked at her and shook his head. Ella laughed delightedly. Dutch had a feeling that his life would never be the same again.

Chapter 21

Temptation and the Dream

Dutch and Ella camped the first night near Lost Cabin, where Ella bought supplies at the commissary. By late morning the next day, the horses had labored up the steep wash that led to Cottonwood Pass. A few spring-fed meadows formed little green oases along the dry wash. They stopped once to water the horses and let them feed on the still green grass.

At the pass Dutch turned the team off the main road and headed up a steep trail. "We'll take a little detour here to view some scenery," Dutch said as the buggy bounced up the rocky trail, the horses struggling with their footing in the loose rocks of the washed-out road.

Dutch halted the horses at the top of the hill. "Oh my gosh, Dutch! We can see the whole world from here!" Ella jumped down from the buggy to gaze at the panorama.

"Look at the Big Horns." Dutch pointed to glistening, snow capped peaks far to the north. "Winter has already started there."

"Those two hump-backed shapes beyond the Big Horns are the Pryor Mountains in Montana. Three days ride from here. Cookstove Basin is near there. Notorious outlaws that we knew used to hide out there! I wonder if Butch ever dug up the loot we buried when we camped there back in the 90's?"

Ella looked to the southwest. "That must be the Wind River Mountains. It seems I could almost reach out and touch them. Oh Dutch, I love this open country." She spread her arms as though to grasp the vista.

Dutch pointed out other mountains in every direction. "Those granite domes are along the Sweetwater River. That jagged skyline is the Absaroka Mountains. They go right into Yellowstone Park."

There was so much to see that they were reluctant to move on. Then a breeze, brisk and cold, reminded them that the days of Indian summer would soon be over.

"Lead on, McDuff."

Ella looked at him in puzzlement. "What did you say?"

"Oh, it's just a quote from an old friend of mine. A fellow by the name of Shakespeare."

Back on the main road the horses broke into an easy lope as the road dropped into the drainage of the Nowood River. Their buggy clattered past cedar cloaked red bluffs and along valley meadows. As they passed by a precipitous canyon cut through a ridge of folded limestone, Dutch pointed down the valley. "The Nowood store is just ahead. We'll stop and buy some grain for the horses."

Inside the tiny Nowood store they were surprised to find fresh fruit and even tomatoes. Noting their wonder the storekeeper explained. "Just came in today. You're lucky you got here before the sheep-camp tenders. Won't last long when they show up."

A little later their buggy clattered into the narrow canyon incised through Mahogany Butte. The soaring cliffs of limestone were folded into a giant arch. On the slopes and high ledges, silvery green mountain mahogany bushes made a pleasing contrast against the light gray limestone.

"Dutch, look at that! A giant hand must have squeezed the earth." Ella pointed at the warped layers of rock.

"I bet you're right. I've seen smaller folds like this in some of the mines but this one is magnificent."

Ella had ridden through country like this in the wilder days of her youth, but this was the first time she had observed scenery for the pleasure of it. She wanted to melt into this countryside and become part of it for the rest of her life. Especially with Dutch.

In the canyon the clear waters of the small mountain stream were barely visible beneath the thick, green clumps of chokecherry bushes, which bent over the deep pools with the weight of ripened clusters of chokecherries. Nearby, a small meadow opened up to the creek.

"Let's stop here for the night." Dutch said, "We still have some time to catch a few fish."

"I'm ready. I'm tired of being jounced around on rough roads. I'll start a fire while you catch our supper." Ella stretched and breathed in the evening air. She watched in girlish wonder as growing shadows of twilight emphasized the sculpture of the soaring canyon walls. High above, nighthawks maneuvered in daring flight. "BzzzzzzZZoup, bzzzzzzZZoup." The sound of their wings echoed off the rock walls as the alacritous birds swooped to glean bugs from the evening air. Ella felt she could stay here forever. As night claimed the canyon, she sat close to the fire, clasping arms around her knees. Dutch rolled the fish in cornmeal, then dropped them in a skillet sizzling with hot bacon grease.

After supper they sat snuggled together, taking advantage of the fire's last glowing embers. A cool breeze came up suddenly, bringing the colder air down from the higher mountains and swirling a wisp of ashes from the cooling fire. The old *Delicious* jelly pail that served as a teapot simmered with a lazy, singing sound. Dutch and Ella were content to sip their tea and gaze at the brilliant heavens.

"Dutch, what kind of ranch are you looking for? I've seen giant spreads like Stokes', but JT was so driven by ambition that he never had time to enjoy life. Then I've seen the squalid little dry farm places with hollow-eyed homesteaders who worked themselves to death before their time. Surely there must be a right size in between. Something we can afford with our savings and work the rest out."

"I've got that gold waiting to go to work. We can buy a large spread and not spend your savings."

"Are you sure you want to finance your ranch with the gold?"

Dutch detected a frown in Ella's voice, though he couldn't see her face. "Well heck, I don't know why I shouldn't. Cat and I risked our lives for that gold. It was thieves' gold in the first place. We weren't stealing someone's life savings."

There was no answer and the embers of the fire gradually faded with the silence. Finally Ella stood up and stretched. "I'm going to bed. I'll see you at breakfast. Goodnight." Gone was her bubbly happiness.

"Good night, Ella." *Damn! I would have thought she'd be happy that I'm putting the gold to good use.*

Long after Ella had gone to sleep, Dutch tossed restlessly in his bedroll, listening to the stream babble over the flat limestone pebbles. The gold's glitter swirled in his mind like a nightmare. *Maybe I should give the damn stuff back to the thieves.*

The sound of the creek took on the voice of his old mental nemesis, Temptation. "You need it for the ranch. You can buy any ranch in this valley with that gold."

Dutch ran the alternatives through his mind. *It would be impossible to strike a deal with the original thieves. Half the gold is missing and they'd always be convinced that I'd stashed the other half. They'd be on my tail forever. Besides they don't know I have it. At least I don't think so. The railroad is interested only because they didn't like to have someone get the best of them. They'd throw the book at me if I confessed. No, it would be best to put the gold to good use for me, for us. Dammit, that's what I'll do.* Again the tinkling stream answered, this time it was Conscience. "No ranch is worth an anchor around your neck!"

It was barely light as Dutch built a fire for their coffee. He and Ella sipped the coffee hurriedly in the chill morning air and broke camp as the orange glow of sunrise touched the uppermost rim of the canyon. Dutch harnessed the horses to the buggy and they left the verdant little meadow. It was but a short drive when they emerged from the mouth of the canyon. They rattled across a wooden bridge and rode along a green hay meadow bounded by gentle hills of sagebrush. Straight ahead a solid wall of red sandstone sprinkled with scattered juniper bushes rose hundreds of feet above the valley.

As the sun rose so did Ella's mood. "My gosh, Dutch, it looks exactly like the Red Wall over at the Hole in the Wall." Ella's enthusiasm had returned.

"I imagine it's the same rock formation. It was probably continuous before the Big Horn Mountains folded up. Pretty soon we'll see some white limestone cliffs where canyons cut the Big Horn Mountain flank. This is the country I was telling you about. Little Canyon Creek, Big Trails, Otter Creek–it's beautiful country all the way to Ten Sleep and beyond."

For two days, Dutch and Ella talked with ranchers from Big Trails to Ten Sleep. Not one of the ranches with big spreads from the low country badlands up to the lush summer grazing meadows on the mountain was for sale. The ranchers were friendly, though, and each evening they were invited to have supper and stay the night. It was impossible to refuse the sincere hospitality. Late on the second day, the proprietor of the grocery store in Ten Sleep mentioned that he'd heard of a ranch for sale in the Paint Rock country. "I'll come back later and look at that place, Ella, I think we've looked enough this trip. It's two days back to DePass. I don't think we should push our luck with the weather."

Dutch and Ella left Ten Sleep early the next morning. They hoped to reach their previous campsite at Mahogany Butte. Riding along the Nowood valley, Ella watched as a breeze sent yellow and orange leaves fluttering off the box elder trees in a rustle of sparkling color. "I'm sorry we didn't find a place, but it was worthwhile just to see the country. I agree that this would be a nice place to settle down."

A few miles south of the Big Trails store and post office the road skirted around high cliffs of red sandstone. It was a place where the summer rains must have lingered. Grass along the road was lush and green.

Across the broad valley below the road a stream flowed from a deep, rugged canyon. The boisterous creek entered the broad meadows below the canyon, then became a lazily meandering brook. The valley widened and another stream joined the first. As though reluctant to leave the chiseled depths of the mountain slope, the enlarged stream gained strength and turned, dropping into another gorge of towering white walls.

On a small rise at the confluence of the streams perched a large log cabin surrounded by bushes and a garden. Its weathered logs blended so closely with the surroundings that the cabin was barely visible. Nearby, a grove of box elder trees glistened gold in the low autumn sun. A wisp of smoke drifted out of the cabin's chimney.

A rutted, red dirt track led towards the cabin from the main road. Ella exclaimed. "What a beautiful place Dutch. Lets stop in and see who lives there."

A neat grass yard was edged by the remnants of summer flowers–' bright orange marigolds, a few roses and drying stalks of hollyhocks. Chickadees flitted to and fro amongst tall drying sunflowers, picking out one seed at a time, then hurrying away. The little yard was protected from encroaching cows by a pole-topped fence. Along the fence, large rhubarb plants lined the yard. A flagstone path led from a rustic wooden gate to the front door.

A tall man in Levis and a large Stetson stood beside the gate, leaning his elbows on the fence rail as if he had been waiting for them. A black and white collie sat quietly beside him, wagging her tail as if she too was glad to see company. Ella could see that the man was probably in his seventies. A square chin accentuated his rugged, deeply tanned face and laugh wrinkles radiated from the corners of his eyes. He raised his hand in greeting.

Ella could see he was a man who had spent his life out-of-doors and loved it. *He has the face of a good man. I think we will like him.*

The rancher doffed his hat in a courtly gesture, revealing snow-white hair. "Howdy, folks. Hop down and come on in. I was just ready to put on a pot of coffee. Matter of fact, I've baked a batch of cinnamon rolls and was wondering how I'd eat them all. The Lord must've heard me and sent ya'll to help!" He spoke with a pleasant, resonate Texas drawl.

He opened the gate. "I'm Frank Hayden." He shook their hands with a firm grip. Dutch introduced Ella and himself. The collie put her nose into Ella's hand, wagging her tail.

"Well now, Miss, Marmie has taken a fancy to you. She's usually sort of shy with strangers."

Ella could see the touch of a woman inside the cabin but doubted if one lived here now. A few cobwebs draped from the ceiling and a picture was slightly tilted on the wall. She guessed that Hayden was a widower. Hayden invited them to sit at the kitchen table. "You have a lovely place here," Ella said as she petted the collie.

"I love it here. Sometimes it gets mighty lonesome, especially in the evenings after my chores. My wife passed away a few years ago. I keep busy reading or writing letters to our kids. My daughter Mary lives in town and Ben is a captain in the army. I guess they didn't inherit my love of ranching." He passed a piece of cinnamon roll to the collie. "Miss Marmalade and I get along fine here, don't we Marmie?"

Ella laughed. "That's an unusual name. How did she come by that?"

"Well, when she was just a pup she knocked a jar of marmalade off the table and ate most of it. She got her name right then!" He rubbed the collie's ears and she seemed to laugh with him. "I'm glad you folks dropped in. It's always nice to visit with new people. We don't get many strangers passing by."

Dutch explained, "We've been looking the country over. I'll be back to look at buying a ranch in the Paint Rock country. Ella thinks you've got the nicest place we've seen all along the mountain, so we stopped."

"I'm lucky to have this place. I would go out of my mind if I couldn't keep busy with a few cows and walk these hills and canyons. Folks, it's too nice to sit inside. How about a tour?"

Behind the cabin they walked past a modest garden patch that contained the withered remnants of the past summer's vegetables. Only a few drying tomato plants and wilted green carrot tops showed the neat alignment of the garden's plants. Further away, corrals and a small barn showed the same attention to neatness. On the far side of the creek a tiny log cabin sat slightly higher on the slope. The roof projected over a porch containing a rocking chair.

Hayden saw Ella looking at the cabin. "That's my reading and thinking studio. It was the original homestead cabin and I've sort of fixed it up. It has a nice view out over my valley and the lower canyon. I like to spend evenings there." He paused and a cloud passed over his face. "My wife used to go up there and paint. Those are her paintings in the house."

Walking under the box elder trees Ella felt as if she were in a fairy-tale setting. She could see up the mountain slope where patches of pine were intermixed with golden aspen. She knew why Frank Hayden loved this place.

"Folks, I know you're anxious to get on the road, but the day is almost gone. It's going to be cold tonight for camping out. Why don't you spend the night? I have plenty of room and you can get an early start in the morning."

It was dark and cold the next morning when they bid their farewells to Frank Hayden. "I hope I'll see you folks again, soon. Good luck on finding a ranch but one like you want is tough to find around here. You might try over in the Owl Creek country."

"That's good to know. If that place on Paint Rock doesn't pan out I'll head on over there."

Later that morning, as they rattled through the canyon at Mahogany Butte, Dutch turned to Ella. "I've been thinking, Ella. I will find a ranch and I want you to be part of it. I can't, I won't, live without you." Then he added. "If you'd have me that is. I reckon I'm asking you to marry me."

Ella put her arms around Dutch and held him close. "Yes! Oh yes, Dutch." She kissed him soundly. "I could never again be happy without you." She slid a ring off her finger and taking Dutch's hand, slipped it onto his little finger. "I want you to wear this. It will be a sign of our new life together. No more running from the past."

Dutch pulled Ella close and kissed her. "I think I like this new life." The bouncing buggy separated them for a moment but Dutch pulled Ella close to him and kissed her again.

"I like it, too. But I'm afraid. Just when I think the bad things are in the past, some vestige of them threatens me again. Dutch, please let's forget the gold and leave it in its grave."

Ella, I'm sure that when I find a ranch and we get settled down things will be different. The gold was destined to no good anyway. You saw what happened to Cat and Stokes when they used it for bad things. We'll put this half to good use."

"Dutch, I don't like the thought of mortgaging our future with the past. I'd rather begin our new life with our own poverty than the wealth of others."

"I understand, but I'd be an old man before I could save up the kind of money it takes to buy a ranch."

"Dutch, you're not an old man and I don't want to be a girl in a gilded cage."

Well, anyway, when we get back to DePass, I'll ride over to Quien Sabe and pick up just enough gold to make a down payment when I find a place. If anybody asks, I'll say I was a miner and brought the gold from Mexico. I'll put it to a higher use than the first thieves had in mind."

Ella looked at him. "Are you trying to convince me or yourself?"

Chapter 22

Choices

The day following their return to DePass, Dutch rose early, anxious to retrieve some of the gold from Quien Sabe. He was convinced that the gold held the key to buying the ranch he wanted. Ella's reticence to use the gold lurked in the back of his mind, but he was certain she would relent once he found the right ranch. *At least it won't hurt to use enough for earnest money.*

Ella wasn't up yet, unusual for her, but the trip had been long and tiring. Dutch made a pot of coffee and fried bacon. He ate a few slices with toast and packed the rest for lunch. Before leaving he called to Ella. "Ella, I'm on my way to Quien Sabe."

"Be careful, Dutch."

"If I get the gold loaded early, I may go directly to Paint Rock and check on that ranch." He held his step for a moment, waiting for her answer, hoping she would come out to see him off.

"Okay, if you must." Ella answered from her room but didn't come out.

Damn, she's still upset about the gold. Why can't she accept that the gold will be our ticket to a good life together?

THE TROUBLE WITH GOLD...

Dutch walked out of the hotel, an unsettled feeling dragging down his spirits. At the stable he saddled Rosinante and put on the sturdy leather saddlebags that would hold fifty pounds or so of gold. *Enough for earnest money.*

The horse, sensing Dutch's urgency, broke into a gallop and they arrived at the Quien Sabe Ranch in an hour. Again there was no one there. He searched for signs of anyone else in the area. There was no life except for an occasional cottontail rabbit and raucous magpies swooping from tree to tree.

Dutch couldn't focus on the task at hand. All he could think of was Ella's terse farewell. *Maybe I should leave the dang gold where it is and go back to the mines or settle for being a dollar a day cowboy.* "Doggonit, Rosinante, we need a cup of coffee to clear my head."

He started a fire in the cabin's iron range. While the stove was heating up, he went down to the creek and scooped up a bucket of water. Walking back to the cabin he breathed in the autumn scents and for a brief moment he felt happiness. Inside, the fresh wood crackled in the stove and the iron creaked as it expanded. Dutch put on the coffeepot and ladled coffee grounds into the water. As the stove heated Dutch smelled the familiar aromas that brought back memories. Today they only made him feel lonesome. *Lonesome? Hell, what's wrong with me? I've been lonesome all my life. I should be used to it by now.*

He picked up a 1912 Harper's Magazine and sat down with it while the coffee brewed. He aimlessly leafed through the pages, finally realizing that nothing he looked at had registered. Pouring a cup of coffee, he walked outside. The mountain crest stood out sharply against the brilliant blue sky. Closer to him, gold and red aspen colored ravines on the mountain's slope. The mountain's ruggedness was accentuated by long shadows of the low sun. The mountain beyond the cabin was a maze of canyons and ridges, with smaller criss-crossing crevices separated by knobby granite spires.

Up there is the key to my ranch. That it will be! His mind made up, Dutch swallowed the remainder of his coffee and placed the cup back in the cabin. He closed the damper on the stove and hurried outside. "Let's go find us a ranch Rosy." He swung up into the saddle and rode into the maze of black, knife-edge slates and intruded granites of Tough Creek.

* * *

Charlie Surcingle had been camped at an old line-cabin on upper Hoodoo Creek for two weeks. He wanted to be at his ranch in New Mexico, but he had been lured back to search for the Cripple Creek gold by a promise of a substantial bonus by the dubious owner of the lost gold. Charlie was convinced that much of the stolen Cripple Creek gold was still buried somewhere in the mountain breaks above the Quien Sabe Ranch. Every day he rode out from his little range cabin, systematically searching every nook and cranny in the rugged country around Hoodoo and Tough creeks.

Each day, in the off chance one of the bandits might return for the gold, Charlie would stop on the high divide between the two creeks and scan the countryside with his field glasses. He had watched Cat Teason a year before and knew about where Cat he picked up his gold. So far he'd seen no one but cowboys down at the Quien Sabe Ranch. His search for the gold turned up nothing, but it was rugged country and Charlie scoured the mountain with steady patience.

Several times he had almost given in to the impulse to ride over to DePass and visit the beautiful Ella Price. So far he had resisted, not wanting to tip his whereabouts. This morning he felt a hint of fall in the air as he sat against a sun warmed rock and scanned the countryside.

THE TROUBLE WITH GOLD... 249

Two more days, then I'll visit Ella and head home. Except for a visit from an occasional cowboy checking on the mountain pastures, he had talked with no one. Most especially, he'd not seen any women. He missed their company.

As he glassed the badlands along the mountain front he thought about Ella. *I'd bet she's ready to move on. Maybe with a little gentle persuasion she might consider marrying me.* "Yep! I think she might!" He chuckled to himself. Feeling good, now that he had made the decision to see Ella, he leaned back and closed his eyes to let the sun shine full on his face. He was tired. The unproductive results of his search had worn him down.

When he opened his eyes and resumed looking over the vast panorama in front of him, he saw a rider leave the Quien Sabe cabin and ride toward the mountain. At first he rode directly towards Charlie then veered slightly to the west, toward Tough Creek. The horse was moving briskly, as though the rider, bent on a mission, was urging him on. Charlie studied the man, his clothing, riding posture, the horse and anything else that would tell him about the man and his motives. This man didn't have the relaxed bearing of a cowboy. *Perhaps a rancher or maybe...*

The rider headed directly into the rugged canyons of Tough Creek. Through the glasses Charlie could see the firm set of the man's jaw and alertness that suggested a cautious concern about his surroundings. *I don't think he's looking for cows.*

Charlie crouched lower and adjusted the field glasses. Squinting his eyes, he studied the man closely. It wasn't Cat Teason, but the face looked familiar. He peered intently through the glasses. The large mustache was missing, but as he watched, Charlie wondered if this could be Dutch Wyatt. He'd speculated that Wyatt might be one of the gold robbers. Not because of any evidence, but aside from Butch Cassidy, Dutch Wyatt was the only one smart enough to pull off the gold job the way it had been done.

I'll just wait and see. If it is Wyatt, I won't lose the man or the gold this time.

Charlie watched Dutch ride into Tough Creek canyon then found a lookout where he could watch all the exits from the steep canyon where he had last seen Dutch. *By dang, that's the place that Cat rode into and came out of with a loaded packhorse!* Charlie checked the cartridges in his rifle and settled down to await the reappearance of the outlaw with his gold. After weeks of searching the myriad of hidden canyons, glens, and caves, Charlie had the area well mapped out in his mind, even though he hadn't yet found the hidden gold.

* * *

It was only mid-morning by the time Dutch had filled his saddlebags with about fifty pounds of the gold ore from the hidden crevice. He reckoned he could make thirty miles by dark if he didn't return to DePass. He didn't like the thought of not seeing Ella before he left, but it would mean getting back a day earlier. In the meanwhile perhaps she would come to her senses about the gold.

As Dutch tied the saddlebags on behind the saddle, Rosinante suddenly raised his head with his ears spiked forward. Dutch could see or hear nothing, but trusting his horse's senses he took off his boots and climbed to the top of the granite wall above the meadow. Staying low, he crawled into the shadows of a spreading juniper and surveyed the mountain heights. The air was still and peaceful. The sky was deep blue. *It's a good time to go out and buy my ranch.* After ten minutes, Dutch could not see or hear anything. Below, Rosinante had resumed grazing. Dutch started to slide back down when he saw a glint of light from the high granite ridge several hundred yards above him.

Freezing where he was, Dutch slowly raised his field glasses and studied the spot. Once again there was a brief flash as something reflected in the sun. As he watched Dutch saw a slight movement, something small. Maybe a hat crown. *Hell, somebody is up there. From his location he would have seen me ride out from Quien Sabe. He'll know I'm down in this canyon.*

Suddenly the mountain stillness was broken by the angry wavering whine of a bullet as it ricocheted off a rock just in front of Dutch. He dropped flat onto the rock and scooted into a shallow depression. Another shot showered a cloud of broken rock splinters over him.

Damn. Sure as hell that's Charlie Surcingle. He's got the range and I'm pinned down. I've got to move before he has a chance to box me in even worse. Dutch weighed his options. If he didn't move soon the shooter could work himself closer and trap him on the rim of the canyon. *If I try to make a break for it, I'll be in Charlie's gun sights. He'll nail me before I take one step.*

Dutch rolled over a little to move a dead juniper branch that was gouging his back. He looked at the stick. *Okay, Charlie, here's your chance.* Dutch removed his hat and placed it on one end of the stick. He pushed it across the rock as far as he could reach. Taking out his revolver he slid it up over the rock, aimed it in the general direction of Surcingle, and pulled the trigger. The report echoed like a barrage off the granite walls of the canyon. Quickly Dutch raised the stick so that the hat was just above the concealing rock. A split-second later, the hat sailed off the rocks as Surcingle's bullet picked it off the stick. Dutch yelled, as though in pain, and shoved the stick and a loose rock over the edge. They clattered loudly as they bounced off the rocks.

Dutch waited. An excruciating five minutes passed before he heard the faint scraping of a boot heal on rock. That meant that Charlie was working his way down off his high lookout. *He won't be able to see as well when he gets lower.* Still lying flat, Dutch pushed himself back over the edge until he found a crevice for his bare foot. For a nervous moment he was in sight of the high point where the shots had come from. There was no shot. *Charlie must have moved, all right.* Dutch dropped onto a ledge and slid on down to the canyon floor.

He found his hat at the base of the cliff, a hole neatly punched through its very top. He laughed silently. *I know old Charlie is a crack shot, so at least he wasn't trying to kill me! If I don't get out of here soon, he'll have another chance.* Dutch knew that Surcingle was probably moving to a point where he could better see both the upper exit of the little canyon as well as the way back to Quien Sabe.

As if in response, a voice floated down to him from somewhere above. "Hey down there. I've got you covered, whichever way you come out. No point in me shootin' you over a little bit of gold that ain't your's anyway."

I wonder if he's just checking to see if I'm still alive? Hell, I'll let him wonder for a while.

"I reckon that might be you down there, Dutch. I don't s'pect my aim is gittin' so bad that I killed you, so I'll just wait for you to come out. I've got all day."

Dutch grinned, but that quickly faded as he realized that Charlie did have the upper hand, having both ways out covered. What worried him even more was the certainty that Surcingle would be stealthily closing the noose, rather than waiting. After a moment's thought, Dutch took the reins and quietly led Rosinante down the grassy-floored gorge, away from the two exits from the meadow.

Further down, beyond where Dutch had entered the gorge from Quien Sabe, the rock walls of Tough Creek squeeze in until they are only a few feet apart. Wild roses and thorny gooseberry bushes appear to make the place totally impassable.

Butch Cassidy had pointed out the precipitous canyon years before. "You can get through there if you have to, but you'll have to suck in your gut and your horse will be apt to get wedged in if you ain't careful. With all them thorns you'll look like you been fightin' wildcats, but you can get through. I did once."

* * *

Charlie Surcingle silently swore when his boot scraped noisily on the rock. Stopping, he sat down and removed his boots. Quickly and silently he hurried to a vantage point where he would be concealed, but could watch the most likely avenue of escape that Dutch might use. He yelled down to his prey, just to let him know he was watching. Through a gap in the rocks he could see the entrance to the narrow canyon where Tough Creek slipped out of the mountain breaks. Carefully he laid his rifle across a rock and aimed it at the spot where an outlaw might think he had a perfect escape route. He didn't have to wait long before Dutch appeared at the narrow gorge. Carefully, Charlie took aim and squeezed the trigger. As he shot, Dutch threw his arms into the air and fell into the brush covering the creek.

* * *

When Ella heard Dutch ride out of the corral at the hotel that morning, she felt a sharp pang of remorse for giving him a cold send-off. Suddenly anxious, she ran outside, but he was already galloping away and out of earshot. The exhilaration she felt when he came back into her life drained out of her like life's blood from a ghastly wound.

Dejectedly she walked inside to her room, where she sat on the edge of her bed and let the tears come. *What have I done? Have I lost him? How could I be so thoughtless? My God, I do love him. Why didn't I tell him?* The disturbing thoughts clanged dissonantly through her head.

It's that bedeviled gold. I can't go back to a life where I fear every day that the law may knock on my door. I don't want my future to be built on a fraud, dulling every joy. I don't think I could live with that. No. That fear would poison the happiness of our life together.

Ella forced herself to work in the kitchen, but she found herself constantly looking down the road. "I can't stand this." She finished washing the breakfast dishes, put a lunch together, and dressed in her riding clothes. Hurrying outside she whistled for her gelding, shaking oats in a can that brought him on a run. She swung into the saddle even before she thought about her destination. Without thinking she started for Quien Sabe, then stopped. *Dutch won't be at the ranch; he'll be back where the gold is hidden. I'd never find him. Maybe he won't want to see me anyway.* Her heart felt leaden, her usual joy withered by its weight.

Instead Ella rode up the road over De Pass. From there she turned onto a dim trail and rode to the peak of the mountain.

Ella could see deer and elk tracks on the trail. In the deepest shadows patches of snow remained from the last snowstorm. *It was after that storm that Dutch first came to the hotel.* Now, the happiness she'd found with Dutch was melting away like the bits of remaining snow.

Reining her horse to a stop, Ella slid off and led her horse up the mountain, anxious for the thought-erasing tiredness the steep climb might bring. As she reached the treeless mountaintop a chipmunk scurried for cover, scolding her soundly. Ella froze and waited. In a few seconds the chipmunk reappeared, looking at her curiously with its tail twitching as it chirped. Ella fetched a small piece of bread from her saddlebag and sat on the ground holding the bread out in her hand.

"Come on Chippy, have some lunch with me." The chipmunk looked at her intently, trying to decide if this strange animal was a threat. His nose wiggled, as he smelled the bread. In a short burst he moved closer, then stopped and again moved towards Ella's hand. As he neared, he lost his nerve and scampered back to the safety of his rock, stopping on top.

"Don't be afraid. I promise not to grab you."

Chippy, becoming used to Ella's voice and presence, moved almost to Ella's hand. Then he made his decision, and in a flash took the bread and dashed back to his rock where he sat and ate the bread as though it was an everyday happening.

Ella laughed in delight. For a few minutes she felt content. She rose to her feet to take in the view from her aerie. She could see a hundred miles in every direction. As she turned she could see the stream gorges that ran through the Big Trails country where she and Dutch had been only two days before. The memories brought an involuntary sob as Ella's sadness returned. *Dutch said he was going to Paint Rock, I wonder if he would come across these hills.* For several minutes Ella scanned the countryside, then realizing the futility of her hope she mounted her horse and rode down the back side of the mountain. Far below she could see a willow-lined stream running through a narrow band of green meadow. *This must be Joe Johns Basin. A good place to contemplate my future. I have to stop feeling sorry for myself.*

Despite the late fall chill, the tiny stream still played musically over a jumble of pebbles, reflecting the sun in flashes of light. Ella put a rope halter on her horse and tethered him so he could graze in the luxuriant grass next to the stream. She took her sack of lunch once again from the saddlebag and sat in the shade of a gnarled diamond willow bush next to the quiet burble of the stream.

Ella unwrapped the brown paper from her lunch but had no appetite and laid her head back against the willow trunk. The dappled sunlight through the yellowing leaves warmed her. A few leaves fell, loosened by a soundless breeze wafting past. The sweet smell of the ripened willow foliage permeated the air. She closed her eyes and thought about that happy evening in the rugged canyon of Mahogany Butte a few days before. *Dear God, why must happiness be so elusive? Perhaps it is impossible to truly start anew, to change one's course.*

Finally Ella's exhausted mind gave in to sleep. She dreamed of Dutch. He was on his horse, much larger than life, then becoming tiny and indistinct as he moved ever further away, finally disappearing through a gap in red sandstone cliffs. The gap closed after him. A giant chipmunk looked at her angrily, tail twitching with reproach, and angrily chattered something, but no words were there. Ella heard Dutch calling and tried to reply, but her voice was mute as well. She heard him again and struggled to awaken before he could leave, maybe forever. "No!" she cried out as she opened her eyes.

The sun was low. She jumped up. *I've got to hurry back and tell Dutch how much I love him before he leaves for the Bighorn country.* She mounted her horse then remembered that he'd said he would ride directly to Paint Rock. *Maybe he changed his mind.*

When she rode into sight of the hotel she looked in vain for Dutch's horse. It had been a day of disappointments for Ella. It might be days before Dutch returned. *I know what I have to tell him when he returns. The days ahead won't change my mind.*

*   *   *

As Dutch approached the tight gorge of Tough Creek, he could see that the stream splashed against both sides of the narrow crevice. Pushing through the brush at the mouth of the gorge he jumped for a rock in the middle of the creek. Too late he realized that the rock was covered with slippery moss. He fell hard into the water. Just as he fell he heard the whine of the bullet and the bellowing echo of a .30–30 rifle. Rosinante jumped in surprise, plowing through the brush and into the shadows of the gorge. Dutch, grimacing in pain with a bruised hip, followed, crawling down the creek in the water. He hoped the brush would conceal his escape.

* * *

It was hours later and shadows were cloaking the valleys in a deep purple twilight when Dutch reached the headwaters of the Nowood River. Scratches covered his arms where he had fought his way through the thorny passage of Tough Creek gorge and his hip had a massive bruise but at least he had escaped Surcingle. Guffy Peak, not far from DePass, was but a dark, looming silhouette in the distance. *I wonder what Ella is doing at this moment?* He missed her terribly.

As the vast Bighorn Basin darkened, Dutch stopped and made camp in the shelter of a small bluff. He gathered up dead sagebrush and built a pungent fire for his tea. Miles to the west, peaks of the Washakie Needles picked up a rim of gold from the sun as it slid behind the mountains. Individual stars winked into sight overhead. Later, before sleep overtook him, Dutch looked up into the Milky Way. This time he could see Ella's face.

Dutch woke to a glimmering of red over the Bighorns. He rose and started a small fire for coffee, looking at the crimson sunrise with concern. *I hope that doesn't mean a storm.* The line from the old sailor's advice came to his mind.

"*Red sky in the morning,
Sailors take warning!*"

"Rosinante, my old steed, we'd best get tracking. With luck we'll buy that ranch and get back before a storm blows in."

The day had warmed by the time Dutch reached Mahogany Butte. He stopped at the place where he and Ella had camped, but only long enough for his horse to drink from the cold stream. *I don't like this place without Ella.*

Later, as he rode past the red bluffs above Frank Hayden's ranch, he looked down and saw Hayden herding some cows across the stream near his house. *I'll stop by and visit with him on my way back, he'd be a good neighbor to have.*

It was late that day when he rode into the little town of Ten Sleep. He stayed the night at the town's small hotel. The next morning he rode out to the Paint Rock ranch that he'd heard was for sale. Dutch rode through the log arch at the entrance to the ranch in high spirits. He looked up at the mountain slope at Paint Rock Canyon, then rode through the lush meadow where the creek meandered through after leaving the mountain. *I am going to like this place.* He reached back and patted the saddlebag that held his rich cargo of gold.

Dutch found the rancher working on a corral at the edge of the creek. "Howdy, I'm Dutch Wyatt." He swung down out of the saddle and shook the man's hand.

"I'm George Wilson. If you're looking for work, I sure don't have anything now. Come next summer I could use an irrigator though."

"Guess you might say I'm looking for work in a way. I'm looking for a ranch to buy and understand yours might be for sale."

The man shook his head. "I'm sorry, Mr. Wyatt. I thought I was going to have to sell. Heaven knows I didn't want to, but the banks were going to call everything in. Thank God I managed to negotiate an extension. Wish I could help you, but I don't know of another place for sale in this valley."

Dutch felt a sense of relief. He had been dreading that he would have to explain the gold he had planned to use for earnest money. Leaving the Paint Rock ranch, he rode his horse at a steady cantor, driven by an overwhelming

THE TROUBLE WITH GOLD...

urgency to get back to DePass and Ella. *I'll stop the night at Frank Hayden's ranch and get to DePass late tomorrow.*

Dutch's thoughts kept returning to Ella. He wondered if she were still worried about using the gold to buy a ranch. Dear *God! What if she leaves while I'm gone? I should have tried harder to convince her that I have to use the gold or buying a ranch will be years down the road. Hell, by then I'll be too old.* He urged Rosinante to go faster, but the heavy bag of gold slapped against the horse's flank. Dutch was forced to slow down, cursing the extra weight as he did.

It was dark as he rode down the dusty road to Frank Hayden's ranch. The smoke from the log house's fireplace floated over the little valley, pressed down by the cold of the evening. Ominous looking clouds were building over the Big Horn Basin.

"Hello, anybody home?" Dutch called out so as not to surprise Hayden with his sudden appearance.

"Howdy! I'm over here at the barn. Who is it?"

"Frank, it's Dutch Wyatt. I was here a few days back. Remember?"

"Well, heck, I shore remember. I'll be right over. I'm just finishin' up the chores for the night. Bring your horse on over, I'll put him in the barn for the night and we'll have dinner."

Dutch rode over to the barn. "I've been down to Paint Rock but that ranch wasn't for sale. Just thought I'd stop by and say hello."

Frank Hayden came out of the barn. "You timed it just right Dutch, bring your horse on in. I've got plenty of stalls. Put your horse in here while I get some oats. We'll have some supper in a bit."

Inside the cabin Hayden added wood to the fire in the kitchen stove. "Dutch, you get comfortable while I get this old range heated up. I reckon it's going to be a cold one tonight. You stay put and I'll carry in some wood."

"Tell me where the wood pile is and I'll take care of that."

"Thanks, Dutch. I find myself moving a little slower on these cold days. Doggoned bones are getting' weary, I reckon."

When Dutch returned with an armload of wood Hayden was building up a pile of kindling and wood in the fireplace. "Dutch, I reckon you're in luck. I've got a big pot of beef stew all fixed up, just waitin' for company. I'll get a pan of cornbread into the oven and we'll be all set."

The gasoline lantern hissed warmly as Hayden and Dutch sat down to their meal. The fireplace crackled and the chill was soon gone from the little log house. "Frank, I came through this area a couple years back. A partner and I did a little prospecting up on the mountain. We didn't find any gold, but I decided this is where I wanted to stake my picket-pin."

"What about Ella? She strikes me as one in a million. I could sure take a shine to that girl if I was about thirty years younger." Hayden laughed, "No offense Dutch. I expect you see her as pretty special."

Dutch grinned. "I was going to tell you Frank. Right after we left here the other day I asked her to marry me." Dutch felt a pang, hoping his statement was still correct. That Ella still wanted to marry him.

Hayden grinned, "Dutch, I feel like I've known both of you forever. I reckon that makes me pretty darn happy."

After they washed the dishes, Dutch and Hayden sat by the fireplace where the glowing embers of the fire served as a pleasant background for Hayden's stories of his early days on cattle drives from Texas to Montana and Wyoming. "After that I was lucky and got a job with the Spectacle Ranch over on the Powder. It was a good outfit too, but the winter of '86-'87 almost wiped them out. I didn't have anything better to do so I stuck it out, and the owner made me range boss. I did okay until times got worse again after the little ruckus between the big ranches

THE TROUBLE WITH GOLD... 261

and the rustlers in '92. How did you come to this country Dutch?"

"I was an orphan kid when I came to Wyoming to be a cowboy. I hoped to put together a poke to buy a little ranch. I soon figured out that I wouldn't live to see the day on a cowpoke's wages. Then I discovered I could make a lot more money doing other things. I convinced myself that the railroads and banks were robbers of a sort so it would be okay to take from them. I reckon Butch Cassidy taught me a thing or two along the way.

"I spent some time over on the Powder too." Dutch laughed. "I wasn't a rustler, mind you. I tried to start a homestead there but couldn't really find a place I wanted and some of the bigger ranches still weren't too friendly to us nesters after the rustler war. I'd mixed in with some of the so-called rustlers. That branded me as undesirable with the big ranches.

"Frank, I'm not proud of some of the things I did, but the excitement got into my blood. The trouble was, money seemed to get spent as fast as it came in, and what I did keep I didn't feel right about. I got tired of my conscience always bugging me, so I decided to try mining."

Hayden looked closely at Dutch. "Do you reckon we might have met? Over on the Powder?" Not waiting for Dutch to answer, he shook his head and answered his own question. "No, probably not. Anyways, that was more than a few years back. I've thought about those days. There were a lot of strong feelings. Sometimes a few hotheads started things that many of us regretted. Guess most of us were guilty of something back then, even when we thought we were right."

Both men sat watching the dying flames. Hayden tapped the ashes out of his pipe on the fireplace. "Dutch, I hope you stay around these parts. You and Ella. You've already seen that places around here are hard to find. You may have to range a little further out. Maybe over on Owl

Creek. Just be careful not to buy in on one of them alkali flats."

"I'll keep looking, Frank. I'm sure something will come up if I'm patient."

A sudden gust of wind tore at the cabin. A puff of smoke blew back from the fire. "Sounds like a storm could be moving in. You might oughta think about staying here 'til it blows over."

"Let's see what it's like in the morning. If I get an early start I can get ahead of the worst of it. Ella's alone at DePass and I know she'll worry if I don't get back when I said I would. I'd better hit the sack and get up early."

Chapter 23

Blizzard

Later that night more gusts of wind wakened Dutch. He turned over and set his mental clock to rise well before first light. He slept soundly until the smell of coffee woke him. He found Hayden in the kitchen. "Good morning, Frank. That coffee smells mighty good, but don't you ever sleep?"

"Mornin', Dutch. I figured there wouldn't be any use in tryin' to talk you out of goin' so's the least I can do is send you off with something warm in your belly." He poured a cup of coffee and dished up a bowl of oatmeal. To finish off the meal Frank set a plate full of eggs, bacon and biscuits in front of Dutch. "I'll pack some food for your trip. Beef jerky and a few biscuits. That will tide you over for a couple of days if you get stuck in a storm. I don't like the looks of it out there."

"Thanks, Frank. I'll be all right. I brought my old buffalo robe coat just in case. I should make it back by tonight anyway. Ella will be expecting me."

After breakfast they walked to the barn. A light snow was falling but the wind had stopped. Dutch saddled up his horse, put the rations in his saddlebag and shook hands warmly with Hayden.

As Dutch settled into the saddle, Hayden reached up and slipped an envelope into the saddlebag. "This is a painting my wife did. If she was around to know you and Ella I know she'd want you to have it. Drop me a line and let me know when the big event will be. I'd sure like to be there."

As Dutch rode out of the yard Hayden called after him. "Give my best to Ella and good luck on finding that ranch."

Dutch raised his mittened hand in a salute as he rode up the hill toward the main road. It was still too dark for the sky to even be somber. The snow began to fall heavily with large flakes that were quickly covering the ground. He pushed Rosinante into an easy canter that would cover the miles rapidly. The sky was barely light as Dutch rode through the canyon in Mahogany Butte. The snow showed no sign of letting up. The camp spot of week ago now looked cold and uninviting.

The big cottonwoods at the Nowood Ranch were but somber, skeletal shapes through the falling snow. The store where he and Ella had bought tomatoes was a dark shape looming alongside the road. Puffs of wind swirled the fallen snow into small eddies around sagebrush, collecting into little drifts that blew away to another drift, each growing larger as the gusts came more frequently. Dutch pulled his hat down tighter and urged his horse to a faster trot now that he could make out the road. For the first time he felt a concern that the snow might not quit soon.

At Bates Creek the main road turned south up the long slope towards Cottonwood Pass, six miles distant. Dutch knew if the wind became stronger he would not be able to keep sight of the road. An alternative was west up Bates Creek and then over the top of Lysite Mountain. That route would cut miles off his ride to DePass, but the flat, open heights of Lysite could be wicked in a storm. The inner pull to get back by the end of this day–to see Ella–made his decision for him. He turned Rosinante toward Lysite Mountain.

Near the ranch on Bates Creek, Dutch heard a moan, beginning low and increasing in its intensity, then wavering and stronger again. The mournful wail seemed to intensify the cold, and Dutch felt an ominous chill crawl up his back. He reined in Rosinante and realized the howl was wind blowing across the barren heights of Battle Mountain, hidden in the swirling snow. For a moment Dutch considered stopping at the Bates Creek Ranch to wait out the storm, but the thought of Ella overcame his instincts and he headed up a small creek on the flank of Lysite Mountain, his mental compass set for DePass.

An hour beyond the ranch the snow became so deep that Dutch couldn't see the trail. Even the dark undersides of the sagebrush were drifted over so that they no longer marked the change from sky to ground. Except for the occasional shadow of a rock or gully bank, all was white. Dutch could only give the horse his head to pick his way up the wind-blown draw.

As they neared the rim of Lysite Mountain the wind roared over the edge with a ferocity that challenged Dutch to take the summit. Dutch cursed himself for being so foolhardy as to try this route in a blizzard. In good weather he would be in DePass in little more than two hours. Now DePass might as well be on the other side of the world. *I've weathered out this kind of blow before, but I'd better turn around and find a spot to hunker down in until that wind lets up.*

Suddenly Rosinante slipped on a hidden rock, his hooves flailing for footing on the frozen ground. Desperately the horse lunged ahead, but slipped again and fell, the weight of the swinging bag of gold putting him off balance. Dutch jumped but plummeted headfirst onto the snow-covered rocks. He struggled to rise, but his limbs refused and an encompassing blackness drew him into its fold. He slumped into the drifting snow. The screaming wind found another form to drift its snow over. Soon, only the brim of his hat and a widening red stain in the snow marked Dutch's inert form.

* * *

Ella rose early the morning that the storm started. She watched the falling snow and hoped that Dutch was waiting out the storm at some ranch. For the first two days after he had left she fretted about the gold and wished that Cat or Stokes or even Surcingle would dig it up and haul it away. Once, when her spirits were at their lowest, she considered packing up and leaving. *No, I'm not good at running away from a problem. And I love Dutch too much to leave him.*

By late morning the wind began. At first it was little gusts that swirled the snow off the roof and plastered it down on the windows. She opened the door and looked outside, hearing the distant, eerie wail as the wind blew across the heights of the surrounding mountains. Soon it screamed mournfully around the abandoned mine buildings, flapping loose metal and boards in dirge-like screeching and clattering that plucked at her raw nerves. A shiver ran the length of her body. She shook her head to rid herself of a rising sense of premonition that constricted her chest.

To ease her mind, Ella busied herself until she realized she had dusted some spots three times. Every few minutes she looked down the road and up to the pass but couldn't see even a hundred yards. This blizzard was far worse than any storm since she'd been here.

Ella slept fitfully that night, wakening every time the wind changed pitch. There were brief lulls when the storm taunted her with hints to its end. The end did not come and the storm would rage again with renewed fury. Gusts shook the building with loud "WHUMPs" as though trying to rip through the walls. Ella's wakeful spells were an endless nightmare of nagging worry about Dutch, and her short periods of sleep were filled with bad dreams.

At daybreak Ella became so frustrated that she put on her coat and walked a few feet out of the hotel. The snow whipped across her face so violently that she gasped with the sudden cold and inability to see. She ran back into the hotel and shut the door against the blizzard, realizing the futility and danger of venturing out. She resolved to set out a series of chores and jobs to fill the time and purge her mind of worry.

First she brewed up a pot of strong tea to settle her nerves. *I shouldn't worry. Dutch knows how to take care of himself.* She knew though, that one of these storms could pound with its fury for two or three days. *Why is it that the men I have known at this place have disappeared?* She shuddered at the thought.

Drinking her tea she chided herself. "Get busy Ella." She watched the steam waft from her tea. There were two loud thumps on the front porch and Ella jumped to her feet, feeling a sense of relief and elation. She threw the door open. "Dutch, I've been worried!" She leaned out into the swirling snow but there was no one there. Then she saw that a large cornice of icy snow had fallen from the edge of the roof onto the steps. She shut the door and walked back to the kitchen, her mind numb with disappointment. Dread enveloped her body like a cloak of lead.

*　　*　　*

Dutch felt a warm touch on his face. "Ella?" He mumbled, "Thank God, I've been having a bad dream." He raised his hand to feel hers, only then realizing that Rosinante was nuzzling his face through snow that had drifted over him. He struggled to waken himself to reality. Icy snow sifted through his open collar. His head throbbed where he had struck a rock in the fall. When he tried to open his eyes he couldn't. They were stuck shut with icy blood.

He was weary and chilled. A spasm of shivering shook his frame. *Just a little bit of sleep and I'll be all right.* He let his body relax into the snow, feeling warmer as the wind swept a blanket of snow once again over his face.

Then a stronger urge signaled him from an inner realm of his mind. He could hear Ella's voice, "Come home soon, my love."

My God! I've got to move before I lose the will. Summoning all of his strength Dutch pushed himself to his knees, then dug the bloody ice from around his eyes. When he could once again see, he slowly stood, feeling unsteady on his feet. *That was the hardest part. I've got to find shelter, and soon.*

Grasping Rosinante's reins he murmured into the horse's ear. "Thank you, my old cayuse, I must have trained you well, or maybe you're just smarter than me. I was dumber than a brick to get us in this fix." Once again he started up the barren wash, this time leading the horse into the teeth of the storm. Suddenly he stopped. "Hell's fire, I just remembered. We passed a little grove of aspen just a ways back."

Turning around, Dutch found that the drifting snow had already covered tracks they had just made. Navigation was purely by chance now. He tried to remember how far back the trees were, but his steps were so uncertain as he struggled through the snow that he had no idea. "We have to keep moving, Rosy." *We have to stay in the bottom of the draw. To wander up the hill in either direction could be a bad mistake.*

Dutch pulled his bandanna tight over his hat and held part of it over his nose. His feet felt like wooden clubs. He stomped them vigorously to get the circulation going. "We've got to find shelter soon, old horse, or we're in trouble." He barely heard himself speak, for the wind whipped his words away.

Then he saw the blurred outline of the aspen grove, the white trunks blending into the storm. The darker branches above seemed to float in space. Further into the grove the trees coalesced into a gloom only a little grayer than the blowing snow.

Next to the aspen a thick patch of willows filled in the draw below a small cliff of rock. Still leading Rosinante, Dutch slowly made his way down the steep hill, sliding and often falling as he stepped on icy rocks or frozen grass. At the bottom he found a tiny spring next to an overhanging ledge of rock. The spring's bubbling waters formed a small pool rimmed by an icy border.

Dutch removed the saddle from Rosinante and put it under the ledge near the spring. Removing the bridle he slipped a rope halter on the horse and tied on his lariat. He tied the other end to a tree next to the ledge. Unfazed by the storm Rosinante immediately started pawing through the snow to find the dry grass.

His hands numb with the cold, Dutch broke off a large bundle of small twigs from a dead willow and dug around the base of the bush where he found some dry bark. He piled the kindling under the rock ledge. With his flint and steel he tried to strike a spark into the shredded bark. Several times the steel fell from his senseless fingers. Finally he managed to get a tiny ember glowing in the bark, only to lose it when he blew on it too vigorously. The next time he was more patient and, with a few careful puffs, nurtured the ember into a flame. He placed the twigs on top, smaller ones at first, then gradually larger branches. The fire grew into a crackling sign of hope.

He built the fire large, adding branches until the flames licked against the back wall beneath the ledge. Holding his hands towards the fire, he alternately warmed them and rubbed them with snow to ease the pain as circulation returned. As feeling returned to his hands, he felt Ella's ring and a sudden pang of loneliness made him forget the blizzard for a moment. He caressed the band, feeling a connection with Ella that surpassed the distance between them. *I'm glad she's safe at DePass.*

When the fire had soaked deep into the rock, Dutch raked the coals and burning branches out to a spot in front of the overhang. He found two large dead aspen branches nearby and dragged them to the fire, placing them on top of the burning wood.

The wind roared overhead but the grove of trees and the nearby willows muted its force before reaching Dutch's shelter. Clouds of smoke swirled around him but eased as the logs caught and burned with a heat that partially defied the wind.

Dutch spread the buffalo robe over the warm floor between the back wall and the fire. Only then did he realize that the wound on his head was dripping blood. He gingerly cleaned the gash with a handful of snow and bound it with his bandanna. Dragging his saddle up for a headrest, Dutch lay back on the robe. The warmth spread through the robe and Dutch settled down, exhausted, feeling the sharp ache in his fingers and toes as the cold left them. His head pulsed with pain and he slept fitfully until the fire burned down and the cold crept back into his shelter. Raising his head he could see that only a few embers remained. He had no idea how long he had slept but it was pitch dark and the blizzard still roared over the trees. As he rose to stoke up the fire he felt as though his whole body had been dragged over the frozen prairie.

After he had gathered in more wood and built up the fire he realized that he was starved. He hadn't eaten since the breakfast Frank Hayden had started him off with. "Thanks Frank," he said, and reached into the saddlebags for the jerky and biscuits. As he rummaged for the food he found the envelope that Hayden had given him. It was addressed simply, *"Best wishes to Dutch and Ella."* He smiled as he placed it carefully back in the saddlebag and took out the food.

He was pleasantly surprised to find that Hayden had also put in a small jar of black tea leaves. He opened the jar and was greeted with a pungent smoky aroma that overpowered the smell of tea. He laughed, "Ah, lapsang souchong. This will keep me going." He dug out the can that he used for a coffeepot and dipped it full of spring water, setting it at the edge of the fire to boil. With warmth gradually returning to his shelter, Dutch felt comfortable for the first time since he had left Hayden's cabin. As he ate a biscuit and jerky he sipped on the bitter hot tea. *Ella, I wish I could be drinking tea with you right now. But you might prefer a more civilized brew.*

A Blizzard Refuge

Chapter 24

Defining Points

As he stared out into the swirling storm, Dutch's thoughts returned to the gold. Reaching into the saddlebag he felt the bag of precious metal. It was as cold as the blizzard's heart. He took a piece out. It was different now. It didn't have the warm, spellbinding glow he remembered when he and Cat had looked at it before they buried it.

"Lord Almightly! That was more than two years ago. What has it bought? Not a darn thing! I've frittered away that much of my life on account of it, is all."

Precious time, he thought, at this point in his life. *Without this baggage of gold flopping we might have made it over Lysite Mountain before the blizzard hit with its full force.* He remembered how the horse had floundered before falling. Rosinante might have recovered had it not been for the weight of the gold swinging them off-balance.

Heck, I still don't have a ranch either. Maybe Ella is right. He remembered what she had said when she was expressing her reluctance about using the gold. "I don't want to mortgage our future with sins of the past." There was something else she'd said – "Dutch, you're not an old man and I don't want to be a girl in a gilded cage."

Then he remembered the full passage that Ella had referred to.

THE TROUBLE WITH GOLD...

Her beauty was sold for an old man's gold.
The Girl in the gilded cage.

Suddenly the gold seemed like so much lead. "Damn! What have I done?"

Dutch's head throbbed and he lay back against his saddle. He pulled the robe over him and tried to find sleep. For a moment he allowed himself the luxury of fantasizing that Ella was here, sharing his shelter-Love and the warmth of their bodies fusing them into one being, oblivious to the storm.

Abruptly Dutch snapped back to reality. *My God. I may have lost her forever.* He walked out into the open, wondering if he dare start out for DePass. The storm was still raging over the trees. *I've got to wait. It would be folly to ride now.* Feeling the need to move about, he shrugged on his slicker and brought in more logs, keeping the blazing fire well in sight as he searched a few yards out in the trees.

After he had hauled in several large branches, his head throbbed painfully. He crawled into his shelter and leaned back against the robe. Sleep eventually found him but again it was fitful, with disturbing dreams wakening him often. He was glad when morning came. The storm appeared to be abating but the sky had only begun to lighten when it turned dark. Snow and wind returned with renewed vigor.

As Dutch put more logs on the fire, Ella's words about the girl in the gilded cage taunted him. Suddenly, clearly, he knew what he had to do. He forged and tempered his resolve like a piece of fine steel, until he knew it would stand up to any test of temptation. He breathed deeply. The cold air cleansed his mind of all thoughts but the task now at hand.

Shrugging on his coat he reached into the saddlebag and pulled out the cumbersome bag of gold. He started to climb the steep slope next to his sheltered overhang, dragging the bag of gold with him. Several feet up his boots slipped and he grabbed a sagebrush to stop himself. He felt a sharp pain in his shoulder as he hit the ground. The gold slipped from his numbed fingers and plummeted down the slope into the willows. Patiently he slid back down and retrieved the heavy bag. He worked his way back up the bank, this time carefully kicking out toeholds so that he wouldn't slip.

At the top he found what he had hoped for–a deep, foot-wide crevice that had been pried open by the Wyoming elements over the centuries. He opened the bag of gold and, without hesitation or ceremony, dumped it into the crevice. He could hear the gold as it slithered and bounced to the bottom. Dutch figured that the crack must be at least twenty feet deep. *Deep enough to put Temptation out of business.* He shook the last loose grains out of the bag, then kicked rocks and loose dirt into the crack. He felt no regret, only a great sense of relief. *The trouble with gold is that one looses his common sense when it has its sway.*

The storm lasted two days, finally wearing itself out in the late hours of the second night. The wind stopped with a suddenness that woke Dutch from an exhausted sleep. His shoulder throbbed and he carefully moved it about to limber it up. When he crawled from the overhang to add more wood to the fire, he could see a few stars between the last thin clouds. Now the real cold would come. He could feel it settling deep into the rocks and trees. Into his own body. Even the fire didn't put off much heat. Dutch piled on more dead branches and logs until the flames burned high and warmed the deepest part of the cave. He set the tea can to simmer on the embers at the side of the fire and impatiently waited for first light.

*　　　*　　　*

Ella awakened as the storm stopped with a jarring suddenness. When the sun came up she looked out on an altered landscape, its roughness softened by rounded drifts of deep snow. She anxiously watched the horizon above the mine. Then she realized that wherever Dutch had waited out the storm it might be all day and maybe tomorrow before he would be able to fight his way through the drifted draws. *If he's okay.* She was immediately angry with herself for having doubts. She set about improving her mood by fixing up a large kettle of chili.

Ella heard her horse whinny from the corral. Scratching a peek hole in the thick frost on the back door window she could see her horse looking up the draw towards De Pass. She pulled hard at the frozen-shut door until it opened with a sudden lurch. Ella's heart leaped in relief and joy as she saw a horse and rider slowly making their way down the pass road. She waved and shouted a greeting. Then she realized the horse wasn't Dutch's horse. The rider, bundled to a shapeless lump, slumped low against the bitter cold. Ella watched the approaching visitor and felt a chill colder than the snow. She shut the door and moved the coffeepot to the warmer part of the stove to await her unwelcome visitor.

The man removed his heavy overshoes on the veranda and stepped inside as he removed his large Stetson. He hung his hat on a hook and unwrapped a wool scarf from round his neck. Finally he shed his long sheepskin coat. Rubbing his hands together briskly, he turned to Ella. "Howdy, Miss Price, I was wondering if I might get some coffee and maybe a few hotcakes and some good fat bacon. And pour the extra grease over them flapjacks."

In spite of herself Ella laughed. "I put the coffee on the stove when you came into sight, Mr. Surcingle. I can fix breakfast in a minute. To tell you the truth, I wasn't expecting any customers. Most folks don't ride around in this kind of weather."

"I was holed up in an old cabin just over the pass in Joe Johns Basin. Been there since the storm started and was getting mighty tired of my own company. There ain't too many ways to fix beef jerky, either."

"This place isn't exactly on the main road anymore, Mr. Surcingle. You must have some reason for coming through here other than coffee." Then she added innocently, "Are you still looking for that outlaw you were after a year ago?"

Charlie Surcingle looked surprised by Ella's direct question. "I'm sorry to say that fellow got away. The fact is that I was on the verge of nabbing his partner a few days ago at Quien Sabe. I had him in my sights, but he gave me the slip. I recognized him, though. I know him from the old outlaw days. He rode with Butch Cassidy, and he's just as clever. I didn't think he even knew I was close until I shot at him. At any rate, he slipped out over the mountain where I couldn't see him.

Ella struggled to hide her relief and a quick lie came to her mind. "Why, there was a man through here just the other day. His horse, a chestnut roan, was overloaded. He wanted to buy one of my horses, but I wouldn't sell."

"Describe the man to me, Miss Price."

"Please call me Ella. He was tall, clean-shaven and had a firm set to his jaw. I thought him rather good looking." Ella smiled, blushing slightly.

"Tarnation, I reckon that was likely him. What day was that, Miss Price, I mean, Ella?"

She wrinkled her brow. "That would have been Tuesday. He left that same day. Said he was going to catch the train. He seemed to be in a hurry."

"Shucks and dagnabit! That was him all right. The same day I saw him. He sure gave me the slip. I was sure he'd gone over into the Thermopolis country. Did he mention where he was headed?"

"He said he was a prospector and headed south to Mexico. He mentioned taking a load of rock samples to an assayer on the way."

THE TROUBLE WITH GOLD...

"It wasn't rocks, Miss Ella. It was gold. Bags of stolen gold from down in Colorado. More than one man and his horse could manage to carry. I figured them bandits split the loot here-a-bouts and went in different directions. It seems strange that they both stopped here at DePass."

Ella laughed, "I guess it's because I can fix something better than beef jerky! They sure didn't leave any gold here." Then she turned contemplative, "That man you were after last year. He didn't seem rich. In fact I think he lost almost everything he had in poker. Including his horse." Then nonchalantly she asked, "You said that you know the man who came by here this week?"

"I don't for sure, but I've got an idea. He's clever, real clever. Like I said, I think it was one of Butch's former cohorts." Charlie paused to sip his coffee, then looked intently at Ella with his steely blue eyes. "Dutch Wyatt. He was a protégé of Butch's. Darned near as clever as Butch." Charlie continued to look piercingly at Ella. "There's been times when I wondered if they were one and the same. Maybe Butch didn't die down there in Bolivia." Then quietly he asked, "Don't 'spose you ever met Butch Cassidy or Dutch Wyatt, Miss Price?"

Ella looked at Charlie with an uncomprehending expression and shook her head. She laughed. "No, I haven't, unless the man who stopped by here the other day was one or the other." She smiled. "Will you be wanting a room for the night, Mr. Surcingle? If you do stay for dinner, chili is the best I can do. There isn't much left in the pantry." She hoped her voice sounded matter-of-fact and didn't betray her desperate hope that Charlie would move on.

Again Charlie Surcingle peered at Ella intently, as though he hadn't heard her. "Miss Price, I said before that I thought we'd crossed trails once before. Well, I reckon I remember and I'm surprised you don't." He smiled confidently, so sure of himself that Ella felt dread as cold as one of the large icicles hanging from the eaves.

"And where was that, Mr. Surcingle?"

"I wish you'd call me Charlie. It was over in Idaho. I was helping put down a miners' uprising at Wallace. I only saw you a few times, but I was smitten, Ella. I'm sorry to say I had to leave suddenly on another job in Colorado. I'm sorry if I wounded your heart."

Ella shook her head. "Charlie, I've never been in Idaho."

Surcingle raised his eyebrows, as though not believing her. "Well, maybe not, but that doesn't mean I'm not smitten with you, Ella. I don't have time to waste or words to spare. I watched you when I was here before, and I'm convinced that you and I would make a good partnership. You're alone at this desolate place and I'm alone at a nice ranch in New Mexico. Come with me. If you'd have me, we can get married in Denver."

Charlie's sudden proposal left Ella momentarily breathless. She gasped and put a hand over her mouth. The sincerity of his proposal was so touching that she felt tears come to her eyes. "Charlie Surcingle, you are a romantic. Maybe I should have met you years ago. But I must tell you that I'm going to be married in a month. He's a cowboy on a ranch over on Bridger Creek."

Charlie nodded his head sadly. "I'm sorry to hear that, but happy for you Ella. Thank you for being in some nice dreams for the past year. I'm sorry we didn't meet a long time ago. I would have wooed you proper!" Charlie pulled out his pocket watch and noted the time. "I'd like to stay a little longer, but I reckon I'd better head to Lysite and catch the train for New Mexico." He took her hand and looked into her eyes. "Goodbye, Ella. My best wishes to you in your marriage."

Ella felt sorry for him–he seemed suddenly old and lonely as he bid her good-bye. In a sudden fit of compassion Ella hugged him and kissed his cheek as he opened the door to leave. She watched him disappear over the hill on the road down the valley, moving slowly through the deep snow.

* * *

Before he passed out of sight over the ridge, Charlie Surcingle stopped and turned in his saddle. "Goodbye, Etta. I hope your new life with your "cowboy" will be happy. If only we'd met in those early days when I saw your photograph with Sundance, I would have won you away and made you happy." He pulled his wool scarf tighter around his neck and rode out of the mountains.

* * *

Later that day Ella could not stand the wait any longer. She donned her heavy winter wraps and saddled her horse. Keeping to the ridges blown free of snow, she worked her way up the mountain. When she reached the top, only scant daylight remained.

From her lofty lookout Ella searched the snow draped hills and the shimmering slopes of Lysite Mountain until her eyes watered from the strain. As the sun lowered in the west, lengthening shadows of the ragged ridge top shot out across Bridger Creek valley like swords of night, stabbing out the last sunlight of the day. Ella looked again, this time with her field glasses, but there was nothing but the endless snow. Ella's hope emptied from her heart and a surge of despair gripped her mind. Sadly, she turned her horse back toward the mine.

Then she heard three shots. Her heart swelled in her breast. Hurrying back to the top of the hill she waved frantically. She focused the glasses and scanned the ridge along Bridger Creek. This time she saw a movement, barely visible at first, then recognizable as someone leading a horse. As she watched, the rider headed straight for her. She swung down from the saddle, waving and yodeling in joy. He probably couldn't hear but she didn't care. She knew it was Dutch.

Man and horse progressed slowly through the drifted snow. Ella trained her field glasses on them until darkness overpowered twilight. Reluctantly she urged her horse back to DePass. Dutch wouldn't arrive for hours, but she wanted to stoke up the fires and heat the kettle of chili. She would have time to fix her hair and change into the dress that Dutch liked.

Chapter 25

The Wages of Virtue

Ella waited, the time dragging by slowly, until finally she saw him coming down the moonlit slope above the mine. It had been hours since she had seen him on Bridger Creek. Ella put on her wraps and ran out to meet him. They held each other until the cold drove her back inside while Dutch fed Rosinante and rubbed him down. At supper they were both tired and were satisfied just to be together again. Dutch told the highlights of his ordeal. After a glass of red wine and bowl of chili, Dutch banked up the fire and they turned in.

As he started up the stairs, Dutch said, "Ella, I have lots to tell you in the morning. Good things. I'm just happy you're still here."

Ella laughed. "How did you know I had a chance to leave?"

Dutch looked at her with a question wrinkling his brow. "Well, it seems you have some things to tell me as well. I can hardly wait until morning." He hesitated then came back to Ella and put his arms around her. "Good night, my love."

Ella awakened the next morning with the sun shining through the heavy frost on her window. No sound came from Dutch's room as Ella started a fire in the kitchen range and stoked up the pot-bellied stove with more coal.

The coffee was brewed when Dutch appeared. He walked up behind Ella and hugged her. She turned and kissed him, lingering in his arms.

"Tell me everything, Dutch. She poured two cups of coffee and taking him his hand led him the chairs by the roaring stove. I've never spent a longer week in my life. You must have found something to spend the gold on. I don't see any heavy saddlebags." Ella sat down and looked at Dutch in anticipation.

"Ella, I have a confession to make. I set out to find that gilded cage, but along the way I lost it and found something much better. As Machiavelli said, "Virtue and riches seldom settle on one man."

"You have me completely baffled. Tell me what you found that's so much better."

"Well, I didn't find a ranch, but while I was waiting out the storm in a smoky cave I found wonderful piece of mind. I dumped the gold down a deep crevice. It's too deep to ever retrieve, and what's left at Quien Sabe will stay there. When I made that decision I felt as though a great burden had been lifted from my shoulders."

"And from our future together, I might add." Ella moved to Dutch's lap and hugged him tightly. "It was too late to tell you last evening, but Charlie Surcingle came by yesterday morning. He was making one last try to run down the gold. He thought I might have seen or heard something. My heart stopped for a minute when he told me he thought he had shot a man with the gold. He saw the man fall and was mystified that he had vanished into thin air when he went to the spot to look for him. Was that you?"

"Providence smiled on me when I slipped and fell a split second before he shot. He'd shot at me once before and I think he was just trying to wing me.

"But what did you tell him?"

"Why I told him a little fib–at least partly. I said a man came through here on the same day he saw you. I told him the man's horse was overloaded and when I wouldn't sell one of my horses he rode south, saying something about Mexico. Surcingle told me he had been to Thermopolis looking for you. He was riding back across the mountain and had to hole up in an old cabin when the blizzard blew up."

"Do you think he was suspicious?"

"Dutch, he scared me to death when he said he remembered me, but he mistook me for a girl he'd met a long time ago. He wanted me to marry him and move to his ranch in New Mexico. I told him I was already engaged to a cowboy. He was gracious but terribly disappointed. I honestly felt sorry for him. He is a nice man."

Dutch smiled and shook his head. "Well he does have good taste in women. It's funny, in different circumstances, I think Charlie and I would have been good friends."

That evening they celebrated with a candlelight dinner and a blazing fire in the stove. After dinner Ella found a bottle of good sherry and two crystal wineglasses. They snuggled together in one of the leather chairs and discussed their future, oblivious to the bitter cold outside.

"I figure I can go a couple of directions, Ella. I can go back to work in a mine–maybe up at Butte or somewhere in Colorado. I can make more money there than cowboying. With what I've saved, we'd have the money to buy a little place in four or five years."

"I've saved what I've made here at the hotel. I haven't done too badly until now. If we are going to spend the rest of our lives together I want to help with my money."

"That would be wonderful, but I guess I ought to ask you if you would be happy on a ranch?"

"I'd love it. Just don't go to work on the railroad!" They both laughed.

"I could maybe work on a large ranch, one where we could also run some cows on our own. With luck and hard work we might do pretty good. In time the right kind of place, a small one, will be for sale."

"That's a good idea. I want to help. There's bound to be a school close by. I can teach. Right now I don't care. I'm just happy you're back safe and sound. We can make out here for the winter. But tell me about the storm. I couldn't imagine you might be out in it."

"I'm almost ashamed to tell you about it. I was so cozy and safe that I wished you could have been there!" He told her about the little cave. "I have to admit, though, I was a lot more comfortable on account of Frank Hayden. He sent me on my way with grub and tea that came in mighty handy."

"He is one of the nicest gentlemen I have ever met, Dutch. I hope we will get to see more of him. Is he okay?"

"He's doing fine, but I can tell he is mighty lonesome. He wanted me to wait out the storm at his place. Maybe I should have, but then I wouldn't be here yet if I had." Dutch paused, remembering the envelope. "Frank sent along a gift. It's in my saddlebags. He wanted us to open it together." Dutch took the envelope from the saddlebag and handed it to Ella.

Ella opened the envelope and pulled out a piece of heavy paper. "Dutch, look! It's a watercolor of the canyon below Frank's place. It's beautiful."

"Frank's wife painted it. He said she'd want us to have it. I'm sure it must have been hard for him to part with it."

"Now I know what our first piece of furniture will be. A gold leafed frame." Ella leaned the painting against a vase on the table. "Oh look, here's a note in the envelope." Ella smoothed out the folded paper and read.

THE TROUBLE WITH GOLD...

Dear Ella and Dutch,
    I want the two of you to enjoy this painting as much as I have. I have several others and I want you to have this. Perhaps I can visit if you aren't too far away and admire it again.
    May you both be as happy in your marriage as I was in mine. I wish you the best in finding your ranch. If I hear of anything over in this country I will let you know.
    Dutch, I hesitate to mention it, as I know you are looking for a good-sized spread, but if you should change your mind and decide to settle for a smaller ranch I would be delighted to have you as a partner. I would give you the option to buy me out when you are ready. One condition would be for me to have a lifetime lease on the cabin across the creek.
    I know my place doesn't fit your requirements but I'd be pleased to discuss it further if you have any interest.
    I wouldn't miss your wedding for anything, so will see you then.

            Warmest regards, Frank Hayden

Speechless for a moment, Dutch looked at the letter. "Well, my soon to be wife, I think we just found our ranch!"

Ella put her hands to her face in delight. "That's better than all the gold in the world! I think you made a liar of Machiavelli!"

Epilogue

Dutch picked up the laughing baby and held her in his arms. He thought how much his life had changed for the better in two years. "Ella, I reckon Annie is a pretty good dividend to go along with the ranch?"

"You'd better pinch me, Dutch. Even better, kiss me and tell me this isn't all a dream. Don't ever wake me up if it is."

Dutch and Ella had married at a big community affair at DePass and moved to Hayden's ranch at the foot of the Big Horn Mountains. Ella had applied her creative touch to Hayden's former house and felt as though they had always lived there. Their baby daughter, Annie, was a happy surprise and now the focus of their lives.

Frank Hayden was happy in his little cabin up the mountain slope. Ella spoiled him by having him down for dinner at least twice a week.

Often weeks would pass without Dutch thinking of his outlaw days. Even the buried gold at Quien Sabe was a fading memory. Occasionally he had a dark thought that his past might catch up with him and wreck this happy existence. The specter scared him. He could never kill to keep his secret, and now, with Ella and little Annie, running was out of the question. But years had gone by since the gold robbery, and the only one who knew his secret was Cat. He wondered what had happened to him.

A rolling boom of thunder sounded as a summer storm moved up the mountain front. Large drops of rain splattered against the windows, then grew into a downpour as the storm moved in rapidly, hastening darkness before night.

"I hope Frank makes it to town before the rain catches up with him." Ella worried over Hayden as a daughter would her father.

"I'm sure he'll be all right, Ella. He said he'd call when he got to town. If phone is working. Half the line is on fence posts and the lightning plays heck with it."

The phone jangled erratically in confirmation, making Ella jump nervously. "I know he's all right, but these spring storms scare me."

Outside, nothing was visible beyond the lantern light that streamed through the window, making slanting lines of the rain as it slashed through the darkness. Dutch peered out. "We'll have some flooding if this keeps up for long. I'm glad we're well above the creek. Frank was thinking right when he built this place."

Flashes of lightning exploded out of the darkness with thunder following almost immediately. Annie whimpered slightly and Ella comforted her with a warmed bottle.

Marmie looked at them for assurance and her tail wagged nervously. Suddenly her ears perked up, and her lips drew back as she snarled menacingly at the door.

Dutch patted her head. "It's okay, Marmie, the lighting won't get us in here."

The collie wagged her tail nervously. Suddenly she barked and hair stood up on her back. She crouched low and moved closer to the door.

Dutch felt his own hackles rise. "Ella, take Annie back to the bedroom. I'll go out on the porch and check things out. This storm's bad enough to scare anybody." He slipped on his slicker and took his rifle off the rack. Before Dutch could open the door, loud thumping footsteps on the wooden porch were followed by a pounding on the door.

"Who is it?" Dutch's voice was calm but he gripped the rifle tightly.

"Just a soggy traveler who needs a roof and a hot cup of coffee," answered a muffled voice.

Dutch set his rifle against the wall within reach and opened the heavy wooden door. The yellow light flooded out to reveal a tall man wearing a large Stetson that drooped with wetness along with his scraggly white mustache. Dutch could see sadness in the eyes beneath the brim of the hat.

Suddenly recognition lit up the man's eyes. He looked as though he was seeing a ghost as his soulful expression quickly changed to one of disbelief. "Dutch?"

Dutch strained to recognize the man. "Well for Almighty's sake! Cat, is that you? Hell's fire, for a minute I thought old Charlie Surcingle had caught up with me!

"Ella, come on out and see who came for supper." Dutch grasped Cat's hand, then gave him a bear hug.

"Ella?" Cat paused, confused, "You mean...Etta? Ella. You and her?"

"Yep, you're looking at the luckiest man in the world." Dutch took Annie from Ella. "And meet another member of the family. This is Annie!" Cat was totally dumbfounded. He swept off his dripping hat as he searched for words.

Ella laughed. "Hello, Cat, you look like a drowned rat." Ignoring his wet clothes, she put Annie in a highchair and hugged him. "You're just in time for supper and we have a bunkhouse that you can sleep in."

Cat shook his head. "My God, I can't believe it, finding you two here. I didn't know. I've been travelin' around quite a bit. I just came from South Dakota. They didn't agree with the way I dealt cards, so I decided to head south for the winter. Thought I'd swing by DePass to settle up accounts with Stokes, then buy an automobile. I hear there's money in runnin' booze, and I dare say that I know more about gittin' around the law than these kids that think they're so clever."

Dutch and Ella exchanged a puzzled glance at Cat's mention of Stokes. "Sounds like you know something about the DePass Mine that we don't, but we can talk about that later." Dutch shrugged on his slicker. "I'll take care of your horse while you change into some of my dry clothes."

After supper, Ella tucked Annie in for the night and brewed a pot of tea. Dutch lit up his pipe and held the match for Cat while he puffed his hand-rolled cigarette to life. "Cat, you mentioned stopping by DePass to settle up with Stokes. It's going on two years since Ella and I left there. The place was a ghost town. I wouldn't have thought there was any chance of that old mine going again, not without Stokes. Have you heard some news about him or the mine?"

Cat's eyes opened wide in disbelief. The embers of his cigarette faded as he held it, forgotten, in his fingers. For a long moment he was speechless as his mind attempted to reconcile his long-held image of golden riches with Dutch's statement. "But the mine was rich. It was almost to the main ore when I left. Hell, I got a bunch of stock. Stokes told me just before I left that the stock was bound to go up a lot more."

Ella brushed back a loose strand of hair. "Cat, Stokes disappeared the same time you did. I thought that there was some reason that you and he left together, but I couldn't imagine why." She paused, "Unless there was a serious problem in the mine that involved both of you."

Cat, looking alarmed, vigorously shook his head. "The last time I saw Stokes, he came by where I was holed up and left a bottle of whiskey. He said he was going down to a lower level and that he would stop by on his way out. He never showed up. After a few hours I decided I'd had enough of that black hole and rang for the hoist to take me up. Somethin' went wrong and it stopped at the one hundred level. I climbed the rest of the way out."

It was Ella's turn to look surprised. "That's odd. The hoist man said that the same thing happened to Stokes, but you said he wasn't with you."

Cat laughed nervously. "No, he wasn't. When the hoist stopped the hoistman called down. He must have thought it was Stokes. I figured if he thought it was Stokes, so much the better, so I answered, knowing that my voice would be muffled in the shaft. I supposed Stokes was still down in the mine since the hoist came up from a lower level. I was surprised, because I thought he had already come up."

Ella wrinkled her brow. "Something else is strange. The hoist man said the hoist was only called one time. That must have been you, but Stokes' horse was missing and showed up the next morning with the reins tied over his neck. We assumed Stokes came up and rode off on his horse. But what could have happened that the horse come back with the reins tied over his neck?"

Cat fidgeted. "I can explain that too. When I came out of the mine I couldn't find my horse, so I borrowed Stoke's horse and then turned him back when I found mine a couple of miles from the mine. I reckon this all sounds like a tall tale, but that's what happened. I had no idea Stokes had disappeared.

"I don't suppose there's much chance of selling my DePass stock."

Ella shook her head in sympathy. "I had some of that stock too. I'm sorry, Cat, but it's not worth a penny a share."

"Cat, I believe you." Dutch assured his friend. "But there is something else. I found some evidence that Stokes had been salting the mine with some rich Cripple Creek ore. I figured he must have got that from you?" Dutch left the statement hanging as a question waiting for Cat's response.

"Shi-oot. I might as well tell you the whole story about me and Stokes. I suppose Ella has told you about me getting shot by Surcingle, but she didn't know about the gold or the scheme Stokes cooked up to raise money by saltin' the DePass mine. But hell, I wouldn't have done it if I hadn't been sure that the mine really was a rich lode that only needed a little priming. Are you sure the stock isn't worth somethin'?"

Dutch shook his head. "Are you telling us that you and Stokes used all of your gold for salting the mine?"

Cat pulled at his ear and looked embarrassed. "Not quite. I dropped some of it down the shaft."

"You what?" Dutch was incredulous.

Cat told about smelting the gold into ingots. "Shi-oot, Dutch, that stuff was even purtier than the raw gold and nobody could have told where it was from. I had an ingot in a saddlebag over my shoulder when I was climbing out of the shaft. I got tired and the darn thing slipped off my shoulder. When I grabbed for it, the ingot slipped out. It was so heavy it went like a bullet right through the landing. I heard it splash after a while. Damn!"

"Cat, how much gold have you got left?"

"Not much."

Dutch looked at Ella. "It would seem that JT Stokes fell into the River Pactolus as he had feared he might. We'll never know for sure, but the DePass Mine is probably his final resting place."

Cat shook his head sadly. "I don't reckon there's anything to stop for at DePass. Maybe I'll try my luck in Colorado." He stifled a yawn, "Well, guess I'd better get to bed. I should leave early in the morning."

* * *

The next morning Dutch and Cat walked down to the barn where Cat saddled up to leave. "Dutch, as soon as I win a few pots I'll buy that automobile and learn to drive. Prohibition could be a good thing." Cat swung up into the saddle and reached down to shake Dutch's hand.

"Cat, you're always welcome here. Come back and see us once in a while."

"You're the wise one, Dutch. You used your poke smart and now you've got what you want. The trouble with gold is that it had lots of promises but brought me nothin' but grief. Just when things were about to go right, they suddenly got worse. Hell, even my last nugget got me rolled with a lump on my head."

Dutch watched Cat until he reached the main road, where he turned and waved. For a moment Dutch thought about calling him back to tell him about the gold still in the crevice at Quien Sabe. Instead he raised his arm and waved farewell.

Ella came out of the cabin and waved as Cat turned and rode up the hill. "Did you tell him about the rest of the gold at Quien Sabe?"

"I was going to tell him, but Cat's gold got him nothing. Why bring down more trouble on him? He'll get into enough scrapes on his own. Maybe one day someone will find that treasure from Cripple Creek and do something good with it."

Ella stood on her toes and kissed Dutch. Taking his hand she led the way back to the cabin. "Speaking of treasures, our daughter is calling for her father."

The End

THE TROUBLE WITH GOLD...

GLOSSARY

THE TROUBLE WITH GOLD...

GLOSSARY

adit A horizontal passage from the surface into a mine. Sometimes referred to as a tunnel, although strictly speaking a tunnel is a passage open to the surface at both ends.
assay A test performed on a sample of ore, rocks or minerals to determine the amount of valuable metals contained. In the case of gold and silver, a fire assay is usually performed which melts down the sample with chemicals and the resulting metal button is weighed.
back The ceiling of a drift, crosscut or stope.
bead A small metal knob on a firearm used as a front sight. Thence comes – "I got a bead on him."
breccia A rock composed of angular broken rock fragments held together by a mineral cement or in a fine-grained matrix.
cage The conveyance used to transport men and equipment in a shaft..
carbide lamp Uses the reaction of water on calcium carbide to produce acetylene gas. The gas is ignited with a striker wheel and flint and the light is focused by a concave metal reflector.
calaverite A pale bronze-yellow or tin-white mineral of gold and tellurium.
cribbing A structure of interlocking timbers that forms a brace between the roof and floor of a mine.
cupel A small shallow porous cut esp. of bone ash used in assaying.
cupellation Refinement of gold and silver in a cupel by exposure to high temperature in a blast of air by which the unwanted metals such as lead and zinc are oxidized and partly sink into the porous cupel.
diatreme A breccia filled volcanic *pipe* that was formed by a gaseous explosion.
drift A horizontal underground passage that follows along a vein. Advancing work in a drift is referred to as drifting.
face The end of a drift or crosscut in which work is progressing in a mine.
geode A rock cavity partly filled by a lining of inward-projecting crystals such as quartz. A vug.
grifting Obtaining money illicitly, as in a confidence game.
highgrader One who steals rich ore, especially gold, from a mine.
hoist The machine used for raising and lowering the cage in a mine shaft. In most cases, a cable wrapped around a large, powered drum.
hydrothermal Hot water, the action of hot water or the products of this action, such as a mineral deposit precipitated from a hot aqueous solution.

GLOSSARY (cont.)

lagging Planks or small timbers placed on ribs or roof timbers to prevent rocks from falling rather than to support the main weight of the overlying rocks.

level A working horizon in a mine. Levels are generally established at regular vertical intervals, generally 100 to 150 apart in the shaft. Level six would normally be at a depth of about 600 feet.

muck Ore or rock that has been broken by blasting.

ore A mixture of minerals and rock from which at least one of the metals can be extracted at a profit.

portal The surface entrance to a tunnel or adit.

pyrite A yellow, glittery mineral of iron and sulfur (sulfide.) Sometimes mistaken as gold by amateurs. It does often occur with gold.

quartz Crystalline silica (SiO2). Quartz is a common mineral in ore deposits. Occurs in transparent crystals or crystalline masses.

range detective Troubleshooters of the late 1800's and early 1900's who worked the range independently or for agencies such as Pinkertons. Clients included the government (in pursuit of bandits such as Billy the Kid,) cattlemen (discouraging rustlers) and mining companies (strike breaking.)

round The advance accomplished in a mine opening by blasting a single set of drilled holes. The ore or rock broken by the blast.

salting The act of introducing metals or minerals into a deposit or samples, resulting in false assays. Done either by accident or with the intent of defrauding.

scorification A process employed in assaying gold and silver ores. The operation involves roasting, fusion and formation of a slag.

stope An excavation in a mine from which ore is being or has been extracted.

tellurides Compounds of the element tellurium with gold, silver and other metal. Calaverite is a telluride in some gold and silver deposits; Cripple Creek, Colorado is a notable example.

Troy ounce The normal unit used in weighing gold. One troy ounce equals about 1.1 avoirdupois ounce or 31.1 grams. There are about 14.6 troy ounces in one avp. pound. (Hence Cat's confusion!)

vein A mineral filling of a fault or fracture in a host rock in a tabular or sheetlike form.

vug A cavity in a vein or rock, usually lined with crystals of a differing composition than the enclosing rock.

winze A downward opening like a shaft but starting from a point underground rather than from the surface.

THE TROUBLE WITH GOLD...

Glossary Sources

Bates, Robert L. and Jackson, Julia A, Editors (1980) *Glossary of Geology.* American Geological Institute.

McKinstry, Hugh Eston, et al (1948) *Mining Geology.* Prentice-Hall, Inc.

Various contributors (1968) *Mining Explained.* Northern Miner Press Limited.

Acknowledgements

Four years ago or so, the late Dr. J. D. Love suggested I write a novel incorporating my experiences and knowledge of the Copper Mountain area of Wyoming. Dave had been my friend and wise mentor for fifty years, so I took his advice. We both grew up in remote ranch country of Wyoming and shared empathy of similar roots. I had the benefit of drawing on Dave's encyclopedic knowledge of Wyoming history, people and geology throughout my life, first as a geologist and most recently as a writer. Dave had the patience and selflessness to endure reading several drafts. His constructive critiques always spurred me on to do better. I owe an immeasurable debt of gratitude to Dave, so this book is also in his memory. Thanks also to Dave's wife Jane and daughter Francie, who read the manuscript with Dave during his last few months.

In 1998, Verna Davis, my mother, at age 96, wrote and published a memoir of her life, *My Chosen Trails*. Her example and encouragement, in deed and in word, has been a real factor in my writing. At age 100, she continues to urge me on.

Joyce Fuller generously provided photos and her father's (J. Herold Day) valuable notes on the DePass and Bridger Creek area.

To some authors, the art of writing is a mostly solitary endeavor, but to me the constructive criticisms by fellow writers in the Southwest Denver Critique group have been invaluable. Over time there were many who participated, but those who helped from the beginning include Mary Ann Kersten, Christine Cary, Anne Pettis, Avis Halberson and Judy Kundert.

Mary Ann Kersten did a thorough job of copy-editing. As a result of her efforts this is a much better book.

THE TROUBLE WITH GOLD...

Daughter Amy Martin did meticulous proofing and was right on with editorial advice where the story needed some bolstering.

A special thanks to my wife, Dorothy, for her patience and understanding, essential and appreciated elements in my endeavors.

My sister, Dorothy Redland generously painted *The Gold Train* for the cover.

Jack and Sally Savoy and Shawn LaVergne of Savoy Color Imaging were an essential part of the cover design.

My appreciation to family and friends who gave encouragement and seldom asked if I'd ever finish. Sometimes they even promised to buy a copy!

The Cover

The Gold Train portrays the outlaws' mule train bearing gold from the train robbery in Wyoming to their hideout. Dorothy Redland, the artist, grew up in Wyoming and is widely known for her work, which captures the mood as well as the beauty of the Wyoming mountains and the Texas hill country. She splits her time between Uvalde, Texas and the Big Horn Mountains of Wyoming. A signed and numbered print of *The Gold Train* without text can be ordered from www.deepcreekpress.com.

ABOUT THE AUTHOR

Jim Davis lives the countryside he writes about. As an exploration geologist and prospector he has traversed the hinterlands of the western U. S., the Patagonian hills, the jungles of Sumatra and places between. He never saw a rock he didn't love.

Growing up in the mountains of Wyoming, he heard stories of the frontier west that were still warm and real. Old mines and intriguing landscapes are rich fodder for his stories–both fictional and true.

Jim and his wife, Dorothy live in the foothills of the Colorado Rockies. They have two daughters, Gail and Amy and five grandchildren, Emily, Hannah, Julia, Erik and Brian.